ADVANCING ON CHAOS

MICHAEL T. TUSA JR.

ISBN: 1539473651
ISBN 13: 9781539473657
Library of Congress Control Number: 2016916981
CreateSpace Independent Publishing Platform
North Charleston, South Carolina

For Rosemary, Madeline and Nicholas.

Special thanks to Gary Gautier for his proofing and suggestions.
All errors are mine.

TABLE OF CONTENTS

Chapter 1
NOM DE GUERRE

Randolph Moates chose the nom de guerre Zarathustra the Second ("II") for himself because of his affinity for all things related to the 19th century philosopher Friedrich Nietzsche, who wrote a book called *Thus Spoke Zarathustra*. Nietzsche, according to Zarathustra II, had blazed a wide trail in search of a "truth" that would save him, and western civilization, from what he perceived as moral dissolution. It was a path, Zarathustra II would later tell me, which anyone could follow, if they were willing to take on the risks associated with that "never ending journey."

"The search for truth is a form of self analysis and that is a lonely endeavor," he said. He would end his comments about man's search for truth somberly, anticipating a rebuke for having voiced his opinion.

"We are forced to find truth on our own terms; there is no appetite for naked reality, because, as Nietzsche said, mankind's desire for distracting illusions is stronger than its desire to find the truth."

Zarathustra II carried a tattered and dog-eared gray and orange paperback copy of Nietzsche's book, *Thus Spoke Zarathustra*, with him at all times. The pages of the book were filled with studied penciled underlines, and small pencil printed notes with his thoughts were in the margins. Normally, he kept the book in one of the exterior pockets of his oversized tan trench coat, along with several number 2 wooden pencils, a pencil sharpener, and a hand size tan spiral note pad, in which he had printed out certain thoughts of his own, and the selected quotations of others.

The note pad had **Zarathustra the Second** printed on the front cover in large black marks-a-lot letters of ownership. The cardboard cover of the note pad was stained with darkened half circles from Styrofoam homeless shelter coffee cups.

When Zarathustra II could sit still long enough, which was not often, I would sometimes see him around town sitting on the ground, or on a bus stop bench, re-reading the book. He would be smiling while he read it, ignoring the whistle call of the world around him, pulling on his mustache and reciting fragments of sentences from it out loud, the words apparently affirming something for him.

I often wondered, back then, what the book was about and who he was, or who he had been. I had never seen a homeless person reading a book. It was only later, after all of the events I am going to tell you about, that I read it.

One of the first things I learned from Zarathustra II was that God had been declared dead by Nietzsche in *Thus Spoke Zarathustra*. According to Zarathustra II, Nietzsche had claimed that man had murdered God. I thought that was a pretty ridiculous thing for someone to say when I first heard it.

"Can you imagine how difficult that was?" he asked.

"What do you mean?"

"Telling the world that God was dead. How that crushing truth must have pressed down on him," he said.

"How can anyone murder God? That doesn't make any sense to me."

"Nietzsche had no choice but to report it. One has to bear witness to one's truth or you lose your integrity," he concluded.

"No choice?" I asked, uncertain that I heard him correctly.

"No choice. But either way, once he felt assured of such an overwhelming truth, he was doomed."

"You keep talking about truth. What truth? Nietzsche's truth of God's death? Is that a truth?"

"Truth can be a cultural creation, or a metaphysical realization. It can also be a lived experience. The lived experience is the most powerful."

"I thought truth was like things written down in the Bible?"

"That's a static orthodox Christian view. I prefer a more Gnostic view that truth is dynamic." I did not pursue the issue further with him, unfamiliar as I was with the Nietzsche or with the idea that there were different types of truth.

While Zarathustra II informed me of what Nietzsche had written about God's death, he also told me, and anyone else who would listen to him, a slightly different story about what he believed had happened to God; the truth as he saw it.

"So you agree with this guy? How do you pronounce his name?"

"Nietzsche. No. Not completely. Nietzsche mistook God's absence in our lives for His death. And he got his substitute Dionysian morality completely wrong. We do need to do away with organized religion, and the Grand Inquisitor's distorted version of Christianity. He was right about that. But we should not do away with the Christ's original message of selflessly helping others," he said.

"Grand Inquisitor?"

"Sorry, a Dostoyevsky reference to the church's distortion of Christ's teachings."

To tell his story about God's disappearance, Zarathustra II used the traditional books of the Christian Bible in a linear fashion, starting with Genesis and ending with Revelation. He used the chronology in the stories to show God's gradual disappearance in the daily lives of mankind; meaning that He has an early active intervening role in the biblical story, but over the timeline of the Bible, His involvement decreases and then ultimately it ceases. Zarathustra II buttressed his disappearance argument with numerous biblical quotes about God 'hiding his face' and with the inexplicable tragedies of life, which he thought a loving and active God would not countenance.

Zarathustra II was a small breakable man with a big heavy story. It was not a story about mankind murdering God, or about who the chosen people were, or about the alleged broken biblical covenants between God and man. Instead, the story he was compelled to tell, his truth you might say, was about the disappearance of God. Man does not murder God. Nietzsche was wrong. Rather, Zarathustra II said, God walks away from man. He disappears.

Chapter 2
PRELUDE TO CHAOS

The first time I saw him he was standing alone in a late summer New Orleans rain, near the corner of Basin Street and Canal Street, close to the Saenger Theater and Joy Theater. The morning sun was bright and yet it was raining. It was a soft slow summer rain, with big drops. The kind of rain that local residents knew would not last long, and which caused steam to rise up weakly from the hot concrete.

He stood next to a large pothole in the Canal Street crosswalk, talking excitedly to himself, or to someone that only he could see. He wore an oversized tan trench coat which was stained in spots and badly wrinkled from sleeping in it. Those humid summer days were not good days to be homeless. A faded blue checkered flannel shirt and heavy rumpled gray dungarees hid beneath the trench coat.

He was wearing worn high top red Converse tennis shoes. His unkempt hair was black and curly, matted, and fell 8-10 inches below his shoulders. He wore a dark blue moth eaten knit wool cap pulled down tightly on his forehead. He wore this wool cap, flannel shirt, dungarees and trench coat despite the oppressive summer heat and humidity.

His hands, which were constantly gesturing, were dirty, and he had an olive, perhaps Mediterranean, complexion. He was unshaven, with an untrimmed full mustache covering his upper lip, and an uneven black and gray speckled beard. Not a big man, he was thin, hard, but fragile, only about 5'6" and 125 pounds "soaking wet," as he would sometimes describe himself. I would learn later, when we finally spoke, that he called himself Zarathustra the Second.

As I stood under my umbrella, on the neutral ground in front of the Simon Bolivar statue, and watched that day, he paced back and forth, methodically placing each step, undisturbed by the rain, in the faded yellow lined cross walk, in the middle of Canal Street. Cars slowed in annoyance to maneuver around him.

His back was bent unnaturally, and his head was bowed in homage to some greater mystery, as his hands, when not in motion, periodically held each other in a disjointed comfort behind his back. As I came to know him, he was always moving hurriedly; his mind willing his beaten body to follow, like the biblical ascetics of old. Then just as suddenly, he stopped pacing. He stepped out of the street up onto the curb and then collapsed down heavily onto the graffiti covered bus stop bench, on the Canal Street median. He lowered his head into one of his hands. There were people crowded together under the eaves of the Saenger Theater, across the street from him, to avoid the rain, in the low spark of the morning, pretending not to notice him, as they waited to cross the street to catch the bus to go to work.

An elderly and heavy set black lady, the color of new charcoal, with her hair in pink foam curlers under a white hair net, walked slowly and stolidly from the Saenger Theater, when the rain momentarily stopped, and sat down harshly on the wet bus stop bench, unconcerned, near him. She held a partially broken red umbrella over her head, and set a brown plastic Rouse's grocery bag at her feet. She wore a neatly pressed, but threadbare at the hem, black dress and what looked to me to be frayed pink print bathroom slippers on her flat and painfully oversized feet.

Zarathustra II rose from the bus stop bench immediately after the lady sat down, stepped to the curb, and spread his arms wide at the shoulders in a childlike anticipation of a long withheld parental embrace. Traffic stopped, started and strained angrily in front of him. Looking to the sky, as the rain started to fall again he spoke loudly, in a voice of internal exile, and to an inattentive audience.

"In Deuteronomy, God told Moses, 'I shall hide my face from them. I shall see what shall become of them.' And that is what He has done. He has hid His face. He has left us." At this point Zarathustra II stopped speaking and simply stood there with his arms still outstretched looking skyward, like he was waiting for an answer to his siren call, waiting to catch something with his entire being. The black lady and I both watched him.

"Bonhoeffer was right when he wrote that 'The God who makes us live in this world without using Him as a working hypothesis, is the God before whom we are ever standing.'"

The black lady on the bus stop bench, stirred, leaned forward and stared hard at him. She fidgeted slightly, furrowed her brow, exhaled deeply through her flat nostrils, and then deliberately slid her bulk down away from him, in disapproval, toward the far end of the wet bench. She continued to stare at him, through the small flames of her eyes, as he stood there looking skyward.

"What is you talkin' bout you fool? Get way from dat street b'fo you is hit!" she said forcefully. Several of the people huddled under the eaves of the Saenger Theater, who may have heard her, looked over in early morning disinterest. Zarathustra II, however, did not acknowledge that he heard her. He continued to look skyward in apparent distress, with his arms spread wide.

Even then, before I knew him, I could tell that there was something about what he was saying; something about his belief in the disappearance of God, or his role as the messenger of that disappearance, that weighed on him, like the unexpected betrayal of a first love. He turned and looked around for a second, before resuming his skyward gaze. A motorist honked her horn while driving by, because Zarathustra II was almost standing in the street.

"The question," he then continued dogmatically in that soft rain, "for each of us," and he emphasized the words *each of us*, "is what does it mean?

What does the disappearance of God mean for us?" Zarathustra II's voice, previously spellbound, seemed to break on this last question. He lowered his arms in momentary defeat. His shoulders sagged in sorrow, but his eyes continued to look skyward.

"Disappearin! My Lawd! What kinda fool is you! Gawd ain't no disappearin," the black lady said in uncertain disgust, seemingly to herself, but loud enough to be heard. She then stood up slowly, with apparent difficulty, holding her broken umbrella above her head with one hand and pointing a chubby charcoal finger on her other hand at Zarathustra II. She took one step towards him.

"You dere! Hey fool! I'm talkin to you fool! My Gawd talks to me all da time. He be here rite now wit you an me. An rite now He's a tellin me dat you is a damn fool. Now gets way from dat street b'fo you is hit!" she said, in a more agitated tone. "Come here!" she then commanded, as she dropped back down abruptly and slapped her hand hard on the wet bench next to her.

Zarathustra II lowered his head, searching the contours of a sadness, of a lifetime of discouragement, he knew well. The large rain drops started to come down harder. His eyes welled with tears. He timidly bent over. His hands clutched his knees, as if this was necessary to hold up himself and some other weight which he bore. He seemed suddenly to be in agony. The world moved by him, silent, refusing to speak to him, as if he had been shunned for some unspeakable crime.

"We are trapped, trapped by God's silence. Silence can be a great teacher, but only if we take the measure of that silence," he then said in a quivering voice, to the pavement, while still bent over. The black lady remained under her broken umbrella on the bench watching Zarathustra II closely, wanting to coax him out of the street, but perhaps wondering if he might be dangerous.

"Lawd, whatcha give me t'day? Dis fool dis mornin, an da RTA bus be late agin. What be next?" she mumbled to her disinterested morning diety. Then she stared back at Zarathustra II. She decided to try once more.

She recalled a biblical verse that her Pastor had read at mass one Sunday about Christians needing to look out for the lame, the sick, the blind and others with mental deficiencies. She tried unsuccessfully to bring the exact words of the verse to her mind. She only remembered the general idea; something about kindness to others.

"Hey you! You dere! You knows dat you is a mighty fool!" she then said, passing judgment. "Don't be a blasphemine round me t'day as I goes to da work. Talkin' bout my Gawd an ya disappearin nonsense! You keep leanin in dat street an you is gonna disappear on da hood of a car, on da killin floor!" She stood up again, laboring, to make her point more emphatic and reached her hand out toward Zarathustra II. I saw the brown lightness of the palm of her hand and it trembled slightly.

"Now puts ya narra white ass on dis bench nexta me an gets outta dat street b'fo I comes ova dere an hasta drag ya here!" she said sternly. "Where is da policeman in dis here city whens ya be needin one of dem ta show up an do sometin fa ya?" she then asked herself rhetorically.

Another passing car, decorated in faded black and gold Saints' Super Bowl memorabilia, honked its horn at Zarathustra II, as he was still standing bent over right on the curb near the traffic lane. "Get out the street asshole!" the driver yelled hitting the pothole and splashing water onto Zarathustra II's trench coat and pants legs.

Slowly, ever so slowly though, as the black lady continued to hold her hand out to Zarathustra II, and as I watched, transfixed by some hidden longing for a disaster or a miracle, he pulled his hands into his body. Then standing up as straight as he could, emerging from the rubble of an internal darkness and stepping into the light, with a deep shapeless sigh from that little body, he stepped away from the curb toward the bench, faced the black lady, wrapped his arms around his torso and he hugged himself. Like a motherless child who felt momentarily loved, he rocked back and forth in his own embrace. His hands held tightly onto his torso. And then, for the first time; a child having opened his first Christmas present, I saw him smile a wide yellow gap toothed unshaven smile toward the lady.

"Dats it! Dats it, honey. Now moves way from da street so you don' git ya lil' sef hurt," she said reassuringly to him, as she signaled for him to sit down on the bench. Zarathustra II moved a few stilted steps of approbation toward her, with his arms still wrapped around himself.

"Thank ya Jesus," she then said, as the RTA bus came into view.

Chapter 3
BIBLICAL LITERALISM

As I mentioned, Zarathustra II relied on the biblical chronology to tell his story of God's disappearance, but he did not believe, like Evangelicals and those who call themselves fundamentalists, that the Bible was "literally true" or "inerrant."

"Anyone who knows the different biblical manuscript streams, Masoretic and Septuagint, and how the Bible was actually put together, could not possibly believe that it was literally true," he told me.

Zarathustra II did, however, believe that the Bible was instructional, and that it was filled with what he called "theological" or "mythological" truths, a thought that seemed contradictory to me at the time, because I thought a myth was something that was always false. It was later that he explained to me that the idea that myths were false was a modern scientific interpretation, and not what biblical writers, or pre-modern man, thought. The power of myth, he said, was substantial for pre-modern man.

"It was more powerful than a mere factual truth, because it also helped explain the philosophical, cosmological and existential implications," he said. Anyway, one of the Bible's theological truths, he preached, was found in God's diminishing role in His people's lives over time.

"How is God's supposed disappearance a theological truth?" I eventually asked him. He smiled a mischievous smile in response.

"It is the most difficult of truths, because we have to ask ourselves why He disappeared. And the 'why' questions are often the most formidable," he told me.

He was the first person who ever told me, in support of his view that the Bible was not literally true, that the Bible was riddled with translation problems, contradictions and with some dittography.

"Dittography? What is that?" I asked, because I had never heard the word before.

"We have all done it. You are copying a line from a book, look away or get distracted, and accidentally copy the same line twice."

"Where is that in the Bible?" I asked, doubting him.

"Well, probably the best example is in Kings where it indicates that the army of the King of Assyria *'went up and arrived'* at Jerusalem and then in the next line *'went up and arrived'* again."

"I never heard of that. And you also said there are translation issues. I thought all Bible translations were the same?"

"There are many different versions of the Bible: King James, NIV, Jerusalem. And many differences in the different versions. Which version of the Bible is the literally true one and which ones are not? And how do you know?"

"I thought there was only one Bible manuscript, the one that 70 or so scholars interpreted identically," I told him.

"Ah! The legend of the Septuagint. But it's not the only manuscript stream. There are significant differences in the manuscripts that different versions of the Bible relied upon. For example, the chronology of the Masoretic text has Abraham being born about 2,083 years after creation. But the chronology in the Septuagint text has him being born about 3,549 years after creation."

"Is that important? When someone was born?"

"Not to me. But both can't be factually correct. So by definition one is wrong. Which one?"

When he told me these things I was doubtful. I had never heard about different biblical manuscript streams, different Bible translations, or contradictions.

I confess that I really did not understand much of what he meant back then. Like most individuals raised as a Christian, I knew virtually nothing about how the Bible was pieced together and who played a part in such things. It was not a topic I ever recall from Sunday school, or Church sermons, even though I was raised as an Evangelical. We were just told that the Bible was "God-breathed" and inerrant. I guess I naively assumed that the Bible was somehow written by men, from start to finish, in one sitting, as God hovered nearby instructing them on what to write.

It was later in our friendship that I learned from Zarathustra II that the biblical canon, at least the New Testament as we know it, had only begun to be put together by the Church in response to a fellow named Marcion compiling his own New Testament biblical canon. When he compiled his own biblical canon, excluding Matthew and John from the Gospels, he was condemned by the leaders of the nascent Church. In fact, Zarathustra II told me that even though Mark was written first, Marcion thought Luke was the only authoritative Gospel.

Marcion had also concluded that the God of the Old Testament and the God of the New Testament could not be the same God; they acted too differently. Nor could the principles espoused by those two Gods be reconciled.

"Two different Gods?" I recall puzzling.

"Marcion compared the Old Testament admonition by God of an eye for an eye with the contradictory New Testament statement by Jesus about turning the other cheek," Zarathustra II told me.

"I always thought that was odd," I replied, uneasily, but not able to identify the source of my discomfort.

"You have to admit that the Old Testament God was portrayed as a pretty mean and arbitrary guy," Zarathustra II said, with a hint of adolescent admiration for the school yard bully.

"I wonder why?" I asked, in the early days of our friendship.

"I think it was simply an attempt to explain things--natural disasters, misfortunes, and other things---that man did not yet have the science or philosophy to understand. It made sense at the time to attribute these things to a sometimes malevolent God. That does change a bit, however, once religion absorbs some Greek philosophy."

The emerging Church and its leaders did not agree with the version of the Bible that Marcion had prepared, with what he put in and what he excluded. So they prepared a competing version, which was the start of the Church's version of the New Testament. According to Zarathustra II, the Bible, as most Christians now know it, with some variation based on denomination, was not in place until about three hundred years or so after Jesus' death.

Zarathustra II knew all these things, and though it was disorienting at times to listen to him. I came to appreciate his intellect and his willingness to share his thoughts with me.

Chapter 4
BIOLOGICAL NEED

There is something else you should know when considering the story I am going to tell you. It is a personal observation. I believe that Zarathustra II's belief in God's quitting man became an emotional weight for him, like the lingering memory of childhood abuse. He could not easily set it aside, or pretend that it was otherwise. He had an urgency to tell people about it, an almost biological need to alert them to it, as another might do with information about a potential natural catastrophe. There were days when his belief in God's disappearance defined and bound him, as if lamenting on a threshing floor, and other days, more pleasant, when he was temporarily freed from its insatiable demands, like a child given free rein to play without parental supervision.

I have since learned that Nietzsche, Zarathustra II's hero, went mad during the last decade of his life, after declaring that God was dead. Darwin, Tolstoy, and many others who had, in earlier times, argued against the dominant religious paradigms of their time, were also disfigured by the weight of their ideas, or, perhaps, by the weight of the cultural resistance to their ideas.

Zarathustra II was aware of the burden he had placed on his shoulders. He discussed with me the dilemma of his effort to get Christians to confront the truth of God's disappearance. He told me that a philosopher named Kierkegaard felt that most Christians turn away and avert their eyes and their minds from difficult truths, from things that might contradict the apparent comforts of easier less examined 'truths.' I learned from him that Kierkegaard, despite this comment, was a devout Christian. Instead, Zarathustra II said that it was unfortunate, but most Christians pursue, what the Catholic Saint, Thomas Aquinas, called "cultivated ignorance," an ignorance which they purposely nurture so as to not have to deal with uncomfortable realities.

That was apparently not how Nietzsche lived. And, as you will see, it was not how Zarathustra II lived.

One thing about Zarathustra II, he knew his biblical scripture. He could quote it as needed for any purpose. But, as I have since learned, Shakespeare wrote that even the devil can quote scripture for his own purposes. And as he became more widely known, through the events I will tell you about, some people said that Zarathustra II was in fact the devil, or the so called "anti-Christ" predicted by the Book of Revelation. That is, at least, what he was called by Reverend Jessie Ray Elder. And Reverend Jessie Ray Elder also knew his biblical scripture very well.

Chapter 5
FIRST APOSTLE

The things I write about Zarathustra II I know because I became his apostle, Luke C. Bukowski. I know that sounds really strange in this day and age. I wonder how the word "apostle" sounded in Jesus' day. That is not my given name, of course. Rather it is the name Zarathustra II gave to me on the day we first met, when he unexpectedly named me his first apostle. I was initially humored by him naming me his first "apostle." It seemed pretty harmless at the time, like getting a goofy nickname from a new friend. Eventually, for reasons I will try to explain, I embraced him as my friend and mentor.

I was born late in my parent's marriage, apparently a rhythm baby, when my mother was 44 years old and my father was 47. My parents had tried unsuccessfully for years to have children. And as the story went, when they stopped trying, I was born. I was never sure if my parents were happy about my late, and unplanned, arrival into their well ordered lives. I often felt like the undertow which would eventually drag them down. On several occasions when I was growing up, I overheard my father lament to friends the energy that it took to raise a child at his age. "The boy wears me out," he would often say.

When I was in grammar school I was tall and skinny and not very athletic. My curly red hair, as well as my pale white complexion, was a natural source of some childhood bullying. One classmate, Evy McCabe, used to call me "light bulb" when I was in 4th grade, because of my very pale skin. A few other classmates picked up on the nickname, but eventually they just left me alone because, try as they might, I refused to fight back, which prompted some boys to also call me "super sissy." As a result the nicknames were sometimes combined and I was called "super sissy light bulb." It apparently made sense to 4th graders.

I was only beaten up three times, that I recall, while still in grade school. I never threw a punch in response. Because I was ashamed of getting beat up, I lied to my mother each time.

"What happen'd ta ya?" she would ask, when I returned home from school bruised.

"I fell down playing with the kids at recess," I would tell her.

"Well, be mo careful," she would respond.

Once I got to high school, the bullying got a bit rougher. Mostly it was just derogatory remarks after they realized I would not fight back. Only beat up twice, but not too badly. A few derogatory things on Facebook that I was told about, but never saw because I was prohibited by my father from having a Facebook page.

Shortly after I started high school I was often sick, fatigued and nauseated. My mother dutifully took me to see a series of different doctors at Ochsner Hospital, to my father's increasing frustration. The doctors never really came up with a definitive diagnosis. One of them thought it might be Epstein Barr, but that was rejected by another doctor. Another doctor thought it might be chronic fatigue syndrome. I just remember wishing so hard and praying, as best I knew how, every night, that they would find something to make me feel better. But it didn't seem that my prayers were answered, as I remained sick without a definitive diagnosis off and on throughout high school.

My symptoms mostly abated after I graduated from high school and moved away from home to attend Delgado Community College. Interestingly, as I got to know Zarathustra II, and quietly confided to him about how I was ill a lot when I was in high school, he had an immediate diagnosis.

"You had neurasthenia like William James. A not uncommon problem for someone who is brilliant."

When I try to recall those high school years, even though it was not that long ago, I don't seem to be able to remember too much, other than staying in bed a lot and watching DVDs of old movies my mother owned.

My father was the dominating dogmatic figure in my childhood and adolescent world, the foreboding shadow that was always cast over me at home or in school. He often fought with my teachers, and the school board, over the curriculum at our high school, deeming it too secular. He had wanted me home schooled, but my mother refused to do it.

"You should do this for me," he told her.

"Ya must be crazy! I ain't no teacher," she said to him.

He resented me reading secular books assigned by my teachers and would routinely tell me that something I excitedly told him I had learned in a class was wrong. He would portray the fight over the use of a particular textbook, or a particular reading assignment, in moral or biblical terms. He would rally other church parents to his cause and they would disrupt school board meetings with prayers and singing. I recall that he succeeded in getting *The Catcher in The Rye* and *Brave New World* taken off of our senior reading list. So I never read those books. The school personnel quickly tired of his objections and, as you might expect, his actions did not endear me to my teachers or classmates.

I do recall that my parents' lives were full of activity when I was growing up, mostly associated with their church. Church members were often at our house, planning, or preparing, for upcoming church events. But I felt mostly invisible to the adults in their world, in my room, not feeling well. Only my mother's best friend, Mrs. Rosemary Matthews, who was not a church member, seemed to genuinely care about me. She would sometimes come to my room, when I was sick, just to visit, to watch part of a movie with me, or to see how I was feeling and to tell me a funny story or a joke. On occasion, if she knew my father was not home, she would bring over her Pete Fountain or Al Hirt CDs to listen to with my mother and re-tell me stories of high school dances she attended when she was a girl.

Even when I grew out a beard my senior year of high school, no one seemed to notice except my father, who told me disapprovingly, "You look like a damn Hasidic Jew." So Zarathustra II's recognition of me, naming me his first "apostle," as odd as that may sound, felt nice. I never thought anything would come of it.

My full name, Luke C. Bukowski, was given to me by Zarathustra II when he named me his first apostle. The name came to Zarathustra II in a natural enough way. He told me that the author of the Gospel of Luke was also the author of Acts, in the Bible. Those were two parts of the Bible he, like Marcion, really liked a lot. And, since I was instructed by him to write "The Story of Zarathustra the Second," he wanted me to model myself on the author who used Luke's name.

Although he did not tell me at the time, I think he borrowed my last name, Bukowski, from the poet Charles Bukowski. Zarathustra II mentioned him to me on occasion. He was called the Skid Row poet. Zarathustra II said, however, that he was one of the few modern writers who had seen the human condition, including the effect of the disappearance of God, clearly. I am not sure where the middle initial "C" came from.

I confess I really did not understand how I would write a story about him, though his confidence in me to do so was mildly uplifting. Frankly, I never really thought I would have to write anything. It seemed kind of a goof at the time. I had to research some dates, and read further on some of the ideas that he had told me about, to get these correct in the story. I also talked to others about conversations they had, or recalled having, with him or about him.

Initially I was going to write his story without any personal commentary, like an impartial historical narrative. I couldn't do it. So sometimes, in the course of the story, I do tell you what I think. Being able to express my own opinions is something I learned from Zarathustra II.

When Zarathustra II named me his first apostle he did so in a very formal manner. I was about 6 or 7 inches taller than Zarathustra II, so he stepped up onto the side of a fallen metal trash can in a convenience store parking lot and faced me. After playfully pulling on my beard, he placed his weathered hands on my shoulders ceremoniously for a moment and looked at me directly in the eyes. He then dropped his arms down to his waist, told me my apostle name, and gave me a piece of advice from Nietzsche.

"My advice for you today, on becoming my first apostle, is from Nietzsche, who wrote: 'Our faith in others betrays in what respect we would like to have faith in ourselves.' Take this to heart," he concluded solemnly, while he scratched himself impolitely.

My real name is Nicholas Jerome Elder. My father is the Reverend Jessie Ray Elder, the founder of the First Church of the Recalcitrant Covenant on St Charles Avenue in New Orleans, Louisiana.

Chapter 6
WRITE THE STORY

When I jokingly asked Zarathustra II if he wanted me to write his story under my real name, or under the apostle name of Luke C. Bukowski, he told me to use the name Luke, and then he said something else I had never heard before. Zarathustra II told me that the author of the Gospel of Luke was not actually Luke the apostle, but someone else who had used Luke's name to give his gospel added credibility. This, he said, was a common practice by writers at that time in history.

"It was not intended to be deceptive, as we might suspiciously think today," he said. Although I was raised in a Bible based church, no one had ever told me such a thing about the gospel authors and I was having trouble believing him.

"That's not true. Each Gospel was written by an Apostle," I countered.

"None of the Gospels: Mark, Luke, Matthew or John, were written by those apostles. Besides, the name of the actual author is not important anyway," he said to me dismissively. "The thing that is important is the theological truth which they sought to convey in their individual Gospels."

He then told me another odd thing. He told me something else I had never heard in church or in Bible studies. He said that each Gospel author sought to convey a "different theological truth" in their stories. "John most of all," he said distractedly, as if this was a self evident fact to anyone who had ever spent a few moments to consider it.

"A different theological truth? How can there be different theological truths? Didn't they all write about the same things?"

"There are different theological truths because each gospel writer had a different notion of God, a different relationship with God, and each was trying to address different problems in their different communities."

"I don't understand," I said.

"God is not monolithic. People don't want to think about that. He is experienced differently by different social classes, and by the needs of different communities. That is true now and was true for the Gospel writers as well," he said. "Remember theological truths are ultimately only about human experiences, and those experiences vary."

"Theological truths. Mythological truths. Factual truths. Cultural truths. Lived truths. This doesn't make any sense. How can there be so many truths?" I asked, frustrated with the diversity of his thoughts.

"Some overlap, where the same purpose is served. But truths have many different basis and serve many different purposes. I hope I can convince you of that before my time here with you runs out," he replied kindly, ignoring my frustration.

Chapter 7
THE RITE OF SPRING

By the way---and let's get this clear from the outset---as far as I know, nothing I write about Zarathustra II is "God breathed" or inerrant, as Evangelical Christians like to say about the Bible. At least I don't think so. How could you really know anyway? You certainly could not rely on the mere fact that I told you so, or that I told you that God told me to tell you so.

And another thing. I lived these events with Zarathustra II some years ago, at a time when my own formal education and understanding was quite limited. There were many things I did not understand during that time, but believe I better understand now. So to remain honest in this story, I admit the things Zarathustra II told me that I did not then understand. I have tried to address those deficiencies in my knowledge over the years since these events, and I even returned to college and obtained a degree in creative writing to help me tell his story better.

So, if my presentation of the story is a bit uneven at times, it is because I lived it at one point in my life, one point in my personal development, but I am telling it at another. Looking back on life's past experiences inevitably gives a distorted view of the experiences. It is not always easy to see the direction in which our perception is skewered, since it is often shaped by our current needs, which we do not yet have the necessary distance from to understand.

Finally, I want to say this up front, before I tell you Zarathustra II's story. Some people have suggested to me that Zarathustra II was crazy or, perhaps, even schizophrenic. A few people thought, because of his predictions, that he was something of an ascetic wise man, or prophet, like Amos in biblical times. He certainly was intelligent. In fact he had a photographic memory of things he had read and would often recite these from memory. Other people, naturally, were unsure of who or what he was. Again, how would you know? What, if anything, separates madness from divine revelation? One person hears voices, like Saul approaching Damascus, and it is treated as a revelation by millions and millions of people over the centuries. Another hears voices, like John Hinkley, the guy who tried to assassinate President Reagan, and he is regarded by everyone as mad and put in a mental hospital.

Here is what I think on that subject, one of those personal observations I told you I would make from time to time. Life is so often lived, and by so many heard, as a single familiar repetitive, but comforting, musical note, a note that like tinnitus, the ringing in one's ears, you have grown accustomed to hearing. That tinnitus can often become the sound track of the prejudices imbedded in our personal narratives. And narratives are hard to change. When we meet someone who lives their life in five or six different musical notes, notes to which we are unaccustomed, what are we to make of them? Some people will hear the five or six notes as unsettling noise without rhythm, like the initial rioting crowd at Igor Stravinsky's *The Rite of Spring* concert. Others will recognize the five or six sequential notes as a more complex melody and hear, without fear, a new musical form, and maybe a new way to hear rhythmic structures; a new approach to living.

Chapter 8
AUTHOR, AUTHOR

Zarathustra II had read a lot of books. Despite his prodigious memory he kept a good many quotations from those books printed down neatly in his note pad, like a diary of someone else's reflections, interspersed with a few of his own. The quotations were squeezed numerously on to each page, in small neat lead pencil print. When I asked him about why he wrote the quotations down, he replied quietly, almost as if he was ashamed, that he feared one day he would start to forget his beloved quotations. So he wanted them handy, in case he started to forget.

The books he had read seemed to frame up something for him. Or maybe the books, and the ideas in the books, and the thoughts these engendered, filled the space in him that had been created by God's disappearance. He seemed his most calm and secure, most at peace, when discussing the ideas in these books, and most self assured using a quote from someone else to explain a larger point.

Here is another one of my opinions. Everyone seems to have a gap, or void, within themselves, a space between the happiness we pursue and the extent of our reach, between our dreams and an overarching disappointment. I'm not sure what to call it, or why we all have it. I now know that the writer Salman Rushdie called it a "God shaped hole," while the philosopher Jean Paul Sartre referred to it as a "hole in being."

Maybe it was created by our separation from God as told in the biblical Fall. Or by the death of God as Nietzsche claimed, and our failure to find a transcendent replacement. Or by our gaining self knowledge and consciousness of our own future death. Or by the collective loss of our one time unified primitive religious view of the world. Ultimately, in differing degrees, I think it's probably about loss of meaning, however you define meaning.

Zarathustra II said something to me once that might be relevant here, a metaphor of sorts that could explain the feeling of the gap, the feeling of alienation from our own vision. He was talking about cosmology, specifically the big bang theory.

"Remember before the big bang Penrose says that there was a singularity."

"A what?" I asked.

"A 'singularity.' I like that word. And the loss of singularity did not just happen to the physical universe. I think it also happened to us as well, with the loss of a collective meaning and the pursuit of individualism. We were once part of a whole, a singularity, bound to each other completely with a unified view of our place in the world, the chain of being, our relationship to God, the order of the universe, and the meaning of it all. Now we are just splinters from that unified beginning. And unfortunately, like the universe, we are accelerating away from each other, emphasizing our apparent individual differences, instead of recognizing our common origin."

"How did that happen? Why do you think we are accelerating away from each other, as you say."

"It is a complicated story. The enlightenment lit the fuse to our shared disintegration. But the tinder was already there," he replied.

Anyway, I think Zarathustra II may have used the many books which he read, and what he learned from those books, for that purpose. It was a filler of sorts for him that minimized the chances he would fall too deeply into that hole; into despair with himself or with humanity.

As a result Zarathustra II knew the names of lots of authors and he spoke of them to me often. Besides Nietzsche, he also spoke to me about Kerouac, Ginsberg and a writer named Richard Brautigan. There were others he mentioned as well that I have forgotten. Often when he mentioned a particular writer to me he would strike a dramatic pose, as if on stage, and recite some lines from one of their books. For example, when he mentioned that Brautigan fellow he would recite:

"In watermelon sugar the deeds were done again as my life is done in watermelon sugar." He always smiled widely across time after he recited those lines.

As I told you, he would also mention the poet Charles Bukowski. At the time I was not sure what he had written. Zarathustra II liked whatever Bukowski had written. He would laugh when he mentioned his name and pretend that he was tipsy.

Once he told me that he used to write a lot, that he had published a few things, and aspired to be an author of important books, but no-one really read what he wrote. At the time I wasn't sure that he was telling me the truth.

"Writing helped me to organize the chaos in my mind," he said, by way of explanation.

When Zarathustra II talked about these writers, I listened politely. He seemed to genuinely enjoy talking about them, as if each was an old friend he had traveled with, had helped to form their ideas, and recalled fondly, but had not been asked about in a while. Outside of required school reading assignments, and the few books my father read, I never knew anyone who read much for the purpose of learning ideas, or to see if their own ideas were shared by others.

I asked Zarathustra II once why he read so much, and why he thought everyone should read. I think his answer helped me to understand him. As best I can recall this is what he said:

"Well, the ideas we get from reading are what keeps our imagination alive."

"Why is that so important?" I asked.

"We need our imagination, our creativity, to defend ourselves, and to create an independent intellect."

"Defend ourselves? From what?"

"From everything that conspires to dumb us down, to make us just accept what we are told."

"Accept what we are told? I recall asking.

"Mass culture destroys our integrity, our intellect. So we need that imagination, and exposure to different ideas, even those we disagree with, to learn to think for ourselves, which is our last line of defense for our independent intellect."

"That sounds like you reject everything related to our current culture?"

"I reject anything that anesthetizes our compassion or intellect, that dumbs us down and makes us focus only on our material selves and not on helping others."

Growing up, most of the ideas I was exposed to were sifted and filtered by my father. He made it clear that he saw no reason for me to read broadly. Indeed, because my father said the Bible was inerrant, he told us that thing's like geology, cosmology and other sciences were simply wrong.

"That contradicts the Bible and is wrong," he would simply say, without further explanation.

As a result, based upon my father's reading of scripture, there was no reason for me to study these other subjects. I was, therefore, not encouraged to expose myself to ideas, or to read anything secular. Rather, based upon my father's reading of the apostle Paul, I was told that pursuing earthly wisdom was counterproductive to our personal salvation. In fact I was taught that the wiser one was in secular matters, the 'profane' my father called it, the more difficult it was to maintain one's faith.

"It will undermine you and your spiritual beliefs," my father had often said firmly, in one way or another, to me and to our Sunday school class. "As Augustine wrote: 'It is not necessary to probe into the nature of things.'"

That was fine with me, when I was younger, because I did not care to read that much anyway. I would rather watch old movies or TV shows. If religion gave me a reason not to read, so much the better.

When I told Zarathustra II what my father had said about Paul's writings in the Bible, and there being no need to pursue secular wisdom, he grew despondent.

"Nietzsche was right, God has been used to 'darken the heavens, to blot out the sun, cast suspicion on joy, to deprive hope of its value, to paralyze the active hand,'" he replied.

Chapter 9
COUNTRY BOY

Before I met Zarathustra II, I regularly attended the First Church of the Recalcitrant Covenant, or the "CRC" as its members called it. It had been started by my father as a small store front church in a rented space on Magazine Street. That part of Magazine Street was filled with local artisans, handmade furniture, retro clothing stores, bohemian restaurants and coffee shops. The church seemed an odd neighbor in the old Rocky's Pizza location next to the Greek restaurant and across the street from the Breaux Mart. However, the church membership grew quickly, along with my father's reputation as a preacher, until its members purchased a former Catholic church on St. Charles Avenue near Tulane University, that had been shuttered after Hurricane Katrina.

The CRC was an independent Evangelical church. It was loosely associated with the Fellowship of Evangelical Churches, a group of Protestant churches that traced its start to a break with the Church of England during the times of Queen Elizabeth I. It was a Bible based church.

Although it had an elected Board of Trustees, my father's word, as its pastor, on matters big and small, was usually final. Its official membership, under his tutelage, eventually exceeded 800 people. The CRC's Sunday services were broadcast every week on a local cable access channel. The broadcasts had given my father a small regional following. It was not uncommon to have a few tourists, who were visiting New Orleans for another reason, attend his Sunday services. Plans to open a grammar school for children of church members, with an "Evangelical curriculum" approved by my father, and a day care center next to the church, were in the works.

Once I was old enough, I was required to attend every service at the CRC where my father, the Reverend Jessie Ray Elder, vividly brought the stories and lessons of the Bible to life through his sermons. He insisted that my immersion in his church services was necessary to offset any secular influence from my parochial school education.

Attending my father's sermons was like going to the movies and being swept away by the unfolding grandeur of the story. He had a way of telling the stories, of dramatizing scripture and explaining the meaning in terms that were simple, but seemed relevant to everyday life. Even if not immediately clear, you felt something as you listened, some emotional kinship with the story and his message. Although I did not like being required to attend all the services, I did like the way he told stories from scripture during his sermons.

In fact, he and Zarathustra II knew the scriptures better than anyone else I had ever met. But my father read the stories in the Bible very differently from the way Zarathustra II read those same stories. My father often said that he read the words of the Bible plainly, as the writers intended, that there was really no other way to read them, and that anyone could read the words and learn what he had learned.

"One need not be college educated to understand it at all," he would say.

He often bolstered his view of the ease of biblical understanding by telling his parishioners that he was "just a country boy, with little book learning." But he told them, he was someone that had "taken the time to read the Bible carefully, which anyone can do."

I remember him telling me when he finished reading the Bible from cover to cover for the 27th time. His goal, he said, was to read it 50 times all the way through before he died. His father, he said, had read it 32 times before he had passed on.

The part about him just being a "country boy, with little book learning," was a white lie, however, as he grew up in downtown Jackson, Mississippi and had attended Mississippi State for one year. He later returned to school in his early 40s, after losing his job, and was one of the first graduates from the Southern Evangelical Seminary and Bible College, with a degree in Evangelical Studies.

His father and his uncle were both small town preachers. Indeed, his father, whom he always referred to as "Reverend Elder," was an itinerant preacher in the South for many years before settling down in Jackson, Mississippi, in his later life, to raise my father and his siblings. My father learned about oratory and exhortation from attending numerous revivals with his father and uncle. Traveling with his father, he told me more than once that he saw the great Evangelists Reverend A.A. Allen and Reverend Milford Buckler, among others.

It was his father that Reverend Jessie said was the motivation in his life; the history he could not escape. Often, when there was conflict between us, he would refer to his relationship with his father to express his disappointment with me.

"I always did what Reverend Elder asked. I never questioned his wisdom," he would say sharply.

Anyway, he seemed to think it important, in telling his parishioners about the Bible, to downplay his formal education.

I tried to read parts of the Bible when I was young in an attempt to duplicate my father's efforts and get his approval. Despite what my father said, the meaning of biblical passages was not always that clear to me. I sometimes thought passages were contradictory in places and even, at times, downright boring. For example, I never could get the story of Noah and the flood straight, and it seemed to me to be told in at least two different contradictory ways. The same thing was true with the creation story in Genesis.

"This is confusing. There are two versions," I said once, when re-reading the second version of creation in Genesis.

"If it is confusing, it is because you are obstructing your own faith. Think less and believe more," he cautioned. Thereafter, to avoid conflict with him, I never said anything about my confusion, or the possible contradictions in the Bible, to my father.

I think that's why I preferred to just listen and let my father tell me what the writers of the Bible said, and what the words really meant. There was something comforting, when I was young, in acceding to his authority, in accepting his wisdom.

Zarathustra II was actually the first person I ever met that confirmed for me that he also believed various Bible stories were contradictory. He had a formal explanation for the contradictions. He told me that the contradictions in the Pentateuch, the first five books of the Bible, were best explained by something theologians called the "Documentary Hypothesis." As best I understood him, at the time, it meant that most stories in the Pentateuch were cut and paste jobs, combining different oral versions of the same stories from different tribes. In fact theologians had identified the different authors with letters like "P," "E," "J" and "D." I remember that "P" referred to an author theologians believed to have been a priest. I think "J" was for the author who always referred to God as "YHWH" and the "E" was the author who always referred to God as "Elohim." As an example, he told me that "P" wrote the first version of creation in Genesis and the author known as "J" wrote the second version.

Chapter 10
A RIGHT TO BE MAD

The way my father---I think I should call him Reverend Jessie from now on---read the Bible, God had not vanished over time, as Zarathustra II preached. Rather, He was here every day, behind every catastrophe, every wish, every event of personal or world-wide significance. Not only was He here, but God was not very happy with mankind, because mankind had broken all of the covenants He had made with them. God, according to Reverend Jessie, had a right to be mad with us, because we had failed so often, and, because we were inherently prone to evil, to sinfulness.

I had to admit that this seemed right to me when I was younger, as, on a personal level, I never did quite succeed at stuff that I tried to do, often losing interest along the way and not completing the desired task. I thought some of the science we studied in school was interesting, until Reverend Jessie told me it was all incorrect. I barely graduated from high school, rarely applying myself to my studies, though I always tested in the top 10% of the class. I dropped out of community college after completing only one semester. I sometimes thought that the intellectual weakness Reverend Jessie pointed out to me, in my misunderstanding the Bible, was mirrored by my physical weakness in often being sick and fatigued.

Ours was not a relationship built on shared experiences, on bonding, or learning about life together as father and son. Rather, as I think back on it, it was a one dimensional relationship, and that one dimension, the only one for which Reverend Jessie had language, was about the difference between right and wrong, as he said was set forth in the Bible. His opinions and fatherly advice, when offered, were cast as biblically inspired judgments, from which he would brook no dissent. If I wanted to connect with my father, as all sons long to do, it had to be on his terms, and in territory with which he was familiar. That territory, the enclave within, in which he lived, was the Bible.

I never did succeed at reading the entire Bible when I was younger. That was another personal failure, a moral failure, considering how many times he had read it. I promised myself I would do so on more than one occasion, but never succeeded. I would start to read it, but late in Genesis, or maybe early in Exodus, I would get bored and stop. I skipped around a few times, but never read it in its entirety. Most Christians I knew, though they did not like to say so publicly, were like me. They held the Bible in high esteem, or at least said that they did, but never bothered to read the "word of God" from beginning to end. They just preferred that someone else, who claimed to have read it all, tell them about it.

Chapter 11
PROCLIVITY TO EVIL

At the CRC Reverend Jessie preached that, because of our corrupt nature, what he called our "proclivity to evil," salvation was impossible for us alone. It was, he always said, like someone trying to outrun a trained marathon runner. Even if we were in the best shape of our lives, the "best spiritual shape" he would say, the result was predetermined.

"God saves us by His grace. We do not save ourselves, though we must strive as best we can to do His work while here on earth," Reverend Jessie would often say. We were all "sinners and transgressors," he told his congregation. But, he said, someone named Rushdoony had written that "the solution is faith and obedience."

Reverend Jessie also liked to quote Augustine, whom he first read on his own, while in Bible College, about the fallen nature of man, and how thoroughgoing our corruption was, as a result of the Fall, the civil disobedience in the Garden of Eden. Reverend Jessie taught that there was an actual Garden of Eden, and that the Fall occurred as written, because Adam and Eve ate the forbidden fruit from the tree of knowledge. He told us that Augustine had set all of this out clearly in his writings, as well as the ramifications of that Fall for all of mankind: original sin.

Augustine's *Confessions* and Rushdoony's *Institutes of Biblical Law* were the only books I ever saw Reverend Jessie read, other than the Bible. When he periodically re-read parts of Augustine's *Confessions* he would get excited by it, and would tell us what it said. It seemed to have a powerful effect on him, even though Augustine was a Catholic saint and he had no use for Catholicism. However, he rarely discussed the content of the Rushdoony book and when I asked about it once, trying to engage with him, he started to tell me about something called Dominion theology, but abruptly stopped, saying I wouldn't understand it. He told me I should just stick to reading the Bible, as I was not likely to ever need to understand the other book.

Reverend Jessie would often sit at the dinner table with a fork in one hand and one of the three books--Augustine's, Rushdoony's or the Bible--in the other hand, or spread open on the table. Reverend Jessie liked to eat. He was a big powerful man, over six feet tall and overweight, which he often blamed on my mother's cooking. His legs were stocky, and too short for his barrel chested torso, something he called being "long-waisted." He had a ruddy complexion, one you would associate with a natural red head, which he was, and a tendency to perspire profusely when nervous.

"This man understands the sinner. He understand our failings and our desires," Reverend Jessie often said, in one fashion or another, to my mother and I, at the dinner table, while re-reading *Confessions.* Other times, in reference to Augustine, he would say quietly, as if speaking directly to Augustine, "My, how closely our struggles mirror each other."

It was not uncommon for him to pose a spiritual question to us over dinner, and then provide us with his version of an appropriate answer. If my mother made a comment about what he had read, or attempted to answer the question he posed, as she used to do, Reverend Jessie often ignored her. Other times his facial expressions, or his curt response, suggested that he was disappointed with the simplicity of whatever she expressed.

"That is not correct," he would sometimes say dismissively, without looking up at her. I learned quickly not to answer the questions he posed and, instead, to wait for him to provide us with the right answer. Anyway, like Augustine, Reverend Jessie told us that he felt that of all the sins men committed, of all those temptations, the sins of the flesh were the worst sins of all.

Chapter 12

THE 3H'S SERMON

Once a year Reverend Jessie gave his highly anticipated 3H's sermon at the CRC on the "Evils of Hedonism, Homosexuality and Hollywood." He would usually be interviewed by the religion editor for one of the local papers the week of his 3H sermon. It was that popular within the Evangelical community.

I remember vividly when I was little boy, and he was still preaching at his store front church, that he would stay up most of the night reading scripture, and praying out loud, the night before he gave that sermon. He always got worked up when he stayed up alone at night and read scripture. Often, while I lay in my bed, I would hear him in the silent darkness through the thin paneled walls, between my bedroom and the kitchen, which doubled as his reading room, saying, "Amen." Other times his voice would break through the quiet, compliant and crystallized, and I would hear him say: "Yes, Lord." I would lay awake frightened when this happened, wondering if God was in the next room. Especially as a young child, I worried about this, because God never spoke to me. Never. At least not that I could tell.

Sometimes, when I was trying to decide about something, the voice in my childhood head would pretend to be God by saying: "This is God." I always knew that it was just my own voice, and that part of me was trying to trick the rest of me into believing that my own voice was God's voice. But when that happened, I was never able to trick myself. So I lived uncomfortably in Reverend Jessie's prophet like presence, a failure, as God never spoke to me.

That is another reason why I think that I just listened to what Reverend Jessie told me about the Bible. God spoke to him, which is undoubtedly why he was so sure of things that did not always seem so clear to my young mind.

In church, for his 3H sermon Reverend Jessie would always be dressed magnificently, in a brightly colored expensive suit and tie. The brightly colored suits were an anomaly for a white southern preacher in an Evangelical church.

"There is nothing wrong with honoring Jesus with a little color in our lives," Reverend Jessie would tell his parishioners, if they questioned him about his attire. On sermon days Reverend Jessie would always wear a white carnation in his lapel, and his full head of graying red hair was always slicked back with hair gel.

When I was young my mother would get carnations for him from a neighborhood florist, Ms. Zoe Skyler, who was a member of the church. She would cut the stem, put it in his lapel with a straight pin, and she would always give him a final inspection before he went out of the house. Then she would give him a kiss on the cheek for good luck.

"I'm so proud a ya Jessie Ray," she would say. "Ya really doin well."

But years later, when she stopped coming to church, she stopped her inspections and her flattery. My mother also started to complain about the cost of the suits, which he had made by a tailor named Joseph Smith, until a parishioner began to buy the suits for him as part of his tithe to the church. Anyway, according to Reverend Jessie, the 3H's--Hedonism, Homosexuality and Hollywood--are all related, intertwined and all three led to eternal damnation.

The funny thing is that Zarathustra II had something of a 3H sermon as well, though he did not give it such a name. In it, on Royal Street, or Canal Street, or from one of the Jackson Square park benches, he talked to tourists, the street kids, and to the homeless, about "Hobos, Hooch and Ho's." It was not as frightening as Reverend Jessie's sermon. In fact Zarathustra II's 3H sermon was kind of funny, but still thought provoking.

Whenever he talked about "hooch" he would invariably mention that writer Brautigan, who, apparently, drank because of a difficult childhood and killed himself.

"Hooch," Zarathustra II would say in his 3H sermon, "should not be used to fill the space reserved for the divine spark in our lives."

When he talked about "hobos" he would mention that Beat writer Kerouac, the one who wrote a book called *On the Road*, about traveling around the country on a journey of self discovery.

"Self discovery should be an element of all religious practices. To own nothing like a hobo, is to lose your material self and find your spiritual self. Jesus owned nothing. He was a hobo. As the Gospel of Thomas says 'If you do not know yourselves, you dwell in poverty,'" he would say in a pastoral voice.

Finally, he would mention that other writer Charles Bukowski when he talked about "Ho's." In fact, he sometimes recited pieces of poetry by Bukowski, during that portion of his sermon, which referred to such women as the poet slept with, who threw empty wine bottles at him, or who drove him around in a red Porsche while he was drunk. Zarathustra II never said anything bad about "Ho's." In that part of his 3H sermon he would mention that the biblical prophet Hosea married a prostitute, as did the Emperor Justinian.

"We all prostitute ourselves on occasion, from the businessman to the housewife, though we hate to admit it. The question we must always ask ourselves, when we succumb to being a prostitute, is whether when doing so we are suppressing our true identity to please someone else's ego. You should never kneel on someone else's altar," he would say.

Zarathustra II may have lived such a life, drinking, wandering with purpose, and living on the rails as a hobo. At the time I didn't know. I knew he was homeless, had been homeless for awhile, and he often hinted at other prior unrevealed troubles. In any event, Zarathustra II said that all three cases--hooch, hobos and ho's--involved choices, choices each of us had the ability to make, and for which we were ultimately responsible.

"We are not responsible because of some inherited passed on original sin of an imaginary guy named Adam, who was created from dirt, and ate an apple he was not supposed to eat," he would say, frowning. "That's a cop out. We are solely responsible for all the choices we make. We don't get to decide after the fact, depending on the result, whether we are responsible or not."

It was from Zarathustra II's 3H sermon that I first learned that "Adam" in the Bible, at least as he read the story, referred not to a particular man but, rather, to mankind in general. I think he told me, when I later asked, that Adam, or "Adham" as it was properly spelled, simply meant "mankind" in Hebrew. He chuckled and told me that "Adham" was also a play on words by the biblical writers, as it had a secondary meaning which was "dust" or "dirt."

"There was no one named Adam, and no 'once upon a time' geographic location named the Garden of Eden," he said to me.

Anyway, according to Zarathustra II, there is no right or wrong choice that we can make in life, though, as a practical matter, some choices will work out better than others. Zarathustra II came back to this point often.

Displaying the breadth of his knowledge of literature, he would say, "As Hamlet says, 'there is nothing good or bad but thinking makes it so.'" Reverend Jessie strongly disagreed with him. For Reverend Jessie, every choice we make, and even some we don't make, is about good and evil.

Chapter 13
OLD MANI

The sermon of Reverend Jessie that I remembered most vividly from my childhood was his "Black and White" sermon. It was easily his scariest sermon for me as a child. It was also very easy for me to understand. Perhaps, that is why I still remember it so well. Or maybe it was the fear it instilled in me, the childhood uncertainty, that made an indelible impression upon my young mind. In the Black and White sermon he talked about the choices we each have to make in life. It was not the way that Zarathustra II talked about choices. Reverend Jessie said that the only two choices we had in this life were between good and evil. He said it had always been this way, and he traced the idea back to the Essenes and to a hermit of sorts named Mani. Mani was an ascetic, who apparently lived in a cave for awhile with nothing else to do but think about good and evil.

Mani attracted followers, later called Manicheans. It is thought that Mani did not leave any writings about his beliefs behind. But his followers did write down some of his teachings. In his sermon Reverend Jessie told us that fragments of these teachings were found with the Dead Sea scrolls in the 1940s. Augustine, whom Reverend Jessie liked so much, had even been a follower of Mani for a short while.

"Old Mani was inspired by God about one thing," Reverend Jessie would say, lighthearted, but serious. That one thing Mani was inspired about, was that this world was a place where the battle, between good and evil, was constantly at play. Rejecting what Reverend Jessie told his parishioners some "pointy headed intellectuals" called "post-modernism," he said that there were absolute standards by which we could judge all behaviors as either good or evil, as "blessing or curse." Those standards were all found, had to be found, he said, in the Bible.

"It is all right here," he would say decisively during the sermon, tapping on the cover of his Bible.

At that point in the Black and White sermon he would thrust his Bible high above his head, in his right hand. It was a worn black leathered version of the NIV study Bible.

"Our choices in this world are between black and white, between the light and the darkness!" he would thunder. "Everything. Everything, is black and white," and the proof, he said, was in the Bible. "This cover on my Bible is black, but its pages are white," he would say simply, still holding up that Bible. Sometimes in the sermon he would look at the church pianist and ask her to play a few notes on the piano.

"The keys on that piano, on that glory of harmony, are either white or black. There are no gray keys, no sir, not on a piano," he would say. "Ms. Valerie, play the gray keys," he would jokingly ask the pianist. There would be silence, and calm in response. Ms. Valerie would shrug her shoulders, followed by the knowing smiles among the congregation. People would then reply, "Amen," or "Yes, Lord," in response.

"In Deuteronomy it is written, 'See, I have set before you this day, the choice: good and evil, the blessing and the curse, life and death,'" he would say triumphantly, ecclesiastically, to prove his point.

He would then walk from one end of the raised dais in front of the church altar to the other end, just holding the Bible aloft. People would gradually stand up and shout, "Amen!" Some in the congregation would clap, or hold the palms of their hands to the sky. A general murmuration, a soft and knowing undertone, would arise. He would keep walking back and forth on the raised dais, sweat streaming down his face, holding the Bible aloft until he felt the moment was right.

"It's all black and white! Life or death! Forces of light and forces of darkness!" he would rumble repeatedly, until the entire congregation was standing. Some members of the congregation would call out: "Tell it Brother Jessie!" But the problem in this battle between good and evil, Reverend Jessie would finally say to quiet the congregation, in a voice that was hypnotic, as he lowered the Bible in his hand, "is that we are naturally inclined toward evil, infected by that old original sin."

When I told Zarathustra II, somewhat proudly of my adolescent memories of Reverend Jessie's "Black and White" sermon, he looked at me sadly. His face looked weary. I was confused by his facial expression, unable to quickly decipher its fight or flight message. He looked away from me, and then momentarily down at his feet, searching for a remembrance, stumbling hard to find the right words.

"You can't pass judgment on others without it also being a judgment on yourself. All harsh external judgments flower from internal insecurity," he finally said. I struggled to understand what he meant, the sincerity of his words seemed profound, an experience he had lived.

"And the person who sees the world only in black and white does so in order to avoid having to think critically, or deeply. Absolutes trap the believer behind emotional and intellectual walls that cannot be easily scaled. Nietzsche, the atheist, thought it was a form of pathology, and Bonhoeffer, the theologian, thought it was an attempt 'to put a grown man back into adolescence.' My own view is that salvation should not be based on fear," he said slowly, searching, wanting me to understand his thoughts.

Chapter 14
MRS. RAISSA IVANOV

Although I had seen him as a summer time fixture near the Saenger Theater, and on Canal Street, on numerous occasions, preaching to anyone who would listen, the first time I actually met Zarathustra II was one afternoon when I was leaving the CRC. I had just attended the church's adult choir practice. I was not a good singer like Reverend Jessie, who had a deep melodic and dark baritone voice. I just unlocked the church before practice and locked it up after their practice. It was a job Reverend Jessie had unilaterally assigned to me, when I dropped out of community college.

I didn't mind the assignment. I actually liked to hear the calm of the singing in church. It was part of that sense of a larger community, brotherhood, that being a church member provided to me, though I am not sure I realized that at the time. Some aspects of religion, at least the rituals and the singing, are as much about the comfort of being part of a community, as about the substance each may represent. Although many Christians might claim their membership in a church is solely about their spiritual beliefs, I think it's also about belonging to something larger than themselves, about having a shared historical, or spiritual, narrative with others.

The adult choir director at the CRC was Mrs. Raissa Ivanov. She was originally from Russia and spoke broken English, dropping certain words, with a thick Russian accent. However, she sang in a beautiful soprano, which was unaffected by her accent. She had immigrated to the United States with her husband, Nikolai, and son, Mikhail. They ended up in

New Orleans because it was a port city and Nikolai had always dreamed of working on big ships, something he had been prohibited from doing in Russia.

Mrs. Ivanov was short, plain and sturdy, with large vacant brown eyes and a round weathered peasant's face. Her broad nose and angular jaw line held tightly the suffering of generations, and her face seemed to lighten only when she sang. Her straight black hair was cut in a bowl and she tended to dress very simply, her cotton skirts sometimes hanging awkwardly on her broad hips. She may have even made her own dresses. She always seemed harsh in her demeanor to me--not affectionate, but emotionally distant, unsure, and opaque.

However, she was one of Reverend Jessie's biggest supporters. She was often at CRC church services. In fact, it seemed like she was there for every daily service after her husband left her and their son for good to live and work on a merchant marine vessel.

She and her husband had often quarreled openly at the church, before or after, services, much to the discomfort of other church members. When they were angry with each other, which was often, their arguments were conducted in their native language. Once their argument broke out during the middle of a church service, interrupting a prayer being offered. Mrs. Ivanov was clearly embarrassed and dragged her husband by the arm out of the church, as if to the school house detention room.

I recall Reverend Jessie intervening and trying to counsel them at various times, at Mrs. Ivanov's insistence. They would meet him at the church after church services, to discuss their marital problems. Reverend Jessie told them that marriage was "a spiritual commitment to and before God Almighty" and as a result it could not be broken.

"Regardless of your problems, you cannot break your personal covenant with God," Reverend Jessie admonished them.

"Even if it become prison sentence?" Mr. Ivanov had asked him, in halting English, in one of their meetings. "What I do to deserve this prison sentence? Since you talk to Him you ask please, God this question

Reverend? What I do?" Mr. Ivanov asked, the dry cigarette wrinkles visible on his face.

At that point Mrs. Ivanov normally started to yell at her husband in Russian, so I was never sure what she said. As she continued to yell Mr. Ivanov would get up slowly and leave.

"I cannot reach him. He not religious man like you Reverend. He very stubborn," she would say. "What I do to make him more like you?" she had asked hopefully.

"Not like me," Reverend Jessie once replied, unenthusiastically, to her request.

Mr. Ivanov would go stand outside the church and, with languid movements, smoke filter less cigarettes until Mrs. Ivanov came outside. They would then leave together in an angered silence.

After her husband left her, Mrs. Ivanov would bring her reluctant son Mikhail with her to church services. She attended each 6:00 a.m. morning service and evening services Saturday and Sunday. Her son was two years older than me and unruly. I often saw him with his chin on his chest, asleep in a church pew during those morning services. At some point during his senior year he was expelled from high school. He immediately moved out from living with his mother into the French Quarter somewhere, and stopped coming to church services with her. I think she felt ashamed about it. It did seem she prayed even more vocally at church services after her son stopped coming to church with her.

Chapter 15
A HIGHER EXAMPLE

As the choir members and I left the CRC that afternoon, I saw Zarathustra II stretched out and sleeping on the red-tiled cement steps in front of the church. A street car went by and I heard the clanking of the wheels on the rails as it came to a stop to pick up passengers.

As the choir members started down the steps, Zarathustra II stirred and then stood up quickly. He seemed a bit unsteady.

"A song! A song for a troubled soul!" he yelled, in a voice that sought to recall an untroubled prior existence. Everyone stopped for a moment, not knowing what to do or say, surprised by him, as if his shape were a startling apparition from a long wished forgotten dream. His request went unanswered. The momentary silence was then pierced again by the sound of police sirens, as two NOPD police cars rushed down the street.

Zarathustra II raised his hands, like an orchestra conductor, and began to conduct an imaginary orchestra, tapping his right foot to a silent melody. I thought that it was funny and laughed. As he did so, I noticed that where his coat opened, it revealed that he had tied shoe strings together to make a belt around the waist of his slightly too large dungarees.

"A song! A song! A song!" Zarathustra II yelled out again and again, shuffling from side to side in front of us, in an improvised dance step, that blocked some choir members from immediately leaving. Several of the choir members regained their composure and, stone faced, walked around him.

"What disgrace!" Mrs. Ivanov rebuked him. "Get away from church! You don't belong here!"

"What is the cost to belong?" Zarathustra II asked cleverly. "Can you spot me a few dollars to join?"

"I say you don't belong here. Get away!" she replied, annoyed, turning her gaze away and brushing past him.

"Do you know any John Prine? How about Lucinda Williams?" he asked the departing choir members, unfazed by Mrs. Ivanov. No-one answered him, or acknowledged his question; like most homeless folks he was a ghost, he didn't exist.

Zarathustra II then laughed a silent laugh, and leaning over slapped his knee hard with one of his hands, as if he were imitating Harpo, in an old Marx Brothers movie. Straightening up, he cleared his throat loudly.

"OK, I'll sing for you." Zarathustra II turned and sang in a hungered voice to the choir members retreating images. The only words from the song I still remember are:

"...make me an angel that flies from Montgomery...."

I stood at the top of the church steps, watching him and smiling. There was something about him that I could not name, that I did not then understand, to which I was immediately drawn; there was something in his alienation which I also owned. Or, maybe, I simply realized he was not a threat to me. I had seen him several times preaching on the streets and did not fear him.

Chapter 16
EGG AND CHEESE SANDWICH

After Zarathustra II stopped singing I clapped a few times, timidly, not used to being noticed. He acknowledged my applause with a slight bow, tipping an imaginary hat to me, as if he were concluding a 1920's vaudeville act. I was the only one still standing on the church steps when he finished his song. He sat down, and immediately invited me to sit next to him, on the steps. He used the side of his hand to ineffectively brush away a few leaves and some dirt from where he wanted me to sit.

"Come join me. There is no fee," he said with a chuckle, patting his hand down on the steps to indicate for me to sit. I walked over and sat down. Zarathustra II ignored the normal feigned pleasantries of initial conversations. He immediately began to tell me about his theological beliefs.

That day I met him on the church steps, Zarathustra II also asked me to buy him something to eat. He said that it was a down payment on what he would teach me. I wasn't sure if I was being conned or not. I admit I was naive about such things. But I agreed. It was the start of our friendship. As we walked to the neighborhood convenience store on Prytania street, near the church, he asked me some brief questions about my religious upbringing, but always he quickly returned to what he wanted to teach me.

The convenience store had been flooded during Hurricane Katrina, and had, thereafter, changed ownership several times. The store was a run-down cinder block design, where many undocumented workers, who sought work in New Orleans, gathered in small groups each morning to wait for potential laboring jobs, or to meet with representatives of the New Orleans Center for Racial Justice.

When we walked into the convenience store, the cashier became agitated.

"Mas te vale tener dinero para pagar hoy!" the cashier yelled out. "Betta have money!" he followed up with, when Zarathustra II did not respond. Zarathustra II went directly to the cold food freezers and picked up a pre-made packaged egg and cheese sandwich and a 7UP.

"Pay the man," he said to me with another chuckle, pointing at the cashier, as he walked briskly out the door without stopping. It cost me $7.26.

When I emerged from the store, after paying the cashier, I found Zarathustra II seated in the parking lot on the curb near a parked car and an overturned blue and white metal trash container. It was a very hot summer day, yet he was still wearing his trench coat and wool cap. He had already finished the sandwich, or had put it in his pocket. I was not sure which, but I did not see it. He pulled the pop top off the 7UP can and in three long guzzles he drank it all down.

Before belching loudly and unashamedly, Zarathustra II told me that honesty dictated that he reveal to me that he was not the first person to notice that God had disappeared. He mentioned that a German Lutheran pastor named Dietrich Bonhoeffer had also written from his imprisonment in a Nazi concentration camp about the disappearance of God.

"Who was Dietrich Bonhoeffer?" I asked, tentatively.

"One of the twentieth century's greatest theologians."

"I never heard of him," I replied, standing with my hands tightly in my pockets, still tentative. Zarathustra II remained seated on the curb.

He told me a bit about Bonhoeffer's life, his escape from, and then voluntary return to, Nazi Germany, and his founding of the Free Church in opposition to the Nazi's takeover of the German Christian Churches. The Nazi's had appointed their own bishops, with little opposition from the Catholic Church, who preached a gospel of accommodation.

"I didn't know that history. I wonder why the religious folks cooperated with Hitler?"

"One of the difficult questions of the twentieth century. But unlike the Catholic Church, Bonhoeffer's truth required that he return and confront the Nazis as a witness, regardless of the personal cost," he said.

"What happened to him after he returned?"

He told me of Bonhoeffer's eventual imprisonment during WWII and the theological impact of the letters he wrote from prison, now studied in various seminaries. He told me about Bonhoeffer's eventual execution at the Flossenburg concentration camp, just weeks before Hitler's suicide, one last act of vengeance by a defeated regime. I was surprised to hear that a pastor had been part of a conspiracy to kill Hitler. I removed my hands from my pockets, relaxed my shoulders, and slowly lowered myself to the ground.

"Dietrich Bonhoeffer," Zarathustra II said, "wrote that we had to learn how to live without a present God."

"I don't understand. I thought you said he was a theologian. Was he an atheist?" I asked, confused.

"No, not at all. He was a devout Christian, but he read scripture to indicate that God had disappeared and wanted us to learn how to live without Him," Zarathustra II said. "That was his genius," he said proudly, before belching again in a way that sounded like a word from a primitive tribal language.

"Sounds kinda like he was an atheist," I replied, trying to act nonchalantly, pulling my knees up to my chest.

"Well, it did prompt the advent of what was called 'radical theology' in the 1960's, which was atheistic Christianity," he replied, in an equally distracted response.

"Atheistic Christianity? That doesn't make sense," I puzzled. Zarathustra II stretched his legs out in front of him on the ground.

"It comes off a bit like Zen Buddhism," Zarathustra II replied, staring at the 7UP can in his hand. Then he closed his eyes.

"Om Mani Padme Hum," he said, or something like that, three times. He then stood up hurriedly, gently placed the 7UP can on the ground, walked around it in a circle three times with his hands folded in prayer and then stomped on it with his heel, crushing it. He took the crushed can and put it in the torn outside pocket of his trench coat.

"Thomas Altizer was probably its original proponent. He thought the crucifixion was symbolic of the death of the Old Testament God," he said, looking down at me, but offering his hand.

"I have never heard of this," I said, grabbing his hand to steady myself as I stood up.

"Of course not. Modern day Evangelicals do not want you to be exposed to anything that contradicts them. You know it was not always that way. Evangelicals actually had a stronger intellectual tradition in the 1800s, but not anymore. Mark Noll wrote a good book about it which you should read called *The Scandal of the Evangelical Mind*."

"Scandal? What scandal are you talking about?" I asked, again confused, but feeling engaged.

"'The scandal of the Evangelical mind is that there is no Evangelical mind.' I think that is the opening line of his book," Zarathustra II said, posing, as I was to learn he often did when he recited something he had read.

"How do you know all of this stuff?" I asked, skeptical, unsure he wasn't making things up.

"You have to educate yourself. Modern man is becoming less and less literate and there is a heavy price for that indifference."

Several Hispanic workers walked towards us. Their faces were dark and their hands dirty from hard laboring work. One of them made eye contact with Zarathustra II and nodded his head knowingly with a slight toothless smile. Zarathustra II smiled back.

"Hola Z!" the worker said to Zarathustra II.

"Hola, Miguel. Como estas?" Zarathustra II asked.

"Bien. Y tu?"

"Muy Bien," Zarathustra II said in an exaggerated fashion, and then broke into another impromptu dance step in response. The workers laughed and one of them affectionately placed his hand on Zarathustra II's shoulder.

Zarathustra II then asked if I could lend him $5 to buy a meal later on that night. I pulled out my wallet and handed him my only $5 bill. Zarathustra II smiled widely looking at the $5 bill in his hands.

"A five to stay alive," he said. It was then that he decided that I would be his first apostle and stepped up on the overturned trash can to tell me so.

Chapter 17
LOCAL NEWS

That night I turned on the television to watch the local news. I had a small 19 inch television set which my mother had won at a church raffle several years before and given to me when I moved away from home. I did not pay for cable TV, but one of the prior tenants had illegally rigged up some cables that allowed the apartment to get Cox's basic cable package free.

Reverend Jessie was on the local news being interviewed in front of the Jax Brewery, near Jackson Square, about the upcoming Southern Decadence Festival in the French Quarter, over the labor day weekend. The Southern Decadence Festival was the annual New Orleans Festival for all things gay, lesbian and transgender. It was one of the countless festivals and parades in and around New Orleans each year that was a brush stroke on the cultural canvas of the city. Since its inception, it had become the signature national event for the gay community in New Orleans, attracting many visitors from out of town.

Reverend Jessie had a running battle with the city, and the festival organizers, concerning the Southern Decadence Festival. It became one of the focal points of his ministry each summer.

For several years it had been the centerpiece of the ministry of another local Pastor named Grave Southern. In those days Pastor Southern was the face of the protest and was often on TV reciting scripture and trying to rally others to his cause, his condemnation. Then it seemed he disappeared from public view. He was arrested, some years later, for sitting in his van and masturbating near Lafreniere Park.

Numerous other itinerant preachers protested the festival thereafter, but without much personal notoriety. The City eventually passed an ordinance trying to halt religious, or political, proselytizing in the French Quarter, but it was declared unconstitutional after some street preachers were arrested for violating it during the Festival. So opposition to the Festival was popular in the local Evangelical community. In the aftermath of the Supreme Court's recognition of gay marriage it became an even more urgent issue for Evangelicals. But none of the preachers, over the years, garnered the attention that Reverend Jessie did when he picked it up as a cause. He was strenuously opposed to the Festival and claimed that it represented one example of this "country's moral crisis" which we faced as a "Christian nation."

In this cultural battle over the Festival, Reverend Jessie's principal weapon was the Bible. He preached the Word as the moral basis to condemn the Festival, its organizers and homosexuality in general. The City government mostly ignored Reverend Jessie, but its weapon in this annual cultural battle was capitalism--the revenues generated for local merchants, and the sales taxes generated for the City by the tourists it attracted. The City, in essence, played the role of Caesar and asked that it receive its due. The gay community's weapon, in combating Reverend Jessie, was a combination of contempt and humor, and an occasional court injunction.

"This so called festival is pure evil, and it's a reflection of the moral decline of our Christian nation. Homosexuality is against God's law, and it is a violation of the deep rooted Christian ethic of this country," Reverend Jessie now told the female reporter, Clarice McComb, who was interviewing him.

"Who decides what is God's law?" the reporter parroted in a staged dramatic tone. She held the microphone up to Reverend Jessie's face awaiting an answer. Reverend Jessie smiled. He held up the copy of his black leather NIV Bible. The one I had seen him carry my entire life.

"It is all right here. This is the inerrant word of God Almighty!" he said, with his Evangelical voice rising, in a tone enunciating the precipice between salvation and damnation, as he shook the Bible in his hand and looked directly into the television camera. "And in no uncertain terms it says in Leviticus that 'If a man lies with a male as with a woman, both of them have committed an abomination!'"

There was a small crowd of people standing behind Reverend Jessie as he spoke to the reporter. They were all older white men. I recognized a few as CRC church members. Several people in the crowd carried neatly printed placards or handmade hoisted signs. On one sign someone had written, "Homosexuality is a sin." Another sign someone held up read, "Gays go to hell." One more sign said, "Jesus is love." A smaller poorly handwritten sign, on a torn portion of a cardboard box, held by someone I did not recognize, who appeared homeless, read, "Anything will help." The reporter turned away from Reverend Jessie, stepped towards the camera and wrapped up her story about the upcoming festival.

"Reverend Jessie and his supporters will be conducting rolling prayer services throughout the French Quarter to bring attention to what Reverend Jessie has described as quote, 'the undermining of the Christian ethic of our nation,'" she said, reading from her note pad. The Festival organizers were already threatening court action, according to Ms. McComb. The Festival was weeks away, but Reverend Jessie and his supporters, as they did every year, were starting early to try to bring their message to the people throughout the city.

Chapter 18
DISCALCED

It was about the time that I turned off the television that I heard a constant knocking at my apartment door. I lived in a one bedroom apartment on the second floor of an old two story raised wooden house on Toulouse street, in the Mid City neighborhood. It was a salt box looking house that had been built after World War II and converted into four apartments in the 1970s. Since its conversion it had cycled through the penniless hands of many poor college students. The first floor had been flooded during hurricane Katrina and was partially repaired before the owner's Road Home money ran out. The green paint on the exterior of the building was peeling and the second floor was not well insulated.

There was an air condition unit in the den window with peeling silver duct tape holding it to a slightly damp and rotting window frame. The apartment had space heaters in the upstairs apartment, which were the only source of heat. For some reason, each summer, it also had fleas. Plenty of fleas. It had been my home for almost a year after I quit Delgado Community College and as I held an assortment of menial jobs. At the moment I was unemployed again, but still receiving a weekly unemployment check, along with occasional cash from my mother. I had just used two Raid Flea bombs that morning, so there was a slightly poisonous smell in the air.

I still do not know how Zarathustra II found out where I lived. It was that night that he moved in with me. He did not really own anything, except the clothes which he was wearing, his copy of *Thus Spoke Zarathustra*, his pencils, pencil sharpener and the note pad in which he neatly printed his thoughts. My sofa, an inherited threadbare green and brown print artifact with scarred cherry stained wooden legs, which had been left in the apartment by a prior tenant, became his bed. My sense was that, other than perhaps at the Ozanam Inn or the New Orleans Mission, which were the local homeless shelters, he had not slept in a bed for awhile.

When he walked into the apartment he immediately stepped past me, too familiar and without introduction, and scanned the apartment's sparse furnishings, chipped white paint on the walls and dull hard pine wooden floors.

"You are lucky to live so simply," he said, as if I had made a conscious choice to reject a large inheritance to do so. I noticed that he was barefoot.

"What happened to your shoes?" I asked.

"I gave them to someone who needed them more than I did," he replied.

"Isn't that hard on your feet?" I asked.

"Yes. But now I shall be discalced," he replied.

"Dis..calced? What is discalced?"

"Discalced, from the Latin *discalceatus*. It is part of my desire to share in human suffering," he said.

Then, without any further preliminary small talk, he started talking to me about the Bible again, the way that he read it, what it should mean, and how we should use it. It seemed important to him that I, as his newly designated first apostle, understand exactly what he believed. For Zarathustra II that meant understanding things at a level deeper than most people live their lives. To know him meant attempting the journey to his level of understanding, beyond the mystery, miracles and magic underlying most people's beliefs, to the distant shore, perhaps too far, of the house of reason. You could not do it, learn and grow, by safely listening to him from the shoreline. You had to take your uncertainty, confess it, and get in the boat and, despite the ominous sky, go out into turbulent deeper blue waters with him and risk capsizing.

In some ways, I guess, we all wish to be understood. However, from Zarathustra II I learned that for those intelligent individuals, with intellectual curiosity, who have been abused, or marginalized, belittled, by family or by society, their need to be understood is at a deeper, and, perhaps, impossible to satisfy, level. For such individuals tearing apart issues of truth, ethics and experience, and sharing that intellectual journey with others, is a safer form of intimacy, removed from the threat of possible emotional harm, which they need reciprocated. It is their attempt, perhaps, to stand up in the unsteady boat and proclaim to the inattentive world: "I am here. I deserve to be. And you should acknowledge my right to be."

Chapter 19
NO PERSONALITY

As I watched, cautiously, and unsure, Zarathustra II walked barefoot in small circles around my living room, three times. He then sat down on the sofa and pulled his knees up to his chest, in a seated child pose, putting the soles of his feet on the sofa. The bottom of his slightly too long dungarees were worn off, frayed and dirty at the cuffs, from being stepped on and dragged on the ground.

"God left us with silence. It is when our prayers are not answered though that we can experience our own growth. His silence is our tree of knowledge, from which we must dare to eat," Zarathustra II said.

His theme of God disappearing was one I already knew and I told him so, annoyed that he had just shown up at my apartment. If he sensed my annoyance he didn't acknowledge it. But now he started to fill in another layer of the biblical story, as he read it. It was about why God quit the scene. It was also about our growing responsibility for ourselves and for each other.

"You have probably noticed," he then said, as if he was an actor in a one man play, "that in the Genesis' story Adam and Eve, prior to eating the forbidden fruit, are very primitive, insubstantial, one dimensional characters."

"One dimensional characters?" I asked, unclear what he meant.

"Milton gave both of them some depth, of course," Zarathustra II said distractedly, ignoring my question. "'Sufficient to have stood, but free to fall,' Milton has God say in *Paradise Lost*, referring to Adam and Eve. And Kierkegaard thought Eve was only created because Adam was already bored with paradise," he giggled, as if revealing a childhood secret he had been waiting all school day to tell to a favored classmate at recess on a school yard playground.

"What do you mean by one dimensional characters?" I asked more clearly, still a half beat behind him, and realizing that a part of me wanted to engage him in the discussion, despite my initial frustration.

"Well, Adam and Eve display virtually no emotion, no depth, no personality, no real forethought or consciousness," he replied quickly, as if reciting from memory a story he had often told as part of a tribal oral tradition. "From a factual standpoint they are unemotional stick man characters that a grade school child could have drawn for his first art assignment," he continued. "Their theological value, of course, is significant, but it's not in the alleged factual narrative. Rather it is in the development of human consciousness, which they represent," he said.

"Development of human consciousness? I thought they were fully formed by God?"

"Noah was the same way. He is as thin a slice of humanity as the parchment his story was first written on, and has no conscience at all, though he does at least get drunk," he continued with a wide smile. "Can you imagine God telling you that he is going to kill everything and almost everyone on the planet and saying or doing nothing to stop it?" he asked incredulously, as he shook his head.

"You are talking about Noah?" I interrupted, to be sure that I was following his reference.

"Yes," he replied patiently.

"Well, really what could Noah do. God is all powerful. I mean he could not stop God from doing what He was going to do with the flood," I said uneasily, certain but unsure, in Noah's defense. Zarathustra II placed his hands on his knees, which were still pulled up into his chest. He looked away from me and then stood up, and began to pace again in unhurried circles around my den.

"No, you are right. Noah could not. But that's because humanity at that time of the allegorical story, was not yet emotionally or intellectually developed enough," he finally said. I walked over and sat down on the sofa confused.

"But once we get to Abraham, and then to Jacob, all that changes. Abraham does negotiate with God. Abraham and Jacob display reason, personality and thought," he said, in an animated fashion. I continued to sit quietly watching him in his one man play, trying to decide if I should still be annoyed with him for just showing up at my apartment.

"So you see," he said, after a contemplative pause, "the biblical story is about man's evolution from the one dimension of the instinctual stick people Adam and Eve, prior to eating from the tree of knowledge, to the rationality of Abraham, where he actually appeals to God's vanity and even argues with him." At that point Zarathustra II smiled sheepishly.

"Remember Abraham plays to God's ego in the story and cleverly questions God: 'Will you sweep away the righteous with the wicked? What if there are fifty righteous people in the city?' He then goes on to say, 'Far be it from you to do such a thing,' appealing to God's vanity and then challenges, 'Will not the judge of the earth do right?' Adam could never have said such a thing to God, and Noah, for all his supposed righteousness, cannot either. And then Moses gets him to feel remorse and change his mind. Remember in Exodus, 'Then the Lord relented and did not bring on his people the disaster he had threatened.' And there is Jacob and Joseph. Joseph is a fully developed self-conscious human. He thinks. He contemplates his situation. He plants the seeds for the future enlightenment. He fails and succeeds in ways that Adam, Eve and Noah could not," Zarathustra II said excitedly, as if he were relaying the facts of historic events that he had actually witnessed. I was unfamiliar with his version of the narrative, but gradually at ease with him.

"I don't mean to offend but so what? Even if you are right what does it matter?"

"What we are seeing in this character development is the pre-scientific biblical writers struggling to explain the evolution of human self consciousness and human identity, from lower instinctual forms, like the animals around them, to higher forms of consciousness. It's a great evolutionary story. It starts with the allegorical Eve eating the forbidden fruit, which represents reason or knowledge, and develops from there. And once self consciousness develops sufficiently our need for meaning emerges," he said, almost to himself.

"I thought you were going to tell me more about why God disappears in the Bible and leaves us on our own," I said stubbornly. "What does all this character development stuff have to do with that?" I asked, assuring myself, with an uncertain self confidence, that I had properly pointed out a digression.

"It is an overlay. It's part of the reason that God disappears over time," he said softly, but emphasizing the word "reason" by adding extra syllables in his pronunciation. "You can't possibly understand the disappearance of God, and why He walked away from us in the story, disappeared, without also understanding the related human development, and the evolving self consciousness that occurs over the time line. Once we come of age, God disappears," he concluded.

"Wait. I don't understand. So are you saying that God disappears because we don't need Him anymore?"

"Let me clarify. Man's self consciousness grew over the story's time-line to the point where we developed the ability to take on the responsibility for each other, without the idea of a God to be appeased, a God as a constant intervener or final arbiter in our everyday affairs. But, instead of pursuing a collective good, we have pursued individual agendas in a futile search for personal meaning, and have continued, sometimes directly, sometimes more vaguely, to ask God to handle the responsibility for our fellow man. Our development of self consciousness had the eventual unintended consequence of us pursuing individualism at the expense of our commitment to others. We evolved, but we took a wrong turn."

Chapter 20
THE FALL

Zarathustra II traced the beginning of this character development in the biblical narrative to Eve's "heroic act" of eating the forbidden fruit of knowledge. "That is meant to represent mankind's first act of free will in the story, our first act of self consciousness. From that point on, we were no longer condemned to act as merely instinctual animals. That is the beginning of our story, not the end of it, as so many preachers, who are fearful of reason and human desires, want us to believe," he said. He remained standing as he spoke. I tried to place what he said within the context of what was known and familiar to me. His comment about Eve almost seemed too intimate. It made me strangely uncomfortable.

I cleared my throat and decided to object. "I thought that our Fall was from God, from his presence, and it was Eve's fault," I said, a bit urgently, in my best impression of what I remembered Reverend Jessie teaching us in Sunday school. I had the sudden realization that I was mouthing what I had been taught and that while I knew such sayings, I knew nothing about the theological basis, if any, of what I was saying. I recalled Reverend Jessie talking about the fall of mankind often. "It was due to the devilry of Eve," he had always told me.

Zarathustra II scoffed when I finally said all of this. He then resumed his pacing in circles on the hard wood floors; three times around again.

"Fall from what? From being treated like unthinking children?" he asked unusually stern, but understanding, as he made the third circle around the den. "Original sin is Augustinian nonsense, based upon Jerome's incorrect Latin Vulgate translation of Romans. If only Augustine could have read Greek better," he then said more thoughtfully.

I did not understand the significance of Augustine's inability to read Greek. At that time I knew nothing of the biblical manuscript streams and the faulty Latin translation that Augustine had relied upon in crafting his doctrine of original sin. Augustine was apparently unable to read Greek and relied upon language in Jerome's incorrect Latin Vulgate translation of the Bible in creating his doctrine of original sin. Zarathustra II knew these things, and patiently explained it to me. When he mentioned Augustine I pictured Reverend Jessie seated at our kitchen table with Augustine's *Confessions* in his hand.

"Luke, the story of the Fall of Adam and Eve should not be read literally, but as a metaphor or allegory. It is an attempt to explain unexplainable things, scary things, in a pre-scientific culture. The story is not about some guy named Adam who ate an apple he wasn't supposed to eat, or about a talking snake" he said. "A talking snake." He giggled at the thought. Zarathustra II then knelt down on the hardwood floor.

"When God tells Adam that if he eats from the tree of knowledge, 'Thou shalt surely die,' what the authors are trying to convey is that knowledge leads to self consciousness, and through self consciousness man will become aware of his eventual death. That's what 'Thou shalt surely die' means. Man will then carry the knowledge of his eventual death with him everyday henceforth. He can no longer live totally in the present, like other instinctual animals, unaware of the future, but, instead he will live with the stress of that uncertain future, and the weight of his past," Zarathustra II explained. "The eating of the forbidden fruit is the line of demarcation, indicating the roots of our self consciousness. And one more thing. The metaphorical eating of the apple is also the beginning of human morality, which cannot exist without self knowledge," he repeated.

I was unsure what to say further in response. He had shown up at my apartment unannounced and began to lecture me about the Bible. Maybe,

I thought, I had let him get too familiar. Still, I felt comfortable around him and I enjoyed being able to ask questions without ridicule.

"I don't know what to say. Some of what you are saying is interesting. I never heard anyone say anything like that," I replied simply. He smiled without judgment.

"It is such a shame that the Fall, the foundational story of Christianity, is read in such an anti-intellectual manner," Zarathustra II then said sorrowfully. I looked at him, as I continued to sort my thoughts

"Anti-intellectual? What do you mean by that?" I asked.

"The story of Adam and Eve's fall into self consciousness has become an anti-intellectual story for most of Christianity and is used by too many preachers to denigrate reason and pander to our lesser angels. If you eat from the tree of *knowledge*, and learn to think for yourself, as a result, you are then banned from paradise," he responded slowly. "How ridiculous."

"But what about Eve's role?" I asked.

"The female remains the scapegoat, doesn't she. Organized religion has so often been used as the enforcer of cultural values and women have suffered so much as a result," Zarathustra II said quietly, but with a pained expression on his weathered face. I saw his compassion for others at that moment. "Christianity has too often given women the false choice of being either the deceptive Eve or the virginal Mary. How absurd," he whispered with difficulty, as if a part of him wished to deny what he had concluded.

I had the sudden sense that he was not really talking to me at the end, but instead, had disassociated and spoke only to himself. I had this feeling at various times when Zarathustra II spoke to me. I remember wondering early on if God spoke to him, like He did to Reverend Jessie. He assured me, with a slight laugh, when I finally asked, that God did not.

"I'm not offended by His silence. Most people don't speak to me," he added.

I still did not agree with his comments about Eve, though he had said much I had never heard before. And I finally confessed to him that I had never really thought about the development of self consciousness for the people in the Bible.

"You'll get there. You're smart," he replied. "Where is the bathroom?" he asked, as he absentmindedly scratched the hair on his face. I pointed down the hall. He started to walk down the hall shaking his head at me in mock frustration. "If you are going to be my apostle you are going to have to figure these things out," he said. "After all, it's not like I am Jesus speaking in parables," he then said, his voice trailing off. It provoked a smile from me.

Chapter 21
PLANS

I had previously promised Reverend Jessie that I would attend a meeting he had organized at the church to discuss his plans for an upcoming protest march directed at the Southern Decadence Festival. The church always had meetings, meals or gatherings, of one type or another, each week. Such gatherings were the unspoken backbone of that sense of community and belonging I mentioned, which was offered by the church to its followers.

When I walked into the church's anteroom there was a crowd of people present. Some of the ladies of the church had baked cookies and homemade pies. I smelled fresh coffee, chicory, being brewed. Reverend Jessie was in front of the group, dressed in a blue suit with a yellow print tie loosened a bit at the collar. He was talking about the plan to divide into two groups so that the church could cover both Bourbon Street and Royal Street in the days leading up to the Festival. He was going to email the local radio and television stations each group's itinerary, along with a statement of the church's position on the festival, so as to try to maximize media exposure. Reverend Jessie told us that proper media exposure for a cause was a lesson that he had learned from reading about the Civil Rights movement. One person from each group, on each street, would be designated to talk to the media, with Reverend Jessie being the principal spokesperson for the church.

"We are charged with dominion over this world and we must take the necessary steps to turn this land into the kingdom of God on earth, ruled by godly men," he said to Mr. John Henry Calvin, one of his older parishioners. "At least that is how I view my charge from God."

I was assigned to go with Reverend Jessie's main group on Bourbon Street. Reverend Jessie just pointed at me as he was calling out names. "You, Mr. Bonnett, Mr. Daigre and Mr. Calvin are with my group." Early on in the meeting it was decided by Reverend Jessie that none of the women would come into the French Quarter. "This is our God given responsibility men. We will not expose our women to this immorality," he said.

"Thank you Brother Jessie," Mrs. Ivanov responded. The women, instead, would be in charge of making the signs; the placards, that the men would carry during their march. Reverend Jessie told them the size and colors of the signs he wanted, and that he would help them come up with the language for the signs.

I was watching this, but for the first time did not really feel like I was a part of it. In hindsight, I think that my exposure to Zarathustra II had put the worm of reason in the apple of my conformity.

In light of his comments at my apartment about how people misread the story of the Fall and other parts of the Bible, I had asked Zarathustra II directly about the potential dangers of relying on reason instead of faith, and about pursuing secular knowledge. I wanted to know more since Reverend Jessie had always discouraged the pursuit of secular knowledge. As I listened to Reverend Jessie talk about the protest against the Festival, my throat tightened and my mind drifted to the conversation I had the evening before with Zarathustra II.

"You said that Christianity is often anti-intellectual, or something like that. But isn't all that thinking, reading and reasoning, dangerous to one's faith? Isn't it just an obstruction of faith?" I had asked.

"It is an important question to ask," he had said.

"So why should anyone do it?"

"Because the alternative, complacent conformity, is worse."

"How can it be worse?"

"Reason can be a tool to destroy the walled prison of prejudice and dogma. It allows you to try to change your narrative of self and not live with a predefined definition that someone else imposed on you."

"I was always told that it was dangerous and would obstruct my faith in God."

"Luke, it is not a choice of either reason or faith. You can have both. Indeed, you should have both. It is dangerous to only have one. I know."

"How can you have both?"

"Because they address different things. Reason can tell us how and faith may help us determine why."

"Why and how," I recall repeating to myself, trying to understand, to feel, what it meant.

I returned my attention to Reverend Jessie, who was still discussing the protest march. Reverend Jessie did not know that Zarathustra II had moved in with me and was sleeping on my couch. He certainly would not have approved. Reverend Jessie had never visited my apartment and I was not concerned about him discovering it. Anyway, even though I felt some distance from it, I intended to go along with what Reverend Jessie was asking me to do concerning being with him to protest the Festival. I had followed his directives and acceded to his authority my entire life without question and it did not enter my mind that this would ever end.

But Zarathustra II was teaching me that using reason and questioning authority, even God's authority, was part of living and was even sanctioned in the Bible. Abraham, Isaac, Jonah, Abel, Aaron, and so many others had done so. I never knew that a history of independent thought existed in the Bible, independent thought that showed faith and reason were not necessarily inapposite.

Chapter 22
FORBIDDEN FRUIT

"Remember that after eating the forbidden fruit God says, 'Here the human has become like one of us,'" Zarathustra II said to me, while he was laying on his back on my inherited couch. The yellow foam padding on one of the cushions of the couch was sticking out where the material covering it had become too thin and had split. The support springs on the couch also sagged a bit in the middle, so Zarathustra II seemed to be lying in a slight hole. However, he had his hands behind his head with his fingers entwined, oblivious to the condition of the sofa, like he was in a hammock on a Caribbean beach, soaking up the sun in a long anticipated vacation. I had just woke up and was standing in the adjacent kitchen in my faded Winnie the Pooh pajama bottoms, trying to decide what to do about breakfast, as I had no food in the apartment. The kitchen faucet dripped sporadically behind me. The air condition window unit emitted a low fragile hum, as it strained to put forth cold air in the humidity of a New Orleans summer morning.

I told Zarathustra II, in a voice of disinterest, that I was familiar with that part of Genesis.

"For the moment ignore the problem of who God is talking to and what it is meant to convey when He says that Adam has become *like one of us*," Zarathustra II said, in a matter of fact tone.

I stood frozen for a moment feeling the cracked and damp linoleum kitchen floor on my bare feet. The faucet dripped again more noisily into the porcelain silence of the stained sink.

I had never really thought about who God might be talking to when He said that Adam had become "like one of us," and I could not remember Reverend Jessie ever discussing it. I tried to focus, to remember anything I was ever told on the subject and came up blank.

"I---never thought about that. Seems kind of odd," I finally managed to say.

Zarathustra II told me that such conversations by God, if the Bible was read literally, undermined the claim of monotheists of a single god, though as a non-literalist he was unconcerned.

"Joseph Smith, the founder of Mormonism, famously preached in 1844, as a result of this and other biblical language, that there was more than one god, though his current followers don't like to admit that," he told me.

He stood up and walked into the kitchen and opened and closed the refrigerator door several times to fan himself. He finally leaned over and looked into the empty refrigerator, having apparently already forgotten that I told him it was empty. The refrigerator light flickered off and on.

"The biblical authors were planting the seed of us becoming our own gods. The idea of the raging Old Testament God was going to disappear, over time, and we were going to have to become our own gods in order to deal with our new consciousness and new responsibilities," he said, still standing with his hand on the open refrigerator door and staring into the empty refrigerator.

I stood there and thought about what he had said, but could only manage to say that I would have to think about it more. "It's hard to think on an empty stomach," Zarathustra II said, closing the refrigerator door.

"I have some of my unemployment monies left. Let's go downtown to eat," I suggested.

"I like your thinking," Zarathustra II responded, walking immediately to my apartment door to leave.

Chapter 23
CHRISTIAN COMPLACENCY

Zarathustra II and I left my apartment to catch the Canal Street streetcar, a few blocks from my house, to head downtown to the French Quarter for breakfast. The street was still wet from the prior evening's rain, and the morning dampness mingled with early morning heat and reminded me of a lost childhood summer day, sitting with my mother on the lakefront's cement steps, fishing in Lake Pontchartrain. My parents had a fight that morning in front of me, which was unusual, and my mother suddenly announced that she and I were going fishing, something we had never done. The "fight" was really just my father repeatedly correcting my mother's grammar, her syntax, and telling my mother, Madeline, that she was not being a good minister's wife and was unsupportive of him. She had tried for several years to get rid of the accent, her dialect, to please my father, who told her it "evidenced a lack of culture." But, eventually she ceased trying. Shortly, thereafter, she stopped coming to church.

"I have grave responsibilities. You don't understand. I am responsible for the soul of each and every member of my church," he told my mother, when she complained, in response, about his frequent absences from home.

"What bout ya responsibility fa ya wife an ya child?" she had countered, in her Chalmette accent where "this" and "that" became "dis" and "dat," to his growing frustration.

"Sometimes we have to make choices Madeline."

"An ya neva choose ya family. I'm tellin ya dat ain't rite," she said.

I had been ill most of that school year, perhaps adding additional stress to their lives. The doctors simply told my mother that I should get plenty of bed rest and relax. My father was not happy about my illness, which he doubted, and periodically diagnosed as having "lead in my ass." So that morning my mother took me with her to Puglia's Sporting Goods store and bought two inexpensive Zebco fishing rods and we went fishing. Thereafter, that one summer, we would periodically go to the Lakefront, park near the Southern Yacht Club, and fish on the bottom of the lake using dead shrimp she bought from a man on the side of the road, whose white panel van had a sign indicating that he sold "SWIMPS BY THE POUND." What we did not use as bait she would bring home, peel and use in her etouffe. We would sit on the steps of the Lakefront silently for long periods of time, her mind trying to frame up her life, her present and maybe her past.

"Ya fatha means well," my mother would eventually say to me, in defense of what she probably thought indefensible. "He has lots a stuff on his plate, but he loves ya, just member dat. Dat's important ta know," she would tell me. "Yes, ma-am," I recall saying, when she told me my father loved me.

By the time we reached the Canal Street streetcar stop, Zarathustra II seemed to have forgotten about eating. He told me that he felt it was important for him to be in Jackson Square today to tell people about God's disappearance and our growing responsibility for each other as a result. He moved incessantly back and forth, restless.

"We must battle ingrained Christian complacency," he said, before sneezing into the palm of his hand and then wiping it on his trench coat. I told him, more calmly, I would catch up with him, but was going first to Café Du Monde to get some coffee and beignets.

Zarathustra II seemed increasingly agitated the longer we waited for the streetcar. His mood seemed to be changing, as I was to learn it often did with no warning, like the summertime weather in New Orleans. Mostly it was small mood swings, but on occasion there could be some large brief and jarring dips, like hitting an unexpected pot hole while driving. He paced, three times in a circle to the right and three times to the left, around the covered waiting area for the streetcar. And he kept mumbling. Others waiting for the streetcar stared uncomfortably at him.

"What's with everything in threes?" I finally asked.

"What?"

"You circle around three times. You repeat things three times."

"Sorry. I'll stop," he said embarrassed. I felt suddenly guilty for raising the issue.

"It's OK. I just didn't know why," I said.

"Thanks. I'll try to stop. Forgive me."

As I stood waiting for the streetcar I turned away from Zarathustra II and looked into the nearby cemetery. His restlessness disturbed my lethargy and was difficult to watch. I saw the countless cement head stones, fallen concrete angels and sacrificial ornaments, rising above ground. New Orleanians were buried above ground because the city was below sea level, something of a submerged island, bordered by the Mississippi river, Lake Pontchartrain, and the not too distant Gulf of Mexico.

I thought again about the fact that I had seen Reverend Jessie the night before at the church gathering. I knew he was going to be in the French Quarter at some point today to continue his condemnation of the Festival, but I did not know where he was going to be, or when he was going to be there. I thought that, after I finished eating, I could walk around and probably find him.

When the streetcar finally dropped us off on the corner of Canal Street and Decatur Street, Zarathustra II and I started walking silently toward Jackson Square. Zarathustra II walked much too fast for me to keep up with and eventually I lost sight of him. He was Olympian in the physical and mental pace which he set for himself each day. He was always in a hurry to get somewhere. Of course, once he got to where he was headed, he was in a hurry to leave. He just had trouble staying in one place for very long, like a falsely convicted prisoner who is finally free from confinement, but who can never wash off the indelible fear that his freedom was a mistake.

Chapter 24
MRS. ROSEMARY MATTHEWS

When I got to the Café Du Monde, I did not see Zarathustra II anywhere. I walked by a street musician who was seated on a bar stool near the entrance to the cafe playing a saxophone. I saw an open table inside the cafe, sat down, and eventually ordered some beignets and cafe au lait. I realized that my money was tight and that I should probably consider getting another job. But I didn't feel motivated to look for one. As I settled into my chair, I could hear the horn of a tugboat, pushing something up, or down, the nearby Mississippi River.

Almost immediately after the waitress came back with my order of coffee and three beignets, and before I could take a bite, my mother, Madeline, and her best friend, Mrs. Rosemary Matthews, walked up unannounced and sat down at my table. They had been playing video poker down the street and decided to take a break and get some coffee. The two of them were exact physical opposites. My mother was short and thin, her hair an unnatural beauty parlor golden brown. Mrs. Rosemary Matthews, who had played volleyball in high school, was tall and had grown heavier over the years, because of her 'menopausal middle' she said. Her hair was a red not found in nature and she had a lifetime smoker's deep raspy voice.

My mother, as was often the case when she went out in public to play video poker with Mrs. Rosemary Matthews, was wearing a white cotton scarf over her hair with a wide brimmed red hat over the scarf. She also had on thick black framed sunglasses. It was one of her daily disguises so as not to be noticed in public playing video poker, since she was the wife of Reverend Jessie. The problem was that Mrs. Rosemary Matthews, who had no reason to disguise her appearance, took to dressing the same way as my mother on these outings. In fact, they always talked before going out and matched their outfits. No matter the weather, the two of them would be wearing identical pants suits, scarves over their hair, with a brightly colored matching hat on top and dark sunglasses. It would have been harder to come up with outfits that were more noticeable. Indeed, instead of appearing nondescript, the outfits drew immediate attention to them. Something which Reverend Jessie said was "an intentional and passive aggressive act."

While my relationship with my father was devoid of sentimentality, my mother and I shared a kind of forced intimacy, as evidenced by our fishing outings that one summer. But I had not attached emotionally to her, felt nothing I could identify as the love one might expect in a mother-son relationship. My father was such a domineering presence in my early life that the normal expected emotional bond between mother and child was smothered at birth. Her role, early in my life, was simply one of duty, which she understood, and believed, to be love. It was a love, or duty, that mostly manifested itself in doing what needed to be done for me and in an occasional reassurance. We never fought or argued, never discussed life's expectations, but there were also no overt expressions of love or affection between us.

As they sat down at my table, they continued a conversation they had apparently been having, as if I was not present. Mrs. Rosemary Matthews, without asking, took one of my three beignets and placed it on a paper napkin in front of her and started eating it. My mother did the same.

Mrs. Rosemary Matthews and my mother had been friends since their early childhood growing up in Chalmette, Louisiana. Both of their fathers were commercial shrimpers, who worked together on the same boat out of Delacroix, and their families lived down the block from each other, near the local chemical refinery. Both were the only child in their family and they grew up as playmates and then as schoolmates.

The life of a shrimper was hard, often dependent on the weather and other things beyond their control. When it wasn't shrimping season, or when the catch was bad, their fathers would go offshore together to work as roughnecks on oil rigs in the Gulf of Mexico. The families grew up rough, often poor, but connected closely to nature and always with a sense of the importance of what they understood, vaguely, as divine providence.

At age 15 Mrs. Matthews had moved in with my mother and grandparents after her mother committed suicide by jumping into the Mississippi river off the old Huey P. Long bridge. Her mother did not leave a suicide note, so no one ever knew the reason for the suicide. Because her father was either offshore, or gone for days at a time shrimping, her move in with my grandparents became permanent. The move cemented the friendship with my mother.

They started playing video poker together as soon as it was legalized by the Louisiana legislature. They played every week, much to the dismay of Reverend Jessie. I never objected because my mother often gave me her video poker winnings, so as not to have to deal with my father on what to do with the money.

"It's our religion, ain't dat rite Madie?" Mrs. Rosemary Matthews would say laughingly, to anyone who asked her about video poker. This was sometimes followed by a nicotine induced coughing spell. My mother, who remained concerned about making a public scene as the wife of a minister, would try to calm her.

"Not so loud Rosemary, if Jessie hears ya say dat . . . God forbid." Actually, it was more like "Gawwd fo-bid," when she said it, and she would roll her eyes behind those dark sunglasses.

Mrs. Matthews was often at our house when I was growing up. She seemed to show up whenever my father was gone. I recall once, when I was a young child, asking Mrs. Matthews if she read the Bible, and why she did not go to church, something I heard my father complain about to my mother.

"Gawd an I ain't on no speakin terms. When He tells me why my mutha jump'd off da Huey P. I'll go visit Him in da church. Now hush ya mout an go outside an play," Mrs. Matthews told me.

"Do you read the Bible?" I asked again.

"No. I'm mo worried bout livin ma life in da present den I'm bout how doze people lived dere's in da past," she said. "Na go outside."

My mother read scripture when I was younger, but she did not know or live scripture the way my father did. When I was young my father and mother would often sit quietly together, each evening, at our kitchen table reading from their own Bible. My mother's Bible had a red leather cover on it and was a wedding present from my father. My mother knew, or remembered, a few biblical stories and often told Mrs. Rosemary Matthews and me that she especially liked the ones involving miracles.

"Can ya believe, Rosemary, dat Jesus fed all a dem people wit just doze few fish?" she would say. "I really like dat miracle."

"Dat's only cause ya Jessie wadn't dere. Oh Lordy, dat man eats so much doze utta folks would a surely gone hungry if he'd a been dere!" Mrs. Matthews would reply.

"Rose-maree!" she would say sternly, trying to shame her friend, "ya ought ta be shamed a ya-self. Jessie woiks hard an he builds up a appetite." When my mother was pretending to be outdone with her friend she pronounced her name, "Rose-Mareee," stretching it out.

"An like all dem free loadin ministers he specially woiks up a appetite when someone else is doin da paying!" Mrs. Matthews would say.

"Oh, Rose-Maree!" my mother would say, in mock frustration with her friend.

"If Jessie had been dere wit Jesus it would a been called da two miracles a da fishes. Da first one ta feed Jessie, da second one ta feed all doze utta people," Mrs. Rosemary Matthews would say unrepentant, as she started to laugh. My mother would not want to, but she would start to giggle like the young girl she could still be around her best friend. Before long one or the other would have to dab their tears with a handkerchief from laughing so hard. I never knew what to make of those conversations when I was younger.

Reverend Jessie had tried for years to convince my mother to part ways with Mrs. Matthews. He called her: "That sinful child of Eve."

"She is garrulous and she is a bad influence on you," he would say indignantly.

"We all chilren a Eve. An besides she's ma friend," my mother would reply to his badgering, and in her attempted defense of her childhood friend.

"Speak proper English Madeline, for goodness sake. It is important. You are the wife of a minister and it reflects directly on me. Rosemary is the reason Paul wanted women to remain silent in church," my father would bellow back, in the beginning of the end days of their relationship.

"Paul who?" my mother asked.

"Paul the apostle, Madeline."

"Paul didn't know Rosemary, she aint dat old. She's ma age," my mother responded.

"Madeline don't be so dense. I never said they knew each other. Oh!..." Reverend Jessie responded frustrated.

"Well," my mother would say, again stumbling to the defense of her friend as best she could, when confronted with my father's reliance on scripture, "No matta. Paul don't got ta worry none, cause Rosemary don't go ta no church."

She would confound my father by continuing her lifelong friendship with Mrs. Rosemary Matthews. When it came to a choice between compliance with Reverend Jessie's way of reading scripture, his absolutes, and her friendship with, and fondness for, Mrs. Rosemary Matthews, my mother always chose her best friend.

Chapter 25
HURRICANE CALENDAR

Besides playing video poker together, and making mild fun of Reverend Jessie, Mrs. Rosemary Matthews and my mother shared one other intense interest: hurricanes. They knew the names of all the hurricanes that had ever hit New Orleans, or the Gulf Coast, during their lifetime. Hurricanes were the background music to their lives, the way that politics, religion or a job, might be for others. Hurricanes provided constant and immutable reference points for them. It was how they measured things, memorized and organized time. It was as if they kept their internal calendars, the rhythm of their lives, based upon hurricane season, and their memories of the past, and their place in it, could only be recalled in their version of hurricane time.

As we sat at the table, and I ate the only remaining beignet, Mrs. Rosemary Matthews asked my mother a question about a wedding ceremony of a friend that was held near the moon walk, behind Café Du' Monde, on the Mississippi river levee.

"Dat was bout eight years afta Hurricane Betsy hit," my mother answered. As if on cue a paddle boat on the nearby river sounded its horn, indicating it was departing from the dock. At some point in the continuing conversation, in reference to something else, Mrs. Rosemary Matthews said, "Don't ya recall Madie, dat was bout six months befo Hurricane Camille hit."

In this world of hurricane calendars, and long before the weather channel was on television, both women, as natives of the area, believed that they were adept at predicting storm paths and the severity of storms. There was always a hurricane tracking map from one of the local TV stations, held in place by religious figure magnets, on our refrigerator door when I was growing up. My mother would carefully plot the course and coordinates of all storms each hurricane season on the tracking map, using a #2 pencil, regardless of whether the storm threatened New Orleans. When she removed a tracking map from the refrigerator, at the end of each hurricane season, she would gently fold it up for safe keeping. She kept prior year's hurricane maps in a manila folder in the cabinet with her good china. I think she had at least 30 years of such maps, along with newspaper clippings about different storms in that manila folder. On several occasions I came home from high school and found my mother and Mrs. Matthews in the kitchen reviewing a tracking map from a prior year, discussing the storms from that year, and comparing storm paths from other years to try to discern patterns. They often quizzed each other about hurricanes from previous years, their own private version of trivial pursuit.

As a result of their interest in hurricanes both women had strong opinions about the local weathermen. They believed that they knew, from experience, which local weathermen were always wrong and which were right, about the projected paths of storms. They were openly suspicious years earlier when the first female meteorologist appeared on local TV. Ultimately they reluctantly accepted her and the female meteorologists that followed her.

"At least dem weatha girls deze days don't dress like dem hussey's on dat Fox news. All legs up in ya face. I bet some a doze women was strippa's," Mrs. Matthews said

"Strippas? Maybe dey was dancers like da girl in dat *Flashdance* movie, cause dey sure like showin dere legs," my mother replied.

Mrs. Rosemary Matthews called one of the local weathermen "Chicken Little."

"Da sky is fallin evry time dat idiot opens his mout," she said. She called another of the weatherman, who had a noticeably acne scarred chin and cheeks, "Da Face." When I asked her "Why?" she replied: "Dawlin, cause evry time I see his face I tink a ma first husband's pot marked ass."

Of course none of the weathermen were as good as Mrs. Rosemary Matthews' hero, Nash Roberts. Nash Roberts was the icon of weather in New Orleans in the 60's and 70's.

"If only Nash was still here he could tell us what dis here storm was goin ta do," Mrs. Matthews would say, whenever she was stumped. My mother would always nod in agreement. Nash Roberts was an old school weatherman, trained in World War II, who used marks-a-lots and colored pencils on poster boards to show hurricane paths. He educated entire generations in the city of New Orleans about barometric pressure, wind shear and the intricacies of hurricanes. Even after he retired, and would occasionally appear on WWL TV during hurricane season, he opted to use the poster boards and marks-a-lots to show his predictions, instead of the new computer graphics. Other people idolized presidents, soldiers or religious figures. Mrs. Rosemary Matthews, idolized retired New Orleans weatherman, Nash Roberts. According to Mrs. Matthews, Nash Roberts had never made a wrong prediction.

"Hon," my mother then said to me placing her hand on my arm, "did ya hear dat dere's a nutta storm off da coast of Africa?"

"No, Ma'am," I replied.

"It's just formin, but it'll be a tropical depression soon, an if'n it becomes a hurricane it'd be a name startin wit a B. It's supposed ta go up da east coast. No threat ta us," Mrs. Rosemary Matthews interjected, eating the last of the beignet she had taken from my plate. She had the beignet's white powdered sugar around the bright red lipstick on her lips, and it looked a bit like poorly applied clown makeup.

"August and only the second storm. That's low," I said somewhat offhandedly. The two ladies then began to discuss the number of storms that had occurred in other years.

"I have da trackin maps at home ta show ya if ya ever wants ta see dem," my mother said to me, perhaps hoping I would develop a shared interest.

"Anyway, it'll be a B name, for Bera...Hurricane Bera," Mrs. Rosemary Matthews said, testing the sound of the name on her tongue, as if she was trying to determine the spices in a fancy dinner entrée.

"Dat's a odd name," my mother said curiously, "I wonda if it's a male or a female," she said, referring to the fact that storms bear the names of people.

Historically, storms were only named after women, but at some point, for sake of political correctness, men's names were added to the list of possibilities. Now hurricanes were named after both men and women. Ms. Rosemary Matthews and my mother were still not sure how they felt about that change, and it remained a topic they would return to periodically.

"It was mo special when dem hurricanes was only named afta women," Mrs. Rosemary Matthews would say. My mother usually agreed.

"It's mo like our personalities den dere's, cause we're kinda breezy," my mother would respond. "Da men is mo like dem tornadoes in da midwest," she offered.

"Some a dem men I've known was mo like a drizzly day, if you know what I mean!" Mrs. Matthews would reply and they would both laugh a bit at the comment.

They always discussed the names of hurricanes, as if the name bestowed an actual personality, made the storm human, and understandable. I recall one year a Hurricane named Dominic was formed in the Caribbean. Mrs. Matthews' second husband, a part time bookie, was named Dominic.

"Well, we ain't got ta worry bout dis here storm," she immediately announced. "If it's anyting like it's name sake it'll hang round an do nuttin fo awhile an den head up da east coast ta Atlantic City an disappear." When Hurricane Dominic in fact skirted Florida and went up the East coast Ms. Matthews told my mother: "What I tell ya?"

"OK, Rosemary. What bout 1998?" my mother asked after finishing her beignet. "Watch dis hon," she turned and said to me.

"Oh, dats an easy one Madie," Mrs. Matthews replied. "Bonnie, Danielle, Earl---Earl was just a Tropical Storm ya know, uh...George, Ivan, Jeanne, Karl, Lisa, Mitch and Nicole," Mrs. Matthews concluded.

"Ya right. Bonnie. I always did like dat name," my mother said wistfully. "You mighta been a Bonnie, if you da been born a girl," she said turning to me.

"Hey, Rosemary, member Bonnie Macaluso, lived down da street from us when we was kids growin up?" my mother then asked.

"Do I member her? She slept wit ma first boyfriend in high school afta a dance at St. Bernard civic," Mrs Matthews replied unashamedly. "I wonda what eva happen ta her?" she asked. My mother reached over and took a sip of my coffee. Mrs. Matthews pulled out a small mirror and after wiping the powdered sugar off, reapplied her lipstick.

"Well, dey have dat facedbook now. You could maybe git on dat an sees if you could find her dat way. But maybe not, cause Jessie says dat facedbook leads people ta commit infidelity," my mother said.

"Den I don't need it. I had nough a dem infidels in my life awe ready," Mrs. Matthews replied, returning her lipstick and mirror to her purse.

"Hurricane Bera. I don't know bout dat name Rosemary," my mother then said, curiously, weighing the letters carefully. She then counted out the four letters on her fingers: B-E-R-A.

"Wasn't there a guy named Bera in the Bible?" I asked, unsure of my recollection.

"I don't know. I hope not," my mother said, without further explanation.

"It's probly one a dem foreign Muslim names like Abdul or Mohommad," Mrs. Rosemary Matthews finally said in reply. My mother nodded her head in agreement as if that explained it.

Chapter 26
BERTRAND FINCH

I looked away from my mother and saw a crowd of people across the street, walking down the pedestrian mall, next to Jackson Square, moving in unison past the rows of artists, tarot card readers and street dancers. The crowd bobbed unsteadily toward the traffic light at St Ann and Decatur Street. There were TV cameras set up at the curb of the street, next to the horse drawn carriages. As the crowd got closer I saw that Reverend Jessie was in front, at its center, leading the marchers. He was dressed in a navy blue suit, unbuttoned at the waist, with a starched white shirt and a matching blue tie. There were numerous neatly lettered handmade signs being carried aloft by the people in the crowd accompanying him. Some of the signs related to opposition to the Festival, or set forth words from scripture. It was like a crowd scene I recalled watching in the Spencer Tracy movie *Inherit the Wind*.

"Look it's dad," I said.

My mother turned around in her chair and saw the crowd, and Reverend Jessie, across the street.

"Heck, Rosemary let's get outta here," she said, quickly getting up from the table and knocking her chair over. She and Mrs. Rosemary Matthews grabbed their white plastic K-Mart shopping bags and, without a word to me, began to shuffle off, back in the direction of the video poker parlor. I leaned over and picked up the chair and pushed it back against the table.

The crowd across the street, which looked to be about 40 or 50 people, had come to a stop at the street corner. Reverend Jessie, now standing near the TV cameras, buttoned his suit with a smile and then slowly turned to face the crowd and raised his hands above his heads to quiet them.

I got up after paying my bill and began to walk across the street to get a closer look. There was a stale smell in the air, not uncommon for a morning in the French Quarter, a mixture of the smells of last night's spilled alcohol, summer humidity, the Mississippi river, and the diesel smoke from tug boats on the river.

On the opposite corner from Reverend Jessie a counter demonstration of sorts suddenly broke out. Five or six clean cut Tulane fraternity pledges from Delta Kappa Epsilon, a fraternity often in trouble with the university for its antics, stood with cardboard signs held around each of their necks by string, on which was written: "The Asshole Brothers." The pledges began a drunken chant.

"We are assholes, you are too, we will do our cheer for you." Each of them, holding a plastic cup labeled "Huge Ass Beer," than broke into a Bronx cheer. They were accompanied by older fraternity brothers. It looked like a fraternity initiation. Some of those in the crowd following Reverend Jessie watched the cheer disapprovingly. Prompted by the older fraternity brothers, the Asshole Brothers than crossed the street to get closer to the TV cameras.

A reporter, from the local independent cable channel, held up his microphone, and waited for the signal that they were about to go on the air live for the fifteen minute mid-morning news broadcast. The independent channel was the home of reruns of *The Brady Bunch*, *Gilligan's Island* and shows like *Jerry Springer* and various spin offs where rootless people yelled at each other in incomplete sentences, threw punches, denied parenthood, or accused each other of being unfaithful. The reporter smiled a too practiced and insincere smile. Reverend Jessie stood by him relaxed and waiting to be interviewed.

"This is Bertrand Finch reporting live from Jackson Square. I am here today with Reverend Jessie Ray Elder...." At that point a majority of the crowd, as if on cue, with arms raised in victory, broke into a rhythmic chant: "We love Jessie! We love Jessie!" drowning out the reporter. Reverend Jessie again turned and calmly raised his hands, smiled widely in acknowledgement of the chant, and quieted the crowd.

"Reverend, we know that you plan to demonstrate again this year during the upcoming Southern Decadence Festival in opposition to homosexuality, but...." Bertrand Finch paused awkwardly here. I had seen some of his reports on TV before and recognized him. He had been in the New Orleans market for about a year having arrived from a smaller market in Mississippi. He had an odd preference for plaid suits, solid color ties, and pants that were too short. He seemed physically fit, but it appeared more an orchestrated attempt to be what he was not. He tried to project young and hip, but simply appeared comically outdated, and with his obvious toupee and dyed black mustache, he came across as a caricature.

"But what if...what if homosexuality is not a choice, but is part of a person's DNA?" Bertrand Finch finally blurted out. I had heard Reverend Jessie in the pulpit, in recent years, reject this claim many times. He was adamant that homosexuality was a choice to defy God's wishes, and not the result of genetics. "A choice to pursue evil and sin!" he would say.

"God," he said firmly in a voice that brooked no doubt, "does not make mistakes." The crowd behind him murmured its support. Several people clapped and two or three shouted, "Amen!"

"Are you saying that all homosexuals are a mistake?" Bertrand Finch quickly asked. The dampness in the air was palpable. There was an uncertain hostility in a brief breeze from the river.

"Homosexuality, as scripture tells us, is an abomination and anyone who chooses this lifestyle," and now Reverend Jessie began raising his ministerial voice as if preaching from the pulpit at a Sunday morning sermon, "is making a sinful mistake!" The crowd chanted its approval. There were a few smatterings of "Amen!" and "Tell it brother Jessie!"

"Why would...why would someone choose this lifestyle...as you say?" Bertrand Finch then asked, as a strong wind blew up the side of his toupee. He quickly smoothed it down. Reverend Jessie paused to answer. Just then

I noticed a man, barefoot, in a too large and worn tan trench coat, with a knit wool cap on his head, standing next to Reverend Jessie. He had slowly moved from the fringe of the crowd into the range of the TV cameras. It was Zarathustra II.

"Choose to be gay? I ain't choosing to suck no dick," an Asshole Brother said adamantly to one of his compatriots, before taking a swallow from his "Huge Ass Beer" cup.

"Are you sure you couldn't be convinced? You could just be on the down low," one of the other Brothers said.

"You got a purty mouth," another brother replied with a fake southern drawl.

"Man," Reverend Jessie said prophetically, "is essentially inclined toward evil. He...." At this point, Zarathustra II was in full view of the camera.

"Stone all the gays!" Zarathustra II yelled as Reverend Jessie spoke. The first time he yelled it, while standing next to Reverend Jessie, he was facing in the direction of the camera. Reverend Jessie stopped speaking for a moment and turned, somewhat stunned, to see who had interrupted him.

"Stone all the gays!" Zarathustra II yelled again. He then stepped away from Reverend Jessie, turned and facing the crowd, exhorting the crowd to repeat it. He yelled it again, and again, as Reverend Jessie stood there, momentarily silent, staring at him in bewilderment.

Zarathustra II pounded his right fist in his left hand, like a seasoned cheerleader at a ball game. He cupped his hands to his mouth.

"Stone all the gays! Stone all the gays! Stone all the gays!" he yelled. Quietly at first and then louder, a portion of the crowd began repeating his chant. The TV cameras recorded the chanting, as if the crowd was deciding between life or death for gladiators in a medieval coliseum.

"Stone all the gays! Stone all the gays!"

Reverend Jessie stumbled out of his silence and turning to face the crowd, became very animated, waving his hands over his head trying to calm the crowd down.

"Stop! Stop!" he yelled, as he continued to wave his hands in the air, like he was a referee frantically signaling an incomplete pass. Reverend Jessie was visibly upset. It finally worked and the crowd quieted, though it seemed collectively unsure what it had done wrong, and why Reverend Jessie was upset.

Bertrand Finch, sensing a larger story, now turned away from Reverend Jessie toward the suddenly quieted Zarathustra II. Zarathustra II stood demurely with his hands in his trench coat pockets.

"Are you a supporter of the Reverend?" Bertrand Finch asked. Zarathustra II did not answer the question.

"We all support the Bible!" Zarathustra II yelled, thrusting his right fist into the air. The crowd erupted again in support, as Reverend Jessie got red in the face.

"Tell it brother Jessie!" someone from the back of the crowd screamed, thinking Reverend Jessie had made the statement.

"And the Bible says, stone the gays!" Zarathustra II yelled, while the crowd was still reacting to his comment about supporting the Bible. Zarathustra II tried to start the chant again. "Stone all the gays!" he yelled. One or two of the people picked up the chant and clapped in rhythm, but others were unsure, looked away, shuffled their feet.

Reverend Jessie was enraged and grabbed Bertrand Finch's microphone and pulled it and Finch toward him. Reverend Jessie looked directly into the TV camera ready to set forth his redemption.

"Wait! Does it...does it say stone the gays in the Bible?" Finch asked Reverend Jessie.

"Yes. Yes. But...listen, I don't know this man!" he said, pointing at Zarathustra II. Reverend Jessie then tried to step in front of Zarathustra II, but was blocked in his attempt by Bertrand Finch, who stiff armed him. Reverend Jessie's remarks about not knowing Zarathustra II were initially drowned out by the crowd which had found its voice and begun mumbling, but without much conviction: "Stone all the gays!"

I looked around and noticed that a larger crowd, some angry, some curious, had continued to gather, encircling Bertrand Finch, Reverend Jessie and Zarathustra II. It seemed to now include a menagerie of the artists and street musicians who make their living near Jackson Square, as well as a few shop owners and some tourists who had stopped to see what the commotion was about. The Asshole Brothers also looked on silently sipping their beer. The mime, painted silver from head to toe, who always stood motionless near the pedestrian mall alongside Jackson Square, with a bowl for tips at his feet, continued to stand perfectly still. Nearby a bald headed man, with a scruffy white beard, bent and twisted long colorful balloons into a myriad of shapes for tourists and their children. Indeed some of those now watching Reverend Jessie and Zarathustra II had hats made of colored balloons on their heads.

"So you...so you advocate killing all gay people?" Bertrand Finch interjected trying to be confrontational. Zarathustra II, playing Prometheus, did not answer the question.

"The Bible also says to stone disobedient children...adulterers and women who are not virgins when they marry!" Zarathustra II yelled, cupping his hands over his mouth, to the crowd.

"Stone the disobedient children!" Zarathustra II then shouted, trying to start another chant. "Stone the disobedient children!" he repeated again sternly. The crowd quieted, reticent.

"I'm screwed now," one of the Asshole Brothers said.

People in the crowd looked at each other, disconcerted, to see if, perhaps, the person next to them understood what to do.

"Stone the disobedient children!" Zarathustra II yelled a third time, as the crowd squirmed uncomfortably. Feet shuffled again and people began to look away, or at the ground. Another person lowered his sign, which read, "The Devil is a Dyke." The sign holder looked momentarily defeated, as if some personal failure of his had now been made a public fact.

"Geez, is that...is that also in the Bible? Stoning disobedient children?" Bertrand Finch asked. Reverend Jessie ignored the question, focusing instead on Zarathustra II.

"Listen, I'm telling you I do not know this man."

"Yes, but...," Finch started to respond.

"Stone the adulterers! Stone the adulterers!" Zarathustra II then bellowed, drowning out Finch. Two or three people in the crowd fervently picked up this chant, but no one else did. "Stone the adulterers!" Zarathustra II repeated, now bringing his knees up high and swinging his arms, marching in place like a High School drum major as he did so. Reverend Jessie continued to stare angrily at Zarathustra II. Bertrand Finch, now silent, held his microphone close to Zarathustra II as the cameraman filmed them both.

"And as Bob Dylan sang 'Everybody must get stoned!'" Zarathustra II then shouted out amusingly, as he continued, left-right, left-right, to march in place. In fact he may have sung "Everybody must get stoned," instead of just yelling it. He then started to laugh oddly, but stopped after a few too large to maintain giggles. "Everyone must get stoned," he repeated softly to himself. Bertrand Finch just stood there like he was lost in deep thought.

"This is ridiculous," Reverend Jessie finally said, grabbing Finch on the shoulder and pointing at Zarathustra II to try to get his attention. "This man is obviously a lunatic."

"But are...are these things he mentions in the Bible, about stoning children and adulterers?" Finch again asked Reverend Jessie.

Reverend Jessie, in no mood to answer, looked away from Finch and back at Zarathustra II.

"Do we have enough stones? Who brought the stones to throw?" Zarathustra II called out to the gathered crowd. One of the Asshole Brothers cupped his hand over his crotch.

"Hey! I've got two stones here!" he yelled.

"Everyone better check their stones," one of the older fraternity boys, accompanying the Asshole Brothers, quickly instructed the pledges. All of the Asshole Brothers then placed one hand over their crotches and held it there, while holding their Huge Ass beers in their other hand. The remainder of the crowd was silent in response. The mime then moved and struck a new frozen pose in which he appeared to be throwing a rock. Zarathustra II saw the mime, laughed and smiled a gap toothed grin.

"But Jesus said 'Whoever is even angry with a brother or sister is liable to judgment,'" Zarathustra II said loudly, but in a clear, calm pastoral manner. "So which is it, violate the nomadic tribal rules of Leviticus and be judged, or get angry with someone like the Reverend wants and be judged?" Zarathustra II paused and searched the crowd. "Listen to me. Such harsh judgment of others is just a shield from self judgment," Zarathustra II told the crowd collectively, as he slowly stepped back and extended his outstretched arms and then innocently shrugged his shoulders. The crowd encircling him pressed in. The mime shifted poses again, scowling and pointing his finger in mock judgment.

"We are all God's children. If one of us is a mistake, we are all mistakes. None of us should judge. None of us should throw stones. Our duty is to care for each other, not to judge and not to throw stones. To love God means to be responsible for each and everyone, not to condemn others," Zarathustra II concluded. Bertrand Finch now smiled slightly, as if he had just understood an inside joke. The cameras kept rolling.

"God is the judge!" Reverend Jessie then said, regaining his voice and gesturing as he faced the crowd in this impromptu debate. "If God does not have dominion over us, if He does not pass judgment on our sins, then He is meaningless and that...that is absurd!" Sweat poured from Reverend Jessie's brow and the veins in his neck bulged in anger. Zarathustra II remained calm. "As Rushdoony said, 'We cannot use our thoughts and feelings as a standard: only God's word is the test!'" he then dogmatically stuttered out admonishing Zarathustra II, and preaching to the larger crowd.

"Don't be silly! You use your thoughts and feelings every time you interpret the Bible! You should be encouraging people to have a confrontation with the difficulties of the biblical text, not seeking an easy accommodation with it," Zarathustra II replied, pointing his finger at Reverend Jessie. Reverend Jessie seemed stunned by the theological rebuke.

"What? You are wrong! You can't challenge me! I rely on God's infallible word to tell me what to believe," Reverend Jessie responded, aggressively, as he stepped toward Zarathustra II.

"Oh! Come on Reverend. You rely on your interpretation of those words. Your God is just a symbol of your personal narrative," Zarathustra II said calmly, challenging Reverend Jessie before the crowd. Reverend Jessie glared at Zarathustra II. His upper lip curled in a slight sneer. Bertrand Finch seemed unsure whom to question.

"In the absence of your angry God, who no one has seen, and who you say judges us and condemns us, we are all god. God wants to see if we will be vindictive or compassionate towards our fellow man. If we will rise above our individual self interest and intolerance," Zarathustra II said directly to Reverend Jessie.

"We are all God! That is...that is blasphemous! We are fallible! He is not! We are sinners. He is not!" Reverend Jessie then screeched back wide eyed.

"Oh, Platitudes! Think for yourself Reverend!" Zarathustra II barked back. Reverend Jessie's face was almost crimson.

Bertrand Finch then turned to face the camera.

"This is Bertrand Finch live from Jackson Square. We have an interesting development in the Reverend's annual protest of the Southern Decadence Festival. As you have seen here first, there seems to be a power struggle developing in the ranks of Reverend Jessie Elder's supporters over the issue. This is Bertrand Finch reporting. Back to the studio." As the signal was given to the camera man to stop filming for the noon broadcast, you could hear Reverend Jessie suddenly pleading with Bertrand Finch.

"What? That's not true! I told you I don't know this man!" he said, looking around the crowd for someone's affirmation.

As I watched this all unfold I realized that I had no emotional response to Reverend Jessie's angst. I was not angry at Zarathustra II, or saddened by the exchange. I found some of Zarathustra II's antics slightly amusing, but his challenge to Reverend Jessie, if that is what it was, evoked no supportive response from me.

Chapter 27

14 DAYS

Reverend Jessie sought to regain control of the situation. He ran his hand through his hair several times, pursed his lips momentarily, and then tried to run Zarathustra II away.

"Get behind me Satan! You will not corrupt vulnerable minds while I am around! I am the Lord's bulwark and because of His will you cannot break me!" he said in a booming priestly voice, swatting his hand demonstratively and dismissively in Zarathustra II's direction. Zarathustra II stood silent, facing Reverend Jessie with his hands in the exterior pockets of his trench coat, like a child purposely pretending he was unaware that a parent was speaking to him.

"I said be gone Satan, or repent your sins right now before your savior Jesus Christ!" Reverend Jessie yelled, stepping menacingly back in front of Zarathustra II and looking down at him. Reverend Jessie was at least 6 inches taller than Zarathustra II and twice as heavy, but Zarathustra II did not seem intimidated.

Unbeknownst to Reverend Jessie, when he started to confront Zarathustra II, Bertrand Finch had signaled his cameraman to begin filming again. The crowd slowly began to understand, as a group, that Reverend Jessie was confronting the fellow in the wrinkled tan trench coat.

"Get outta here!" one member of the crowd yelled at Zarathustra II. Another one, who was carrying a sign which read, "Michael Jackson was a homo," yelled hoarsely, "Leave you moron!"

"Are we assholes or morons?" one of the Asshole Brothers with blonde hair asked his buddy contemplatively, before sipping his beer.

"I'm an asshole, you're a moron," his buddy replied, as all of them continued to hold their crotches with one hand and their Huge Ass beer with the other.

"Yea, but it's ok, you're *our* asshole," the blonde hair pledge responded.

Slowly, Zarathustra II turned away from Reverend Jessie as if he was going to oblige and walk away. "Be gone!" someone in the crowd chirped, but without much conviction. Reverend Jessie stood staring at Zarathustra II, even as Zarathustra II turned away from him. There was enmity in his eyes. Reverend Jessie held up his Bible in his right hand, demanding, so that it was between him and Zarathustra II.

"Just like Jesus did with the demons in Gadarenes I cast you out! You are a polluter of men with your false ideas!" Reverend Jessie hollered at Zarathustra II, shaking his hand with the Bible in it. Indeed, Reverend Jessie was so angry that his lips were now trembling as he spoke. Perspiration ran down his forehead into his eyes and the veins in his neck still bulged.

Zarathustra II took three steps away from Reverend Jessie as if he was leaving, but instead of being run off like some charlatan in a western movie discovered hawking the latest sham mineral oil cure, he calmly stepped up on to the half wall holding the wrought iron fencing surrounding Jackson Square. He now stood above Reverend Jessie and he turned and looked down on Reverend Jessie and the crowd. He pointed directly at Reverend Jessie.

"You will not send me into a herd of swine, nor will I rush head long into the sea for you!" Zarathustra II responded, while Finch's cameraman kept filming. Reverend Jessie seemed puzzled for a moment by Zarathustra II's knowledge of scripture and involuntarily lowered the hand holding the Bible.

"I speak the word of God!" Reverend Jessie finally retorted in a hollowed response.

"No. No, you speak in stereotypes which dehumanize those with whom you disagree. There is no lived experience in your words, only fear," Zarathustra II replied, from his higher perch.

Before Reverend Jessie could respond further, Zarathustra II spread his arms wide again, like he was holding up the entire blue-white sky above him.

"I am Zarathustra the Second, hear my words, all those who have ears to hear, let them hear me!" he yelled. At this point he paused for effect, as Finch's cameraman zoomed in on him. The crowd moved collectively a few steps closer to where he stood. Reverend Jessie looked up at him uneasily. "In 14 days a storm shall come to this city and destroy it...!" he began. Reverend Jessie now interrupted him.

"Blasphemy! Blasphemy!" he yelled as loudly as he could, while stepping towards Zarathustra II and raising his Bible high again. "Do not listen to this man!" Reverend Jessie screamed out frantically, turning towards the crowd as he spoke. "He is insane. He is the anti-Christ, a false prophet sent by Satan to lead us astray from the challenges we now face in this city with this sinful festival!"

"14 days and this city will be destroyed, I tell you!" Zarathustra II repeated loudly, ignoring Reverend Jessie, and forewarning the crowd, while he continued to hold up the sky. He then stepped down from the retaining wall and lowered his arms. The crowd parted for him and watched as Zarathustra II moved off hurriedly, and alone, deeper into the French Quarter.

The crowd was again confused. Not everyone had understood what Zarathustra II said. "How can 14 gays destroy the city?" someone in the back of the crowd asked. "Hush up," someone replied sternly. "Yea, you moron," the fellow with the Michael Jackson sign said.

"Well, hell, I guess we have some drinking to do in the next 14 days," one of the Asshole Brothers said to his mates. They broke into another

Bronx cheer, while still cupping one hand over their crotches. The people standing around me began to slowly disperse.

Reverend Jessie turned to face his followers. He looked exhausted.

"We have dispensed with this agent of Satan, but there will be others, hostile to us, who will try to divert us from our task. Others will try to subvert the message of the Lord, but the Lord always prevails!" he told them breathlessly. The crowd of followers encircling him seemed to accept that explanation.

"Let us now bow our heads and pray that Jesus will get us through these tribulations," Reverend Jessie said, lowering his head and, trembling, clutching his Bible with both hands close to his chest. He then led his followers and others in the crowd who stayed, in a recitation of the Lord's prayer. Bertrand Finch's cameraman captured it all on film.

Chapter 28
PARK BENCH PREDICTION

That night, on the local news, brief stories ran on all the TV stations about the rally by Reverend Jessie and his followers to protest the Southern Decadence Festival. Reverend Jessie had been interviewed separately by each station during the course of the day. Bertrand Finch's television station, however, also ran a story in its 5:30 and 10:00 p.m. broadcasts, in which Bertrand Finch discussed, "dissension in the ranks of Reverend Jessie's church during the annual protest of the Southern Decadence Festival."

In the story Bertrand Finch wrongly reported that Zarathustra II was a former member of the CRC who had recently returned to the city and was in a power struggle with Reverend Jessie for control of the CRC. Finch suggested that anonymous sources had claimed that Zarathustra II was an ascetic, and some of the CRC Trustees were supporting Zarathustra II in the conflict. I laughed out loud when I saw the story. It was completely made up.

There was footage of Zarathustra II's park bench prediction. They continued to show the clip when Zarathustra II said, "In 14 days a storm shall come to this city and destroy it!" This was followed by Reverend Jessie yelling, "Blasphemy! Blasphemy!"

The story even ended with the station's local weather man, the one Mrs. Rosemary Matthews called Chicken Little, seated at the anchor desk being interviewed by Finch discussing the storm season and the likelihood that New Orleans would take a hit from the storm in the Atlantic.

"Well, right now the spaghetti models forecast it to head into the open Atlantic and die out. But 14 days would put it hitting the city near the anniversary of Hurricane Katrina, so you never know, this could be the big one!" he said. Other local and national weathermen, in their normal weather forecasts, and without reference to Zarathustra II's prediction, had said there was virtually no chance that the storm would even get into the Gulf of Mexico, much less threaten New Orleans.

We saw the broadcast of Bertrand Finch's story that night on the small TV in my apartment. Zarathustra II turned somberly to me, after the broadcast, and said, "'If any want to become my followers, let them deny themselves and take up their cross and follow me.'" I recognized the biblical quote Zarathustra II used from my Sunday school classes. I did not know if Zarathustra II was trying to claim he was Jesus, or that he was like Jesus. It concerned me. So I asked him what he meant by that quote from scripture, because I really wanted to understand. He looked at me appreciatively.

"Things are about to get hairy," he said.

Chapter 29
LUKE C. BUKOWSKI

The next day, I now know, at least one person in the crowd posted a YouTube cell phone video of Zarathustra II and Reverend Jessie's confrontation. Bertrand Finch also added the entire video to his station's Facebook page and sent it out on his twitter account. It had apparently gotten a few thousand hits overnight.

I am not sure how the other news stations in town learned that Zarathustra II was staying at my apartment. I had not told anyone at all. Apparently, Bertrand Finch's story, or perhaps the You Tube video, or Facebook posting, had sparked competition, among the local TV station news managers to get the rest of the story. The next morning I awoke to a knock on the door. When I finally opened the door there was a cameraman and a female news reporter standing on the stairwell landing outside my door. The reporter asked to speak to "the Zarathustra guy." I recognized the reporter as one of the local WDSU weekend anchors, Clarice McComb.

I often saw her picture in the society section of the Time Picayune newspaper at various charitable functions with her husband, a rock musician who played in a popular local band called "The String Theory Messiahs." Ms. McComb, before she became a news reporter, would dress up in a beaded bustier, a mini skirt and knee high boots and sing with the band, using the moniker "Kitty Love." In those days the band was known as "Kitty Love and the String Theory Messiahs."

I was still in my pajamas and was not sure of the time. Ms. McComb did not apologize for waking me up and then asked more formally again if "the fellow who calls himself Zarathustra" was here. I turned to see if Zarathustra II was on the sofa, where he slept, but he was not there. I told Ms. McComb that he was not home and that I did not know where he was this morning.

"How did I get this bonehead assignment?" Ms. McComb then said to the cameraman, in blonde frustration.

"Beats me bow head," replied the cameraman. She then composed herself and asked if I would answer a few questions on camera. With the camera rolling, and me in my pajamas, I complied.

"Is this where the one who calls himself Zarathustra lives?" she asked melodramatically, already knowing the answer, and thrusting the microphone towards me.

"He stays here, but he is not here right now," I replied simply.

"Is he a member of the CRC?" she asked.

"No," I replied.

"Do you know whether he and Reverend Jessie Ray Elder are battling over control of the CRC?" she asked.

"I don't think so," I responded.

"And do you know Reverend Elder?" she asked.

"Yes, he is my father," I replied.

"Are you in cahoots with this fellow?"

"In what?" I asked.

"Cahoots. Oh never mind. Look, are you seeking control of the CRC?" she asked.

"No," I replied quickly. I then yawned and it appeared Ms McComb was offended by my breath. She backed away slightly.

"What is your name?" Ms. McComb then asked, keeping a safe distance, but extending her arm with the microphone to me so that I could be heard. It seemed like a simple enough question. I hesitated. She looked at me with disdain, which I did not appreciate.

"Is that a difficult question?" she asked sarcastically.

"... uhm, I am Luke C. Bukowski," I finally said in response and jokingly.

"I thought you said you were Reverend Jessie Elder's son?" she asked confused. "Anyway, what is your relationship to this Zarathustra fellow?" she then asked, in a tone that made it clear she did not care what my answer was. I stood up as straight as I could.

"I am his first apostle," I said as a goof, thinking she might laugh and change her tone.

"His what?" she asked, like she was not sure she heard me correctly.

"His first apostle," I repeated, more unsure.

"I got it," her camera man said, as she lowered the microphone.

"Just what the world needs, a vagrant with idiot followers," she said, as she turned to walk down the stairs. She did not say goodbye.

The interview ran on her station's morning broadcast as part of a story about Zarathustra II's prediction in Jackson Square. Ms. McComb indicated that Zarathustra II was not a member of the CRC and that Reverend Jessie and his son were estranged. But otherwise Ms. McComb suggested that the real story was Bertrand Finch and his flagging TV station's news department trying to create a story where there was none.

"In this reporter's opinion Mr. Zarathustra, or whatever his real name is, has as much chance of predicting the future correctly as our New Orleans Mayor, Shemp Wanek, has of being elected President of the United States," she concluded.

Chapter 30
THREE FULL DAYS

I did not see Zarathustra II the rest of that day. The reporters from other TV stations and radio stations began calling my cell phone to see if he was there for an interview. I was interviewed twice more, including on the air by a local morning DJ comedy team. One of the DJ's kept asking if Zarathustra II could predict when he would get laid next.

"If he could do that, I'd follow him anywhere," the DJ said, to canned laughter.

"And if he can get you laid that would be a miracle, right up there with the parting of the Red Sea," his co-host opined, again to canned laughter.

The last reporter that called was from a local low wattage Hispanic AM radio station and wanted to know if I knew from where Zarathustra II got his predictions.

"Does he have visions of the Blessed Virgin?" the reporter asked.

"I don't know, you would have to ask him," I said politely to him over the phone.

"Do you know if he gets the stigmata?" the persistent reporter wanted to know.

"I don't know, you would have to ask him," I replied again.

That night the reporter did a story on Zarathustra II and misstated my apostle name. "One of Zarathustra the Second's followers, Duke Brunowski, said there was no doubt that the Blessed Virgin appeared regularly to the Prophet," he reported.

I did not see Zarathustra II for three full days. His absence prompted several comedic references by the local news media. The video of me being interviewed by Ms. McComb was picked up as part of two other news stories on other stations.

I now know that he had gone to the top floor of the Canal Place parking garage and stayed in a corner of the stairwell. It was a safe spot he knew from his many homeless days in the city. He told me later, when I asked about being homeless in New Orleans, that he had slept there often at night and then spent part of one day every week at the Tompson Center, a drop in center for the homeless off of Tulane Avenue.

"I like to shrink the world down in size when it gets too big for me," he said candidly. "And it is starting to feel too big again. But don't worry; I never do it for too long."

When I asked seriously, what he was doing for three days in a parking garage stairwell, he looked at me as if he was weighing the significance of the question and his possible answer. His eyes saddened. He then somberly quoted Nietzsche, as he often did when he was in need of an explanation.

"'When you look into an abyss, the abyss also looks into you.'"

After showing up briefly at my apartment to explain his disappearance, he went back to a park bench in the French Quarter in Jackson Square. I went with him downtown so I could eat breakfast at Café Du Monde.

A waiter at the Café Du Monde greeted me when I walked in to get breakfast. "Hey, you're the apostle guy. I saw you on TV," he said with boyish laughter. I smiled and nodded back, feeling embarrassed.

He then volunteered, when I bought some coffee, that he thought Zarathustra II was going to be good for business today. "I saw that he is across the street getting ready to preach. People want to hear predictions about their future. It gives them the perception of control," he said philosophically. In fact, I watched him put up a hand written sign near the entrance of Cafe du Monde, trying to capitalize on Zarathustra II presence in Jackson Square. The sign read, "See the Prophet of Jackson Square predict the future, and enjoy a cup of black coffee. All for just $2.99."

Chapter 31
MIKHAIL IVANOV

Zarathustra II walked back and forth for a few moments. The St. Louis Cathedral stood behind him, like a picture postcard frozen in papal judgment, on an overcast New Orleans morning. He stopped, contemplative, and looked down at the green wooden slats on the half circular park bench beneath his feet. The park bench was actually four black wrought iron benches pieced together in a half circle. There was a small crowd seated in front of him. The distant distorted musical sounds of some street musicians outside the square floated on the still breeze.

"Hey, that's the guy that was on TV," I heard someone say, and then laugh.

"Is he the one that predicted the storm would hit the city?"

"Yea, I think so."

"This will be fun. Let's go see what this idiot has to say."

I watched as the people speaking walked up and sat down to listen. Others joined them. The crowd was reticent. Most appeared to be about my age. Two older disheveled homeless men slept, unaware, on the grass behind the park bench, near a grocery cart filled with stained blankets, plastic bags, hoarded newspapers and other lost and found things. I noticed that one of them was wearing Zarathustra II's red high top tennis shoes. A very thin brown and white dog, of indeterminate breed, was tied to the cart with a long piece of frayed rope, which was also fashioned around his neck as a collar. The dog's hair seemed as frayed as the rope and scratched incessantly behind its ears. Zarathustra II looked up at the two homeless men for a long moment.

Zarathustra II then turned to face the small crowd. "We emerged from our infancy into adolescence and then adulthood long ago, and God then withdrew His presence from us. We must evolve. The time is long past for us to became responsible for ourselves and for each other. To learn the folly of our adolescent delusions. There is no final arbiter to whom we can now appeal and get a response, or a reprieve. We must learn to live without Him, or His comforting image," Zarathustra II said. He waved his hand driving off an annoying fly and paused, watching the crowd for a response.

This time, however, instead of mumbling to himself, he had a crowd of about 15 or 20 people seated in front of him on the sidewalk in Jackson Square. A few more people began to walk up once they saw him on the park bench.

"This withdrawal of God from our presence is the beginning, not the end of our lives. The exciting thing is that we now get to define ourselves. As opposed to a story of Luther's predestination, where we have no options, no say in our own destiny. Instead we get to define our essence and who we are," he said, as he fidgeted with something in the right pocket of his trench coat. He stopped speaking and pulled out a piece of crumpled notebook paper from his pocket and read from it silently, as if it held some important message he needed to decipher, and then he carefully folded it and slipped it back in his pocket.

A young man, heavily tattooed, with his head shaved, wearing oil stained blue jean cut offs, a black Electric Ladyland and Tattoo T-shirt, and black flip flops, was seated on the sidewalk in front of Zarathustra II's park bench. He raised his hand as if in class to ask a question. He was seated with several other heavily tattooed individuals. A few had visible piercings in their lips, nose or ears. One was drinking from a bottle wrapped in a paper bag. Zarathustra II paused, looked at the young man and nodded his head slightly, giving him implicit permission to speak. The young man stood up to ask his question.

"So what about the storm that's supposed to be coming this way to destroy the city, dude?" the young man asked. In doing so he drew out the word "dewwwd," when he spoke. A few young people sitting next to him muttered in group-think, as if this was something they also wanted to hear. The young man high-fived the person sitting next to him as he sat down, proud of his question, like it was the singular accomplishment up to that point in his life. Zarathustra II paced the park bench a few times more, looking down awhile before responding.

"They want to hear more about the hurricane and my predictions," he said out loud, but speaking to some alter-ego.

"Yes," someone seated up close said. A couple of people in the crowd clapped and one fellow whistled loudly. A few people laughed.

"We are required to look at how we live our lives, at how we treat the least among us," he continued, turning to look again at the two homeless men still sleeping on the grass. As if on cue the thin dog barked hungrily at him. "There are many homeless people in New Orleans living under the Claiborne overpass and others by the New Orleans Mission," Zarathustra II said, trying to return to his topic and ignore the question. The crowd fidgeted as one. A low rumble arose.

"What about the storm, butt-head?" the tattooed fellow interrupted, with a harshness in his voice. He stood up again and turned to look at those around him, trying to rally them to his cause. "Fuck the homeless!" he then said, eliciting delayed stoned laughter from the people sitting next to him. Zarathustra II did not react to what the fellow said. He paused. The tattooed fellow remained standing.

"We are victims of our own myths and narratives. If you are unable to love, you cannot see past the stereotypes and you end up using easy labels that dehumanize both yourself and those you accuse," Zarathustra II finally said quietly, almost to himself.

"What's this dickhead talkin' bout?" the tattooed fellow then said loudly to one of his friends.

"Will it be like Katrina?" a neatly dressed women seated nearby yelled out anxiously. Zarathustra II looked at her. He became sullen, dispirited, and paced again.

"Sorry," she replied, sounding like a spouse accused.

"Tell us about our responsibility for the least among us," a person standing a few yards behind the crowd yelled out. The people seated up front turned in unison to look at him.

"Who is this dill weed?" the tattooed fellow asked no-one in particular, as he sat down, staring menacingly at the kid who asked the question.

I recognized him as the son of Mrs. Ivanov, the CRC choir Director. His full given name was Mikhail Bakunin Ivanov, but his mother would sometimes call him by his middle name "Bakunin," after the 19th century Russian anarchist. She would chastise him in her thick Russian accent. "You my Bakunin. You rebellious for no reason and ruin all us one day," she told him once as church services ended.

Mikhail Ivanov took his mother's words literally and, while a senior in high school, tried to form the "Chalmette High School Anarchist Club." He painted "Chalmette High School Anarchist Club" on a T-shirt in acrylic and wore it to school one day, in apparent violation of the dress code, and put up flyers at the school soliciting members. As a result, he was expelled from school. Advocating anarchy was not allowed, according to the St Bernard Parish School Board. It was rumored that the police had also found a pipe bomb in the garage at his mother's house and that only Reverend Jessie's intervention with the authorities kept him from being charged with a crime.

Ivanov was two or three inches taller than Zarathustra II and he was very thin, "heroin thin" I had heard someone at the CRC say suspiciously of him one time. His skin was very pale, like mine, the type that would easily sunburn. He wore his jet black hair long, to the middle of his back, but short on the sides. He had a self-punishing demeanor, which was reflected in his small black eyes, a broad flat boxer's nose and a clearly visible scar that cut through his right eyebrow. He was clean shaven, but had sprouts of hair below his lip. I noticed that his right ear was pierced in two places and each had a small silver loop earring. The clothes he wore all appeared to be second hand and well worn. A chain ran from his belt loop to the wallet in the back pocket of his faded jeans. He wore scuffed black leather motorcycle boots and a faded yellow T-shirt that had "Baker-Gurvitz Army" written on the front, a band from the 1970s I later learned.

I understand that after being expelled from high school he left home and squatted for awhile with some street kids in an abandoned warehouse on the other side of Esplanade Avenue. A few months later he moved into a one room studio apartment in the French Quarter with some street musicians, trying to learn to play guitar. He then got his GED, hung out with the street kids who often passed through town, and took a job at local radio station WWOZ. It was a listener financed station and he mostly ran errands and answered the phone, but on a few occasions he filled in for absent DJs in the early morning hours. He enrolled at the University of New Orleans where he took courses randomly, selecting them based on his interest and not as part of any specific curriculum requirement.

Zarathustra II looked up at Mikhail Ivanov. The crowd now came to attention. There was an air of mild frustration, yet some hope that he would still explain his hurricane prediction.

"When we diminish another's humanity, we diminish our own. We must come together, not be pulled apart. Recognize ourselves in the homeless and in others. In our singularity. That's the true collective Christian ethic. Not in pursuing our individual egoism," Zarathustra II said. Zarathustra II paused again, as if collecting his thoughts.

"So is the hurricane's going to destroy us, or the city, because of the Southern Decadence Festival?" another member of the crowd asked earnestly, ignoring Zarathustra II's response to Ivanov.

"No," Zarathustra II said immediately, and unusually harsh. All the enthusiasm he had shown in response to Ivanov's earlier question disappeared. He stood mute, and I thought he was trying to decide whether to continue.

"No," he finally repeated quietly, distressed. "Don't you understand?" he said raising both his hands in a questioning gesture and facing the crowd. He then removed the knit wool cap for a moment and held it tightly in his hand.

112

"God is gone. He does not send us hurricanes to punish people. We have evolved beyond such simple minded understandings of the universe. We need instead to talk about our responsibilities and our actions, not about God's," Zarathustra II said dismissively.

"What about homosexuality and the admonitions of Leviticus in the Bible?" Ivanov then asked. Some members of the crowd turned again and looked at Ivanov. "What about the condemnation of homosexuals in it?" he then asked Zarathustra II more plainly. The sound of a solo saxophone drifted from in front of Jackson Square. I noticed that the damp smell of the river still hung in the morning air, as another five or six people walked up to listen.

"What about it?" Zarathustra II parlayed back rhetorically. He stepped down off the park bench and then nervously back up on it again three times. "The Bible should not be about all of the nomadic tribally required 'Thou shalt nots.' It should not be read as a story about condemnation, or a listing of personal prejudice," Zarathustra II then said cautiously. "Instead, the Bible stories, read properly, are about the transfer of responsibility for our lives from God to us. We should replace small minded intolerance with enlightened understanding."

"But why homosexuality? Why are the Evangelicals like the Reverend and his church so hung up on it?" Ivanov asked in a conversational tone, as if no one else was present but he and Zarathustra II. Zarathustra II looked down at his feet. He put his knit wool cap back tightly on his head.

"You have to understand that currently the tap root of Evangelicalism is cultural fear and despair. That despair has prompted condemnation and dogmatism, instead of acceptance of differing views. Their homophobia has much to do with that despair, along with Evangelicals marginalization of women, and their almost paranoid fear of their own sexuality," he said in a low voice, as if he wished it otherwise.

Zarathustra II looked around for a spark of acknowledgment. The crowd did not respond. Zarathustra II stepped down off the bench and without explanation stepped away from it. People started to get up, stretch, and leave.

Off to the right, partially hidden behind some azaleas in the square, I recognized another face. It was the reporter Bertrand Finch with a baseball cap pulled down low to try to cover his eyes. His camera man had filmed everything.

"I thought he was going to talk about the hurricane," the tattooed young man said, disappointed, as he stood up. "And what was that shit about hating women? Man, I love the whores," he said loudly with a laugh.

"Hey, let's roll a doobie," his friend replied.

"Good idea!" the tattooed fellow said, punching his friend in the shoulder.

Just then a clatter and commotion came through the Decatur street entrance to Jackson Square, from behind the dispersing crowd. We all turned and looked. It was 5 or 6 people running and dressed in gorilla suits. All of the gorillas had "The Asshole Brothers" signs hanging around their necks. It was the pledges from DKS and they were being escorted by older fraternity brothers for another initiation prank. The crowd that had stood to leave, froze for a moment to watch. One of the gorillas jumped up on the park bench where Zarathustra II had been standing. The other Asshole Brothers jumped up and down near him and grunted pretending to be gorillas. One of the gorillas was smoking a cigar and holding up a copy of Darwin's *The Origin of the Species*. The Asshole Brother gorilla on the bench spoke.

"Hear me! Hear me!" he said, and then beat on his chest to the approving grunts and wild sounding shrieks of his brothers, and the laughter of the crowd. "We are all primates! But we, the Gorillas, are the superior primates! We believe in the big primate gorilla god king---the King Kong of gods! Darwin was right, you and me are all just branches on the big big monkey tree," he said, to the further amusement of the crowd. He beat on his chest and then hooted ineffectively, like a gorilla, before coughing loudly and purposely. His brother gorillas jumped up and down excitedly. The gorilla smoking the cigar blew smoke rings skyward. I looked over at Zarathustra II and saw that he was watching and laughing.

"The imagined glorious past is our future. We must unite against the amphibians, the reptiles, and the single cell creatures who claim to be our primordial kin and who want to evolve beyond their current state. We are superior to them! The gorilla god king has appointed us as the anointed ones! We must return to our glorious past!" he yelled.

The entire band of gorillas now jumped up and down excitedly in unison, beating the chests of their gorilla suits and hooting approvingly. Several grunted out "the past." One of the gorillas turned his back to the crowd, leaned over and kept scratching the butt of his gorilla suit with both hands. The leader then jumped off the bench and started rambling toward the St. Louis Cathedral, in his best impression of a gorilla running. "Reclaim the past!" he yelled as he ambled away. The other gorilla/ Asshole Brothers walked closely behind him, followed by the older fraternity brothers. Several members of the crowd clapped and others laughed.

Chapter 32
DOMINIQUE DAGNY

I walked over to where Zarathustra II was standing after the crowd dispersed. He was grinning, sheepishly, rocking back and forth, childlike, shifting his weight nervously, from one foot to the other, and talking with two scantily dressed women. He may have been blushing when I approached.

"Luke, these are my friends, Ms. Dominique Dagny and Ms. Shiloh Lemoine," Zarathustra II babbled out, stepping slightly away from the women, and gesturing stiffly three times toward me as he spoke.

"Hello handsome," Ms. Lemoine, whose skin was not exactly black, but somewhere between brown and copper, said to me, in a high pitched voice, staring at me, as she twirled the ends of some long white Mardi Gras beads around her neck with her finger. I smiled uncomfortably.

"Ms. Dagny is, uhm, a uhm, big fan of the writer Ayn Rand, and, also she is a member of the world's oldest profession. And Ms. Lemoine is a poet...in the Burroughs cut up style, and she works with Ms. Dagny," Zarathustra II stammered out, embarrassed, as an introduction.

Ms. Dagny looked me up and down, seductively, unashamed. Ms. Lemoine continued to stare at me while twirling her beads. Ms. Dagny was wearing a red silk dress that really looked more like a night gown that barely contained her rage and her eroticism. It was trimmed in black lace at her bosom and on the bottom. A small black leather purse hung from her bare shoulder. She had on lots of dark blue eye liner, that set off her cobalt blue eyes, pink lipstick, and a sun tanned, perhaps slightly orange, complexion. She was wearing knee high black leather boots with stiletto heels. At first glance, and at a distance, her clothes seemed shiny and brand new, but as I looked closer I saw that the black lace was frayed in spots and the knee high boots were scuffed in several places.

Ms. Dagny's natural auburn hair was in child like ringlets to the middle of her back. The ringlets were held in place by some type of heavy hair spray. In the boots she stood about 6 feet tall. She was attractive, in a sort of masculine way, with a muscular face.

Ms. Lemoine was smaller in height and frame. She had soft full bronze lips and large brown eyes full of wonder, like a school girl experiencing things for the first time. She had on the same sort of silk dress as Ms. Dagny, except it was all black with a white frilly trim. She wore fishnet stockings and black motorcycle boots, similar to the boots I saw Ivanov wearing. She was not as broad across the shoulders as Ms. Dagny, and she had a tattoo of two hands folded in prayer on her left shoulder with the words "Praise the Lord" underneath. Ms. Lemoine had on a country girl blonde wig, with two long pigtails, one on each side of her head. She kept slowly popping a yellow tootsie pop in and out of her mouth.

"Is this your first time seeing Zarathustra the Second preach?" I asked, almost unintentionally.

"We're taking a break this morning to show off the goods," Ms. Dagny said in a matter of fact manner, as she passed her hand in front of her breasts like a Price is Right show girl in front of a product to be bid on. "And tourist crowds, business men in town, are generally good for business, though not so far today. Besides we like this preacher man cause he don't judge us," she concluded.

"A preacher man that don't judge. Imagine that," Ms. Lemoine confirmed. Ms. Lemoine then popped the tootsie pop loudly between those bronze lips, again while looking directly at me.

"Is this the disciple boy you told me about the other day?" Ms. Dagny asked Zarathustra II. She started to slowly walk around me with her blue eyes ablaze and her hands on her hips, like she was inspecting merchandise for possible purchase. I heard her stiletto heels click amorously against the pavement with each of her steps.

"Yes. My apostle, Luke," Zarathustra II said, as if he could not say it quickly enough.

"Who is Ayn Rand?" I asked, a conversational moment behind, trying to dispel a rising discomfort I could not explain. Ms. Dagny stopped walking and stared hard at me, in a disappointed way. Her lower lip hung open for a second in mock disbelief, displaying a perfectly aligned set of chemically whitened teeth.

"Disciple boy, you need some educating. You don't know Ayn Rand? Preacher man I thought you told me the boy was smart," she finally said. "And listen, if you have some money, I can begin that education right now...you heard me," she then said with a chuckle. Ms. Lemoine popped the tootsie pop out of her mouth.

"Do it girl! I think the boy needs a lesson plan!" Ms. Lemoine encouraged.

"Ayn Rand was a novelist who also created a system of thought that she called objectivism," Zarathustra II recited. Ms. Dagny stood with her hands on her hips, coy, and listened attentively as Zarathustra II spoke. "Among other things, Rand believed that reason was tied to individuality. The collective cannot reason," Zarathustra II concluded in a tired rote manner.

"The preacher man, he knows some shit. Hey preacher man, all that smarts, that way you got with dem words, it ever get you laid for free?" Ms. Lemoine replied, before looking at me and rubbing the wet sticky tootsie pop around her lips and putting it back in her mouth. Ms. Dagny laughed.

"Ms. Rand's books taught me that to be a selfish capitalist is a good thing. It's about the money baby. I should always look out for No.1," Ms. Dagny said tartly to me.

"That's not very Christian," I replied naively, not sure why I said it, why I didn't stay quiet.

"Ms. Rand was an atheist, disciple boy, so she would not have worried about your Christianity, whatever that means these days...you heard me," Ms. Dagny replied. "So what ya think Shiloh? Does this boy need some educating right now or what?" she asked. I stood frozen in place, stiff, determined not to speak again.

"Don't embarrass da boy! Dem Christian boys have to pretend otherwise in public. But I ain't never had me no apostle to teach. Do they get a holy roller discount?" Ms. Lemoine teased with Ms. Dagny, who continued to look at me. Zarathustra II shuffled nervously from side to side. He buttoned his trench coat and then immediately unbuttoned it.

"Hey! Disciple boy, you like chocolate?" Ms. Lemoine asked me sweetly, pointing at me with her tootsie pop.

"Yes," I replied foolishly.

"Well I got some chocolate for you right here baby," she smiled. Ms. Dagny laughed hard, showing her teeth.

"Country come to town! How much money you got disciple boy?" Ms. Dagny asked directly, pushing an index finger gently into my chest, as she stepped closer to me. I tried to speak but my voice had finally, thankfully, deserted me.

"So how have you incorporated Rand's philosophy into your business, uh, your life?" Zarathustra II asked weakly, momentarily rescuing me. Ms. Dagny stepped back from me, reached into her purse, peeled a piece of bubble gum out of its wrapper and put it ever so slowly into her mouth and chewed it a few times, while looking directly at me, before answering.

"I only fuck who I want, when I want, where I want...and I set the price...you heard me," she replied proudly, as she chewed on her gum.

"That's right girlfriend," Ms. Lemoine responded, with a slow circular grind of her hips.

Chapter 33
DON'T CALL

Reverend Jessie had seen me being interviewed on TV and he now knew that Zarathustra II was staying with me in my apartment. He was not pleased. He called me on my cell phone. Before I could even speak he yelled into the phone.

"You are a pariah! I shun you! Don't write! Don't call me! You are your mother's son and your only purpose, like hers these days, seems to be to embarrass me. You want to break from God and be a 'self made man' with that vagrant, do you? Well, remember, 'a self made man has a fool for a maker!'"

"Dad, I...." He then hung up on me.

I stood perfectly still. The anxiety, the remembered punishment, that had quickly arisen in me as he yelled, caused my heart beat to echo loudly in my ears, as if I was descending too quickly from a higher altitude. When I tried to clear my throat it was dry and I felt a bit light-headed.

Zarathustra II was standing next to me. He overheard what Reverend Jessie had said to me. He looked at me. I thought I saw compassion, concern, in his eyes. He chewed a bit on his lower lip and pulled on his mustache. I was not sure what to say. I stood there fixed, with my heart continuing to beat heavily. My hands seemed to shake a bit and my mouth remained dry. I felt unsteady. I had that vague suffocating feeling, a tightness in my chest, which I distantly recalled from scolding's my father gave me when

I was a child and light headedness which reminded me of the symptoms I had often in high school.

"I don't understand why he would be so mad," I stammered, insecure but certain.

"It is written that 'They will be divided, father against son and son against father, mother against daughter and daughter against mother, mother in law against daughter in law and daughter in law against mother in law,'" Zarathustra II then recited, breaking my silence into shards as he stood facing me. Then he belched, openly, and in doing so said the word "mooove," to indicate that I should move out of his way, so he could get passed me and out of the kitchen.

Chapter 34
DRESS THE PART

"Can you make him more presentable, bathe him, shave him, and dress him up a bit? We have to take the initiative from these other TV stations that are trying to mock me. And for God's sake see if he will wear shoes," Bertrand Finch asserted.

Bertrand Finch was seated, uninvited, on a barstool at the counter in my kitchen. His blue tie was loosened at the collar and he wore a red and green plaid blazer that looked, purposely, one size too small. He was talking about my roommate: "Finch's Fool," as some of the media now mockingly called him. The media had continued to post brief stories about Zarathustra II and his prediction. Most were not flattering. Finch, on the other hand, continued to show video clips of Zarathustra II preaching and was trying to build a story around him.

Zarathustra II was uncomfortable with the attention that he was receiving from Bertrand Finch. He stopped and suddenly looked wide-eyed at Bertrand Finch.

"Why do you worry about my clothes?" Zarathustra II asked, in a tone that suggested he had long ago tired of defending his appearance to others.

"Image is important," Bertrand Finch said dismissively, like a spouse responding to the same tired excuse from their partner. "This is the media age and a little work on your image is a necessity," Bertrand Finch concluded bluntly.

"Fashion and image are a cheap substitute for self knowledge," Zarathustra II announced. Bertrand Finch looked at me for support, but I did not respond. He jotted something down in his note pad.

Finch put his pen down and looked at Zarathustra II. "Listen to me," Finch then said to Zarathustra II. "I don't think about everything like you do. I know that's surprising to hear, but I'm not a deep kind of guy. No one...no one is anymore. With technology it's not necessary. We don't have to think much. But I have learned some things over my years in broadcasting. I am not as young as I look," he said. "People don't really believe in ideas anymore. Do you understand? They only pretend to do so, like they pretend that everyone is faithful in marriage. It's a facade," he said smugly to Zarathustra II. "But they will believe in an image, and they will always believe in a personality. That is as deep as they will go. So if you allow me to work on your image, they will believe in the image we give them," Finch concluded.

Finch absentmindedly pressed his hand down on the top of his toupee. He picked up his pen and wrote in a notebook he had brought with him. Up close I noticed that there were dark circles under his eyes and he had age spots on his hands. I wondered how old he was.

"See what you can do with him. But I want him in a conservative suit so we can begin to fashion a new image. What I envision is a storyline where he will be the former vagrant who is redeemed, kind of like a movie about a homeless guy I saw once on the Lifetime channel," Finch said. I listened and stood there not knowing if I should agree or not. So I remained silent.

It seemed that Bertrand Finch had hatched an idea. He was going to interview Reverend Jessie again about his opposition to the Southern Decadence Festival. He knew Reverend Jessie would not turn down a chance to be interviewed, but Finch wanted Zarathustra II to be there as well for a possible confrontation. He decided to make Zarathustra II's presence at the interview a surprise to Reverend Jessie. It was Bertrand Finch's chance, he thought, at taking another step to create a big story, something unique involving Zarathustra II, which might catch the eye of a General Manager in a bigger television market.

Bertrand Finch tried to get Zarathustra II to give him some personal information to aid in his image creation efforts. Zarathustra II was resistant, not interested.

"When did you become homeless? There must have been some tragedy that laid you low which we can use?" Finch asked. Zarathustra II did not reply.

"Do you have a college degree?" Finch prodded. Zarathustra II would sometimes cite biblical quotes in response to his questions. "You're not helping me much. I will...I will do some internet research on you. You didn't just materialize in New Orleans. These days we all have a history. What is your real name?" Bertrand Finch exclaimed at one point in frustration.

"I am who I say I am," Zarathustra II obliquely responded.

Zarathustra II quickly added that his life story was of no particular importance. None of us were important, he said, except for what we could do for others. He based this view, he told an increasingly frustrated Bertrand Finch, on the Sermon on the Mount, or the Sermon of the Plains as he also called it. He waved off Bertrand Finch's specific questions about the details of his life prior to being the so called "prophet of doom." "It does not matter," Zarathustra II told him.

Bertrand Finch really did not care to listen to Zarathustra II's preaching. He was as indifferent as the biblical Pontius Pilate and he had no interest in Zarathustra II's theology, except to the extent that he thought he could use it for his own benefit. Finch tried again to get me to promise to have Zarathustra II dressed properly for the interview with Reverend Jessie. I made no promises, which Finch seemed to take as my silent assent.

"If you want people to believe in you and become your followers than you must dress the part and in a way that promotes confidence in you," Finch said, sounding like an info-mercial on late night television.

"You just don't understand the importance of marketing. It is the substance of the modern world and all leaders use it. Don't be naive, religious leaders use it *all the time!*" Bertrand Finch said bluntly to Zarathustra II. "So I will handle the marketing aspects for you," Finch said.

Finch reviewed some notes he had taken and scratched through a sentence. He shifted on the bar stool. The faucet in the kitchen dripped noisily behind him, as the air condition window unit continued to strain. "I bet you need to clean the filter on that unit," Finch offered, while he continued to review his notes.

Zarathustra II stood up and then stepped up to the counter and faced Finch. "I have read that as to propaganda 'its effect for the most part must be aimed at the emotions and only to a very limited degree at the so called intellect....The art of propaganda lies in understanding the emotional ideas of the great masses and finding through a psychological correct form, the way to the attention and thence to the heart of the broad masses,'" Zarathustra II recited wearily.

"Wow!" Bertrand Finch said satisfactorily. "That's more articulate than I could say it." Finch looked at Zarathustra II and smiled. "I see you really do understand more about modern man. My mistake. I am glad your readings covered marketing materials. That will make the creation of your image easier," he told Zarathustra II, as he shoved his note pad to the side, convinced of Zarathustra II's sudden doctrinal conversion. Zarathustra II remained standing at full attention, as if in a military formation, waiting to be dismissed by a commanding officer.

"Who wrote that?" I asked Zarathustra II, surprised that his readings had extended to something as dull as marketing ideas.

"Hitler in *Mein Kampf*," he replied. Bertrand Finch, hearing the reference, slowly lowered his head into his hands and pressed down again on his toupee.

"Well...I guess...," Finch, disturbed, tried unsuccessfully to respond.

Zarathustra II then dismissed himself from formation and walked to the sofa to lay down. On the way he replied, "I have no interest in another tortured confrontation. It exhausts me." Bertrand Finch lifted his head and looked at Zarathustra II without empathy, but unsettled.

"Trust me, you need this. I need this. Here is $10. I'll drop off some clothes for him to wear. Just have him there," Bertrand Finch then called to me, as he picked up his note pad, put down the money, abruptly rose, and left my apartment.

Chapter 35
NINE DAYS

Standing on the steps of the First Church of the Recalcitrant Covenant, Reverend Jessie readied himself for the start of another interview with the local media. It was just getting dark. Bertrand Finch had called and arranged the interview with Reverend Jessie's secretary Dolores. He told her it would be a follow up story on the progress of Reverend Jessie's opposition to the festival. Dolores suggested that he decline. She didn't trust Finch, she said. "That clown is not going to do you any favors," she told Reverend Jessie. But Reverend Jessie rejected her suggestion with a chuckle, telling her, "The Lord is watching over me. I can handle anything he tries to do."

Church services had just let out. Several hundred church members were present, milling around, some of them in a receiving line, shaking Reverend Jessie's hand. Others were engaging in communal small talk, waiting to watch the interview. Reverend Jessie was wearing a shiny rust colored suit, white starched shirt and a rust colored tie. He had a rust colored handkerchief in his coat pocket. Even his shoes, which were well shined, were rust colored. His hair was cut and slicked back neatly, but his eyelids seemed to droop with fatigue, and heaviness lay on his forehead. His large frame fit nicely into the tailored suit. If Reverend Jessie saw me, he did not acknowledge that I was there. Zarathustra II and I had been picked up by Finch's cameraman in the TV station panel van and driven to the church. Bertrand Finch stood casually next to Reverend Jessie.

On the day in question Zarathustra II had told me that he decided he did not want to go. When Bertrand Finch called me to confirm that Zarathustra II would be present, I told him he had changed his mind.

"What? He can't do that. It will mess everything up for me. I'm sending a van for him and I'll give him $10 more," Finch replied, ignoring what I told him. When the van driver arrived Zarathustra II was reluctantly ready. His demeanor changed as he got into the van. I saw a sheath of determination strengthen in his face, a temporary veneer over any self doubt.

"Give us just a minute Reverend," Bertrand Finch said deceptively. I saw Mrs. Raissa Ivanov, and remarkably her son Mikhail was there, though they were not together. I also noticed, oddly, that Dominique Dagny and Shiloh Lemoine were there, talking to one of the male camera crew, next to the TV station van. Thunder rumbled overhead once or twice, but it was not raining. Lightning cracked briefly in the sky far off in the distance. As the cameraman counted down from five to start filming Zarathustra II was hurriedly rushed out of the van by an aide of Bertrand Finch, to stand on the opposite side of Mr. Finch from Reverend Jessie.

I had not done that great a job of cleaning him up. He did take a shower. I got a comb part of the way through his curly and matted hair, but the effect was that his hair was now flat on top where I had tried to comb it, but splayed out wildly on both sides, looking like something had set on the top of his head for awhile.

He had allowed me to remove his tan trench coat and replace it with the blue suit and matching pants Finch had bought him off the rack from the Goodwill store. I did not own an iron, so the pants were a bit wrinkled. However, he insisted on having the trench coat draped, Linus like, over his arm. The blue suit was probably two sizes too big and, as a result, the shoulders were too big and the sleeves were too long. Only his fingers showed from the end of the suit sleeves. He wore a clean V neck white T-shirt under the suit. He refused to shave or to wear shoes.

"This is Bertrand Finch reporting live from the steps of the First Church of the Recalcitrant Covenant with Reverend Jessie Ray Elder and Zarathustra the Second," Mr. Finch announced. I could tell from his reaction that Reverend Jessie was caught off guard by Zarathustra II's sudden appearance.

"As you may know the Tropical Depression has now been upgraded to a Tropical Storm. Its exact future path is uncertain. The weathermen say it still appears to be headed into the open Atlantic. In fact it is 100 miles north of the Bahamas, but to my eye it seems...it seems to have stalled just a little bit, a tiny bit, in the last 12 hours. Zarathustra the Second has predicted that it will become a hurricane and hit our city directly. Reverend Elder, what are your thoughts on that prediction?" Bertrand Finch then pointedly asked, confrontationally, putting the microphone into Reverend Jessie's face.

Reverend Jessie was upset. He had been tricked. Dolores was right.

"First of all, let me get something clarified. This homeless fellow is not a member of my church, as you recently said, nor has he ever been. That is false. I'm in complete control," Reverend Jessie said loudly, pointing at Zarathustra II. "And I thought we were going to discuss my protest of the festival. What is he doing here?"

"Can you answer my question about the hurricane, Reverend?" Finch interrupted.

Reverend Jessie seemed to be considering his options on how, or whether, to respond to the question, when Zarathustra II spoke up, quietly but determined.

"The hurricane will hit the city in nine days. The weather forecasts will be proven wrong," Zarathustra II said. He then started to take off the blue suit while still on camera and put his tan trench coat back on. Bertrand Finch stared with his mouth slightly open. Reverend Jessie fumed at the remark.

"Nine days. Fourteen days. Are you going to listen to this street person? Is he now the weather forecaster for your TV station?" Reverend Jessie finally asked, angrily. "This city is about to be in the vortex of sin. Abominations are being paraded around, destroying the very foundations of this Christian nation, and you want me to comment on what this fool has to say?" I had never seen Reverend Jessie so agitated.

"Well, Reverend..." Finch, taken aback, started to respond. Then Zarathustra II said something that silenced Reverend Jessie and drained the color from his face. He said something that raised the theater and drama of the spectacle Bertrand Finch had orchestrated to a level that even Bertrand Finch had not contemplated. In two sentences Zarathustra II gave Bertrand Finch his big story. He gave it to Bertrand Finch like a kiss not expected.

"When the storm hits, this man, Reverend Elder, as you call him, will die," Zarathustra II said, looking around nonchalantly. A communal gasp, a shared incoherence, came from the church members as they watched the interview. Zarathustra II then paused. Reverend Jessie stood there speechless, which was something he was not use to being, though it was becoming a habit at moments around Zarathustra II. While Reverend Jessie and Bertrand Finch stood transfixed, Zarathustra II said, "It will also kill me and you, Mr. Finch." There was then a long period of dead air on the live broadcast.

Once Zarathustra II had finished speaking, and had his trench coat back on, he dropped the blue suit jacket on the ground, where it partially covered the shoes of Bertrand Finch, and he walked over to me.

"Uhm...uh...Zarathustra the Second has made, uhm...another prediction," Finch sputtered inarticulately.

"How did I do Luke? I hope my appearance did not disappoint you," Zarathustra II said, in a child like voice, seeking parental approval. Our roles were momentarily reversed.

"I'm never disappointed in you," I said, as thoughtful as I could sound.

At that moment Bertrand Finch seemed insignificant and conniving to me. Reverend Jessie also seemed suddenly smaller in stature to me, like when one returns after many years to the neighborhood of their youth and notices that the distance between things is smaller than remembered. When Bertrand Finch turned to ask a follow up question to Reverend Jessie, he found that Reverend Jessie had also walked away.

After the cameras stopped rolling and the people started to leave, I saw Mikhail Ivanov go over and pick up the blue suit Zarathustra II had briefly worn and put it on over his yellow Baker Gurvitz Army T-shirt. It looked like it fit him well. Ivanov walked over and began speaking to Ms. Lemoine. She brushed her hand on the front of the blue suit and gingerly turned down the suit's lapel. I saw Ms Dagny stuff some cash in her red bra, which showed through the top of the man's white undershirt she wore, and then she left arm in arm with one of the camera crew headed toward the TV station van.

"Don't leave, I'll be right back...you heard me," she yelled out to Ms. Lemoine, who did not acknowledge that she heard her.

"Can we go now?" Zarathustra II asked me. He was suddenly emotional. I saw tears well up in his eyes. "Can we go now?" he asked again, as if he needed my permission, standing very close to me. I put my hand gently on his arm and guided him away from the church and we walked to catch the streetcar. He wept most of the way home.

Bertrand Finch's TV station ran the entirety of the interview on its 10 p.m. newscast and posted it on its website and Facebook page. Finch ended the story by stating, "In all my years of broadcasting I must say that I have never met anyone like Zarathustra the Second. He is a throwback to the days of old. While other reporters and stations ignore this story, or make fun of him, I will continue to bring you exclusive stories on him and his predictions."

Chapter 36
BIG HARRY'S

The next morning the front page of one of the local papers, *The Times Picayune*, had as its lead headline: "Tropical Storm strengthening to hurricane status, stalling and confounding forecasters." A smaller article was entitled: "Homeless man who calls himself Zarathustra the Second says storm will destroy City and kill him, Reverend Elder of CRC and TV reporter Bertrand Finch." An even smaller article was entitled: "Weathermen now say 10% chance of storm reversing track and entering the Gulf of Mexico." *The Advocate* ran a similar article focusing on the storm's stalling in the Atlantic that also mentioned Zarathustra II's prediction of destruction of the city.

"If dat ting gets inta da Gulf, we leavin town," Mrs. Rosemary Matthews emphatically told my mother. "I don't wanna be standin on no roof agin, like in Katrina, wit my hair in dem curlers waitin ta be rescued no," she said.

My mother was sitting next to Mrs. Rosemary Matthews on a bar stool, playing video poker at Big Harry's Truck Stop and Restaurant in Metairie. Louisiana had long ago outlawed gambling in its state constitution, but it had not outlawed "gaming" and so the legislature in the 1990's passed laws clarifying the mysterious difference between "gambling" and "gaming." As it turned out "gaming" could occur at truck stops, and the legislature thought this legal. But only if the truck stop also served food and thereby became a restaurant. Big Harry's had 50 video poker machines, the maximum allowed by the gaming law in one facility, and a very nice cafeteria style restaurant. Big Harry's was named after a former Jefferson Parish sheriff.

"Where we gonna go dis time if'n it comes ta da Gulf?" my mother asked Mrs. Rosemary Matthews, while continuing to look at her video poker screen. Both ladies were wearing blue hats with white scarves and sunglasses with green frames today.

"I tink we maybe oughta go visit ma cousin Marvin in Atlanta. Dat's ma Aunt Robin's oldest child, you member he was down here ta visit rite b'fo Hurricane Isaac came ashore. He's bout our age," Mrs. Rosemary Matthews said. My mother nodded in remembrance.

My mother and Mrs. Rosemary Matthews had a hunch about Zarathustra II.

"Anyone interested in dem hurricanes can't be all dat bad," my mother had said. "He musta studied da hurricanes. Katrina, Isaac, an others hit durin da last week a August. So he knows his hurricanes an his prediction must be based on dat knowledge," my mother said, philosophically.

"An it ain't too far from da historically busiest day a da year fo hurricanes," Mrs. Rosemary Matthews said. Both ladies then said in unison: "September tenth!" "Ya neva no he might be da next Nash Roberts," Mrs. Rosemary Matthews wondered out loud, hopefully. "Anyone would be betta den dat idiot Chicken Little," she continued. My mother nodded in blue hat agreement.

"Dat Zaratootstra fellow's gonna be rite bout da storm, mark ma words Rosemary," my mother said emphatically.

"Dawlin, come on! A hurricane wit a name startin wit a *B* an a preacher wit a name startin wit a *Z*, tell me dat ain't a *divine intention*," Ms. Matthews replied, popping the gum she was chewing.

"Dat's divine intervention, not intention, Rosemary. At least dat's what ma Jessie calls it," my mother said.

"Intervention, intention, dey's all da same ting," Mrs. Matthews replied. Just then Mrs. Rosemary Matthews won a hand on the video poker machine. "Cha-ching," she said, which is what they would always say whenever one of them won a hand of video-poker. Mrs. Rosemary Matthews winning hand paid $10.90.

Chapter 37
SELECT CARDS

"Da ladies at da beauty pawla yesterday said dat Zaratootstra's gonna be talkin bout da storm agin an makin mo predictions t'day at 10:30," Mrs. Rosemary Matthews said, as though she was revealing the local visit of a national dignitary.

"How do dey no dat?" my mother asked.

"Madie, it was reported by dat parrot faced toupee head Finch on da evenin news," Mrs. Rosemary Matthews said.

"Rose-maree! Really! Parrot faced toupee head?" my mother giggled. "You is too much."

"He needs ta use some a dat supa glue ta keep dat cheap rug a his in place," Mrs. Matthews said, as she pressed a button to start a new game of video poker. "Its worser den ma first husband's."

"I need ta make an appointment at da beauty pawla wit Shirley ta get me some mo color in ma hair. I should a tried ta go ta da beauty parlor wit ya yesterday," my mother replied, touching the side of her head, without looking over at Mrs. Matthews.

"Shirley axed bout ya. She's havin mo trouble wit dat grandson a hers. An ya know she's Eeyore when it comes ta talkin bout her problems," Mrs. Matthews said.

"Eeyore! Rosemary girl ya on a roll t'day. What did da granson do dis time?" my mother asked quietly.

"Stealin coppa from dem houses bein built in one a dem new subdivisions in Gretna ta support his weed habit," Mrs. Matthews replied.

"Did he get caught?" my mother asked.

"Yea, he's not too sharp a bulb. He stopped an NOPD officer an axed if he knew where he could sell suma da coppa," Mrs. Matthews replied.

"Is Zaratootstra goin ta be in da same place as da last time in da square," my mother asked.

"Same place," Mrs. Rosemary Matthews replied, as she hit the button on the video poker machine to select more cards.

"Afta we finish ya wanna drive ova an see him?" my mother asked.

"Sure ting," Mrs. Rosemary Matthews replied.

Chapter 38
MAKING MISTAKES

"Reverend Jessie says that God does not make mistakes," Mikhail Ivanov said cautiously to Zarathustra II. Zarathustra II was standing, hunched over awkwardly, on his Jackson Square park bench, with his hands behind his back and his head lowered. He moved forward and then turned back around. His steps were very short, purposeful, carefully placing one foot in front of the other, heel to toe, heel to toe. Dark nightmare clouds in uneven shapes were spread across the sky. A mid afternoon rain shower appeared headed for parts of the city. The crowd, which had gathered on the cement and grass near the bench, quietly awaited his response.

"We are all evolutionary mistakes," Zarathustra II said, somewhat absentmindedly in response. "I know I feel like one often."

This morning there were probably 50-60 people in attendance, along with a few newspaper reporters, Bertrand Finch and his cameraman. Finch no longer concealed his presence. The crowd was a mixture of young and old. Some were clearly there to hear Zarathustra II. A handful of others looked as if they had slept in Jackson Square that night: street kids, unwashed, broken, pursuing their own notions of freedom and clinging to one another. Others, perhaps, wandered over when they saw the crowd and the TV camera.

Ivanov stood, apart again, at the back of the crowd. He wore Zarathustra II's blue suit over his yellow Baker-Gurvitz Army T-shirt. Off to his right an unshaven vendor in a frayed wide brimmed straw hat, with an unlit cigarette dangling from his lips, opened boxes and was selling brand new gray T-shirts with **Zarathustra the Second's Army** printed on the front in bold black letters. On the back of each shirt it read, **"Everyone must get stoned."**

Shiloh Lemoine was standing right next to the vendor's cart wearing thigh high red stiletto heeled boots, tight jeans and a see through white blouse. I could smell her patchouli perfume from where I stood. She wore a blonde shoulder length wig. The bottom of the blonde hair was tinged in pink. She had another tootsie pop in her mouth, and listened attentively, watching him closely, as Ivanov asked his question.

Mikhail Ivanov appeared interested in a comment which Reverend Jessie often made, in reference to homosexuality, that "God did not make mistakes." Everyone knew that God did not make mistakes. Indeed, Christians were all raised to believe in an all powerful, all knowing, all forgiving God, who was incapable of error.

"What mistakes do you say that God made?" Mikhail Ivanov asked, rephrasing his question, in hopes of eliciting a more complete answer. Shiloh Lemoine moved slowly, fetching, a few steps nearer to Ivanov.

"Who has a Bible?" Zarathustra II suddenly asked, in a slightly professorial tone. He raised his head up and faced the crowd, with his hands still behind his back. Zarathustra II looked tired. His blue eyes sunk a bit further into his unshaven face.

"I do," said a young woman in the front row, near Zarathustra II's bench.

"If you want a biblical literalist's answer to your question read Genesis 6:6 and 6:7 out loud," Zarathustra II demanded, and returned patiently to his obsessive heel to toe pacing on the bench.

The young women stood up and thumbed through her pocket sized Bible. She was freshly showered, innocent, with finger combed long auburn hair, wearing khaki shorts and running shoes, with a large silver cross on a chain around her neck and a small fleur de lis tattooed above her right ankle. She was wearing a brand new gray **Zarathustra the Second's Army** T-shirt.

"Read Genesis 6:6 and 6:7," Zarathustra II repeated. She brushed her long hair out of her face, cleared her throat, and then read:

And the Lord was sorry that he had made humankind on the earth and it grieved him to his heart. So the Lord said, 'I will blot him out from the earth the human beings I have created people together with animals and creeping things and birds of the air, for I am sorry that I have made them.'

The young girl sat down.

"Does that answer the Reverend's statement about the biblical God not ever making mistakes?" Zarathustra II asked Mikhail Ivanov. Mikhail Ivanov shook his head knowingly and smiled. Shiloh Lemoine moved closer to him. The crowd cooed gently in response, like a baby for its parent's attention.

"This story can be read in many ways," Zarathustra II then said. "First, there is no reason, other than fear, or personal insecurity, to require God to be inerrant. But regardless, to read this literally strips it of any significant meaning, except to say that once upon a time God screwed up and was mad at himself for doing so, and as a result killed most of mankind. I am not sure what merit such a reading has, other than to cast God as the originator of genocide. But what it is really meant to show us is that we are all bound to each other and just as we seek to know God, God seeks to know man and the knowledge of the other will always be imperfect. We both strive for a degree of perfection. Neither will achieve it. And in that striving we will be disappointed, in ourselves and in our God. Just as God will sometimes be disappointed in Himself and in us," Zarathustra II said.

Apart from the crowd, but within hearing distance, two separate groups of people were also watching Zarathustra II. Inside the entrance to Jackson Square Mrs. Rosemary Matthews and my mother stood.

"Oh Madie, he's some good, yea. He can member tings. He knew just da rite quote bout God makin dem mistakes. Lordy, I can't even member da ingredients in ma meatloaf recipe," Mrs. Rosemary Matthews said, as she threw the butt end of her cigarette away. "An it's clear ta me dat he's rite," she then said softly, before exhaling cigarette smoke.

"Rosemary, how can ya be so sure he is rite bout God makin dem mistakes? Dat don't sound rite ta me?" my mother asked doubtfully, as she unwrapped a pecan praline from its wrapper.

"Please Madie," Mrs. Matthews said, stretching out the word as "Pleeease." "I got poisonal experiences wit one a God's mistakes. Member ma second husband? Now dat man was a mistake, if eva dere was one," Mrs. Rosemary Matthews replied. Madeline nodded her head, but could not respond because her mouth was full of pralines.

At an opposite corner of the square stood Reverend Jessie. He was not amused. "This is a deceitful use of scripture," he said aloud. He then spoke to the muscular man standing next to him, the church's recently hired Director of Security, Ralph Liddy.

"I want you to find out everything you can about this fellow and report back to me," Reverend Jessie said with emphasis. But while he spoke to Mr. Liddy, Reverend Jessie never took his eyes off Zarathustra II.

Chapter 39
LEIDENHEIMER BREAD

As Zarathustra II left Jackson Square that day, a crowd of 10-15 people followed closely behind him. There was the strong smell of French roasted coffee in the air. I noticed that many of those following him were now wearing those T-shirts that had **Zarathustra the Second's Army** printed on the front. So there was a sea of gray that followed Zarathustra II, with a few other colors mixed in and two ladies in blue hats.

"Let's folla an see where he goes?" Mrs. Rosemary Matthews told my mother.

"Sure. Maybe he'll make anutta prediction," my mother replied optimistically.

The crowd continued to follow Zarathustra II down Decatur Street. I saw Bertrand Finch and his cameraman filming the crowd. Zarathustra II weaved his way through the weekend tourists and walked in front of three black kids who were dancing for tips. They had aluminum cans on the bottom of their worn tennis shoes to create a tap dancing effect. A cardboard box was strategically placed in front of the dancers to receive tips. Two or three tourists watched the dancers in obvious enjoyment. Zarathustra II stopped and improvised a dance with the kids for a few seconds.

"Get outta here Mista," one of the kids told him. "Ya messin wit da show!"

Zarathustra II was oblivious to the fact that he was being followed. He stepped away from the dancers. The crowd was 20 or so yards behind Zarathustra II, but moved gently forward in anticipation.

Zarathustra II stopped at Cafe Maspero's where a young waitress, whose name tag said "Madison," usually gave him french bread discarded by patrons for free. There was a line of people waiting to get inside the restaurant for a table. Zarathustra II stood in the open doorway until Madison saw him. A few moments later, she gave Zarathustra II four pieces of cut and buttered bread on a napkin. Usually discarded French bread was used to make bread crumbs. But since these pieces were already buttered they could not be used, so the wait staff would throw them to the pigeons, or give them to the homeless. Zarathustra II bowed in an exaggerated fashion twice and thanked Madison. "It's the least I can do now that you are famous," she replied smiling, with a sly knowing female wink.

He then stepped back onto the sidewalk, outside the restaurant, near the Toulouse Street corner to eat. Several darting pigeons eyed him hopefully from the curb. The crowd continued to stand as one, 15-20 yards away, and watched him, as did those waiting in line to get into the restaurant. Zarathustra II finished off three pieces of the bread very quickly.

Just then a large white Leidenheimer bread truck with Bunny Matthews' Vic & Nat'ly cartoon characters painted on the side, pulled up on the corner to make its daily delivery of French bread to the restaurant. The pigeons scurried out of its path. Zarathustra II took the fourth piece of bread broke it in half and threw the two pieces on the sidewalk for the pigeons.

"Aint dat nice a him ta feed dem pigeons dat way," Mrs. Matthews warbled, as she cupped her hands to light a cigarette. Zarathustra II then turned the corner to walk away towards Royal Street and at that the crowd stirred from its slumber to follow him.

In the mean time, the driver of the Leidenheimer truck had stepped out of the delivery truck to the rear doors of the truck. He quickly opened the doors and grabbed three large brown paper bags each containing ten loaves of fresh French bread. There were empty go cups, pieces of discarded fruit and other trash in the street near the curb. The driver held the bags in front of him, partially obscuring his view and stepped up onto the curb. The crowd was just a few steps away from him. The driver then slipped and fell, either on one of the pieces of buttered bread that Zarathustra II had thrown on the sidewalk, or on some of the trash near the curb. When the driver slipped the bags of French bread he had been carrying spilled all over the sidewalk, at the feet of the crowd following Zarathustra II. A dozen loaves of French bread were scattered everywhere. The crowd which had been following Zarathustra II began to pick up the French bread and break it into pieces and distribute to each other, and to those waiting in line, to eat.

The driver was not hurt. He got up easily and brushed himself off. He shrugged his shoulders over the lost bread, as if it was meant to be, and went back to his truck to get more bread for delivery to the restaurant.

Chapter 40
MIRACLES

That night there was another ridiculous story about Zarathustra II by Bertrand Finch.

"Zarathustra the Second was said by his followers, now known locally as Zarathustra the Second's Army, to have performed a miracle of sorts in the French Quarter today. His followers are calling it the "miracle of the french bread," Finch reported. "Witnesses interviewed said that he had fed a crowd of about 50 with just one piece of buttered French bread." The video for the story showed a crowd breaking up loaves of French bread, passing the pieces to those in line and among themselves, outside Cafe Maspero's. There was no mention of the Leidenheimer driver slipping and spilling the bread. One woman interviewed, wearing a blue hat and green framed sun glasses, said in a heavy Chalmette accent, with a filter less cigarette dangling from the corner of her mouth, "It was rainin dat French bread on all a us an da sidewalk, an it was real fresh, like it was jus baked. It was kinda a French bread miracle." She then turned for confirmation to someone just out of camera range.

"Ain't dat rite Madie?"

"Rose-maree! Don't call me dat in public," a startled voice off camera could be heard saying.

"Oh!" the woman being interviewed said puzzled, as ashes fell from her cigarette.

"Dat's rite Mrs. Jones, it was real fresh," the other woman confirmed.

"Who's Mrs. Jones?" the lady on camera replied.

"Hush Rose-Maree!" the lady off camera said.

Finch ended his story by claiming that there was a "growing recognition by the public and the media that Zarathustra the Second, despite his shabby appearance, may be a prophet like those from biblical times."

When Mrs. Rosemary Matthews saw the story on TV she told my mother: "I still don't no who was dat Mrs. Jones."

"Hush, Rose-Maree!" my mother replied.

Chapter 41
FALSE PROPHETS

That same evening, at the 6:00 p.m. CRC church service, Reverend Jessie started his campaign in response to the growing media coverage, mostly by Finch's station, of Zarathustra II. He gave a promised televised sermon on the topic of 'false prophets.' The media had been alerted to the sermon topic and Mr. Finch mentioned it in his news broadcast, as further proof of Zarathustra II's battle for control of the CRC. The church was overflowing its 600 person capacity. There were people standing in the aisles and in the balcony. There were even people outside the church who could not get inside. I noticed about a dozen people, who I did not recognize as CRC members, standing in the aisles with rainbow flags pinned to their shirts, and a handful of others with duct tape across their mouths, presumably as a protest against Reverend Jessie's position on homosexuality. I saw Mr. Liddy cautioning those in the aisle to remain quiet.

This was the CRC's weekly church service, which was regularly televised on cable access TV, but in light of the protest of the festival, and word that Reverend Jessie would discuss 'false prophets,' other local networks were there to cover it as well. Even though Reverend Jessie was not speaking to me I attended the service. Perhaps, it was a habit that I did not yet know how to break. I had not seen Zarathustra II since that morning in the French Quarter. I assumed that he was at my apartment, which I now left unlocked so he could come and go as he pleased.

From my balcony seat I caught a glimpse of Bertrand Finch in the crowd, though he did not seem to be with any of the camera crews. I wondered what he might be planning, certain that he was not present just to attend the services. I also saw Mikhail Ivanov there, but not seated with his mother, who was in her usual spot in the first row. Ivanov was still wearing the blue suit which Zarathustra II had so recently abandoned.

Reverend Jessie walked to the podium, smiling pensively, with his Bible in his right hand. He calmly put on his black framed reading glasses. He must have been pleased with the larger than normal turnout. He stood at the podium for a few seconds, opened his Bible to some specific pages and waited to begin. The crowd quieted as a bell rang to signal the beginning of the service.

"Good evening."

"Good evening," the people echoed.

"In Matthew 7:15," Reverend Jessie said, "it cautions us to, 'Watch out for false prophets. They come to you in sheep's clothing, but inwardly they are ferocious wolves.' And in Mark 13:21-23 it provides, 'at that time if anyone says to you "Look, here is the Christ." or "Look, there he is!" do not believe it. For false Christs and false prophets will appear and perform signs and miracles to deceive the elect.'" Reverend Jessie closed his Bible. He walked away from the podium, towards the worshipers in the audience, and stopped midway. He stood among the silence, letting the words of the scripture speak and touch the audience more deeply.

"I am here today to tell you that we have a false prophet in our city, a secular humanist masquerading as a believer; a serpent trying to get people to eat the apple of disbelief," he fulminated. A disjointed drone of approval arose from the crowd, while a few people wearing rainbow pins booed. "Some of you have seen this poorly dressed man, who calls himself Zarathustra the Second, being interviewed by the media." His voice rose, direct, premonitory.

"He has become the elite liberal media's new lion, their latest champion to try to discredit you and I, and our Christian faith." There were a few people who said "Yes" in response. Reverend Jessie moved hurriedly across the raised dais from one end to the other as if to emphasize the urgency of his revelation.

"This man, whose real name is Randolph Moates, is no prophet!" the Reverend said coarsely, stopping abruptly. Reverend Jessie pulled a piece of folded loose leaf paper out of his coat pocket. He glanced at the paper. Again, he stood silent for a purposeful instant.

"I have it upon good information that he was once an English professor at Samford College, but was denied tenure due to an alcohol problem. And before being homeless, which he has been for awhile, he worked as a common laborer at a Monsanto plant on the river." Reverend Jessie paused to let his listeners consider this information. He looked up, frowning, grim but dogmatic, over the frames of his reading glasses, toward the crowd.

"Does that sound like the pedigree of a prophet?" he asked dismissively. Mrs. Ivanov and several others promptly warbled out a desultory "No!" At this point I could see Mr. Liddy, the Director of Security, in a side church pew, with his arms folded.

"He was fired from that job at Monsanto for excessive absenteeism," Reverend Jessie continued dryly, looking back at the piece of paper. "Before that, he worked briefly on a shrimp boat in the Gulf of Mexico. And he lost that job after he had been jailed for vagrancy in Houma, Louisiana. In fact, he has been arrested 9 times in at least 6 different cities for vagrancy!" Reverend Jessie began to pace again, with the piece of loose leaf paper held on high in his hand, in testimony. His voice rose again.

"He has an attachment out for his arrest right now in Atlanta for obstructing a sidewalk. Let's face it, he is a common criminal!" Reverend Jessie said decisively. Reverend Jessie pursed his lips together and shook his head in theatrical disgust at the information revealed.

"Does any of that sound like the pedigree of a prophet?" he again asked. The responding baritone "No!" in unison, was now louder, connected, as more people understood what was expected of them and joined in the chorus.

"He misreads the Bible, for his own purposes, and is seen around town cavorting with homosexuals and prostitutes, does that sound like a prophet?" Reverend Jessie said angrily, shaking the loose leaf paper, the indictment, for effect.

"No!" came the loud collective response. A few people wearing the rainbow flag pins booed. There was jostling in the aisles.

"Don't touch me!" I heard someone yell.

"I am also told that he has a daughter in Atlanta, that he has not spoken to in many years, that he has abandoned." Reverend Jessie snickered. He shook his head again in mock disbelief.

"This poor fellow says that God has disappeared from our lives, but it appears to me that he is the one who disappeared from his daughter's life. Does that sound like the actions of a prophet?" he asked rhetorically.

"No!" came the now uniform braying chorus of the congregation. He paused for silence.

"God has disappeared from this man's life because of the life he leads. Living on the street, homeless, drinking, cavorting with prostitutes. What should he expect?"

Reverend Jessie slowly and methodically folded the piece of loose leaf paper into a square and put it in the inside pocket of his coat. He removed his reading glasses and placed them in the same inside pocket. He then re-trieved his Bible from the podium and held it aloft in his right hand, as he so often did when he preached. He walked around, relaxed, his shoulders at ease, on the raised dais in front of the congregation, looking down and then up at those in the balcony. He finally stopped at one corner, lowered his head, closed his eyes to pray and grasped his bible in both hands.

"Lord, this man is a deceiver of our children, and the weak in faith among us. He has been sent by Satan, to mislead and divert us. We pray heavenly Father that you will remove him from our midst and lift the veil from the eyes of those whom he seeks to deceive," Reverend Jessie prayed aloud prompting a chorus of "Amens!" "Lord, this man claims that he can see the future. The only future I can see for him," and at that the Reverend lifted his head, opened his eyes and raised his voice, "is eter-nal damnation for blasphemy!" "Amen," again came the stern reply, along with more jostling in the aisles.

Then there was a sudden commotion in the middle of the church, as someone objected and yelled out "No! No! No!" Some church members stood, pointed and responded: "Look! Look!" pointing at a man wearing a white sweatshirt and a brand new Saints baseball cap. I didn't recognize him at first. It was Zarathustra II several rows behind Mr. Finch. The hat and shirt must have been given to him by Finch. Several more church members stood and pointed at Zarathustra II. It was Zarathustra II who had yelled "No! No! No!"

"Look! He's here!" one of them yelled out again. Several people standing in the aisle clapped and whistled in approval. Reverend Jessie stepped to the end of the raised dais and strained his neck to see to whom they were pointing. Zarathustra II then stood up, took off the baseball cap, dropped it on the floor and suddenly spoke.

"Jesus said 'Foxes have holes, and birds of the air have nests, but the son of man has nowhere to lay his head.' Jesus was homeless. The homeless today are often arrested for no good reason. I was arrested because I had no home," he said, while remaining standing. The people around him whispered their unease and discontent. Some shoving occurred in the aisles near the rear of the church. I had never seen anything like this before.

Bertrand Finch must have brought Zarathustra II to the church in hopes of another confrontation. Reverend Jessie took large Gulliver steps across the raised dais toward Zarathustra II. His voice boomed.

"Get out of my church! Get out of my church you vagrant! You false prophet!" He pointed to one of the exit doors. "You will not be allowed to practice your deception, your falseness, in the House of the Lord!" The overflow crowd in the church rumbled. Some more people stood up. A few people yelled, "Get out!" Zarathustra II remained standing.

"And you, Reverend, champion our darker impulses!" Zarathustra II yelled, over the rising din and shoving of the crowd. As different people stood up, or turned in their seats to see him, Zarathustra II slowly worked his way towards the aisle, bumping into the grumbling knees of those seated in the church pew. When he got to the aisle he paused in the midst of a sea of disapproval. He looked down dejectedly, for a long moment, as the crowd noise grew.

"Get out!" Reverend Jessie yelled again. "Get out!" Mrs. Ivanov echoed. Zarathustra II looked up and directly at Reverend Jessie.

"I tell you all that a storm is coming to this City and we will both die. Reverend, 'Set thine house in order.'" At that, he turned and pushed his way forcefully through those people in the aisle and shuffled out of a side door of the church. Bertrand Finch and his cameraman followed, a few steps behind him. Some of the protesters in the aisles filed out noisily. More shoving ensued as they exited. I noticed that Mikhail Ivanov also left a moment later.

Reverend Jessie looked very upset. He was perspiring profusely. He wiped his forehead with the back of his hand. He walked inconsolably in semi-circles around the raised dais, while the congregation watched him anxiously. Those who had stood to see Zarathustra II now sat down in waves. The crowd moved noisily for awhile longer, but slowly quieted, as Reverend Jessie continued to pace in silence. He ran the palm of his hand over his mouth and then over the top of his head. He seemed dejected, unsure of a way forward.

A loud gum popping noise then punctured the silence. A few moments later the noise happened again. People in the congregation fidgeted around trying to find the disrespectful culprit. It was difficult in the overflow crowd for me to tell where the noise came from. Reverend Jessie stopped pacing and his gaze fell upon a side pew of the church. His face grew angry. He turned and walked briskly towards those seated there.

"Security! Security!" he yelled, as Mr. Liddy and a security guard quick stepped, as best they could, amidst those in the aisles, towards where Reverend Jessie was pointing.

"Get these hookers out of here! Get these hookers out of my church!" Reverend Jessie erupted, pointing at Dominique Dagny and Shiloh Lemoine. He took his coat off and angrily threw it on the floor like he was preparing for a fistfight. His dress shirt and undershirt came untucked on one side, exposing his stomach. Both women were dressed in their usual work attire, but Ms. Lemoine wore a white bowler hat with an embroidered white handkerchief attached to the hat and hanging down over her face like a veil. It looked like she was wearing a rosary around her neck.

Ms. Dagny had a crimson colored scarf over her hair and tied under her neck. Ms Dagny blew a bubble and popped her gum again loudly. Mr. Liddy then grabbed Ms. Dagny by her arm and pulled her to her feet. Ms. Lemoine stood up as well.

"Let go of my arm. You don't touch me unless I let you. You heard me! I'll slap the shit out of you!" Ms. Dagny replied loudly, trying to pull her arm away from the muscled Mr. Liddy.

"Your church?" Ms. Lemoine shouted at Reverend Jessie as she stood up. "Well, ain't that interesting. I thought this was God's church. Since when did you become God?" Reverend Jessie did not respond, but seemed to struggle for breath.

"Let's get out of the man's damn church," Ms. Lemoine then said to Ms. Dagny. Ms. Dagny hesitated.

"This is no brothel!" Reverend Jessie then yelled, shaking and exasperated, and pointing his finger at Ms. Dagny. He kicked his jacket, which was laying on the floor, in a childlike tantrum.

"And you ain't no damn Christian, preacher man...you heard me!" Ms. Dagny yelled back, picking up her purse and walking sharply, and with exaggerated hip movement, down the aisle, as the people squeezed apart for her. She stepped out the church doors. Ms. Lemoine followed close behind.

"Kiss my black ass!" Ms. Lemoine yelled, while patting herself on the behind, as she also left through the church front doors.

Reverend Jessie bent over and put his hands on his knees. His face looked ashen. He took large gulps of air. I thought I could see his hands trembling. Mr. Liddy stepped up to him and gently escorted him to a chair on the dais. He sat down. The church crowd looked on troubled.

"I'll be alright folks. The Lord does not give us more than we can handle," Reverend Jessie said hoarsely. Mr. Liddy retrieved Reverend Jessie's coat off the floor and put it over the back of the chair. "I'll be alright," Reverend Jessie repeated weakly.

The entire confrontation between Reverend Jessie and Zarathustra II was broadcast on the late night news on several TV stations.

Chapter 42
JOHN ROLAND REYNOLDS

The next morning I got up early and walked, without ambition, to the Rouse's grocery store on Carrollton Avenue and bought a newspaper and a Red Bull energy drink. I felt fatigued, beat up, as if I had overexerted myself, physically, except that I hadn't done so. I needed some slow time. I saw Zarathustra II sleeping soundly on the sofa when I left. I sat down on the curb outside the store, wishing to be elsewhere, took a sip from my drink and began to read the paper.

There were three stories about Zarathustra II. The first was about his alleged duplication of Jesus' feeding the masses. This was Finch's so called "Miracle of the French Bread." Apparently, not to be outdone by Bertrand Finch's report, the *Time Picayune* wrote a mocking editorial story on it. The writer interviewed several people and cited "anonymous sources" concluding the episode was a hoax (which the paper mistakenly spelled a "hoacx"):

> As usual the populace is willing to suspend reason in support of religious fervor. No wonder we are unable to solve the very real problems facing our city and state. You cannot discuss reality with people who believe in fairy tales.

The second story, in the religion section of the paper, was about the dust up which had occurred at the CRC between Reverend Jessie and Zarathustra II. The writer indicated that Zarathustra II had shamed Reverend Jessie, "who seemed apoplectic that this fellow, who calls himself Zarathustra the Second, had taken their ongoing battle into the sanctity of the CRC church." The writer stated that CRC members were concerned about the toll this was taking on Reverend Jessie's health.

There was also a story in the metro section in which a reporter interviewed people from Samford University and the Monsanto plant. Samford University had refused to release any information about a tenure denial, but confirmed that a Randolph Moates had taught there. The newspaper article said that "Mr. Moates had taught Nineteenth Century English Literature classes and had written several professional articles and a self published book entitled *Thus Spoke Zarathustra: a Spiritual Critique.*"

The article indicated that the book was out of print, but that a contemporary review had severely criticized it. The *Times Picayune* quoted the book reviewer as having written: "The author, Randolph Moates, seems overly enamored with the idea that society, with the so called death of God, began to pursue individual meaning at the expense of collective meaning and that this has resulted in the pursuit of self interest over larger collective interests. The author then seeks to smuggle a religious social gospel into the public consciousness out of Nietzsche's misplaced atheistic ideas."

As to Zarathustra II's other employment, the Monsanto person contacted did not recall anyone named Randolph Moates who had ever worked there. "Our laborers come and go and if he was hired through a manpower service we might not have a record of him," Mel Alker, V.P. of Communications for Monsanto, was quoted as saying. The article cited the exact dates and cities where Zarathustra II's had been arrested for vagrancy. It stated that the arrest records indicated that he was homeless at the time of each arrest. As to his arrests in New Orleans, the article stated that he had been cleared of all the charges at the Homeless Court, with the assistance of the Loyola Law Clinic. The writer also indicated that attempts were made to contact Zarathustra II's daughter, but she did not return phone calls.

Finally, I noticed another story in the paper, not related to Zarathustra II, that would not make Reverend Jessie very happy. It was a story about the upcoming Southern Decadence Festival. It seemed that the organizers had decided, for the first time in its history, to name someone as the honorary Festival Drag Queen. The Southern Decadence Festival had a Grand Marshall each year, but never an honorary Festival Drag Queen. The article indicated that the Festival's board decided that the Queen would have to be a drag queen of some notoriety.

The Festival Board, the newspaper announced, had seriously considered several candidates before making its final selection. The Board had considered local drag queen Varla Jean Merman, and also nationally known drag queen Ru Paul. The paper, citing an unnamed Festival Board member, indicated that Reverend Jessie had been considered, but rejected by the Board for his "refusal to acknowledge his inherent drag queen nature."

Instead, the committee had chosen former New York Giants quarterback John Roland Reynolds to be the honorary Festival Drag Queen. Mr. Reynolds, prior to leading his team to a Super Bowl win in February, had told the media that if the Giants won the game he had something to say that would "shock" the world. It was kind of a Joe Namath pre-Super Bowl braggadocios comment. Local sportscasters thought that John Roland Reynolds would announce his retirement after the game, like Jerome Bettis had done some years before. Others in the national sports media thought that was unlikely, as he was only thirty years old.

His team not only won the game, but he was the MVP, completing a remarkable 20 of 22 passes for 337 yards and 3 touchdowns. As a result he got paid $100,000 to look into the camera as he was leaving the field after the game and say, "I'm going to Disney World." In the post game locker room celebration, surrounded by jubilant teammates, who were pouring champagne on each other, John Roland Reynolds made his announcement to the world.

"I'm gay and a drag queen and when I go to Disney World it will be in drag!" he said, and then turned and kissed his center, who was standing next to him, on the cheek. The center, Tom Wenrdihoskieu, who had just emerged from the shower and was wrapped in a towel, punched him, knocking him unconscious.

"You won't be putting your hands on my ass anymore!" Wendrdi-hoskieu exclaimed.

The Giants cut John Roland Reynolds two weeks later and claimed it had nothing to do with his homosexuality. Disney refused to run its commercials of him due to pressure from Focus on the Family and other Evangelical groups. But he was to be the first Southern Decadence Festival Drag Queen. When contacted by the newspaper about his selection, John Roland Reynolds, who had been living in seclusion since his Super Bowl announcement, told the reporter that he was looking forward to being "Queen for a day."

"I will use this occasion to emerge from my self-imposed cocoon and be the butterfly I always wanted to be. Hopefully, it is the start of my new life," he said to the reporter.

Chapter 43
ADVANCING ON CHAOS

When I returned to the apartment, after going to the grocery store Zarathustra II was not at home. I noticed that one of my spiral school notebooks was on the sofa. I sat down on the sofa and opened the notebook. It was the one I had used for Mr. Judice's communications class, before I dropped out of Delgado Community College. I thumbed through the first section of the notebook looking at my class notes and wondering if I would ever return to school. When I turned to the next section of the notebook, behind a dark blue divider, I saw handwriting that was not mine on the first few pages. I recognized it as Zarathustra II's printing, the printing I had seen in the notebook that he carried with him all the time.

On the last page of that section of the notebook, in small printed letters, Zarathustra II had started a letter to his daughter.

Dear Cordelia,
I am not sure how to start this letter to you. I am afraid that people will now try to contact you because of me and where I am presently living (New Orleans). I am sorry if this occurs and have no desire to interfere in your life; a life that I guess I have abandoned.

After your mother's death, when you were four years old, I was broken, singled out like Job for tribulation, and did not believe I could be put back together again. I had started to drink. Then I lost my job, the other anchor in my life, and I was set adrift. My fears briefly became anger with the world. That anger almost destroyed me.

I have lived my life in such an anarchic way, even when sober (and I am sober now thanks to my good friend Luke), that having me as a father would have only brought you ridicule. As a young child, and then as a teenager, you would have suffered from teasing because of how I lived and what I believed. Your mother, who could talk to angels, was the perfect shield for me from the 'slings and arrows' that the world often throws up if you are different and are willing to seek answers to large questions. When she died I lost my compass. She allowed me the freedom to study, to teach as needed, and to live without the materialistic concerns, the chimera of ambition, and the denial myths, which consume most people. Having lost my moorings, I have spent the last 15 years 'advancing on chaos' as Emerson wrote. Some days I see my many mistaken choices clearly and with regret, other days I cling to my intellectual shield as protection from the pain of those choices.

I do not know how to get this letter to you. I have written many such letters to you over the years un-mailed. I carry them with me in my coat pocket for awhile and pull them out periodically and reread them. But I understand you are now in Atlanta. I can only hope that you are well and that you have your beautiful mother's disposition.

I know this will make no sense, but it will all be over soon. You may receive some more calls from people about me, but please ignore them. Live your own life and be true to your own self and your own experiences. And since I will not be there for you in the future, remember this one admonition: 'If you meet the Buddha walking down the road, kill him.'

At this point the letter seemed to end. I closed the notebook and gently placed it back on the sofa where I had found it. Later that night, after Zarathustra II had returned home, I noticed that the notebook was back in my room. When I opened it back up, before going to sleep later that night, I found that the pages where his letter had been written were torn out.

"Reverend Jessie says you have a daughter in Atlanta," I said tentatively to Zarathustra II, who was sitting on the sofa.

"I do have a daughter."

"When did you last see her?"

"Probably 15 or 16 years ago." I was not sure if he wanted to discuss it further so I said nothing in response. At that point Zarathustra II got up from the sofa and his eyes seemed to search the recesses of his mind for a memory.

"Perhaps your father was right about my abandonment of her. I have always tended to rationalize it as having been best for her," he said quietly, with difficulty.

"Who raised her?" I asked.

"I left her with my mother in law," he said with a still distant, rummaging, look. I watched as he held his hands, and perhaps himself, tightly together.

Chapter 44
HURRICANE BERA

There was trouble brewing. Hurricane Bera had defied the predictions of the computer models. It had indeed stalled drifted, unmoored, and then changed course dramatically over night in a westerly direction. The National Weather Service was perplexed that it had been completely wrong about the track.

"Normally our computer models are not this wrong. This storm seems to have a mind of its own. Its why we always have to be prepared," one Weather Channel reporter said, during the noon broadcast. Local weather forecasters were also confused.

"Either someone hacked into the computers, or it was initially given bad information to create these mistakes. The National Weather Service is checking on that. Computers should not be this wrong," the weather-man Mrs. Rosemary Matthews called 'the face' reported. It now appeared that the hurricane was going to cross the Florida peninsula and enter the Gulf of Mexico. It had completely changed direction. It was a category three storm, but it was slowly intensifying.

"We have come to rely on these computer models, and sometimes we don't do our own thinking," the face said, in the same broadcast, staring blankly, puzzled, at the latest spaghetti models. "Ya tink! Nash Roberts neva had such a problem," Mrs. Rosemary Matthews said to her TV screen, as she watched the report.

All of the local weathermen began to report on the latest computer tracking models with an air of skepticism, a hedge against a failed forecast. The new computer models showed about a 25-30% chance of New Orleans taking a direct hit. Biloxi had a 40% chance of a hit and the pan handle of Florida had a 30-35% chance. "But we can't be sure," the face modified. It was still too early to tell the exact path which the storm would take. A lot depended on a low front that might be coming from the northwest. The city of New Orleans might be in real trouble.

New Orleanians and those on the Gulf Coast had lived with the uncertainty, the repressed anxiety, of hurricane seasons their entire lives. The city had been declared dead by pundits more than once: Hurricane Betsy, Hurricane Katrina, the BP oil spill, as examples. Obituaries were written, announced, testified to, and then discarded. Most of the city, prior to Hurricane Katrina, had dulled their senses to the possible danger, ignored that menacing cloud on the horizon. But Katrina and the levee failures had overturned some of that stoicism. There was a nervousness beneath the veneer of even the most hardened hurricane veteran now, which had become part of the city's collective character. It always intensified as the anniversary of Katrina approached.

Attempts to decipher the effects of living in hurricane alley on the psyche of New Orleanians was an inexact science. During hurricane season New Orleans natives lived a daily version of the Rorschach ink blot test sketched on TV stations in the form of hurricane spaghetti models.

When I saw the stories on the change in the hurricane's path, and realized that there was a real possibility that New Orleans could be hit, I developed a headache for several hours and became anxious. Once I saw Zarathustra II again the symptoms slowly abated, and at the same time, and maybe for the first time, it dawned on me that Zarathustra II's predictions about the storm, the damage, and the city might be right.

Chapter 45
FESTIVAL QUEEN

Despite the possibility that the hurricane would head into the Gulf of Mexico and threaten New Orleans, the merchants in the French Quarter continued to prepare for the Southern Decadence Festival. Local bars began to clean up and stock up, readying for the expected tourists, but with an anguished eye on the path of the storm. Capitalism was neutral in matters of morality, or acts of God, unless its bottom line was threatened. In the City that Care Forgot the merchants were happy for any business. Unlike preachers, merchants embraced the tolerance and forgiveness offered by the almighty dollar.

The Festival Drag Queen, John Roland Reynolds, was expected to come to town early to get fitted for his coronation gown and to meet with festival organizers. When he was told by a reporter of the possible storm headed into the Gulf of Mexico he was quoted in the paper as saying, "What a drag!"

Young gay men and old gay men started to be seen together in larger groups in the French Quarter, having made their way to the city before the storm changed direction. Lesbians and a handful of transgender individuals moved effortlessly down Bourbon Street. Reverend Jessie's two different groups from the CRC also continued to walk the streets of the French Quarter with signs and megaphones, proselytizing, imploring people to reject homosexuality, repent, and accept Jesus Christ as their savior. On occasion other street preachers hauling scriptural banners, some benign, some offensive, crossed their path.

The CRC members stayed mostly on Bourbon Street and Royal Street and walked in shifts. They tried handing out pre-printed pages with quotes from Leviticus about homosexuality being an "abomination," and a listing of upcoming services at the CRC. Sometimes there was friendly banter between the CRC members and tourists walking in the Quarter. On a couple of occasions arguments broke out, voices were raised in anger, when Reverend Jessie preached loudly with his bull horn that homosexuality was an "abomination."

"You and your bullhorn are an abomination!" someone yelled.

"That outfit you are wearing is an abomination! You should be stoned for wearing it!" another yelled at Reverend Jessie. "I need to be stoned to look at it!" another replied.

But mostly the groups ignored each other, or talked past each other, speaking foreign tongues, unfamiliar languages.

The pledges from DKE, wearing their Asshole Brothers' signs, used the CRC protest for another initiation prank. They stood on the corner of Bourbon Street and St. Ann, across from the Bourbon Pub. All were dressed in black slacks, black shoes with no socks, starched white oxford shirts with button down collars, wearing thick no lens black plastic framed glasses and with their hair slicked back with styling gel. Several carried different versions of the bible with them. One of them had a copy of the Kama Sutra. Another had a wooden cross around his neck with a rubber Gumby nailed to it.

"Citizens, Countrymen and douche bags of all type! Listen up! We belong to the Church of the Intolerant and Genocidal Almighty!" one of them said into a bullhorn. "My name is Movinious Snoot."

"Amen!" the pledges yelled in a unified response.

"Our God is the ball busting, ego-maniacal and vindictive Old Testament God, not that mamby-pamby out there somewhere New Testament Greek philosophy logos God!"

"Amen, brother Movinious," several of the pledges replied.

"Our God speaks to us."

"Actually he yells at us brother Movinious," the pledge with the Kama Sutra said.

"He has told us that you are all idiots, all reprobates, all destined for eternal damnation. In fact He appeared at our frat house last night and confirmed the stupidity of the masses over a beer."

"It was gin. He was drinking gin brother Movinious," another of the brothers interrupted.

"Yes, Brother Fellatio, it was gin. My apologies," the one with the bullhorn said. "Anyway, God told us that He is depressed by your stupidity. He has not disappeared as the vagrant preacher-weatherman-prophet Zarathustra the Second has said. He is simply bummed out by how you all turned out, like a parent whose only child became a crack head," brother Movinious said. "But if you join us, and you contribute the spiritually correct sum of $100, right now, He told us that you will be born again, free from your stupidity---what He calls the 'Original Stupidity'---with the veil of ignorance lifted from your eyes!" he yelled. The pledge wearing the cross with Gumby on it hoisted a home-made sign that read "$100 all sins forgiven." Another then held a sign aloft that read: "Would you pay $100 not to be stupid?" Several tourists, with drinks in hand, listened attentively to the brothers and laughed.

The CRC members walked by the Asshole Brothers, but ignored their pleas to join the Church of the Intolerant and Genocidal Almighty. "Think of it as complying with an updated version of Pascal's Wager," the one named Brother Fellatio implored them, to no avail.

Chapter 46
WILDEBEEST

Reverend Jessie's revelations and the newspaper coverage about Zarathustra II's work history, arrests, and his daughter, had not, it seemed, dampened people's enthusiasm to see him. Finch's reporting, the numerous YouTube videos, newspaper articles, Facebook postings and online comments about him, probably helped. In addition, the hurricane suddenly changing direction and heading towards the Gulf of Mexico captured people's attention. Indeed, the combination of it all may have made some people more curious about him, as if he was an amalgamation of biblical prophet, magician, and reality TV star.

So they waited by his park bench near Jackson Square for him to show up. Their numbers were growing. There were at least 50-60 people, including several reporters, there the next time he showed up to speak. They seated themselves on the ground in an ill formed half circle around his park bench. They were young and old, lost and hoping to be found, or not found out. Some wore the **Zarathustra the Second's Army** T-shirts, some wore work clothes and others were dressed in their Sunday best. A handful of homeless men watched him hopefully. They no longer badgered him about storm predictions, as a few had originally done.

When he arrived several times each day to speak they sat quietly. They remained so, anticipating, while he paced back and forth on the park bench.

He spoke on his favorite topics, the disappearance of God, our need for collective meaning and our responsibility for ourselves and for each other. He talked more about the social gospel, rejecting stereotypes, and our responsibility to take care of the less fortunate. The homeless men would clap meekly when he talked about caring for others. He talked about Jesus and Buddha. He said there were many parallels in their actual teachings, in their underlying humanity, and those parallels had to do with living a self less life. He also mentioned Confucius, saying that we should be the catalyst of the change we wish to see in the world. Sometimes someone would ask a question about his theology, about how he read the bible. On occasion someone would approach him with money.

Those asking questions tried to get him to reduce his answers to easy to remember bromidic formulas, or phrases. When I pointed this out, he told me he still hoped people would understand everything more deeply.

Zarathustra II rejected any attempt to dumb down his message and when I asked about it, he said, "This is not Luther's catechism." He told me later that he disliked much of what Luther had written, especially his anti-Semitic tracts towards the end of his life. He said that Luther purposely dumbed down his religious doctrine so that illiterate people could more easily understand it and that is what the word "catechism" actually meant, a sort of dumbed down summary. He presented Luther's Catechism like it was an early marketing idea in the history of religion.

"The Catholics co-opted what Luther did, though they had long before softened, leveled and revised, the doctrines of Jesus at the Council of Trent, through their concept of tradition and also because of Constantine's embrace," he said painfully.

I told him that everything would probably be alright if people would just read more and think more deeply. I thought for certain he would approve of my comment. Instead, he got a bit melancholy. He talked again about the delicate balance that was needed in the quest for self knowledge.

Someone in the crowd that day, asked tremulously, "Well, if God is gone, like you say, how are we to live our lives?" Others nodded in fearful unison, like a herd of wildebeest placed on alert, by one of their number, of a nearby lioness.

"The same way you decided things when you thought God was here listening to everything you said, and watching everything you did. Just internalize the principles," Zarathustra II answered. He referred often to Jesus' remark that 'the kingdom of God is within' to support this view. The wildebeests stirred restlessly as a group, uncomfortable with the home-work assignment. He also told them about the Russian writer Tolstoy, and his notion that the entire Bible should be distilled down to the teaching found in the Gospel of Matthew: "But I say unto you, That you resist not evil...."

Chapter 47

RESIST NOT EVIL

That evening at my apartment I asked Zarathustra II if he could explain the 'resist not evil' quote again to me.

"I'm not familiar with that phrase. Where is it at?"

"It's in Matthew."

It was important, he said, that I understand that the King James Bible, which had the "resist not evil" quote in it, had numerous translation errors. The translation errors were apparently discovered when the Dead Sea Scrolls were uncovered. But its language, he said, was poetic, memorable, and, like Shakespeare, it has given us many phrases that have became part of our everyday language.

"It was authorized by King James in 1604. Supposedly fifty four biblical scholars worked on it, and it was completed around 1611. And they used the Masoretic text as their basis. The entire quote is, 'But I say unto ye, that ye resist not evil; but whosoever shall smite thee on thy right cheek, turn to him the other also,'" he said.

"Oh! I know about the turn the other cheek stuff, but I never heard the 'resist not evil' phrase."

"It was an important phrase for writers like Tolstoy, and later Gandhi. For different reasons, Nietzsche thought it the most important saying in the Bible."

"Nietzsche? The same guy that said God was dead?"

"Yes," he snickered.

Patiently, he told me that much of Gandhi's political philosophy of 'truth force,' of passive resistance to the British occupation of his country, sprang from his reading of Tolstoy's interpretation of that one King James biblical phrase: "resist not evil." Tolstoy had written an entire book, *The Kingdom of God is Within*, based on that phrase, which explained how to live such a life. Gandhi had read the book and had been moved by it, as later Martin Luther King would be by Gandhi. Interestingly, Zarathustra II told me, Tolstoy was excommunicated by the Church for his writings.

"But it is not a phrase, 'resist not evil,' in the lexicon of most ministers today. Because organized religion, to attract the mass of men, must contain a large dose of hatred," Zarathustra II concluded, somewhat despondently.

"I didn't know Gandhi was a Christian," I said, displaying my ignorance of all things not Western.

"He was not," Zarathustra II said, looking at me, searching for something in my countenance.

"And I don't agree that there is an element of hate in religion, or whatever you said before," I belatedly rambled.

"Unfortunately, there is," he said calmly, defusing my agitation. "That is the low level marketing aspect of much of organized Christianity. Without the negative other, the object or group to hate, which preachers are all too willing to identify, there is little need for organized religion," he said. I waited for an explanation from him but none was immediately forthcoming.

Then in soliloquy, a few minutes later, he said, "Bukowski was right. Hatred is the mass man's art." At that point something sat between us, unspoken, an experience of Zarathustra II's that I could not yet understand, a flaming arrow that I had never had to deflect. "Hatred is the mass man's art, and religion is too often the canvas on which it is painted," he said to himself, in that same soliloquy.

"Religion and hate. That just doesn't make sense," I protested mildly, knowing there would be a rebuttal.

"It shouldn't. But people want to belong to something. A tribe, a nation, a religion; something bigger than themselves. But that need to belong is the jumping off point for having to define the 'other' in our lives, those we believe are in opposition to us, or to what we believe. And once the 'other' is defined it is gradually de-humanized and hate, which is never far beneath the surface, emerges. Unfortunately, that is a large part of the legacy of organized religion," he said lucidly, but as if he wished it were not so.

"But religion is not supposed to be about hate," I said again, defensively, not knowing if I was defending religion or myself, but feeling compelled to do so.

"I wish it were otherwise," he said in a monotone voice. "What did Christianity do to the Jews, who were cast as its negative other, for over 2000 years? Look what Christianity did to Muslims during the various Crusades. Look at what Muslims and Christians are doing to each other right now in Africa and elsewhere. What about the long hatred between Sunnis and Shiites? Look at the battles between Hindus and Sikhs in India," he rattled. I did not know how to respond. His eyes misted up. "Religion and hatred have often embraced as relatives, at the insistence of our dethroned angels," he said, wiping the mist in his eyes with his hand.

Chapter 48
GIVE ME A SIGN

Try as he might Reverend Jessie did not believe that he was getting the amount of media attention he wanted for his campaign against the Southern Decadence Festival. Although some of this had to do with coverage of the developing hurricane, Reverend Jessie attributed the lack of attention entirely to the fact that the media, led astray by Bertrand Finch, was preoccupied with reporting on Zarathustra II and his predictions. This was exacerbated once the storm had changed direction.

Reverend Jessie sat up all night reading scripture, trying to find some inspiration, revelation, as to what he should do to reverse the trend, while the ghost of his father, Reverend Elder hovered over him. But try as he might nothing seemed to come to him.

Such times were very difficult for Reverend Jessie. I had seen it before when he felt blocked, that the Word was not coming to him from God, or the ever present ghost. He would sit up all night, or walk the halls of the church, apprehensive, concerned that he had made a misstep in the eyes of God, with his Bible held tightly, saying: "Just give me a sign, Lord." Now, since my mother was not involved in the church anymore, he no longer had her in whom to confide his thoughts. And when God was not speaking, he was just like the rest of us, trapped like Lot's wife in salt, trying to figure a way to move, on his own.

The morning after his unsuccessful all night vigil, reading and reciting scripture, he was seated at the kitchen table, still in his suit, with his tie loosened and sweating profusely through his dress shirt. His whole body ached. It seemed as if God's taciturnity was making Reverend Jessie ill. His Bible was on the table and he was trying to drink some ice water to cool off. His hand shook slightly, as he raised the glass to his lips.

My mother came into the kitchen wearing a lime green pants suit, blue hat and green framed sunglasses, pulling her bright yellow suitcase on wheels behind her. It was obvious that she was going somewhere. Reverend Jessie hesitated to ask her anything, such was the unforgiving tension, the fractured nature, of their relationship.

"Madeline, what are you doing?" he finally asked, clearing his throat.

"What's it look like?" she replied defiantly, filling up her large plastic travel coffee mug from Big Harry's in the kitchen sink.

"Where are you going?" he then asked formally.

My mother seemed preoccupied with the task of filling up her coffee mug and did not immediately answer. When she did respond it was simply to herself.

"Let's see, I got da hurricane maps fa 85, 87 an 97 ta discuss. Oh! I forgot ta get da loaf a Bunny bread. I hope dat Rosemary got one."

"Speak proper English!" Reverend Jessie bemoaned.

Reverend Jessie then stood up gingerly, bracing himself against the kitchen table. His face was an unhealthy color and there was a tightness in the lines on his forehead. Stubble was on his unshaved face.

"Where are you going?" he now demanded with as much volume as his tired voice would allow. My mother stopped what she was doing and looked him directly in the eyes, without compassion. She bowed up like a cat readying itself for a fight with a larger cat, but one she had beaten before, and often.

"Foist, I"m goin ta Big Harry's ta meet wit Rosemary," she said sternly.

"With a suitcase?" Reverend Jessie interrupted.

"Let me finish!" my mother said loudly, holding the palm of her hand up to his face in defiance. "Ya neva would let me finish. Dat's aways been a problem," she countered, as spouses have countered each other, damaged each other, across many broken years and white lies. Reverend Jessie sat back down.

"Den we is drivin ta Atlanta ta get away from dat hurricane," she said.

"Why are you leaving, you don't even know if the storm is going to hit New Orleans," Reverend Jessie now said calmly, trying to reason with her.

"Well, I may not know," my mother said, with one hand on her hip and the other shaking a finger at Reverend Jessie, "but dat Zaratootstra fella noze." With that comment Reverend Jessie lost all composure. He stood again, shaking, and tried to reach my mother, speaking in the only language he knew.

"Madeline, don't be ridiculous. He is a false prophet like Matthew warns. I have studied scripture for all these years and I know these things," he implored her, lips trembling.

He did not reach my mother. The distance that had grown between them was now too great to bridge; it could only be fallen into. His words sat like an unexamined bundle between them, tied with an unfamiliar yarn, which then fell unopened, into the divide which separated them.

"Ya know, I tink you was a betta man ta me when ya had mo doubts. But at some point ya only listened ta ya Gawd. An den ya was impossible," she said calmly, tossing away the stone of hope and broaching something she felt she should have expressed years before. "An ya didn't tink ya was above evrybody den."

"I am the same man you married Madeline. No better. No worse," he said uneasily, feeling the emptiness he sometimes felt, painfully exposed, as one can only feel with criticism from someone you have loved.

"An ya loved da Lord so much, ya didn't have no love left fa ya family." She looked at him with contempt; love and contempt.

"Madeline, that is...that is simply not true. I always loved my family... as best I could."

"Well, mostly it neva felt like it," she said, fueled by an inner anger.

"Listen to me Madeline, this fellow is a false prophet. He can't predict the future."

"He's a nice man ta people. Ya should be so nice."

"Madeline, you are being foolish."

"Well, it seems ta me dat Zaratootstra is providin all a us a public type service wit his warnin. If ya want ma advice stead a sittin up all nite readin da Bible ta ya'self, ya could spend some time tellin people what ta do bout da storm," she said, with a serrated, but compassionate, edge to her tone. "An if I was ya I 'd be very careful bout his prediction dat ya was gonna die," she said, and for a moment her voice faltered.

"Madeline, he is a fool. I'm in no danger," he replied softly, feeling her concern, and grasping to find common ground. They both stood silent for a long moment, but neither could find a way to reach across the divide. My mother hesitated. She looked around the kitchen like she was seeing it for the first time, or the last time. She then rolled her suitcase out of the kitchen. He stood up as she passed.

Reverend Jessie felt beaten. His soul no longer had words for this pain. "You can't just be a minister. Your family is not your congregation. You must also be a husband and a father," the marriage counselor had told him. He often wanted to apologize, set down his pride, which he had struggled with, and pick up the burden of confessing, but had not done so. He could not afford to think long about it, or linger on the idea. The effect on him when he did so was palpable, like a heart beat in the throat after a sudden scare. He had to let it pass.

Whether she heard him or not, as she pulled the suitcase over the carpet and out the front door, he said quietly, with his head held lowered, as if offering up a death row prayer, immediately prior to an execution, "Please be safe." And standing there in the kitchen, beaten, dumbfounded and abandoned by my mother, Reverend Jessie had his moment of inspiration.

Chapter 49
THE LIVES OF THE FAITHFUL

Bertrand Finch stood off to the side of the hastily called morning news conference. He was uneasy. He did not know what to expect, as there was no detailed information provided on the precise subject of the press conference. The press conference had been called unilaterally, by Reverend Jessie, who had faxed urgent notices to all of the local TV and radio stations. The notice simply stated that Reverend Jessie had an "important announcement to make that would be of interest to the media, to the city and the faith community, about the hurricane." It was understated and vague. Finch was worried that Reverend Jessie might try to further sabotage his stories about Zarathustra II.

"Any ideas on what the good Reverend's going to talk about?" Finch, awkward, asked reporter Clarice McComb.

"Maybe he is going to announce that he has become a follower of Finch's fool," she replied. She then turned and faced Finch, who had turned his head away at her remark. "What you have set in motion with this guy is not professional. I don't agree with his religion, but he is a minister for God's sake," she replied firmly. Finch winced, and then instinctively patted the top of his head to assure that his toupee was on tight.

"I'm just...I'm...I'm just...giving the public, uh, what it wants," Finch replied, stammering, uncomfortable, hoping the conversation would end.

"No, you're not," Ms. McComb confronted him. "You're trying to create a spectacle and somehow use it to your advantage. I thought my report showing the falsity of your early stories would dissuade you from going further, but I guess not." Finch stepped away, discourteously, without responding, from her and moved to the front of the group of reporters.

It just so happened that some of the media had already been planning to assemble at the airport for another press conference that morning, which was set to begin twenty minutes after Reverend Jessie's requested press conference. It included several local sportscasters and cameramen from ESPN and FOX Sports. When the stations received Reverend Jessie's fax a group email from the media was sent to him and told him that the press conference would have to be at the Louis Armstrong New Orleans International Airport. Reverend Jessie had no idea that there was another press conference already scheduled and attached no significance to the airport location. He thought that the media would be assembling simply to hear his announcement. He was determined to take the initiative in his battle with what he believed was evil. All the camera equipment had to be put up a bit sooner than expected to accommodate Reverend Jessie, and a few reporters straggled in late, so there was a delay when he arrived. A podium for Reverend Jessie was finally obtained from airport personnel and placed in front of the cameras.

"Alright Reverend, they're ready for you," someone with the media group finally said blandly, adjusting the height of the microphone attached to the podium before stepping away. A handful of members of the CRC were present with Reverend Jessie, and stood by his side. On the other side of the camera equipment, standing next to the reporters, there were a half dozen men dressed elegantly in drag. They were the drag queen selection committee and were there early on behalf of the Southern Decadence Festival to greet John Roland Reynolds, whose plane was to arrive shortly and who was set to be interviewed upon his arrival.

Reverend Jessie waited until he was sure all the cameras were on. "Thank you for coming today," he began simply. "In the last week or so the media has given much credence, much air time, to the false prophet who calls himself Zarathustra the Second, but whose real name is Randolph Moates. He has been allowed to make outrageous predictions and to confuse the faithful into believing that he knows the mind of God. This nonsense has been played up by the local media, in particular by Mr. Finch and his station, at the expense of the rock hard faith of simple believers throughout this city." Reverend Jessie paused for a moment to look directly at Finch. "In contrast to this buffoon, I am here today to tell you that the Lord has spoken directly to me. In doing so, he has instructed me to reveal the power of his love and mercy, and to also reveal the chicanery of this false prophet, Randolph Moates, who does not speak for him." Reverend Jessie was perspiring under the heat of the camera lights. He took a handkerchief from his inside coat pocket and wiped his forehead. He continued to clutch the handkerchief in his fist, which he then rested upon the podium as he leaned forward. The media group was getting restless.

"Here is my announcement. The Lord has told me to take a select group of His followers, twelve in number to be exact, and to stay in the French Quarter during the hurricane, in the middle of that den of inequity, near the homosexual bars. He has told me that if I will do this He shall spare and protect the lives of the faithful who are with me, even in the face of the approaching hurricane," he said.

One of the drag queens, wearing gecko green eye shadow and bright red lipstick, who looked like a Cher impersonator, turned to his friend and said in a monotone whisper, "Just what we don't need, more straight people sent by God to be in the Quarter."

"I'm sorry Reverend, are you saying that you now admit that Zarathustra the Second is correct in his prophecy, and that the hurricane is going to hit New Orleans?" Bertrand Finch quickly asked.

"Mr. Finch, the Lord has told me that it is now His will, since it will serve a larger purpose. He will use the storm to punish the wicked and to protect the righteous," Reverend Jessie replied confidently.

"And are you saying you are going to stay in the French Quarter during the actual storm?" Finch asked. Reverend Jessie smiled and patted his brow with his handkerchief.

"Yes. In the French Quarter, unprotected except by the Almighty. The truly faithful who stand with me, the elect, will be spared, Mr. Finch. God has told me He will not allow them or me to be harmed."

"When you say they will stay with you in the French Quarter during the storm unprotected what do you mean?" Ms. Clarice McComb asked dumb founded.

"Ms. McComb, we will stand together in the street during the storm, exposed to the wind, the rain, all of the elements of the hurricane, with the Lord as our one and only protector," Reverend Jessie answered.

"What!" Ms. McComb blurted out. One of the reporters laughed. The gathered media seemed unsure what to ask in response. There was a low murmur of voices and the turning of pages in notepads.

"So you are going to stand outside in category 4 or 5 hurricane force winds?" Finch asked, still unsure.

"That's correct," Reverend Jessie replied calmly.

"How...How do you know this? How do you know you will be protected?" Bertrand Finch finally asked incredulously.

"Mr. Finch, I don't expect you to understand this, but God has told me so," Reverend Jessie replied, without hesitation. "If you knew your Bible, as I hope you will one day, you would not be surprised. God often tests our faith."

"But the police will arrest you. You can't do that," Finch said, looking from side to side to solicit support from the other reporters.

"No. The Lord will handle any other obstacles as well. It is His will and His will cannot be thwarted by man," Reverend Jessie replied.

"Who are the twelve idiots who have volunteered for this assignment?" Ms. McComb asked, disdainfully.

"I'll ignore your sarcasm Ms. McComb. But my followers, and the larger faith community, need to know that I am waiting for further instruction from the Lord on who to select. He will guide me on the selection, as He has always done with other things in my life."

"Hasn't this gotten out of hand between you and this homeless fellow that calls himself Zarathustra?" Ms. McComb asked. "Isn't that what this announcement is really about?"

"It is important that the people's faith be preserved, or restored. I am merely the Lord's instrument here. I have no choice," Reverend Jessie replied.

"You always have a choice," Ms. McComb responded sincerely.

"Not when the Lord asks," Reverend Jessie replied.

"Are you sure the Lord is asking and it's not your pride?" she asked.

"I'm betting my life on it," Reverend Jessie replied, and then cleared his throat.

"Unbelievable!" another reporter exclaimed, as others got on their cell phones to call in the story, or turned to face cameras to wrap up the story being broadcast live.

Reverend Jessie smiled slightly and sensed that he had surprised the media with his announcement. The assembled media moved about like a recently disturbed ant pile. Bertrand Finch stared at his blank note pad and tried to think about whether this helped or hurt his chances of getting noticed by a larger market.

"This story is going to go national and make New Orleans look like the land of nuts," Ms. McComb said to a colleague.

"We'll be The City that Reason Forgot," someone said humorously.

"Hey, a good title for an article. Do you mind if I use it?" another reporter asked.

Just then one of the drag queens screamed. "He's here!" Sure enough about 30 yards up the concourse, behind Reverend Jessie, was Super Bowl quarterback John Roland Reynolds. He was dressed in a dark blue Luis Vuitton suit with a red, white and blue American flag bow tie, but wearing a black cowboy hat and ostrich skin cowboy boots. The six or so drag queens, who had been waiting for his arrival, rushed towards John Roland Reynolds passing between the TV cameras and the podium. When they met John Roland Reynolds one of the drag queens gave him a dozen roses.

With all of them in tow Mr. Reynolds walked right up to the podium for his previously scheduled press conference.

Reverend Jessie just stood there momentarily transfixed, like a man who has been long confined in a dark room and whose eyes could not adjust to sudden light. Mr. Reynolds, not knowing who Reverend Jessie was, extended his hand for a friendly handshake. He was flanked by his drag queen entourage. Reverend Jessie ignored the offer of a handshake. He was aware of the selection of a Festival Drag Queen.

"Lord, even the demons must submit to us in your name!" he said forcefully to John Roland Reynolds, as he walked away from the podium.

John Roland Reynolds did not know what to make of Reverend Jessie or his comment. He stepped up to the microphone at the podium, faced the cameras, like he had just calmly avoided a quarterback sack, and said, "New Orleans, your Drag Queen is here." The drag queens surrounding him shrieked and clapped with delight in response.

Chapter 50
GALVANIZED

Reverend Jessie's press conference had its intended effect on the media. It also galvanized the CRC membership in support of his cause. Reverend Jessie had fallen back on the Occam's Razor of preaching: the simpler the message the better. It was easy to understand things in black and white. Mani had taught the world that lesson.

Reverend Jessie's message was alluring to those who wanted to believe and to a community that increasingly saw itself as being victimized. If you were chosen by Reverend Jessie to be with him in the French Quarter, and presumably God would help Reverend Jessie make his picks, and you were faithful to God, and one of the elect, you would be protected from all harm. This would prove that Reverend Jessie stood in good favor with God, disprove religious critics, and it would also prove God's power and mercy.

What about Zarathustra II's prediction that the hurricane would hit New Orleans and that he, Reverend Jessie and Bertrand Finch would die? Either God would protect Reverend Jessie, or He would not. That made for good theater, and it was easy for people to understand: someone would be right and someone would be wrong. At least that was what I was thinking after I saw the press conference.

Bertrand Finch had been upstaged by Reverend Jessie's announcement. Reverend Jessie had seized the momentum. Every local TV station did a breaking news segment to report on Reverend Jessie's press conference and on his promise to stand in the French Quarter during the storm. Local editorial commentators on television that evening addressed the announcement. Now many people in the faith community, and perhaps the larger community, waited in anticipation to see which twelve individuals Reverend Jessie would name to accompany him.

The national media, as Ms. McComb predicted, had also picked up the story of Reverend Jessie's press conference. The Christian Broadcasting Network immediately christened it as "Reverend Elder and his Christian Soldiers Stand Against Evil" and lauded his efforts to "raise the consciousness of the army of true believers to the evils facing us as a Christian nation." Donations were wired to the CRC from around the country. The CRC received over $20,000 in donations in the two days following the press conference.

National media pundits on CNN that afternoon discussed the matter in round table format yelling each other down.

"Listen to this. An Evangelical minister in New Orleans named Jessie Ray Elder has indicated that God has told him to select twelve individuals and stand unprotected in the French Quarter if Hurricane Bera hits the city," the moderator said to the panel.

"The Reverend needs to find a God not quite so dumb as to put a man in the middle of a hurricane. I didn't think God was a Republican, but this has all the makings of a stunt by the Republican right. This guy will be another Icarus," the Democratic CNN contributor said.

FOX News interviewed several self identified theologians from Liberty University and Trinity International who refused to express any opinion on the wisdom of Reverend Jessie's actions. "Only God and he know the content of their conversation," one of them said. Another Fox contributor, in a discussion group, said the criticism of Reverend Jessie was "further proof that Christians are unfairly demonized by the mass media."

Bertrand Finch was emboldened by the elevation of the matter to the national level. It was what he wanted all along and Reverend Jessie had facilitated it with his announcement. Finch, however, felt certain it now increased his chances of being noticed and moving to a larger market or, perhaps, even the national stage. This was his story. But he had to regain control of it.

Chapter 51
CHRISTIAN BROADCASTING NETWORK

"Good evening fellow believers! We are happy to be joined via satellite hookup by a most remarkable servant of Christ, Reverend Jessie Ray Elder of the First Church of the Recalcitrant Covenant in New Orleans, Louisiana," the announcer from the Christian Broadcasting Network said, reading from a teleprompter. Her name was Sister Sarah and she was seated comfortably on a gold sofa. She had on heavy make-up and wore a short black skirt with her tanned, but slightly too large, legs crossed. She was joined on the sofa by a well dressed non-descript male co-host. Her hair was an odd black-orange color and looked like a too large tabby male cat was curled up asleep on top of her head.

"Good evening. Hallelujah! Good evening to you Sister Sarah!" Reverend Jessie, joining from a local New Orleans TV station, said enthusiastically in response. Reverend Jessie was dressed in a conservative dark gray suit with a yellow tie and a white carnation in his lapel. He had quickly changed from his morning press conference at the airport when the request for the CBN interview was relayed to him by his secretary Dolores. He smiled broadly. Despite his notoriety in New Orleans Reverend Jessie had never received any coverage from the Christian Broadcasting Network.

"The Lord is wonderful, isn't he," Sister Sarah replied, clasping her hands together tightly.

"He's the boss! He knows all! We are not worthy of His love!" Reverend Jessie bellowed back proudly, in an adolescent, reverential, tone.

"Amen!" the male host echoed.

"I have to tell you Reverend that what you are about to do is an inspiration to all of us in the faith community," Sister Sarah said. "So many people in this country, especially our politicians, embrace a vague religious faith that they can't even articulate, but you are going to walk the true faith. We are under siege in this nation by satanic forces and you are standing up to those forces, as all Christians should be doing," she said.

"This will show them who is the real King," the male co-host replied.

"Well, all glory be to God. It was His idea, not mine," Reverend Jessie said, with a hint of modesty. "And as Rushdoony wrote 'The result of becoming tolerant towards sin is that we become intolerant towards God and His word.'"

"Amen," Sister Sarah replied.

"Amen," the male co-host echoed.

"I have to ask this for our viewers with a weaker faith. Aren't you a little afraid about standing outdoors possibly facing hurricane force winds?" the male co-host asked tepidly, grinning.

"Well, the Lord will be with me and as He wrote in Isaiah, 'The one who believes does not flee,'" Reverend Jessie replied.

"Amen! Though I confess I'd have to do something about my hair in that wind!" Sister Sarah said, touching the side of her hair with her hand. The male co-host smiled insincerely.

"You are obviously a man of great faith," the male co-host then said to Reverend Jessie in a manly voice.

"Tell us a little about yourself and your ministry," Sister Sarah asked. Before Reverend Jessie could answer, she interjected, "Yours is an evangelical church---correct?"

"Yes, ma'am. Yes, ma'am. Well, our ministry continues to grow down here. We are the largest evangelical church in the city, and you know this is a very Catholic city," Reverend Jessie explained.

"God is guarding you I can tell," the male co-host interrupted.

"He is. He is. And this is the least that I can do. When God calls on us to mobilize we must answer. We are his foot soldiers in this cultural war. If we don't answer Him now we will have to answer to Him later in the hereafter. He wants us to build His kingdom here on earth. A kingdom of godly men and godly women based on His inerrant word," Reverend Jessie said. "Absolutely," the male co-host replied.

"And have you selected the twelve foot soldiers; the canonical twelve I'll call them, to stand with you in this cultural war?" Sister Sarah asked.

"And that's exactly what it is, a cultural war," the male host added, with a touch of righteousness in his voice.

"No ma'am. I am waiting on instruction," Reverend Jessie said.

"This fellow that calls himself, what is it Zara—Zarathustra? What an odd name. He is the one misleading the faithful. Is that correct?" Sister Sarah said.

"Yes he is. You would have to see this little fellow. He is a vagrant. He looks like he has been homeless for a good while. He has some sense. He is intelligent, but I can't let him cause people to question..." Reverend Jessie said.

"Unbelievable that people could listen to such a man," the male co-host interrupted.

"He is something of a media creation. People are being misled by the local elite liberal media---no offense intended," Reverend Jessie replied.

"None taken. We understand exactly what you mean. The Devil has his minions in all places, including the media," Sister Sarah replied.

"This has been a nice interview," the male co-host said, indicating the interview was at an end.

"Can I say one more thing?" Reverend Jessie then asked.

"Quickly," Sister Sarah said, less enthusiastic.

"Madeline, if you are watching, please...." The screen showing Reverend Jessie went blank cutting him off mid sentence.

"Reverend, we are out of time. Oh, I wish we had more time to further discuss your crusade against homosexuality in detail. But thanks so much for your time and what you are doing. You are in our prayers and we know the Lord will keep you safe," Sister Sarah said.

"What an amazing development! The Lord is showing us His presence," the male co-host said. Sister Sarah shook her head in agreement.

"Can God help you with your financial investments?" Sister Sarah asked looking directly into the camera. "Our next guest will tell us how to use the scriptures, in particular Proverbs, to make your investment decisions," she concluded.

"And after that we will be joined by Louisiana's own Smooth Family Gospel singers doing their rendition of 'Stomp the Devil Down,'" the male co-host said.

Chapter 52
A BARBIE GIRL

The largest gay bar in the city, the Bourbon Pub and Parade, had set up a "Meet and Greet the Festival Drag Queen" party for the night of John Roland Reynolds arrival in town. It was combined with the bar's annual food drive for the Second Harvest food bank, so admission to the party required a donation of three items of canned food.

There were many local dignitaries present at the party, including Mayor Shemp Wanek and City Council President Willa Mae Spinazola. Brad Pitt made an appearance, as New Orleans was his part time home. The music industry was also represented by local rap star X-Mo-Dis who grew up in what was left of the Lower Ninth Ward. His brother, a wannabe rap star, who called himself Seymour 69, was a DJ at the bar. Seymour 69 wanted to be a nationally famous openly gay black rap star, but was having trouble getting a record contract. His style of rapping was called "prissy-rap." It incorporated some of the New Orleans Bounce style of Big Freedia's repetitive rap, along with the brass sound of groups like the Soul Rebels. He had stolen a line from a Mott the Hoople song and released a single entitled "Is that concrete in my head?" The self produced disc had not generated much interest.

John Roland Reynolds showed up on time at the bar in a black stretch limousine, wearing a tight fitting full length gold lame' dress with a faux pink mink stole around his shoulders. His gold-blonde wig matched the dress perfectly and his pink earrings set well with the mink. It was "very

Marilyn retro drag," one of the local drag queens present said when he arrived. As a surprise he brought two women dressed in cheerleader outfits with him. Their cheerleader outfits looked a bit like the colors of New York Giants cheerleader outfits, except that emblazoned on the front of each sweater was the phrase: "Drag-Hag." Local media, ESPN and FOX Sports showed up and filmed his arrival, as if it was a red carpet movie premier.

Reverend Jessie and the Bourbon Street group of his CRC followers stood across from the Bourbon Pub and Parade and watched, transfixed. Reverend Jessie had not yet named his elect group, so the group with him was just the church members chosen to be on Bourbon Street that evening to protest the Festival.

The Christian Broadcasting Network promised to run an update each day on "Reverend Elder and his Christian Soldiers Stand Against Evil." It included contact information for the CRC, where donations could be sent. Supporters from around the country offered to come to New Orleans to help and Dolores, the CRC secretary, was given the task of discouraging them. Liberty University started a prayer chain asking people to pray for Reverend Jessie and his "canonical twelve." A blog was also set up by the Atheist Alliance Organization called "Countdown to Stupidity," which promised to post: "daily dumb remarks by those associated with the Reverend Elder's 'Stand in the Storm.'"

The head of the New Orleans Police Department, Superintendent Ken Spalitta, had initially threatened to arrest Reverend Jessie if he stood outside in the storm, but retracted the threat when the Mayor's press secretary told him it would be bad PR for the city. However, the Police Superintendent advised the local media that "God may protect Reverend Elder and his crew, but the NOPD has jurisdiction over the rest of you and we will arrest any outsiders."

When John Roland Reynolds walked into the Pub, with the two cheerleaders, Mayor Shemp Wanek was there, at the doorway, to shake his hand. Mayor Wanek was something of a comical figure in New Orleans politics. New Orleans had many colorful politicians, and "wanna be" politicians, over the years. Some were corrupt and many inept. Mayor Wanek had won the Mayor's race when the only other candidate in the race, heavily favored Democratic incumbent, Rick "Trout" LeBlanc, who had been leading by 30 percentage points in the polls, was videotaped having sex with two under-age girls. The videotape, which featured the Mayor wearing a diaper and telling the girls: "Call me Wendy," was put on YouTube two weeks before the election sinking LeBlanc's campaign.

The District Attorney had LeBlanc arrested and charged with statutory rape. Turn out on election day fell to just 10%. Shemp Wanek, who had previously run three times unsuccessfully for mayor, ran on his self described "Hemp Ticket." His platform statement read: "Vote for Shemp, he'll Legalize Hemp." Immediately after his election Wanek proposed an ordinance to decriminalize the possession of marijuana, unless the person had more than 50 pounds in his personal possession. The City Council unanimously defeated the proposed ordinance and the Mayor had made no other legislative proposals since.

Mayor Wanek was openly ridiculed by the local media and was criticized by the City Council as being out of touch with the citizens. On this night he was wearing a 1970's green knit leisure suit with a yellow shirt and a wide blue tie. It looked like the entire outfit was purchased from a thrift store. John Roland Reynolds eyed the Mayor suspiciously, but shook the Mayor's hand and then curtseyed to him.

"Where did you find that suit?" Reynolds mockingly asked Mayor Wanek. The Mayor missed the mockery and just grinned in response.

"It's one of my favorites and a big hit with you gals. If you know what I mean," he replied.

Reverend Jessie had seen enough. He spoke into the bull horn which he carried with him.

"The faithful shall be saved in the pending catastrophe. God shall strike down the wicked and the unfaithful. As it is written in Psalm: 'Blessed is the man who does not walk in the counsel of the wicked.'"

The Mayor and John Roland Reynolds, standing in the open doorway of the Pub, heard every word. "That's the man who would not shake my hand at the airport," John Roland Reynolds said, quietly, to no one in particular, as he looked out the doorway towards Reverend Jessie. The management of the Bourbon Pub also took notice and decided that it was time, once again, to seek a court ordered injunction against Reverend Jessie, keeping him from disrupting its business and from harassing its customers.

Seymour 69 was not interested in hearing any more from Reverend Jessie. He cranked up the volume on the bar's sound system and began to play the entrance song John Roland Reynolds had requested.

"Ladies, and ladies in waiting, here she is, your Queen John Roland Reynolds, or as she has asked to be known during her reign, the Decadence Drag Queen of New Orleans," the DJ said. The music started. John Roland Reynolds smiled and walked slowly into the Pub down a strip of red carpet. As he walked in to greet everyone the entrance song he had selected could be heard clearly: "...She's a Barbie girl, in a Barbie world...."

Chapter 53
THOMAS BAKER-GURVITZ

Zarathustra II had spent most of that same afternoon on my couch talking to himself in a rapid cadence, which I could not always understand. He seemed disassociated, leaning over the edge of something. His chills had disappeared for now, but were replaced by a restless mania. Sometimes he would turn, stare blankly, and start talking to someone, but no-one was there. "Coriolanus, why are you bothering me now?" I heard him say. "Shut up Samuel!" he yelled on another occasion, though it sounded like "Shmuwel," as he struck his forehead, disconsolate, with the palm of his right hand several times, as if seeking to dislodge something.

Mikhail Ivanov had stopped by to visit with us. He and I watched, troubled for our friend, but for the most part, Zarathustra II did not seem to notice us. Ivanov began to talk to Zarathustra II peacefully, to try to bring him back from the ledge, even though he did not respond. Zarathustra II would turn and look vacantly in Ivanov's direction, as if he heard his voice, but had temporarily lost his vision and was not sure from where the voice came. Zarathustra II would then turn away to continue the conversation he was having with himself.

"I am curious about other mistakes you claim God made," Ivanov said calmly. But Ivanov's attention to Zarathustra II seemed unrequited. Nevertheless, he kept asking Zarathustra II questions about homosexuality, the Bible and other evidence of God making mistakes. At one point Ivanov said, "I think some of your thoughts are contradictory." Zarathustra

II did not respond, but turned over on the sofa away from Ivanov so that his back faced Ivanov.

"How are you going to respond to his latest claim that God has spoken to him and told him to stay in the Quarter during the storm?" Ivanov then asked.

"I don't know. I think...I don't know. Things are moving too fast for me," Zarathustra II suddenly replied, his speech muffled as his face was partially buried in a sofa cushion.

Zarathustra II now stood up, gently, but abruptly, as if it pained him to do so. I wondered what abuses his body had suffered over the years from being homeless. He looked at Ivanov directly, deliberately, in the eyes. "When the Jews opposed Paul and became abusive he shook out his clothes in protest and said to them, 'your blood be on your own heads! I am clear of my responsibility!'" Zarathustra II said to Ivanov. Then Zarathustra II took off his trench coat and shook it out, like a Mississippi country woman airing out an old blanket in the southern heat. He quickly put the trench coat back on. He stood in front of Ivanov, dark creases running from his mouth, his eyes sunken and burned out.

"Well, I'm not sure what all that means, but you are a friend, so just don't worry about what the Reverend does," Ivanov said. Zarathustra II smiled.

"I shall call you Thomas," Zarathustra II then said to him, weakly. Ivanov looked warily at Zarathustra II. "You shall be known as my second apostle Thomas Baker-Gurvitz," Zarathustra II said, with his hand resting on Ivanov's shoulder. Then in the same formal and ceremonial tone he had used with me, when I became his first apostle, Zarathustra II gave Ivanov his apostolic admonition: "Nietzsche wrote: 'If you would go high, use your own legs. Do not let yourself be carried up; do not sit on the backs and heads of others.' That is my advice to you on becoming my second apostle," Zarathustra II said to Ivanov.

It appeared to me that there was an immediate physical effect on Ivanov. He straightened his back with his shoulders squared. He smiled slowly but appreciatively.

Zarathustra II sat back down hard on the sofa. It was Ivanov who now paced. Zarathustra II closed his eyes and laid back down again to sleep.

"I'm exhausted. Very tired. Need to think," he said quietly, piece meal. Ivanov looked at me and I pointed to the door indicating we should leave and let him sleep.

Chapter 54
PROLONGED PENANCE

Mikhail Ivanov and I really did not know each other. Although I recall seeing him years earlier in Sunday school, and at church, I did not recall ever speaking to him.

"I've never been in this coffee shop before," I told Ivanov, as we walked into a PJ's Coffee in the American Can Building on Orleans Avenue. I could see Bayou St. John through the coffee shop windows. Ivanov looked at me in response, with an unpracticed smile, but did not say anything. I noticed that his faded blue jeans and his T-shirt both had 3-4 dime size holes in them, as if a moth had measured and cut each hole exactly. His tee-shirt was green and had "The Graham Edge Band" on the back.

"I never heard of that band," I said, trying, unpracticed as I was, to kick-start a conversation, while we waited to order.

"Graham Edge was the drummer of the Moody Blues," Ivanov replied, matter of fact, not immediately revealing more of himself.

"After the Baker-Gurvitz Army broke up, the Gurvitz brothers teamed up with Edge for a couple of albums," he continued.

"I don't know much about popular culture," I confessed to him.

"These were bands from the 1970's. Other than punk I don't really like much music made after maybe 1975," he said, and then turned away from me to order a drink that ended in 'mocha.' I got a regular cup of coffee and moved to join him at a table near the windows. I was not sure he was comfortable with me. He seemed dismissive when explaining music.

196

"So how does it feel to be a new apostle?" I asked conspiratorially, still hoping to provoke something, even if I was unsure why.

"I think it is simply his way of conferring friendship," he replied. His response seemed to down play the physical impact I thought I had just witnessed at Zarathustra II's announcement.

"Did you catch my show last night on WWOZ?" he then asked, slightly upbeat.

"No."

"I filled in for about an hour, 'cause Dr. Jazz was running late. He has a fusion jazz show and sent an email to the station on what I should play. I had never listened to fusion jazz before. It is really chaotic and sounds unstructured. At least is seems that way on the surface, at first glance. But under the various sounds, I found that, if I listened closely, there is a raucous structure, an order of sorts. You have to listen attentively for it, but it is there."

"Fusion jazz? I never heard of that."

"There are different types of jazz. Traditional. Smooth or Progressive. Fusion. Dr. Jazz had some Miles Davis on the list of things to play, from *Bitches Brew*, and some things from Chick Corea and *Return to Forever.* Seems like the Davis album was pivotal in enlarging the scope of jazz, to introduce fusion."

"*Bitches Brew?*"

"That's the name of the Miles Davis album."

I nodded not knowing what else to say, concerned about my musical ignorance. Ivanov sipped from his drink. A small foam mustache gathered on his upper lip. We sat silent for a few moments.

"What was it like to grow up with Reverend Jessie?" he asked haltingly. I thought for a moment before answering.

"I'm not really sure what to think of its effect on me. I was sick a lot when I was young and don't remember too much," I said finally, revealing in my words more than I was conscious of at the time.

"What type of sickness?"

"I never got a diagnosis," I replied, feeling my answer was disappointing.

"Too much religion?" Ivanov asked slyly.

"Maybe," I grinned uneasily. "Zarathustra claims it was something called neurasthenia."

"He would call it something we have to look up. Any idea what it means?"

"I looked it up, but seem to recall it wasn't well defined. Something about a stress basis for fatigue and other symptoms," I said. We both sipped our drinks and sat quietly again, letting our feelings catch up with the conversation.

"When my dad left," Ivanov said, opening up, looking at his drink, which he held with both hands, "everything got kind of weird at our house." It was my turn not to immediately reply. "My mother saw his leaving as some kind of karmic punishment from God, for having left her own mother and father in Russia. And then everything that went wrong in our lives thereafter, every mistake I made, was a punishment for some sin which she thought that she, or I, had committed. Our life became a prolonged penance to try to get right with God," he said thoughtfully, as if he had rewritten and revised the words of this sentence several times in anticipation of one day saying it out loud.

"How old were you when your dad left?"

"Sixteen," Ivanov replied.

"Were you close to your father?"

"Not really. He was a pretty emotionally distant guy who never really adapted to American culture. I think he needed a more authoritarian structure," Ivanov said.

"My dad and I were not close either," I offered.

"It's funny, the only advice I can ever remember my father giving me was 'don't marry a saint. If you do the only role left for you will be as a martyr.' He looked up at my mother and said, 'I am no martyr' and then he left the house. That's the last time I saw him," Ivanov explained.

"My mom," I found myself saying without forethought, "got marginalized by my Dad over time. I watched it but I'm not really sure I understood it while it was happening. It's hard to understand the dynamics of your parents relationship when you are a kid."

"I understood the yelling," Ivanov said.

"My parents didn't fight too often, which is even harder to decipher," I replied. "Except when my mother said she was not going to church anymore."

"That was kind of odd when she stopped coming to church. I remember my mom mentioning it," Ivanov interrupted. "Were you embarrassed?" Ivanov asked, "cause I think I was when my Dad left us. As a kid you always wonder if such stuff is your fault."

I tried to bring back a Sunday morning when my mother told my father, for the first time, that she was not going to church anymore. I thought there would be a terrible argument. My father tried to provoke one, but my mother remained relatively calm in response. I recalled that he stalked around her referring to a woman's role as set forth in the Bible and berating her about embarrassing him, while she occupied herself with her duties, dusting the living room furniture. She refused to be drawn into a debate, or to change her mind.

"I don't need ya church no mo. Dere is utta tings in ma life. An besides ya make Gawd so difficult," she finally told him in a somber but certain tone.

"You know, I believe I was proud of her," I then said, surprised, by giving that thought voice. I was not sure why I had said it in response. I had a sudden realization that I had not lived my life, that I had stood apart from it. Ivanov did not reply.

"How do you think this will end," Ivanov finally asked.

"I don't think she'll go back to church," I said plainly.

"No, I mean Zarathustra II's prediction and the storm and all," he replied. It was a good question, but things had been moving too fast to consider it for long.

"I'm not sure," I remember saying.

Ivanov and I sat quietly for awhile, as if we were suddenly self conscious about revealing too much of ourselves. We finished our drinks and headed back to my apartment to check on Zarathustra II.

Chapter 55
A PARAPET AROUND THE ROOF

I decided I wanted to better understand how Zarathustra II read the Bible. He had made it clear to me that he did not read it literally. But I was always told by Reverend Jessie that was the only way to read it and I was struggling to understand how else to read it.

There was so much which was being upended around me, so much challenging my simple narrative. Maybe if I could pick this one thing to really understand, to hold onto, things would seem less chaotic. I always assumed Reverend Jessie lived his life according to the literal language of the Bible, and told this to Zarathustra II, who was now awake, pensive, and sitting up on the sofa.

"If you follow it literally certainly that must be comforting, to know which rules to follow and what to do, or not to do, for your salvation," I said, standing in front of the sofa to present my argument. Ivanov sat quietly, appearing disinterested, on the floor in my apartment, with his legs folded underneath him.

"No one follows the Bible literally," Zarathustra II said, as he stood up and began to slowly pace in a circle around Ivanov. He seemed groggy.

"How can you say that? My father did. Didn't he?" I asked.

"Does your father's house have a parapet around the roof?" he asked me.

"A what?" I asked.

"A parapet. Deuteronomy requires it, if you read the Bible literally," he said. I immediately felt inadequate for the conversation I had provoked.

"Does your father wear clothes that are a blend of fabrics?" he then asked me.

"Probably," I replied.

"Well that is prohibited by another part of Deuteronomy," he answered.

"The Bible as fashion guide," Ivanov mumbled sarcastically.

"Does your father comply with the requirements of Leviticus not to cut his hair at the sides of his head and not to clip the edges of his beard? Of course not. In fact he is clean shaven," Zarathustra asked and answered.

"Wait. There is something about haircuts in the Bible?" I asked.

"Yes, There are countless other things like this in the Bible."

"Seems kind of silly," Ivanov offered more clearly. I did not know how to respond.

"Guys, these rules were designed to keep order in a nomadic tribe that had no central government and still believed God was living upstairs and had to be appeased with sacrifices to avoid his wrath. These are not God mandated decrees to live by today," Zarathustra II said. I sat down on a bar stool.

"So you don't believe any of the Bible is literally true?" I asked, trying to get back to my original question.

"Some of the history and people are accurate. And archeology has confirmed some of the locations mentioned. But that's about it."

"What about the miracles?" Ivanov asked.

"I've seen no miracles in my life, just a wishing in the wilderness. Why would there be none now?"

"Well, if God disappeared as you say, maybe that's why," I replied.

"I doubt any of the miracles, but I don't know. If someone was knocked unconscious and then awoke later, how would pre-modern man explain it? He might think he rose from the dead."

"So if God has disappeared, as you say, and there were never any miracles, God, or the concept of God, is really irrelevant in how we live our lives---right?" Ivanov argued.

"Not irrelevant. But no longer the sole source of meaning."

"What other source of meaning is there?" I protested.

"We are the source of meaning. It's in how we treat others, that's my view," Zarathustra II replied.

"No ultimate meaning, just the here and now," Ivanov summarized, as Zarathustra II nodded approvingly.

"So why do you object to the folks who read the Bible literally?" I asked.

"Setting aside the contradictions in the text, it is because all those I have known, who claim to read it literally, are very selective in what they claim they must comply with," Zarathustra II replied. "And their selectivity is usually based on personal convenience and their own prejudices, which they then impose harshly on others, and use the Bible to justify."

We sat quietly for awhile, and then I went to bed.

Chapter 56
GOD OR MAN MADE

"Come see this," Ivanov called out to me. I walked from the kitchen, where I was eating my last piece of toast for breakfast, to the den, and saw Ivanov standing in front of my television. Zarathustra II was not in the apartment. We were not sure where he went.

Bertrand Finch was on the television screen. He was seated talking with two men on some type of morning talk show. There was a large sign behind all three men that read: *Bertrand Finch's New Orleans' Forum*. It looked like the sign had been hastily prepared; the letters were not all the same size, and it was hung slightly crooked.

"I never heard of this show before," I said.

"I bet he just created it to try to get more publicity," Ivanov responded.

Finch had confided that he was excited about the national coverage Reverend Jessie had generated with his announcement to stand in the hurricane, but was concerned that it was at his expense. Maybe Ivanov was right.

"Let's get back to our topic, which I am sure is of local and national interest. Again, my guests this morning are Professor Slade Tilton of the University of New Orleans Philosophy Department and Reverend Jedidia Beecher from the New Orleans Baptist Seminary College," Bertrand Finch said.

"I know Professor Tilton. I took one of his introductory classes," Ivanov said, as we both stood watching the television screen.

"Please continue Professor Tilton with your answer to the question of whether Reverend Elder is correct in asserting that God causes destruction, like a hurricane, as punishment for men's sins," Bertrand Finch asked.

"Well, as I wrote in my book, *The Evolution of Evil: God or Man Made*, over time we have seen our views on the cause of natural disasters, like a hurricane or an earthquake, evolve from believing that it was caused by any one of the gods for unknown reasons, to believing that it was caused by the monotheistic God as a result of man's transgressions, to finally believing that it is caused by neither, just caused by the laws of nature. This has paralleled the increase in our scientific knowledge and our understanding of the earth. So in that regard I would not agree with what you have told me this fellow Reverend Elder said, that these are God made judgments in the form of disasters," Professor Tilton said to Bertrand Finch.

"Those in Bible based churches, like my Evangelical friends, would not agree with that," Reverend Beecher interjected.

"Does that change in our understanding about the cause of disasters relate in any way with the so-called disappearance of God which Zarathustra the Second talks about?" Bertrand Finch asked, sounding more intelligent than I imagined him to be.

"As I wrote in my book, *The Profane as Sacred*, the human definition of God in Christianity has changed over time as Greek philosophy, and then scientific knowledge, developed and altered our world view," Reverend Beecher said, while pulling on his full Darwinian white beard.

"I don't understand what that means," Bertrand Finch interrupted. He absentmindedly patted the top of his head.

"When mankind believed that the world was a three story universe, as reflected in the Old Testament, God was described in anthropomorphic terms. He talked. He walked the earth. He had hands. He had feet. He had a face. He got angry. He was present in the world like any other human being. But with the rise of Greek philosophy and science such human descriptions were thought by some theologians as too finite, too limiting a description of an all powerful God. The world was no longer just three stories, our knowledge had expanded, and our conception of God had to change to reflect that expanded notion of the universe," Reverend Beecher replied.

"What do you mean by a three story universe?" Bertrand Finch asked, still seemingly confused.

"Well, cosmology in those days, such as it was, posited a universe of Hades, earth and heaven. Three stories, if you will, with God upstairs and hell in the basement. And by the way Christians borrowed the notion of heaven and hell from Plato," Reverend Beecher responded. "Of course, science has proven that world view wrong. So God became less anthropomorphic with these scientific developments. As our understanding of the universe expanded, our definition of God had to expand. He could no longer be the guy living on the third floor who rained down disasters when He was upset. He became the Greek Logos, the idea, less human and instead of God being 'up there,' on the third story of the building, he became transcendent, or 'out there' as some 20th century theologians have written. And a transcendent God, a God out there, may be a God that has disappeared to some. It is certainly a harder concept for most Christians to understand," Reverend Beecher concluded.

"Anthro...Anthrohomo...What does that word mean?" Finch asked

"Anthropos is a Greek word for man," Reverend Beecher stated dryly to Finch.

"Anthropomorphic means 'like man.' An anthropomorphic God is one that is man like and has human characteristics," he concluded, since Finch still looked puzzled.

"The problem of the common man understanding transcendence, or a transcendent God, is one of the reason's I believe that Constantine decided to side with Athanasius against Arian and endorse the Trinity at the Council of Nicea in 325 AD and make Jesus God," Professor Tilton quickly added.

"Excuse me?" Bertrand Finch asked, indicating he had been momentarily distracted. "People could not understand the idea of a transcendent God, a God out there to use Reverend Beecher's phrase. Because they could not visualize a transcendent one, the emerging Church, with

Constantine as enforcer, made Jesus, who was human, God---made him part of the Plotinus' Trinity, so that there would still be a God in human form which people could visualize, paint pictures of, understand and pray to. He reintroduced the anthropomorphic God, in the form of Jesus, through the Trinity and sided with Athanasius over Arius on the issue of Jesus' divinity," Professor Tilton said proudly. "In fact, I think it is safe to say that most Christians believe in Jesus, who they can visualize, and are completely confused by, and only mouth that they believe in, God," Professor Tilton said.

"Athan...Ariola? Who are they?" Finch stuttered.

"Arius was a North African Presbyter who did not believe that Jesus was divine; what was called Arianism. Athanasius was a bishop who opposed him. Each had followers who killed each other over the conflict until Constantine stepped in at the Council of Nicea," Professor Tilton explained.

"Let me just say that I don't agree with your characterization of Christians. Your history is correct, but not the characterization," Reverend Beecher replied.

"Why not?" Bertrand Finch asked.

"That is such a pejorative description of Christians, that somehow an overly simplified doctrine, or definition of God, must be created because they are not smart enough to otherwise understand what they believe," Reverend Beecher said in a mocking tone, again stroking his beard.

"Oh, come on Reverend! You are not running for political office where you have to pander to the masses and suggest they are smarter than they really are," Professor Tilton said caustically. Reverend Beecher's face turned a bit crimson.

"Literacy hasn't changed the average Christian in the last 1,700 years. They still do not tend to think too deeply," Professor Tilton replied. "Most Christians attach themselves to religious symbols, to the idea of miracles, to religious art, or to religious songs. They know little of the substance of their beliefs. Most Christians couldn't identify Arius or Athanasius if their salvation depended on it, and they know nothing about this early skirmish over Jesus' divinity," Professor Tilton said. Reverend Beecher mumbled a disapproving response.

"Huh?" Finch replied.

"Now interestingly some forms of Judaism took a different approach. In Judaism the abstraction of a transcendent God led to a deeper intellectualism in their religion, with midrash and things of that nature. And there was no God in the form of Jesus, as a person, to believe in and soften the difficulty of understanding transcendence," Professor Tilton concluded.

"Who had a rash?" Finch asked.

"Midrash is the commentary on the Torah," Professor Tilton answered.

"You keep talking about transcendence as if it is a new concept that you created, but there is a long history of God being 'Deus absconditus,' a hidden God, an unknowable God!" Reverend Beecher finally responded sharply, ignoring Finch.

"Deuce condom? Is that a brand?" Finch tried to ask.

"It's Latin," Reverend Beecher answered.

"That's largely, though not exclusively, Luther's contribution, so it is relatively recent. But whether we say transcendent, or Deus absconditus, it is essentially the same thing," Professor Tilton responded, calmly, speaking directly to Reverend Beecher and ignoring Finch.

"Gentlemen, let me interrupt," Bertrand Finch said, feeling proud that he had somehow provoked this exchange. "I'd like to ask a slightly different question. One that I think is important to our growing national audience. What do you think about people following Zarathustra the Second and viewing him as a prophet?" Bertrand Finch asked.

"You should know, he is your creation," Reverend Beecher promptly responded.

"Only in part," Professor Tilton replied, as Bertrand Finch looked down at his note cards.

"The public has, historically, been fascinated by the supposed 'madman' or prophet in our midst," Professor Tilton stated.

"Why is that?" Bertrand Finch asked leadingly.

"Because where we see incompletely, on some level, and this was certainly true in a pre-scientific society, we believe that the mad man sees the whole, and that includes seeing the end of things which we so fear, but can't admit," Professor Tilton confirmed, as Reverend Beecher sat with a silent scowl. "At least that was true prior to this media age. But even now we have a large segment of the American public that has not evolved beyond pre-scientific thinking, and are still drawn to such cultic figures," Professor Tilton said.

"The prophet of the old times, the Hebrew prophets, are often portrayed in the Bible as outsiders, or social outcasts, who arrive just in time to advise the public of the reason for the problems they were confronting, the solution to the pending dilemma. So regardless of his veracity, this fellow who calls himself Zarathustra the Second---by the way, a nice Zoroastrian name---appears to be following in that vein," Reverend Beecher said, finally smiling a bit.

"But why now? Why are the people drawn to him now?" Bertrand Finch asked, apparently not hearing Tilton's, or Beecher's, response.

"Well, the times we live in dictate when the mad man becoming the prophet will arise. We tend to think that cannot happen in this modern day and age but it still can to segments of the population because, as I said, the majority of the public still thinks pre-scientifically. But, anyway, there has to be a high degree of insecurity and uncertainty in the air. Sometimes it is economic uncertainty, sometimes it is political uncertainty. It is those who are most insecure with their place in the world, who are fearful and sense conspiracy everywhere, that are the most susceptible to the mad man prophet. A narrow deductive reasoning triumphs over a broader inductive reasoning. The best example is what occurred during the Weimer Republic in the 1920s, where there were countless of such individuals who wore hair shirts, beat themselves, spouted prophecy, and garnered followers. Similar things happened in America in the 1830s and 1840s. And even in the 1970s there were books of prophecy that the public greedily bought," Professor Tilton responded.

"Historically you also need to understand that knowledge has generally had three sources. In biblical times it was based on the authoritative position of the speaker; that is, the King, the Rabbi, the Bishop, etc. After the Enlightenment it could also be based on study and reason, thus it was open to all. But also there has always been that third basis, harder to define or quantify, which is revelation. Revelation has been the basis of most religions; think of Mohammed and Islam or Joseph Smith and Mormonism. The prophet fits under that third, less easy to define, source," Reverend Beecher said. Finch looked as if he had momentarily been hypnotized. Reverend Beecher snapped his fingers in front of Finch's face and Finch sat up straight.

"Wouldn't you agree that Zarathustra the Second is too intelligent to be nuts?" Bertrand Finch asked awkwardly.

"I don't think you understand madness," Professor Tilton answered dryly.

"Or much of anything else," Reverend Beecher echoed.

"Often times the mad man is very intelligent," Professor Tilton replied.

"Exactly," Reverend Beecher again echoed.

"I believe it was the Christian apologist G.K. Chesterton who wrote: 'The madman is not the man who lost his reason. The mad man is the man who has lost everything except his reason,'" Professor Tilton recited. Reverend Beecher nodded in slow agreement, while Bertrand Finch stared blankly trying to understand what he had just heard.

"Uhm, we are out of time," Bertrand Finch then said. "I'm glad I was able to facilitate and lead this discussion. Join us for our next program later today on the psychology of religion and Zarathustra the Second's place in it." As if on cue Zarathustra II walked back into the apartment.

Chapter 57
CHEMICAL IMBALANCES

Zarathustra II moved slowly, weighed down and with difficulty, as he lay down on the sofa. I told him a little about the show Ivanov and I had seen and what the guests had said. Ivanov chimed in with some of the specifics. Zarathustra II did not appear particularly interested.

"Apparently he is going to do another show today about you and the psychology of religion."

"Psychology? Hmm, maybe he can tell me why I am so tired and depressed," Zarathustra II said. I had thought he looked tired, but did not want to say anything.

"My mom didn't want me to take anti-depressants," Ivanov blurted out, as if he had no choice but to reveal the matter, rather than suffer further in silence. His hair was in a braided ponytail and he had on a faded blue T-shirt with "T-Rex" on the front and an album cover design of "Electric Warrior" on the back. Zarathustra II sat up and looked at Ivanov, with worn out compassion.

"She believed that if I would only let Jesus into my heart and pray sufficiently, I would be alright and the depression would disappear," he said plainly, but clearly unconvinced. I was not sure what to say in response to such a private revelation.

"When was that?" I finally managed to ask.

"In high school after my dad left us. Not too long before I got kicked out of high school," he responded, standing near one of the windows.

Zarathustra II stood up like he was going to leave the room, but then turned gently to face Mikhail Ivanov. Zarathustra II buttoned his overcoat and put his hands in his coat pockets. He looked like he was cold again.

"Organized religion views science and psychology as intruding on its turf," Zarathustra II said calmly. "And though most Christians would not admit it, theology has a heavy dose of primitive psychology in it," Zarathustra II said, almost to himself. "Someone should write a book on how the theological 'soul' described by Plato, which Christianity adopted, became the psychological 'self' described by Freud," he then said.

"You think those are the same?" Ivanov asked.

"Probably. Just different descriptions at different times of human development." Ivanov nodded as if he understood.

"Anyway, as a result, with Buddhism as an exception, religion has too often rejected science because it fears it as competition," Zarathustra II continued. "Although stupidly, with things like creation, it has sought to turn the foundations of spiritual creation and the existential truths in the Genesis story, into hard science, which it was never intended to be," he said. He removed his hands from his pockets and lowered himself on to the floor to sit. Both Ivanov and I kept our eyes on him.

Zarathustra II took off his wool cap and scratched his head. I noticed that his eyes still looked very weary. He wrapped his arms around himself for warmth and comfort.

"Besides, as to psychology, if it is right, and if chemical imbalances cause depression and anxiety, what does this say about the biblical notion that we are all created in God's image?" Zarathustra II asked. "Religion does not want to have to answer that question, so it demeans the science."

Ivanov walked over to the sofa, sat down and leaned back hard into the sofa cushion and pulled both knees up to his chest, putting his arms around them.

Chapter 58
OLD TESTAMENT GOD

Zarathustra II rose from the floor. He put his wool cap back on his head but kept his coat buttoned up. Ivanov sat up from a slouch and the springs on the sofa creaked.

"I'm very tired, but in light of what you told me about this television show by Mr. Finch can we talk about the definition of God?" Zarathustra II asked, uncertain, as he began a slow pacing around the room with his hands behind his back, stoop shouldered, as if in deep concentration.

"Luke, give us your definition of God," he said, without looking up at me.

"Definition?" I asked harshly, not wanting to participate. I was tired as well. Zarathustra II was becoming heavy to me, a feeling with which I was not familiar.

"Yes, tell me about the God you believe in. Describe Him so I can understand Him," he said, ignoring what I thought was my clear indication to remain silent.

"Well, uhm, well…I believe in a God as set forth in the Bible," I finally managed to stammer out. At the same time, as was the case with many of my conversations with Zarathustra II, I realized it was not a topic I ever remember thinking about or discussing. After all God is God, right?

"The one in the Old Testament, or the one in the New Testament?" he asked.

"Do you think there is a difference?" Ivanov asked curiously, but as if he knew the answer already.

"Well, Marcion thought so. So did Thomas Jefferson," Zarathustra II responded. "Luke? Your definition?" he then asked, again looking at me.

"The Old Testament God," I answered, more out of frustration than anything else.

"The God who speaks? The God who has feet and walks on the earth like a human? The God who has hands and can make a fist? The God who gets angry if people don't pay enough attention to Him? The God who is jealous of other gods? The originator of genocide? That's the God you envision when you think of God?" he asked pointedly, but gently.

"The anthropomorphic God," Ivanov revealed.

"I don't know any other definition," I finally responded, disappointed with my answer.

"Don't be upset. It is a difficult question. Luke, your image of God is as a human being, but with superhuman powers. Right? A sort of super-hero. Isn't it?" he asked more kindly.

"Well, I guess so. I mean it sounds silly when you say it that way, but how else can I envision Him?" I asked.

"Freud thought that such anthropomorphic definitions were simply human projections. And before Freud, Xenophane famously said that if horses or cows could draw, their gods would look like horses or cows," he explained. The comment lightened the moment.

"Moo! I am the Cow God!" Ivanov said jokingly.

"Exactly," Zarathustra smiled. I smiled as well.

My frustration with Zarathustra II was dissolved by the solvent of his kindness. He was my friend, heavy or not.

"Although many modern Christians are unaware of it, there is a long intellectual history, despite biblical descriptions, that argues God is unknowable," Zarathustra II said.

"One of the professors on the TV show said something like that," Ivanov interjected.

"How can you worship a God that is unknowable?" I asked.

"Well, I'm not sure we should worship anyone, but the point is that we need to contemplate the Godhead, what it stands for, and our part in it. That is what makes us more God like, more tolerant, more compassionate to others," he said.

"The Godhead. Sounds like a great name for a band," Ivanov added.

"We need to be careful in our assumptions about how we use the word 'God.' Most Christians are unaware, but Spinoza's 'God,' for example, is not the same as Luther's 'God' and neither is the same as Bonhoeffer's 'God.' For many it is simply too complicated a subject, regardless of its importance to their faith, and is, therefore, ignored. They use the word, profess their faith in a God, but would be hard pressed to define it," he told us.

"Hard to believe in something you cannot define," Ivanov offered.

"What is your definition?" I asked Zarathustra II. Ivanov smiled a conspiratorial smile when I asked the question. Zarathustra II did not seem to notice.

"I admit it is a complicated question. Nevertheless, for me, I believe that Origen and Tillich had it essentially correct. God is being itself," he said.

"Being itself," Ivanov repeated, almost as a question, trying to understand the phrase.

"What does that mean; God is 'being itself'?" I asked.

"God cannot be a being like you and me, as that would subject Him to the limitations of time and space. Tillich said that God is the ground of being, the power of all being if you will, the power in everything," Zarathustra II explained.

"I don't understand," Ivanov replied. "That doesn't sound like a person at all."

"It's likely not. At least not what we would recognize as human," Zarathustra II replied.

"So how can a God who is a not a person disappear?" I asked, troubled by the definition which I did not really understand. I sensed the same confusion in Ivanov.

"So is God's disappearance simply the change in our definition from the Old Testament superhero upstairs, to the power in everything that you just described? Are you saying that God has disappeared simply because the traditional way of defining Him is no longer valid?" Ivanov interrupted, before Zarathustra II could answer me.

"No longer valid?" I asked.

"Well, the superhero God that lives upstairs. There is no upstairs. There is no Hades in the basement----right?" Ivanov responded to me, but then turned to look at Zarathustra II.

"Excellent question, Thomas. For those who understand the effect of Greek philosophy on the Old Testament concept of God that is undoubtedly the case. Most people, however, have not thought that deeply on the subject. But before I answer further do you have a definition to share?" Zarathustra II asked Ivanov, referring to him by his apostle name. Ivanov again sat quiet and uneasy for a moment. I wished Zarathustra II had given a further explanation of his definition.

"Guys, you probably know this already, but I don't believe in God, though I never heard of the ground of being definition. It's kind of interesting. So anyway, I can't define what I don't believe in," he said openly. "My anarchist tendencies make me reject any master of any type," Ivanov continued.

"You don't believe in God? That's impossible. I don't know anyone who does not believe in God," I insisted.

"You do now. Like Ozzy Osborne sang: 'There are no believable gods,'" Ivanov responded.

"Maybe Thomas you are like the writer Annie Dillard who wrote: 'Of faith I have nothing, only of truth: that this one God is a brute and traitor, abandoning us to time, to necessity and the engines of matter unhinged,'" Zarathustra II, posing, quoted with a smile.

"Sounds like she does not believe, but is mad at Him anyway," Ivanov replied.

"A Jewish theologian once wrote that if God lived on earth people would throw rocks through his window every night," Zarathustra II said in response. I noticed that Zarathustra II's hands were shaking and his facial expression seemed remote.

"You aren't throwing rocks but quotations!" Ivanov replied laughing.

"Wait. If you don't believe in God, what do you believe in? I mean you have to believe in something," I asked Ivanov.

"Well, my answer is evolving," Ivanov replied calmly, unwilling to argue. Zarathustra II and I waited for Ivanov to elaborate. "I don't believe in God. But I do believe in sin, if that comforts you any."

"That does not make sense. How can you believe in sin, but not believe in God?" I asked, not really expecting him to answer.

"Thomas, how do you define sin?" Zarathustra II interrupted.

"For me, I think sin is a word I am comfortable with to describe when someone, or a group, harms individuals, or oppresses individuals, while claiming to be acting in their best interests," Ivanov replied.

"Now, if there is no God what effect does such a sin, as you define it, actually have?" Zarathustra II asked.

"Hard for me to answer," Ivanov said quickly.

"Seems kind of meaningless to me," I said, annoyed.

"Perhaps you are conflating what you perceive as arrogance with sin," Zarathustra II suggested.

"Well, I'm still thinking about it, but it strikes me that it is sinful because it restricts freedom," Ivanov replied.

"So freedom is a state without sin?" Zarathustra II asked.

"Maybe so," Ivanov said. I was bothered by Ivanov's response but I was not sure why.

"I thought sin was sin; like a violation of one of the ten commandments," I said frustrated, but again with a creeping sense that I was standing alone out on a limb, unsure how I got there.

"Luke, there are many definitions of sin. Indeed, what constitutes sin is often just a cultural creation arising from social situations. I personally think that sin may be the failure to give up the personal ego, the failure to put others before yourself," Zarathustra II replied.

"Interesting," Ivanov said, while I sulked.

After a few moments of silence Zarathustra II suggested we go down town. He wanted to speak to people again in Jackson Square. "I'm running out of time," he said.

Chapter 59
CUT UP POETRY

On the street car ride down to the French Quarter, Zarathustra II stood up, child like, on his seat, as the driver told him repeatedly to sit down. The street car lurched on occasion bouncing him, but he remained upright. The passengers glanced at him. Perhaps, some recognized him from the TV stories.

A block after exiting the streetcar, walking past shop owners who were boarding up their windows in preparation for the hurricane, we were greeted by Ms. Dominque Dagny and Ms. Shiloh Lemoine. As we all walked toward the French Quarter, Ivanov and Ms. Lemoine fell a few steps behind us in conversation.

"Hey Dominique, I knew this one in high school," Ms. Lemoine yelled out to Dominique Dagny, who was walking in front of me, next to Zarathustra II. Ms. Dagny stopped walking and turned around. She looked at Ivanov, one hand on a cocked hip, seductively. Ms. Lemoine giggled a bit and ran her hand through Ivanov's hair, purposely messing it up to make him uncomfortable, as we all stopped and stood together. "He was this really shy kid, who nobody hardly knew, and then after I quit school I heard he got like expelled for wanting to blow up the school," she explained, leaning heavily into him.

Dominique Dagny walked towards Ivanov and stood next to him, so that he was flanked by her and by Ms. Lemoine. "I never tried to blow up the school," Ivanov said defensively, as he blushed. "I got expelled for trying to start a school anarchist club," he clarified, slipping both his hands, quickly, defensively, into his pants pockets.

"An anarchist! Now that's sexy," Dominique Dagny whispered in his ear, her lips touching him, as she pressed her body against him. Ms. Lemoine placed her hands under Ivanov's shirt. Ivanov tried to look at ease, but stiffened his body, as both ladies laughed.

"We are not really free," Ivanov said, his voice disjointed and trailing off. "We are imprisoned by religious myths, economic myths and cultural myths. To be free we have to move beyond the myths and symbols blocking our way," Ivanov said, in a rigid rote manner, as Ms. Dagny began to move her body up and down against his.

"You sound like Ayn Rand. You know she lived through the Bolsheviks seizing her family property. She was always distrustful of government. You should read *We The Living*, her first novel...you heard me," Ms. Dagny said.

"Yes, it is probably her most autobiographical novel," Zarathustra II said.

"What's it about?" I asked.

"It's about the evils of an oppressive government and the value of individual freedom," Ms. Dagny replied, glancing at me as she straddled Ivanov with her right leg.

"Hey, you teaching the disciple boy! Imagine that," Ms. Lemoine chuckled.

"Anytime you want a lesson, disciple boy," Ms. Dagny replied.

"And what would you do if you were really free?" Ms. Lemoine then asked Ivanov, a bit seriously, taking half a step back in anticipation of his answer.

"Yea, tell me handsome," Ms. Dagny said. Ivanov hesitated.

"Well, we would undo everything and we would be different people, without many of the fears and the denials that make up our lives. Without those fears we could be more creative, more open, and more supportive of each other. There would be no masters," he said.

"I especially like that 'undo everything' part of what you said. What should I undo on you first?" Ms. Lemoine purred, as she leaned back hard against Ivanov.

"And maybe my ass wouldn't have to go to jail for using my ass...you heard me," Ms. Dagny said laughing, as she continued to press her body against Ivanov.

"I recall you wrote poetry in high school for the school newspaper and were in the glee club," Ivanov said turning to face Ms. Lemoine, their lips almost touching. She seemed surprised by his comment.

"Do you still write poetry?" I asked. Ms. Lemoine then smiled gently. It was not her usual business smile. She stepped completely away from Ivanov, as if her poetry could not be confused with her line of work.

"I keep a journal of stuff, but mostly I just do cut up poetry."

"Cut up poetry. What's that?" I asked.

"You take a current article someone else has written and cut up the words of the sentences and then piece them back together differently."

"That's poetry?" I asked, and then felt embarrassed that my tone suggested a rebuke.

"William Burroughs said 'you cut up the present and the future bleeds out,'" she replied, with a surprising sense of innocence. "Sometimes I cut up articles from the past, and when I do I tell myself that the present bleeds out."

"Interesting. I'd like to read some," Ivanov replied in earnest, with his hands still in his pockets.

"Are you still an anarchist today?" Ms. Lemoine asked Ivanov, breaking up the discussion of her poetry. Ms. Dagny released herself from Ivanov, who appeared to exhale.

"Well, mostly, uhm, I am. But I am also willing to consider the libertarian view on an interim basis," Ivanov said, trying to sound confident and disinterested.

"Perhaps, he will be like Ayn Rand's character Howard Roark in *The Fountainhead* and never make compromises," Zarathustra II said to Ms. Dagny about Ivanov.

"Not likely," she promptly replied. "The world breaks all the Howard Roarks before we ever get the chance to notice them. And then they become bitter at everyone else because of their compromises," Ms. Dagny said, looking directly at Ivanov as if she wanted to make sure he heard her words and remembered them. "You should understand that Preacher man," Ms. Dagny then said to Zarathustra II.

"Do you know what a libertarian is?" Ivanov asked Dominque Dagny. She smiled, a skilled insincere smile.

"Yeah, hot stuff. It's an anarchist who has decided to make compromises," she growled, and then promptly pressed her body up against Ivanov again.

Chapter 60
GLOBAL WARRING

Mrs. Rosemary Matthews drove a refurbished 1977 candy apple red Buick LeSabre with black leather interior and a solid silver chain steering wheel. It had been restored and was owned by her stepson, who gave it to her when he was sentenced, as a multiple offender, to twenty years in prison at Angola State prison for manufacturing and selling Crystal meth. It had gray mud flaps with chrome silhouettes of a naked girl on each, oversized white walled tires and silver curb feelers. A faded bumper sticker on the rear bumper said "Grooving."

She and my mother fit easily in the front seat. The trunk was stuffed with Mrs. Rosemary Matthews' belongings. The back seat had my mother's yellow suit case on it and Mrs. Rosemary Matthews' dog Mathilda. Mrs. Rosemary Matthews also had her cat, Scout, in a kennel and her parrot Johnnie in a cage on the back seat. The bird cage was set on top of the cat's kennel and Mathilda sat heavily between my mother's suit case and the cat kennel. A giant loaf of Bunny bread was stashed above the back seat on the rear dash.

They were on the road, for the second day, to Atlanta to beat the traffic jam expected in the next few days when the evacuation of the city, which they felt certain was coming, was ordered. This was the second time this hurricane season that they had evacuated from the city. The other storm had missed New Orleans. "Dat idiot Chicken Little," is the only explanation Mrs. Rosemary Matthews would offer in response.

The ladies had different theories as to why there were more hurricanes in recent years. "I keep tellin ya Madie dat it's dat *global warring*. All doze bombs bein dropped ova da years in Japan, Vietnam, an utta places like dat, musta changed da air some kinda way," Mrs. Rosemary Matthews said to my mother as she drove.

"It's called 'global warming' Rosemary. An I tink it is from all da cows passing all dat gas," my mother corrected.

"Cows? Da air don't smell no diffrent ta me cept by da Murphy oil plant, an dere aint no cows dere. I'm tellin ya it musta been all doze bombs dat was dropped," Mrs. Rosemary Matthews said.

"Rosemary, it's cow gas, an den people gas dat caused it."

"People gas! Den my ex, Dominic, shoulda been persecuted. Dat man got gas just from drinkin water!"

"Rose-maree! Ya terrible."

"It's true."

"Well, anyway, Jessie says dat dere's no such ting as global warmin cause it aint mentioned in da Bible."

"Madie, I'm guessin dat fartin aint mentioned in da bible eada but it happens."

"Rose-maree! Ya bein sacriligous!"

"Madie, I ain't, but at ma age I'm tired a people tellin me what ta believe in."

"Well, you ain't bein told. Ya aint goin ta no church."

"No, I aint, but doze folks like ya Jessie are messin up evry ting. Just let people believe what dey wants ta as long as dey don't hurt nobody else, dat's what I say. Dere's too much hurtin goin on dese days."

"Some days ya is just impossible!" my mother replied smiling.

"Oh! Madie, before I forget, look what I got us. It's in dat bag rite dere," Mrs. Matthews said, with her hands on the steering wheel but nodding towards a brown paper bag on the back seat. My mother raised up and reached back and grabbed the brown paper bag from the back seat and opened it. She pulled out two gray **Zarathustra the Second's Army** T-shirts.

"Oh, Ro! Dey is adorable...but I can't wear dis. If Jessie saw dis dat'd be it," my mother said.

"Jessie don't need ta know. We'll wear dem unda our blouses. An I know Jessie won't be lookin dere, from what ya tell me," Mrs. Matthews said.

"Oh, Rose-maree! Ya terrible girl!" my mother replied, folding the shirts back up.

Chapter 61
EXHALE

As they drove along, slowly headed to Atlanta, Mrs. Rosemary Matthews suddenly realized that, with the rush of everything that had been going on, she had not asked my mother how she felt about leaving Reverend Jessie behind in the city to face the storm. They had also not discussed Reverend Jessie's revelation, which they heard reported on the radio, after leaving town, that he would stay in the French Quarter during the storm. It saddened her that she had forgotten to ask. Both ladies had on green hats, red scarves and oversized leopard print K-Mart sunglasses. Mrs. Rosemary Matthews looked over at her friend and felt a wave of compassion for her.

"Whateva did happen ta ya Jessie?" she finally asked, like a wrecking ball loosed inadvertently toward its intended target.

My mother sat looking out the passenger window. She held her purse with both hands, tightly, in her lap, as if she feared it would be snatched from her. My mother was short, at 5 feet even, so she had to look up to see out the window and, as a result, seemed swallowed by the car's leather front seat. She fidgeted in the seat with the question hanging in the air between them, like a familiar musical melody that neither could not name. My mother adjusted her seat belt. Mrs. Rosemary Matthews sat quietly. She was prepared to give her friend as much time, or silence, as she needed. Then my mother moved the air condition vent to the left so it would not blow directly on her. She sat for a moment longer without speaking, but with a faraway look in her eyes.

"He was so handsom an so polite when we was first datin, don't ya member," she finally said, answering her friend, while reaching for a recollection.

"I sure do," Mrs. Rosemary Matthews said supportively. "He was betta lookin den my first two husbans put togetha," Mrs. Matthews added, with her hands on the chain link steering wheel of the LeSabre, trying to steer her friend away from despair.

My mother then exhaled. It was a long wounded exhale, full of metaphor. "He," she started plaintively, still looking out the passenger window, "replaced me a long time ago wit his Gawd." A shared nondescript silence sat between the two friends, that years could only confirm and not erase. My mother continued to look out the passenger window in silent meditation. Mrs. Rosemary Matthews reached over and touched her friend on the hand.

"Dat's aright, ma third husban replaced me," and she emphasized the word *"me,"* "wit dat broke tooth skinny bar maid he met at da Ernie K-Doe's Mother in Law lounge." She laughed a deep nicotine toned self effacing; "this one's for you my friend," laugh. My mother smiled and grabbed Mrs. Rosemary Matthews hand and squeezed it tightly.

"At least ya could get mad at da bar maid," my mother then said, more seriously.

Chapter 62
TRANSFERENCE

"Thank you for joining us for our second significant program of the day. This evening our guests are Dr. Carolyn Slaton, the head of the Department of Psychiatry at LSU Medical School and Psychology Professor Jessica Baldwin, from Tulane University," Bertrand Finch said, reading from note cards. The sign, with **Bertrand Finch's New Orleans' Forum**, hung behind him, still tilted slightly, as both ladies sat across from him on what appeared to be a wooden bench. He was wearing the same plaid suit which he wore during the prior TV show.

"Our topic this evening, which I came up with, is Madness or Revelation," Finch said provocatively. The sole studio camera moved in for a close up of Finch. "Let's get to it," he then said. "Professor Baldwin is there a difference...between religious revelation and madness...and if so how would we know?" Bertrand Finch said, reading haltingly from a 5x7 card he held in his hand. It sounded like a question someone had prepared for him.

"Well, I think the simple primer on that topic is probably William James *The Varieties of Religious Experience*, from his Gifford lectures in the early 1900's. A more academic analysis can be found in Richard Swinburne's book on revelations," Professor Baldwin said.

"Can you tell us in a sentence what the William James book says?" Finch asked hurriedly, as he looked into the camera instead of towards his guest.

"No. You'll have to read it," Professor Baldwin said not too subtly. "But one of James' points is that it is actually hard to know the difference. If the authorities lock you up, then society considers you mad. If you spawn a religion, or a host of followers that endures, it will likely be treated as a revelation, at least by your followers," she concluded.

"I think Professor Baldwin is correct. Madness, to use your word, is often a social construct," Dr. Slaton added.

"Please explain," Bertrand Finch responded, while continuing to look directly at the studio camera, so that it would show him asking the question, except that the only TV camera operating showed the entire set, and Finch, instead, appeared to be merely looking away from his guests.

"All of us build up character defenses and these are often based upon a series of lies we tell ourselves. These are lies we need to function, but can rarely acknowledge. Indeed we deceive ourselves into believing the lies are true. And lies may seem too harsh a word. Your listeners may feel more comfortable with the word illusions. Anyway, setting aside chemical causes for the moment, the so called madman is simply the person who can no longer maintain those illusions," Dr. Slaton responded.

"And by underlying lies you mean principally the lies we tell ourselves because of our fear of death, correct?" Professor Baldwin asked.

"Exactly. I think it was Victor Hugo who wrote that 'we are all under a death sentence, but with an indeterminate reprieve.' But, candidly, it can be a broader fear, depending on the fears of the particular individual. But to your point, man is the only animal who is conscious of his ultimate death. He must carry it with him every day. But to face the prospect of that death directly, on a daily basis, would be very difficult and for many render their daily life meaningless. So he lies. He tells himself that he can achieve immortality if he joins a cause, has children, follows a particular leader, or whatever. He denies death that way," Dr Slaton replied. There was a brief silence as Finch stared at his note cards.

"It is like Mark Twain said: 'Don't part with your illusions. When they are gone you may still exist, but you have ceased to live,'" Dr. Slaton said smiling. Professor Baldwin also smiled.

"Dostoevsky mines the idea of the illusions we live under in *The Double*, through the character of Mr. Golyadkin. So literature has also long recognized the issue," Professor Baldwin replied.

"I have always said we are not aware of the life we are actually living, instead we are only aware of the one that we imagine that we are living. The story of our life that we tell ourselves, our personal narrative if you will," Dr. Slaton said.

"I like that. But I think we have to recognize that we are also imprisoned by those very illusions and narratives. Even our knowledge, which we think is real, as Schopenhauer wrote, is mere representation," Professor Baldwin replied.

"That's very Buddhist," Dr. Slaton answered.

"Well, a Buddhist would say the ultimate illusion is the self," Professor Baldwin concluded, leaning cross legged toward Dr. Slaton.

Bertrand Finch nervously shuffled his 5x7 cards and accidentally dropped the stack of cards onto the floor. The cards scattered in front of his chair and underneath it in full view of the wide angled camera shot.

"If I can give you another simple analogy about illusions, that listeners might understand, but find surprising, it would be this. We do not fall in love with the reality of another person. We fall in love with the image we have created of that person. And trouble usually comes when the image and the reality conflict," Dr. Slaton said.

"What you are describing, in part, is an issue of transference isn't it? Transferring our unacknowledged personal needs onto another?" Professor Baldwin asked, as Bertrand Finch began to crawl on the floor picking up his note cards. "Do you believe that most people are aware of it when they engage in such transference?" Professor Baldwin then asked Dr. Slaton, taking over the role of moderator.

"No. Most people are what Kierkegaard called 'immediate men.' They must repress any knowledge of the transference," Dr. Slaton replied. "So it is like what Otto Rank wrote: 'With the truth one cannot live. To be able to live one needs illusion,'" Dr. Slaton concluded.

"Yes. I have thought of it as being on several unconscious levels. First, there is the fear. Next, there is the repression of that fear. Finally, there is the transference, most of which occurs at a level of consciousness we don't acknowledge," Professor Baldwin said.

"A nice hierarchy," Dr. Slaton complimented.

There was a more silence. Bertrand Finch seemed transfixed, as he had sat back in his chair and shuffled the index cards, trying to get them into their previous order.

"I am glad the receptionist put numbers on the cards for me when she wrote the questions," he said to himself, but loud enough for the microphones to pick up his comment.

"So let me ask you how this fear of death and transference could possibly relate to individuals attaching themselves to a religious or political leader?" Professor Baldwin asked calmly, to break the silence.

"Well, most, if not all religions, offer immortality. And the more one fears death, even though that fear is not acknowledged, the more insecure one is, and the more that person will try to fill their world with 'omnipotent father figures', as Becker wrote," Dr. Slaton replied succinctly.

"And religion offers up these omnipotent father figures?" Professor Baldwin stated, as a rhetorical question.

"I think so," Dr. Slaton replied.

"But just to close this idea, it's not all bad. Life, to be livable, has to be infused with imagination and memory. Those things at least give it temporal meaning," Professor Baldwin replied. Dr. Slaton nodded in agreement.

"Temporal meaning. I like that phrase," Dr. Slaton replied.

Bertrand Finch seemed to suddenly awake from his stupor. "So what my many listeners want to know is whether you think that Zarathustra the Second is a madman or not," he finally asked, again looking away from his guests when he asked the question.

Chapter 63
LKHSRDBRD

"Luke and Thomas, I want to spend a few moments talking about the Hebrew language with you," Zarathustra II said. It was late. We had been sitting up talking, late into the evening, as we did most nights. We had watched part of Bertrand Finch's second TV show of the day and Zarathustra II laughed at Finch's questioning about whether he was a madman.

"He tries very hard," Zarathustra II said.

"He's the worst of modern man in a nutshell. He doesn't want to wake up," Ivanov quickly opined, dismayed by what Finch represented, or what he felt he represented.

I was tired and ready for bed. Whereas my days prior to meeting Zarathustra II moved slowly, languidly and without purpose, lately each day seemed to quicken with potentiality. It was more difficult in some ways, yet I felt more engaged in my life. Zarathustra II began his usual slow pacing around the room. Ivanov and I looked sluggishly at each other.

"Can either of you read or write Hebrew?" Zarathustra II asked. Ivanov laughed. I shook my head.

"I know a little pig Latin," Ivanov said in jest.

"I assume you know that the original versions of the Old Testament books were written entirely in Hebrew. This was done once writing became more common and the oral traditions of various tribes had started to fade," he said.

I think I knew that," I said uncertainly, with a yawn.

"Most Christians, however, don't realize that the Old Testament books were originally written in Hebrew. And they don't know, for example, that ancient Hebrew was written without vowels. So the original books of the Pentateuch were written without vowels," he said, as he slowly paced, while staring down, absorbed, at the hardwood floor. "And not only were there no vowels, but Hebrew did not use spacing or punctuation? In other words there are no commas, no periods," he said without looking up.

"So, just a string of letters? How can you read a bunch of consonants?" Ivanov asked. I was struggling to stay awake.

"Exactly. This is the language which Evangelicals claim is literally true, a series of uninterrupted Hebrew consonants," Zarathustra II responded. "Yet the Hebrew had to be translated," he said. Ivanov leaned forward on the sofa and rested his elbows on his knees. I rested the back of my head on the wall behind the sofa and closed my eyes.

"Luke please translate this sentence: LKHSRDBRD," Zarathustra II said carefully pronouncing each letter.

"What?" I asked, sitting up quickly and trying to focus. "LKHSRDBRD," Zarathustra II repeated again slowly, and then a third time as Ivanov wrote the letters on his hand with an ink pen. I fidgeted on the sofa. The springs creaked beneath me.

"I don't know Hebrew," I protested.

"I didn't ask you in Hebrew. I gave you English consonants to use. Please try," Zarathustra II replied. Ivanov then slowly read the letters out loud from his hand.

"Well, I can't do it," I responded, annoyed. What did this no vowel Hebrew have to do with anything, I thought to myself. Who cares?

"I intended the letters to mean 'Luke has a red beard,'" Zarathustra II said. Ivanov looked at his outstretched hand.

"It could also be 'I like his red beard,'" Ivanov then said, looking at the letters on his hand. "Or the 'LK' could be the word Lake."

"I guess it could also be 'Luke has a red bird,'" I admitted reluctantly, as I also looked at the letters on Ivanov's open hand.

"Or a rad board," Ivanov laughed.

"And neither of you could divine my intention from those string of consonants. Imagine trying to do that with all the consonants in the Pentateuch," Zarathustra II said. I started to get up to go to bed.

"I'm done for today," I said decisively. Ivanov stood up to leave. "See you tomorrow."

Chapter 64
SANCTIFIED

Reverend Jessie spoke into the bullhorn to his crowd of supporters, to those passing by on Bourbon Street in the mid morning sun, to the men on the balcony of the Bourbon Pub and Parade, and to those standing like parched laborers waiting for drink in its doorways. "'My prayer is ever against the deeds of evildoers; their rulers will be thrown down from the cliffs, and the wicked will learn that my words were well spoken. They will say, 'as one plows and breaks the earth, so our bones have been scattered at the mouth of the grave. But my eyes are fixed on you O Sovereign Lord; in you I take refuge.'" Reverend Jessie relaxed his arm for a moment and the bullhorn fell softly to his side. There were other CRC members near him holding up signs objecting to the festival.

Near the opposite corner of Bourbon Street, 20 yards or so down St. Ann, close to the other gay bar Oz, but periodically obscured by the gathering crowd moving in the street, another bullhorn sounded.

"Is this on? Testing 1-2. Can you hear me?" the person said to the men on the balcony of Oz, while Reverend Jessie and others looked over through the crowd on Bourbon Street, trying to determine who was speaking.

Someone on the Oz balcony threw the speaker some beads which landed at his feet. He quickly reached down picked up the beads and put them around his neck. "How do they look?" the speaker asked through the bullhorn to the men on the Oz balcony. Several laughed in response.

I was still a half block away, but I realized immediately that the speaker was Zarathustra II. I had lost Ivanov a few blocks back when he stepped into a bar called the Boondock Saint to talk with a bartender he knew. But where, I wondered, did Zarathustra II get a bullhorn?

"He calls me a false prophet," Zarathustra II then said, speaking into the bullhorn again, while standing alone, next to a Lucky Dog vendor's cart, and casually pointing across the street toward Reverend Jessie. "But he is the one who tells only half truths." As I got to within a few feet of Zarathustra II I saw Bertrand Finch and his cameraman under the balcony of Oz. The cameraman was filming. "What he won't tell you about the Bible I will," Zarathustra II continued.

"I've been struck by the spirits," someone on the balcony yelled out.

"Have another drink," someone else muttered in response, as a few men laughed.

"He wants to tell you about the wicked! And he ridiculously picks on homosexuals as the so called wicked, but what Corinthians actually says is 'Do you not know the wicked will not inherit the kingdom of God? Do not be deceived. Neither the sexually immoral, nor idolaters, nor adulterers, nor male prostitutes, nor homosexual offenders, nor thieves, nor the greedy, nor drunkards, nor slanderers, nor swindlers, will inherit the kingdom of God.' That's what it actually says. And combine that with the Bible's many other listings of those who should be stoned and will not get into heaven, like disobedient children, those who take the Lord's name in vain, those who work on the Sabbath and women who are not virgins..," Zarathustra II said into the bull horn.

"What's your point asshole?" someone on one of the balconies yelled.

"And I've got bad news for the Reverend. Those proscriptions, read literally as he likes to do, covers most of us. If he thinks the Bible is literally true, why isn't he condemning disobedient children? Why does he not protest those who work on Sunday?" Zarathustra II concluded, as his voice suddenly broke, tired, overcome by emotion. Zarathustra II leaned more heavily on the Lucky Dog cart, the bull horn clutched in his right hand, his head hung down. The Lucky Dog vendor, who had returned to his cart while Zarathustra II was speaking, reached out with a paper napkin and gave it to Zarathustra II to wipe the tears from his eyes. Zarathustra II took it and blew his nose loudly. The sound of his nose blowing came through the bullhorn, as the "on" button seemed stuck, so the entire street heard it. Several people nearby laughed. Zarathustra II tried to hand the napkin back to the vendor, but he shook his head refusing Zarathustra II's offer. Zarathustra II stuck the crumpled napkin in his coat pocket and again lowered his head.

From the opposite side of the street came a response from Reverend Jessie. "We have been washed, and we have been sanctified, justified by our Lord Jesus Christ. These people, these abominations, have not been." Reverend Jessie again lowered his bullhorn. The men on the two balconies now turned to look at Zarathustra II.

Zarathustra II looked up, tortured, breathed heavily, regained his composure and stepped a few feet towards Reverend Jessie. He raised his bull horn.

"No, you have not been washed and you have not been sanctified. That is one of your delusions. We have been abandoned. No one has seen God, wrestled with God, argued with God, or heard from God in a very long time." There was a background music to this verbal tennis match, a steady but confusing intermixed disco beat from the two bars.

"You are wrong!" Reverend Jessie yelled back into his bull horn. "God speaks to me often. He tells me how to live my life and how others should live their lives. He has told me that he will protect me and my chosen elect. And He only disappeared in your life because of the life you chose," he said firmly.

"Who is the guy that says he talks to God?" a Bourbon pub patron asked. Someone answered him in a low voice which the music drowned out.

"How do you know?" Zarathustra II volleyed back, in a labored, unnatural, voice. "There are many voices in our heads; how do you know it's God talking to you, since all the voices sound the same?" Zarathustra II's question was too vulnerable, but sincere.

Reverend Jessie turned to his followers and laughed. They all laughed. One of them said "kook" and twirled his finger in a circle near his temple, to indicate that he thought Zarathustra II was crazy. Another younger man with a shaved head, standing to the right of Reverend Jessie, pointed at Zarathustra II and laughed.

"Hey, I know who you are! You are the King of the Gays!" the young man who was pointing yelled. Several of the men laughed at the remark and repeated it. Reverend Jessie turned and faced Zarathustra II.

"The difference between you and me," Reverend Jessie said into his bullhorn, somewhat amused, "is that you hear voices because you are crazy. I, on the other hand, hear God's voice loud and clear because I am one of the chosen."

"But how do you know?" Zarathustra II interrupted in that same Tom Waits "Romeo is Bleeding" angst of a voice. While his followers continued to laugh, I saw Reverend Jessie grimace, pinch his lips together, and momentarily lower his head, in reflection.

"But how do you know?" Zarathustra II again yelled, his voice trailing off at the end, as he dropped slowly to his knees. He put the bullhorn on the ground.

At that point Reverend Jessie directed his followers to begin walking up Bourbon Street. "The King of the Gays!" that same man yelled again divisively, pointing at the fallen Zarathustra II.

"Hey! Don't do that," Reverend Jessie promptly castigated the man, who seemed puzzled by the reprimand.

"We have to spread the Word," Reverend Jessie said to get them moving. Reverend Jessie glanced over one final time at Zarathustra II as his group began to walk away. Zarathustra II was clearly shaken. I stood next to him, defiant, but unsure, rebelling but seeking conciliation, staring at Reverend Jessie, while Zarathustra II stayed on his knees. Someone threw another pair of beads to the ground in front of him and, surprisingly, Zarathustra II picked them up and put them around his neck.

Bertrand Finch then walked over to us. Zarathustra II picked up the bull horn and gave it back to him. Bertrand Finch took it from his hand.

"We got it on tape and we'll edit it and put parts on YouTube and my Facebook page shortly. Here, buy yourself a Lucky Dog," he said handing Zarathustra II a twenty dollar bill. Zarathustra II stood up with a sudden burst of energy and stepped over to the Lucky Dog vendor.

"Ignatius, one dog with everything on it."

Chapter 65
LOSE ME

"I recall being drawn to Mikhail Bakunin when I was younger," I heard Zarathustra II say. "I loved the creative force behind his anarchism. He was an artist whose art uncomfortably disrupted others. But ultimately his views did not satisfy my own need for order. He always reminded me a bit of Shakespeare's Coriolanus---he did not understand nuance or compromise. And that was, in a sense, his tragic flaw," he concluded, with a tinge of lament, as Ivanov listened intently.

"I didn't learn about him in school," Ivanov responded. "I had read about Marx on my own at UNO's library and discovered that Bakunin was his most forceful critic. It seems to me that he really pissed off Marx and Engels. So I read a biography on him and whatever else I could find. I read his book *God and the State*. There was not a lot I could find, but I was fascinated by everything I read about him. He seemed larger than life," Ivanov said.

"The principal ideas behind anarchy; that we are deformed by the hierarchical structures of government, and the pressures of society in general, certainly resonate with me. Indeed I am one of its more deformed products. But I think one can only understand this if you already have a heightened sense of freedom and have felt it being oppressed, maybe from an abused childhood, or some other form of alienation," Zarathustra II explained.

"Deformed. Yea. I use that word as well. I've tried to explain it to kids at school to no avail. The street kids seem to understand. But I guess some people are just unaware of the pressures exerted on them by social structures and such," Ivanov said.

"Most people need that structure and are happy to have it," Zarathustra II said, scratching his chin. "Some current writers on anarchism do a pretty good job of explaining the deforming effect," Zarathustra responded.

"I've been working my way through a history of anarchism by Peter Marshall," Ivanov said. "I didn't realize there were so many different variations of anarchism. It reminded me of all the different religious denominations."

"I should have mentioned this to you the other day when you mentioned your definition of sin. The theologian Reinhold Niebuhr believed that sin could be collective and it included society's distortion of individual freedom. He believed that society, the collective if you will, could be immoral," Zarathustra II said.

"Interesting. That is kind of like what I've been thinking when I try to describe my concept of sin, but haven't been able to articulate too well," Ivanov replied. "I wonder how that relates to Marx's view that economics determines a nation's ethics, religion and culture? Maybe it determines or shapes its concept of sin as well," Ivanov asked.

"Well, to the extent that economics is the determining force in society it certainly distorts culture in order to achieve its goals," Zarathustra II replied. "However, I tend to think that it is not economic theory, but man's perceived relationship with the divine, or lack thereof, which has dictated a culture's ethics and indirectly its notion of sin. But it's a close call between the two," Zarathustra II then said.

"I disagree," Ivanov interjected quickly. "It seems to me that economics also defines and distorts religion, at least in America. Like the conservative nonsense, opposing the social gospel, that Jesus would somehow be a supporter of free market capitalism. So any effect of religion on ethics and culture is by a religion that has already been altered by economics," Ivanov said a bit forcefully.

I sat listening. We had walked over to Cafe du Monde from St. Ann and each had a cup of Cafe au lait, which Zarathustra II proudly paid for with monies Finch had given him. He would usually take the $10 or $20 Finch gave him, change it for one dollar bills, and distribute those to the homeless in the Square.

Music flowed from performers at Washington Artillery Park across from Jackson Square and several locals had interrupted our conversation to take pictures with Zarathustra II.

Ivanov had no difficulty putting forth his ideas even if, as he said, the ideas were not yet fully formed. I found that I wanted to join the conversation, to contribute, and wished I had thought more about it and formed my own ideas.

"Anyway, ultimately, I don't think that anarchism can succeed. At least not yet," Zarathustra II said easily to Ivanov.

"It would be tough," Ivanov responded, in a low voice, wishing it were otherwise.

"As a people we have not evolved to the point where everyone could live peaceably, in loose association, without a coercive governmental structure. People do not know themselves, and on some level may actually wish to be unknowable to themselves, except in the most superficial ways. Anarchism, to succeed, would require personal transformation, and asks people to not only know themselves, but to know their fellow man," Zarathustra II replied.

"Well...isn't that what you ask them to do spiritually...to know themselves, and live without the structure of a present God or religion? It's kind of the same thing isn't it?" Ivanov asked. As soon as Ivanov asked his question I found myself connecting the dots between what Zarathustra II said anarchism required of people and what I had heard Zarathustra II ask people to do with their spiritual beliefs.

"Good observation Thomas. It's similar," Zarathustra II said. "But just like you are fighting for something not readily achievable, but which you believe is ultimately for the betterment of all, I am as well. All we have to give in this life is our truth, as we understand it, even if it will be rejected," Zarathustra II said darkly. Ivanov and I glanced at each other waiting to see if Zarathustra II's mood would deteriorate, but it did not. It seemed to momentarily unburden him.

Chapter 66
HUTTERITES

"Perhaps, if anarchism ever gained enough momentum it might at least contribute to creating a less repressive governmental structure," Zarathustra II finally replied.

"You think so?" Ivanov asked.

"Maybe it could be like Buddhism's effect on Christianity. A Christian who absorbs the basic tenets of Buddhism ends up being a better Christian," Zarathustra II said, in a more uplifting tone. Zarathustra II seemed relaxed and happy to be challenged by Ivanov. The fatigue, the chills, I had recently witnessed, had temporarily deserted him.

"How does Buddhism make one a better Christian?" I asked, trying to participate.

"Well, the short answer is that Buddhism asks us to respect all sentient beings, not to harm anyone and to be tolerant of everyone. Those ideas resonate well with the actual teachings of Jesus."

"Assuming Jesus existed," Ivanov challenged, looking at me to see if I would react. I raised an eyebrow and shook my head in a purposely exaggerated fashion enjoying the moment of friendship.

"These ideas we are discussing are all intertwined," Zarathustra II then said, standing up and stretching. Ivanov and I also stood up to leave and all three of us slowly walked outside Cafe Du Monde, over to the steps near Washington Artillery Park, where the Soul Rebels brass band was playing for tips. Even Zarathustra II had slowed his pace.

"I am beginning to see the parallels between coercive government and coercive organized religion. I wonder if we can ever achieve Bakunin's idea of no masters while either are around," Ivanov puzzled.

"Both groups have recognized the other as a possible threat over the course of history," Zarathustra II said.

"I didn't know that," I responded.

"Government has at times co-opted religion for its own purposes to keep its citizenry compliant. Think of the divine right of kings nonsense. On other occasions it suppresses religion as a competitor. And there have been any number of religious groups, for example, who rejected capitalism, engagement with civil society or government, because of its deforming influence on their religious beliefs. Taoists rejected all form of government. The Cathars did not believe in private property. The Anabaptists prohibited its followers from actively participating as citizens in the state. The Hutterites advocated a communal society and rejected capitalism. Some polygamist Mormon groups believe in 'bleeding the beast' and think they can bankrupt government by being on its entitlements," Zarathustra II recited to Ivanov, as we sat on the steps.

"I knew some of that," Ivanov replied. "I know oppressive governments, like Stalin's and Mao's, saw religion as an enemy. I think that's consistent with what you are saying."

"Unfortunately many of the religious groups that pursued such anti-governmental communal structures degenerated into Orwellian societies. They replaced one master with another. Or became the new master. Remember Orwell...'Some animals are more equal than others,'" Zarathustra II said, suddenly giggling.

"But I guess it shows that even some religious groups have struggled with the same issues anarchy tries to address," Ivanov replied.

"To use Bakunin's language, both wanted to be the master," Zarathustra II said.

We fell silent for a moment listening to the rhythm of the brass band. I continued to try to process what they were saying. I had never thought of religion or government in such harsh terms.

"Did you really try to start an anarchist club in high school?" Zarathustra II asked, smiling comfortably.

"Yea. I was doing a lot of blotter acid then to cope with stuff at home. I put my flyers up on May 18th to coincide with Bakunin's birthday," Ivanov explained. "The flyers said 'No Gods. No Masters,' and then, 'Join the Chalmette High School Anarchist Club,'" Ivanov recited. Zarathustra II laughed loudly.

"I bet that went over well with school officials," Zarathustra II said, with a wide supportive smile. I heard Ivanov laugh a little as well.

"Were you really a college professor?" Ivanov asked suddenly.

"Yes," Zarathustra II said more quietly.

"Did you enjoy teaching?" I asked.

"It's all I ever wanted to do and before I started drinking I think I was pretty good at it," he replied.

"Why did you start drinking?" I blurted out. Ivanov looked at me with fleeting disapproval.

"It's ok," Zarathustra II reassured me. "My life was unraveling. My wife had passed. My writings were being rejected. It was one of those times when there was no meaning to hold on to." Ivanov bit at his lower lip in empathy. I felt the distant pain in Zarathustra II's words.

"Well, you have been a good teacher to me, maybe you can go back and do it again someday," Ivanov interrupted.

"I had never heard of Nietzsche before I met you," I said, following the change in subject.

"I promise I will read some of Nietzsche," Ivanov then said in a more serious tone. "It would probably help me better understand things from your perspective,"

"No, that's not a reason to read him," Zarathustra II said, to my surprise. "Read him for yourself. Find your own way. Remember it was Nietzsche who wrote: 'I bid you lose me and find yourselves,'" Zarathustra II scolded slightly. "Remember your own mantra: 'No Masters.' If that works for you, don't make Nietzsche, or me, one of your masters," Zarathustra II concluded.

Zarathustra II then stood up. Zarathustra II said he needed to walk, and without a formal goodbye, headed over to the Decatur street crossing. Ivanov departed several minutes later. The band started another song. I felt uplifted by the conversation and decided to stay and listen to the music and think about what they had just discussed. At least I intended to do so, but shortly after they left, Shiloh Lemoine and Dominique Dagny came over. Ms. Lemoine sat down next to me on the steps, while Ms. Dagny remained standing.

"How you doing there disciple boy?" Ms. Dagny asked.

"Ok," I said.

"We just crossed paths with the preacher man. He was talking to those folks in the Square again about truth."

"Yea, he talks about the different types of truths sometimes. Don't really understand it all," I said quietly.

"All that truth searching, that meaning he talks about, you know what that is all about?"

"Not really," I said, honestly, wondering what Ms. Dagny could really know about such complicated things.

"Truth and meaning. That's just about crossing your fingers and wishing for a happy ending, that's all baby---and by the way if you want a happy ending, I got the back end to do just that--make you happy---you heard me." She turned her back to me and bent over slightly, before turning her head to look back at me over her shoulder. I smiled, still uneasy. Shiloh laughed into her hands. Ms. Dagny then straightened up and stretched her arms in an exaggerated fashion above her head. We sat quietly until the band ended its song.

"Shiloh, so I am asking you again. You getting sweet on that sullen boy Ivanov?" Ms. Dagny asked, still standing up straight, continuing a conversation they had apparently been having as they walked up.

"He's different," Ms. Lemoine replied.

"Different? He's male ain't he?" Ms. Dagny said with her hands in judgment on her hips.

"Yea, but he the only person I ever met that don't ask me for nothin. He just want to talk about music and philosophy and just wanna share it with me."

"That's not all he wants to share. Trust me," Ms. Dagney said.

"He is interested in my poetry....And he gave me a nickname: 'Little Love.' So I call him 'Big Love,'" Ms. Lemoine explained, looking suddenly demure.

"Uh huh. Nicknames. Well this aint no *Pretty Woman* movie, ya heard me. And I ain't seen no halo around that boy's head," Ms. Dagny chided, still standing. "Listen, I got an appointment at the Pontalba baby," she said to Ms. Lemoine. "See you soon disciple boy," Ms. Dagny then said to me as she walked away.

The band started a new song with its leader introducing the song by yelling to the crowd: "It ain't my fault." Ms. Lemoine leaned back on the palms of her hands, relaxing, and stretched her legs out in front of her. I noticed some bruises on one of her legs. I hesitated.

"Shiloh, can I ask you something?"

"Sure disciple boy. You looking for some chocolate?" she said grinning.

"Why do you do what you do?" She looked away from me, perhaps surprised by the directness of my question. She brushed her hand against her leg, thinking, and sat up straight before turning to face me.

"Can you handle an honest answer?"

"Yes," I said, in as masculine a voice as I could muster.

"With paid sex, I find I can relate to others, without having to be intimate. It's kind of like how I feel when I write with my poems using other people's words."

"But I thought sex was intimacy. Isn't it?" She laughed lightly, a smile that uncovered my innocence.

"Baby, real intimacy is the child of love, of letting go and being possessed but not being owned. Sex can be a way to avoid intimacy," she replied.

"But you can relate to others in conversation, by friendship, can't you? You don't have to do what you do...right?" She smiled and looked away again.

"Those things are superficial. Boring. In my life I need to go to the extremes to feel anything," she said without looking at me. She shuffled her feet and gripped her hands together as if to test their strength.

"So do you believe in love? That there is such a thing?" I asked, unsure where the question came from, in a voice with which I was unfamiliar. She relaxed and looked at me.

"There's not a lot of real love in this world, baby, cause we is all living wounded lives. It's mostly pretending and manipulating, and fighting over the proper way to fold towels," she replied, with a knowing grin, expressing some sentiment at the center of her, of who she was.

"Towels?"

"It ain't about towels baby. It's about control." I didn't understand. How could folding towels be about control? But, for some reason, I wanted to continue the conversation.

"What about relationships? Do you think they can last?" I asked, thinking, perhaps of my parents' troubles, uncertain about their love.

"Anything can last. People can endure just about anything. Trust me I know. It's just whether it's worth it; whether there is anything to hold onto to make it worth it. Most relationships are just a broken jumble of white lies bound together by personal needs, like the pieces of a stained glass window. At least that's how it appears from my perspective dealing with lots of so called *faithful* married folks."

"You make it sound like a constant battle. It doesn't seem like it should be that way," I replied, a virgin on the subject.

"Ha ha! One piece of advice baby. In that battle, as you call it. Men generally win the battles. But women, we always win the war." She smiled again.

"How many people have you slept with?" I asked, and then was embarrassed for asking. She looked away from me, furtively, perhaps deciding whether to answer, whether to be offended.

"Too many....And not enough to retire."

I didn't know what to say in response. She remained resting on her hands and then turned to face me directly again.

"Thanks for asking, baby."

Chapter 67
TOO MANY COKES

It seemed clear now that New Orleans was going to be hit by Hurricane Bera. The Weather Channel was reporting that a weak Atlantic front had apparently pushed the storm off its original course and into the Gulf of Mexico. Zarathustra II's park bench prediction, that the storm would hit New Orleans, was going to be right. How could Zarathustra II have known this was going to happen?

There was a chance, some weathermen said, that the eye of the hurricane would go more to the west toward Baton Rouge, or east to Biloxi, but New Orleans would sustain a major hit regardless. The computer models now all agreed on that point. And it was a very powerful storm, evoking comparisons to Hurricane Camille and Hurricane Katrina from local and national weathermen.

My mother and Mrs. Rosemary Matthews pulled into the driveway of the home of Mrs. Matthews' cousin Marvin, after taking their time driving, shopping on occasion, and stopping again overnight. Mrs. Matthews put the car in park and opened the driver side door and got out as quickly as her oversized legs would allow. She did not close the car door but, instead, ran to the front door of the house, as best she could, with one hand on her head holding her hat down, and the straps of her purse secured in the crook of her elbow. Marvin had come out of the house to greet her. Mrs. Rosemary Matthews brushed by him and went straight into the house without speaking, like an exclamation point at the end of a sentence.

My mother got out the passenger side of the car and slowly walked over to Marvin. Her lower back hurt, so she had her hands on her hips in a way to indicate that she was in the discomfort of older age. Marvin raised his hands perplexed at his cousin's behavior and looked at my mother. "Don't worry hon, she drank too many a dem diet cokes while we was driving," my mother said.

"I'll unload your luggage. I have the Weather channel on for you inside. Looks like it will be a bad one," he said, and moved quickly towards the car.

Chapter 68
A COURT ORDER

The management of the Bourbon Pub and Parade had seen enough of Reverend Jessie's bull horn and the harassment of its customers. The bar retained the services of New Orleans attorney Salvatore "Big Sal" Riccobono to try to end the harassment. Big Sal was a native New Orleanian, having grown up in a once predominately Italian-American neighborhood on LaSalle Street, in the waning days when everyone knew each other and a child of the neighborhood was the responsibility of all. Mr. Riccobono successfully ran for state senator at an early age where he served three unremarkable terms. Then he returned to New Orleans and was elected, without opposition, to the New Orleans City Council, where he held office for three terms before "retiring" from politics. His retirement coincided with the shift in demographics, as white flight continued in his district.

Big Sal, who was near 80 years old, was small in physical stature, but affable and well liked. He was always seen, regardless of the weather, wearing his brown fedora over his receding gray hair and chomping on the butt end of an unlit cigar. He was otherwise not a natty dresser, and often had his shirt partially un-tucked, coffee stained, and sometimes wore mismatched socks. It was one of his many colorful idiosyncrasies, which some felt he purposely cultivated.

One well told story was that he once tried a jury trial in Civil District Court with a sheet of fabric softener stuck to the back of his trouser leg.

During his closing argument he looked down, noticed the fabric softener, and without missing a beat, removed it from his trouser leg, crumpled it up and throwing it in a waste basket, suggested that his opponent's claim was like the sheet of fabric softener desperately hoping it could stick to something.

He was street smart and street educated, politically incorrect, which meant that often he could be crude. Again, whether it was real or cultivated was never clear, and native New Orleanians did not care, as sincerity and contrived performance are often confused by the public. He was well known in the legal community, as was his son, "Little Sal" Riccobono Jr., who was a criminal defense attorney.

Big Sal also enjoyed the limelight. Despite his retirement from politics he missed the days where he had unfettered access to the media and where people were always seeking him out for his opinion on issues of the day. So when he had a legal case, or a court appearance of public interest, he contacted his friends in the media to try to get some coverage. The media often complied because Big Sal was 'good copy.' In this case, involving the Bourbon Pub, he had the media meet him at the courthouse that morning, where, standing on the courthouse steps, he announced that he was filing a petition for injunctive relief against Reverend Jessie.

"We are going to keep Reverend Jessie, and his so-called disciples, from disrupting the operations of a legitimate business in the French Quarter, namely the Bourbon Pub and Parade," Big Sal said. A reporter from the Louisiana Digest then asked Big Sal if it concerned him that his client was the largest gay bar in the French Quarter. He promptly replied, "not in the least." When another reporter goaded him further about the dispute with Reverend Jessie and his views on the morality of homosexuality, Big Sal paused, chomped on his unlit cigar for a moment, as if it helped him clarify something.

"As my Sicilian grandfather used to say, people can shovel gravel with their mouth if they want to, it's none of my business," he replied.

Under the rules of civil procedure, since Big Sal was asking for a temporary restraining order, he had to notify the CRC and its attorney that he was headed to court so that the CRC could present its arguments opposing the TRO. The CRC's lawyer was Andrew Lagarde Jr.

Andrew Lagarde Jr. was also well known in the legal community. He had been a promising partner in a large law firm before having a brief psychotic break in which he was hospitalized. Immediately prior to being hospitalized he assured his notoriety in the legal community by having his computer e-mail out approximately 1,200 notices to other lawyers in south Louisiana advising that he would be hosting a seminar on what it was like to be him, entitled "Being Andrew Lagarde Jr." His partners decided to do an intervention and had him sent to River Oaks Psychiatric Hospital for 30 days. The first week he was there he was placed in with a court ordered therapy group of seven fashion design students from Tulane who had been arrested for spray painting graffiti on the mannequins at a Sachs 5th Avenue on Canal Street.

Mr. Lagarde emerged from the psychiatric unit with his legal reputation tarnished but, some said, a better sense of fashion. On this day he was wearing a dark blue Armani suit and a silk yellow tie with a series of red crucifixes imprinted on it.

"My client has a First Amendment right to speak about the issues he and his church deem important to this community. He has no intention of entering the Bourbon Pub at any time," Mr. Lagarde told the assembled media.

"How do you know he has never been in the pub?" a reporter yelled laughingly. Mr. Lagarde frowned disapprovingly.

"I'll leave the comedy to Big Sal," he replied. The lawyers then left the microphones and headed into the courthouse for the hearing on the temporary restraining order.

The duty judge at Civil District Court signed a temporary restraining order that morning which read as follows:

IT IS ORDERED that Reverend Jessie Ray Elder is enjoined and prohibited from entering the premises of the Bourbon Pub and

Parade at 801 Bourbon Street and further prohibited from being within 20 feet of its doorways.

The judge refused to enjoin Reverend Jessie's bull horn on First Amendment grounds. The judge also refused to enjoin any other members of the CRC as there had been no proof that any had been involved in harassing the bar or its patrons. Big Sal immediately declared victory before the assembled media as he exited the courthouse.

"We kicked the Reverend's ass," he said, with the ever present cigar dangling from his lips.

"Big Sal knows as much about the law as he does about fashion," Mr. Lagarde replied. The next morning Oz's attorney filed the same lawsuit and obtained the same restraining order by consent.

Chapter 69
CANCELLATIONS

If the predictions and the computer models were right hurricane Bera would begin to make landfall the evening before the Southern Decadence Festival was scheduled to start its parade. It would land during the time the pre-Festival party, including the crowning of the Festival Drag Queen, was scheduled to take place. Businesses had boarded up. Hotels were reporting a steady stream of cancellations because of the storm, but there were already some tourists in town for the festival. Much of the populace of New Orleans, however, was emptying the city like cats spitting up hair balls; slow, painful and congested.

The contra flow plan was to go into effect on Interstate 10. The state police were going to assist the NOPD with traffic flow and security and the Governor had put the National Guard on notice of a post storm deployment in the city, to assist with crime control. Mayors always stayed in town during a storm to coordinate matters, but Mayor Wanek had announced, while attending the grand opening of a new Ra Shop, that he was leaving.

"I'm happy to be part of the economic boom and weed renaissance my administration has created as evidenced by opening this Ra shop," he told the media. "This is the second Ra shop I have been privileged to welcome to our city. Soon we will be the weed paraphernalia capital of the country."

"Why are you leaving town for the storm?" Ms. McComb asked.

"It's not for me. It's out of concern for the citizens of the city. They need to know that their Mayor is safe during the storm and can come back to help clean up. Besides I don't want to have any Ray Nagin moments."

"Where will you be?" Bertand Finch asked.

"Probably in Lake Charles."

As for the tourists coming into town, Mayor Wanek told reporter Clarice McComb that he did not have an opinion on whether they should come or not, but would have his people study it and let him know what they thought.

"But if you are coming please enjoy our city's hospitality," he said, with an easy used car salesman smile.

Though many native New Orleanians were leaving town to avoid the storm, Shiloh Lemoine and Dominique Dagny were not. They were checking into the Bourbon Orleans in the French Quarter. The hotel was on the opposite side of the street corner from the Bourbon Pub. They had a benefactor, a Dallas businessman, who was in town and had visited with them before. Ms. Dagny described it as "a dress up return engagement." The Dallas businessman decided that he didn't want to cancel the arrangement because of the storm. "He thinks it will add to the excitement," Ms. Dagny said to me.

In exchange for free room and board in his hotel suite during the storm, and $1,500 each, the ladies had agreed to stay with him and "entertain him." "There'll be some play acting involved," Ms. Lemoine told me, explaining their plans.

Chapter 70
AMEN

The Mayor's staff had been meeting regularly to discuss ways of invigorating his diminishing political chances at re-election in two years. The staff felt that the hurricane presented the Mayor with an opportunity to appear in command during the potential crisis. They recalled vividly how the fortunes of other Louisiana politicians were often judged, at election time, by their performance during such natural catastrophes. The Mayor's staff had fought a running, and losing, battle to have the Mayor portrayed as a serious and thoughtful politician by the local media. On each occasion he had thwarted their carefully planned efforts to cultivate his image by veering off script. Several political advisors had resigned since his election because of the Mayor's refusal to adhere to their counsel. Now, with his statement that he was leaving town before the storm hit, they knew there would be a negative response and they would have more difficulty cultivating an in charge image.

"We need to get him out in front on the whole religious issue concerning the storm," the Mayor's most recent media advisor, and former indicted Union official, Antonio "Pipeline" Sorcic, told the staff. Mr. Sorcic was a powerfully built man who had spent much of his adult life working as a longshoreman and then running the local Longshoremen's union. Mr. Sorcic's indictment, removal as Union president, and subsequent federal trial on corruption charges, would have probably ended his nascent career as a political advisor elsewhere. New Orleanians, however, loved their home grown rogues, especially if they beat the rap as Mr. Sorcic did. Despite his acting as a caricature on occasion, he knew and understood local politics.

"Religion in the south, however vague, is the basis of most political authority. It's a litmus test, and the people need to know that the Mayor is a religious man," he offered philosophically. The Mayor's staff concurred uneasily.

It was decided by Mr. Sorcic that too much press was being given to Reverend Jessie and Zarathustra II on the storm and the possible pending showdown between them. The Mayor had, once again, become a political afterthought. So Mr. Sorcic decided to try to refocus the citizenry on the Mayor and called an evening press conference for the Mayor to discuss "storm preparations." Mr. Sorcic admonished the Mayor's staff that he needed to seize control of the religious dimension of the storm. Mr. Sorcic worked up a brief speech for the Mayor, which included several quotes from the Bible.

To further assist with the political goal of the press conference, Mr. Sorcic invited a diverse group of the city's religious leaders to attend the press conference. He specifically excluded Reverend Jessie out of fear that the media would question him, and not the Mayor, and thereby defeat the purpose of the press conference. "Look, the other ministers and religious leaders can't be too damn happy about Reverend Jessie getting all the attention. I know these guys. They love publicity. So let's co-opt them by having them get a special invitation from the Mayor," Mr. Sorcic told the Mayor's staff. "We can use them as a support, and they will be happy to report back to their congregations about how the Mayor asked for them, blah, blah, blah," he concluded. Everyone agreed and the press conference was set up to coincide with the evening news. "Maybe this will deflect some of the criticism about his dumb ass decision to leave town. I tried to convince him to reconsider, but he won't listen," Mr. Sorcic said. The press conference was then quickly arranged by the Mayor's staff and the other religious leaders were invited.

"I want it understood that my administration is mindful of the many spiritual needs of its citizens during this very trying time, and I want the public to know that I often call on God, in private of course, to help me in times of personal need, though He bailed on me when the City Council considered my ordinance to legalize marijuana. Not sure why. I thought we had an understanding," the Mayor said, in a disemboweled street barker's voice from the podium at City Hall, to the assembled media. He was standing behind the podium wearing a pinkish blazer with a green shirt open at the collar, a visible gold chain around his neck, and a New Orleans Zephyrs baseball cap.

Standing on the side of the mayor during the press conference, which was being broadcast live on the evening news of all the local TV stations, was the local Catholic Archbishop Gautier and Rabbi Bohrer of the Lost Tribe of Hebrew Temple. To the Mayor's far right a young lady used sign language to convey the Mayor's message to the hearing impaired. As Mr. Sorcic had suggested, a group of other local ministers and religious leaders, who were invited, stood several feet behind the Mayor, Archbishop Gautier and Rabbi Bohrer.

A black woman in a brightly colored Dashiki, whom I did not recognize, also stood on the podium, off to the Mayor's left side. The Mayor's staff was nervous as they did not know who she was and he had refused to introduce her.

"You'll see. It's the coup of da grass," he told them.

Mr. Sorcic had scripted the entire press conference, but the mayor had arrived with this woman, and two others, including a tragically thin woman in a mini skirt, of indeterminate age, slump shouldered, with lots of make-up, who was also wearing a Zephyrs baseball cap, in his entourage. At the last minute the Mayor had balled up the written text of his speech, telling his staff and Mr. Sorcic, immediately before he stepped to the podium, that he could ad lib it just fine.

"I'm a natural born showman," the Mayor said, turning to the bashful woman in the mini skirt with a wink. The staff sat quietly in anticipated despair. Mr. Sorcic immediately left the press conference telling the Mayor's staff, in disgust, to handle it.

"As a result of my unwavering spiritual commitment to the citizens of our city I have asked Catholic Archbishop Gautier to ask God, Mary, Jesus and all those Catholic Saints, and there's a bunch of them, to spare our city and to send the storm elsewhere…like, maybe to Mississippi," the Mayor stated, unashamed of his comment. "After all Mississippi usually ranks last in everything so it shouldn't matter to them if a couple of house trailers get destroyed," he said. Archbishop Gautier, wearing the proper vestments, looked uncomfortable with the mayor's introduction as he stepped up to the podium. He bowed his head.

"Let us pray," the Archbishop said. "Almighty and heavenly Father, please forgive us our sins this day and we humbly beseech you to spare our fair city and its citizens from another disaster, another black day, unless that be your will, in which case give us the strength to endure and the wisdom to accept what we cannot understand." The Archbishop, with his head still bowed and his hands held in prayer, paused for a moment in silent reflection.

"You forgot to ask them to send it to Mississippi," the Mayor said, leaning towards the Archbishop, but loud enough to be picked up by the podium microphone.

"Amen," the Archbishop said, stepping back, ignoring the Mayor's rueful plea.

Mayor Wanek abruptly stepped back up to the microphone like a public auctioneer as the Archbishop stepped away. "Thank you Archbishop Gautier. It is always good to hear from God's Catholic representative. And now let's cover another base, Rabbi Bohrer, you're on!" Mayor Wanek said, as if directing a game show contestant. The Rabbi was dressed magnificently, wearing a Kippah, Tallit and Tefallin.

"As Jews have done for eons, in times of turbulence, I will offer a silent prayer," he said, gracefully bowing his head.

"Just be sure He can hear you," Mayor Wanek said, with a smirk, stepping next to the woman in the miniskirt and then playfully bumping his hip into her. After a few moments the Rabbi stepped away from the microphone. Mayor Wanek stepped back up to the podium. The Mayor's staff expected him to take questions at this point in the press conference and braced themselves for how he would handle it.

"And finally I have asked my new friend, who I met last night at The Dungeon lounge in the Quarter, the Voodoo Priestess Jolie Marie Brownlee to help us out as well." At that moment the black lady in the Dashiki turned on a portable CD player and a loud percussion began with accompanying chants. The Voodoo Priestess, barefoot, started to dance rhythmically and throw her head back and forth. The Mayor began to clap and stomp his feet out of time, like an uninvited white guest at a black church revival. She lifted a burlap bag from behind the stage and pulled a white boa constrictor out of the bag and held it, with both hands, high above her head. Archbishop Gautier and Rabbi Bohrer, both clearly disconcerted, walked off the stage at this point, followed promptly by the other local whispering religious leaders. The Voodoo priestess danced for another minute or so chanting, but in a language that I could not understand.

Mayor Wanek returned to the microphone before, it seemed, she had finished her dance. She continued to dance in the background with the snake draped over her shoulders, until one of the Mayor's staff turned off the CD player.

"Let no-one question this administration's commitment to God, or to the spiritual well being of its citizens," he said, and then beat out an adolescent disjointed rhythm on the podium with his hands. "Any questions?" the Mayor then asked the gathered reporters, while leaning on the podium with a smile of satisfaction on his face. Some of the reporters were laughing. Others were stone faced, impertinent.

"This is serious business," the Mayor chastised them, frowning, as he pounded his fist on the podium.

"Questions?" he asked again.

"What church do you belong to, Mayor?" Ms. Clarice McComb then asked, snickering. "Well, now missy," the Mayor responded, "that's really not a proper question to ask me as a public official. You know there is that separation of church stuff in the uh, the uh, Third Amendment to the Constitution and you see I represent all the citizens of the city regardless of their faith, so I can't be partial to any particular god. But I can tell

MICHAEL T. TUSA JR.

you that my commitment to God, or whatever his real name is, has never wavered, at least not much." The Mayor looked over at the woman in the mini skirt and winked at her again.

"Does God speak to you, like He does to Reverend Jessie?" Bertrand Finch asked, rather seriously.

"I would rather not say. I think those conversations would be covered by that Executive privilege thing," the Mayor responded.

"Have you reconsidered riding out the storm out here so you can direct city services?" Ms. McComb asked, still laughing.

"No. It's more important to me that I stay alive," the Mayor said promptly.

Chapter 71
THE DISCIPLES

Reverend Jessie was ready to announce the names of the twelve men who were going to ride out the storm with him in the French Quarter, on Bourbon Street between the Bourbon Pub and Oz. This announcement would, he thought, prove the sincerity of his opposition to the Festival and also allow the men to honor God's revelation to Reverend Jessie that He would protect His most faithful followers from any harm.

When Reverend Jessie had originally announced that God told him to stand with twelve others in the French Quarter, during the storm, Zarathustra II had said that things were moving too fast, that he need-ed time to think. I decided, as we learned that the announcement of the twelve was forthcoming, to raise the issue again to see what he thought about it.

"I can't believe he is going to stand in a hurricane," I said. "Why would he do that? It seems like an affront to God. Arrogant. You know, kind of a prove you exist to me."

"This has nothing to do with God. It is about something else," Zarathustra II offered, stoically, carefully choosing his words.

"What else? What do you mean?"

"Something he is trying to solve for himself. Some extreme that he needs. Maybe his faith is not as strong as he claims. I don't know exactly."

"And he thinks you are crazy," I replied. Zarathustra II hesitated.

"Well we may both be. I've decided to be there as well," he replied.

"What! Just because he is acting like an idiot does not mean you have to do the same," Ivanov said, sounding like a parent admonishing a child.

"Perhaps, but we are tied together now. The Yin and the Yang. I'm very tired of this life," Zarathustra II said, resigned, his blue eyes burned to ash.

"It sounds more like a death wish," Ivanov replied, trying to stir the ashes back to flame.

"Maybe. But you will grant that it is my life and I should have the freedom to forfeit it if I choose to---right? You know the freedom you talk about," Zarathustra II said, with a slight edge, a challenge, to his voice.

"Yes. Yes, you do," Ivanov replied, backing down.

Reverend Jessie told the assembled media, before announcing the names of the twelve, that he had prayed over his possible selections and eventually told one and all that God had personally instructed him on each person to pick for the task.

Indeed, Reverend Jessie picked distinguished pillars of the community, and of the CRC, to be the twelve representatives, the twelve elect. He notified the media after the evening news, announcing the names of those who were chosen. They included Philip Harvey Harrison, the CRC's treasurer and long time local banker; Timothy Mark Daigre, who was the Deacon at the church and stood in when Reverend Jessie was unavailable; Rivet David Walker, a local lawyer who had helped finance the building of the church and was the church's largest contributor; James Simon Scott, a former seminarian who oversaw the child nutrition program at the CRC; Martin Luther Blanchfield, who was on the CRC's development committee; Joseph Kevin Hawkins who was a regular volunteer at the church youth gatherings; retired judge Norton Augustine; retired minister, Thaddeus "Spook" Johnson, a former basketball player from Liberty University; Saul Peter Fierke, a highly decorated retired military man; Bartholomew Davidson, who was in the church choir; Shaun Bonnet, a former state legislator and John Henry Calvin. Mr. Calvin was the oldest of the bunch, nearing 87 years of age. He was a recently retired history teacher who had taught at Jesuit High School in New Orleans for over 50 years and regularly volunteered at the church since his wife had died a few years back. Mr. Calvin and his wife had one son, Daniel, who, at 18 years old, was listed as an MIA in Vietnam. His body had never been found. Mr. Calvin still wore a stainless steel MIA bracelet in remembrance of his son.

Reverend Jessie also had the church secretary, Dolores, fax out announcements to the local papers and other media with biographical information about each of the selections. "These men are the elect, the truly faithful, and God has personally instructed me to ask each of them to stand with me and has assured me that He will protect us from harm," Reverend Jessie wrote in the fax.

A short while after the announcement was made, by the other TV stations, Bertrand Finch called me on my cell phone. He wanted to know what Zarathustra II was going to do in response.

"The Reverend is trying to upstage me again. I need Zarathustra to show up there as well," Finch said.

"He said he was going to do so," I replied.

"Good. He needs to designate some disciples to stay with him in the French Quarter during the storm," Finch advised.

I looked over and noticed that Zarathustra II was asleep on the sofa. "He hasn't said anything about that," I replied. "But Ivanov and I will probably be there."

"What about the two hookers? Didn't Jesus have some hookers with him?" Finch asked. "Ask him to think about naming the hookers as disciples," Finch concluded.

Chapter 72
A CORONATION

The *Times Picayune* and *The Advocate* ran articles in their printed paper, and in their online versions, the next day indicating the names of the twelve individuals chosen by Reverend Jessie. "The disciples," the *Times Picayune* article indicated, "would be standing with him in the French Quarter to prove their opposition to the Southern Decadence Festival." The article, which took up an entire page, had photographs of each of the twelve, with a brief individual biographical sketch. It looked like a layout of the starting lineup taken from a Saints football game day program. There was a picture of "Spook" Johnson from his basketball playing days and one of John Henry Calvin from his teaching days.

The article also indicated that Zarathustra II would be accompanied to the French Quarter by "the Russian anarchist Mikhail Ivanov and Reverend Jessie's son," something Bertrand Finch told the paper. "Zarathustra the Second has many followers who wanted to be there, but he has only selected his two original apostles to be with him," Finch was quoted as saying.

While Reverend Jessie's selections were labeled his "disciples," by the paper, Ivanov and I were called Zarathustra II's "undesirables." There was no pictures of either of us, though there was a picture of Zarathustra II standing barefoot on his park bench in front of a crowd under a caption: "Who will God choose?" For biographical information the article indicated that I was "the alienated son" of Reverend Jessie. It also indicated that Ivanov was a Chalmette High School drop-out and mentioned his expulsion for "being an anarchist."

Bertrand Finch did a story on the early morning news about Reverend Jessie and Zarathustra II facing the storm. He entitled the story "Showdown on Bourbon Street," a title that sounded like a 1950's low budget western movie. He reminded viewers that he had first covered Zarathustra II's prediction that the storm would hit the city.

"Not to brag, but I must say my superior journalistic instincts have been right all along." He promised to exclusively cover the confrontation in the French Quarter during the storm.

That same morning Mayor Shemp Wanek announced a mandatory evacuation of the entire city. He said that he had contacted the weather service, his aides had studied the matter, and he was assured that this was the right step to take. As far as shelters for citizens who stayed behind in the city, he said there would be none. "You're on your own folks. We don't have time to take care of everybody," he said in the morning press conference. The city would provide RTA transit buses to go to Houston for those who wanted to go.

The Mayor of Houston, when asked, however, said he had not been consulted about the buses coming to his city and had no idea where those fleeing the storm in city buses would be housed. In light of the poor condition of the RTA bus fleet, Mayor Wanek promised that one bus would carry nothing but spare bus parts, in case any broke down on the way to Houston.

"No-one can say we are not prepared," Mayor Wanek said affirmatively. Mayor Wanek did suggest that if you stayed behind in the city to ride out the storm, "Put an axe and some food in your attic and write your name on your forehead."

Some of the hotels decided to close as well and told guests that they would have to leave. Others, like the Bourbon Orleans, were going to remain open for their existing guests and the media coming to town to cover the storm. The Bourbon Pub and Parade indicated that it would stay open and host a mini Southern Decadence hurricane party and an in house coronation of this year's Festival Drag Queen. It had a propane generator which could run the property if power was lost. The Southern Decadence Festival itself was cancelled, as was the expected Grand Marshal parade.

When contacted and advised of the festival cancellation, Reverend Jessie declared righteously that "God works in mysterious ways. It's another moral victory for believers." However, he indicated that he and his "disciples," as he too had now started to call the twelve, would still make their stand in the French Quarter during the storm. "When God asks, we cannot decline," he said, explaining the decision.

Chapter 73
LOSING ONE'S FAITH

I was in my bedroom asleep when, as if part of an early morning dream, I thought I heard a knock on the front door of my apartment. Then again I heard another knock. I had the slow realization that the knocking was not in my dream. I gradually woke up. I looked at the clock on my night stand. It was 7:30 a.m.

As I sat up in my bed I heard voices coming from the den. I immediately recognized Zarathustra II's voice. I did not recognize the voice of the other man. There seemed to be agitation in the tone of the other man's voice. I heard someone fall to the ground.

"Are you here to kill me?" I heard Zarathustra II ask. I got up quickly and headed down the hall to the den, unsure, and frightened.

I found Zarathustra II laying on his back on the floor. Standing over him was Mr. Liddy, the Director of Security for the CRC. Mr. Liddy looked over at me momentarily, and then dropped a stuffed white envelope onto Zarathustra II's chest. As the envelope hit Zarathustra II's chest it fell open revealing that it was stuffed with cash.

"That which does not kill us makes us stronger," Mr. Liddy said sarcastically to Zarathustra II, as he remained standing over him.

"Do you know Nietzsche?" Zarathustra II asked excitedly. Liddy ignored him and took a step back.

I did not know Mr. Liddy very well. I had heard a rumor that he was a former marine who had been deployed several times to Afghanistan.

269

He had a close military crew cut and a muscled and heavily tattooed physique.

"Several of Reverend Jessie's followers have asked that I give you this money, as seed money, so that you can start a new life elsewhere," Mr. Liddy then said. Zarathustra II sat up and pulled the cash out of the envelope to count it.

"Someone is defecting," Zarathustra II said to me, grinning childishly, a slight twinkle in his eyes.

"It is $5,000. More money than I expect you have seen in years. It is yours if you will just leave town before the storm and announce that you are leaving. You can go to Atlanta to visit your daughter," Mr. Liddy said, watching Zarathustra II continue to count the money. "I prepared a press release for you to use when you leave," Mr. Liddy said, dropping a folded piece of paper next to Zarathustra II.

"Would you give the money to her instead if I leave?" Zarathustra II asked to my surprise. But he quickly changed his mind before Mr. Liddy could reply

"No, no, she needs to be rid of me. Never mind."

"They must really be afraid of what you are preaching, if they are willing to buy you off," I said to Zarathustra II.

"I doubt they care about what I preach. No-one ever has. They are just afraid for themselves. Who really wants to stand outside in a hurricane?" Zarathustra II muttered. Zarathustra II stopped counting the money, which was mostly $100 bills. Zarathustra II remained seated and stared up, penitent, at Mr. Liddy.

"People should be allowed to choose who they believe is right," I said, continuing my defense of Zarathustra II. Mr Liddy laughed at me and then folded his arms, still standing, chiseled, over Zarathustra II.

"Kid, people don't choose their beliefs based on whose right. They choose the God that's necessary for them, the God they need in order to survive," he responded dismissively. Zarathustra II fidgeted on the floor, but continued to stare up at Mr. Liddy.

"What do you mean they choose the one they need to survive?" I asked. Mr. Liddy looked at me with bemusement and mild contempt.

"Which God did you choose?" Zarathustra II asked him confessionally. Mr. Liddy laughed again, but this time the laugh seemed forced. Zarathustra II laughed with him, as if they had once had this discussion before and already knew the outcome.

"A badass one that would protect me and my men in a desert overseas," Mr. Liddy said, revealing for a brief moment, a possible complexity in his character.

"And it appears that He protected you," Zarathustra II said.

"Me, yes. But not all my men."

"And you are left wondering why He disappeared for some, right?" Zarathustra II asked, philosophically, playing his scripted part.

Mr. Liddy then looked down at Zarathustra II peacefully. Tension, doubt and intolerance fell slowly from his face, it lightened. It seemed like he wanted to unload some thoughts he had been carrying around for awhile in his personal rucksack. The anger that he had entered the apartment with, whether real or feigned, seemed to have abated.

"This may surprise you coming from me. Religion is like patriotism. It's the same drink, that 'my country tis of thee' bullshit. But most people ain't fighting no fucking war like we were, so they can believe that kind of stuff." I looked away, unable to meet the tortured blaze in Mr. Liddy's eyes.

"Don't get angry over it. Anger destroys you," Zarathustra II counseled him. Zarathustra II remained seated and continued to look up at Mr. Liddy, like a young child waiting for the punishment to be explained. Mr. Liddy seemed to be considering his response, perhaps identifying something lost, some injury found. Zarathustra II picked up the press release and read it.

"This is funny. It says 'I'm leaving town to start my ministry elsewhere,'" Zarathustra II read out loud. "My ministry. Who knew I had one?"

Mr. Liddy then spoke. But I was not sure to what he was responding.

"Reverend Jessie gives his followers the illusion that they are in this together and will triumph over this life, kind of like the marines do with recruits," Mr. Liddy said quietly, with his arms still folded.

"Reverend Jessie preys upon people's sense of unworthiness, because he himself feels unworthy. It's all projection. Deep down most people feel worthless. He preaches worthlessness, confirming their unspoken fears about themselves and then offers them the illusion of a way out in the hereafter, an illusion that he also needs. Maybe if he convinces others to believe it, it makes it easier for him to believe," Zarathustra II rebutted.

"And you tell them there is no meaning, but what they can create," Mr. Liddy quickly responded, less aggressively, but firmly. "You have no mythology, no symbols, no semper fi, nothing for people to belong to, or hold onto when times are hard. You ask people to turn inward and rely upon themselves, but that approach will not defeat death; in fact, it makes them face it," Mr Liddy said.

"Well, if people will always choose the God which they need then why do you care whether I am here?" Zarathustra II asked, ignoring Mr. Liddy's larger question. There was a long pause, while Mr. Liddy remained speechless. Then Mr. Liddy smiled again, dropping his arms, defenseless, to his side.

"Personally, I don't care," he finally said. "Neither of you will accomplish anything with this latest stunt. The question is will you take the money and leave town."

"I can't. I'd like to, but I can't. I hope you understand."

"It doesn't matter if I understand. I didn't think you would take the deal," Mr. Liddy said. He leaned over and slowly picked up the cash and the press release stuffing both back in his coat pocket. Without saying more, Mr. Liddy turned and walked out of the apartment.

Chapter 74
THREE STOOLS

Bertrand Finch lobbied his bosses at the TV station to allow him to set up a TV set piece on Bourbon Street during the early hours of Hurricane Bera, from which he could narrate the pending showdown between Reverend Jessie and Zarathustra II. Bertrand Finch was sure that there would be a journalistic award in it for him, and the station, and that it would catapult him to the larger TV market which he so desired.

"This story could really put us in the lead for once," Finch told his boss. "It will be an exclusive. We could overtake WWL as the number one station in the market. I, I mean we, could get an award for the coverage," he suggested.

The station manager knew there was interest in this story. Indeed some national outlets, including the Christian Broadcasting Network, CNN and FOX news, had asked to get copies of any film footage. But he was more worried about the hurricane and the massive evacuation underway, and less interested in Bertrand Finch's personal desire for greater stardom, which was well known. As a result, Bertrand Finch was only allocated one cameraman with a retired battery operated camera.

"We're not ruining an expensive camera over this, our budget can't afford it. Just take an old camera, some extra batteries and we will load up the film the old fashion way when you return," the station manager said. "And what about you?"

"I'll be fine. I'll get you the big story boss."

"What about this prediction that you will get killed?"

"Oh, I'm not worried about that. I am going to take shelter after the initial interview," Finch said.

"You're a pain in the ass, but you ginned up this story. Take the old Mardi Gras set pieces in storage for the interview. We were going to replace them anyway," the station manager said.

He had to use the set pieces the station had used over the years for its Mardi Gras day broadcast, which were three bar stools and a pressboard desk front. He immediately made plans to set up on the street corner across from the Bourbon Pub.

Before leaving for the day Finch sent unsolicited emails to several stations in larger markets, with his resume attached. In the email he referenced his discovery of Zarathustra II and his reporting on Zarathustra II's prophecy that the storm would hit New Orleans. He also planned to upload to YouTube and Facebook the storm related film of his interview of Zarathustra II and Reverend Jessie.

Chapter 75
HIDING MY FACE

Zarathustra II was becoming more dour, withdrawing into the wasteland of his anxiety. His chills had returned. He sat on my sofa, with troubled thoughts, while Ivanov and I moved around him, like bees swarming their paralyzed prey. It was as if the tempest inside of him, that constant motion I had always witnessed, was suddenly inert and unsure.

"Could I be wrong?" he said three times, rhetorically, not expecting an answer, probing something deeper in the well. The lines on his forehead squeezed together, more pronounced. He bit at the corner of his lip.

"Thomas," he said, in a barely audible whisper. "Please read from Deuteronomy for me." Ivanov asked for, and I gave him, my Bible. He sat there with it in hand waiting for instruction. "Thomas, please read Deuteronomy 31:17-18 for me," Zarathustra II then said, as he lowered his head into his hands and laced his fingers through his hair. Ivanov turned some pages and then stopped.

"Here it is," he said. Then he cleared his throat. "'On that day I will become angry with them and forsake them; I will hide my face from them and they will be destroyed. Many disasters and difficulties will come upon them, and on that day they will ask, 'Have not these disasters come upon us because our God is not with us?' And I will certainly hide my face on that day because of all their wickedness in turning to other gods.'" Ivanov stopped. He kept the page open. Zarathustra kept his head in his hands seated on the sofa. His own face was hidden from us.

"Read me Deuteronomy 32:20," Zarathustra II then said, in a voice that was a fragmented mumble. Ivanov turned the page of the Bible. His finger ran down the page.

"'I will hide my face from them,'" he read, "'and see what their end will be; for they are a perverse generation, children who are unfaithful.'" Ivanov again stopped and looked up. I moved closer, protective, standing next to Zarathustra II.

"Read me 2 Kings 17:22 and 23," Zarathustra II said. Thomas flipped a section of the Bible. "'The Israelites persisted in all the sins of Jerobaum and did not turn away from them until the Lord removed his presence as he had warned....'" Zarathustra II interrupted, "that's enough."

"I was thinking about your question of why God disappears," Ivanov said, in an effort to pull Zarathustra II out of his well of despair. Zarathustra II did not respond. "Here is what I was thinking: maybe you could say that God has periodically disappeared so that the false images of Him created by mankind will crumble by His non-responsiveness," Ivanov offered. Zarathustra II fidgeted on the sofa. "You know the superhero type image. He can't be a superhero if He never does anything, if he never shows up to save the day," Ivanov concluded.

"Read me Micah 3:4," Zarathustra II then said, ignoring Ivanov's lifeline. I had not ever read Micah and did not recall it being a book in the Bible. Ivanov fumbled with the index to find where it was in the Bible, as I looked over his shoulder. He shifted the Bible in his hands.

"'Then they will cry out to the Lord, but he will not answer them. At that time he will hide his face from them because of the evil they have done,'" Ivanov read. Zarathustra II laid down, gently, painfully, on the sofa. He pulled his legs in tight into a fetal position.

"Jeremiah 33:5," he said quietly.

Ivanov turned pages and read. "'I will hide my face from this city because of all its wickedness.'" Ivanov stopped.

"Psalm 10," Zarathustra II said. Ivanov handed me the Bible. He also seemed distraught, as if through some osmosis he had absorbed Zarathustra II's anguish. I fumbled with it and found the Psalm.

"'Why, O Lord do you stand far off? Why do you hide yourself in times of trouble?'" I read.

"Psalm 44:24," Zarathustra II said softly. I turned a few pages and read.

"'Why do you hide your face and forget our misery and oppression.'" Zarathustra II was weeping and shivering. I set the Bible down and went and got a blanket from my bedroom and returned to cover him. Ivanov sat in front of him, worried about his friend, staring at the ground.

Then Ivanov stood up and moved a few feet from where Zarathustra II lay. Zarathustra II was still shaking a bit from the chills. I reached over, tucked in the corners around him, and made sure the blanket covered him completely. Ivanov cleared his throat, straightened up his shoulders, cocked his head from side to side, as if preparing for a physical confrontation, and brushed some hair off his forehead. He pulled a sheet of paper filled with handwriting out of his pocket and began to read from it.

"'Is it really so difficult simply to accept,'" Ivanov recited, in a sonorous tone, "'what is considered truth in the circle of one's relatives and of many good men, and what moreover really comforts and elevates man?'" Zarathustra II stretched out his legs and slowly sat up. His lips trembled. Zarathustra II wiped his tears with the back of his hand.

"'Is that more difficult than to strike new paths, fighting the habitual, experiencing the insecurity of independence and the frequent wavering of one's feelings and even one's conscience, proceeding often without consolidation,'" Ivanov continued to recite. Zarathustra II then smiled broadly, red eyed, while looking at Ivanov.

Ivanov's tone changed a bit to be more assertive. "'Here the ways of men part; if you wish to strive for peace of soul and pleasure then believe; if you wish to be a devotee of truth, then inquire,'" Ivanov concluded, still standing straight.

"Nietzsche!" Zarathustra II yelled, tossing the blanket aside, as he jumped up clapping. He wiped his tears once more and hugged Ivanov.

"Thank you," Zarathustra II said, holding Ivanov close to him. "Thank you," he repeated with his head firmly against Ivanov's chest. I saw tears well up in his eyes again, but there was no mistake, these were tears of joy.

"You have reminded me of something else Nietzsche wrote," Zarathustra II then said more composed, as he stepped back from Ivanov. "'A very popular error: having the courage of one's convictions; rather, it is a matter of having the courage for an attack on one's convictions,'" he said. "I had almost forgotten," he said. "Thank you," Zarathustra II said again, momentarily redeemed, as if he could not say it enough.

In my childhood home, Reverend Jessie was also reading the Bible as part of his attempt to read it in its entirety one more time before the storm. But he was not focused on passages about God disappearing. Reverend Jessie was reading Revelation. He read out loud. "'I saw heaven standing open and there before me was white horse, whose rider is called Faithful and True. With justice he judges and makes war.'"

Chapter 76
SNOWFLAKE

John Roland Reynolds was just waking up. The last twenty four hours were something of an alcohol induced blur to him. He looked around from the strange bed on which he was lying and saw a half naked male body next to him asleep. This much he did remember. He smiled. He had brought a young man with him to the guest bedroom, which the Bourbon Pub and Parade had given him to use during his stay. The bedroom was part of the third floor apartment at the bar, above the disco.

Nim was the young man's name, but as John Roland Reynolds recalled, he had jokingly said, "Just call me Snowflake." "Oh boy!" John Roland Reynolds thought as he sat up and held his head in his hands, and then lightly rubbed the fog from his temples with the palms of his hands. The young man stirred.

"Good morning Snowflake."

"Good morning," Snowflake replied with a yawn. "Are you ready for your big day? For your coronation?"

"Should be fun."

"I don't guess it's as exciting as winning big football games in front of thousands of people."

"In some ways it's more exciting."

"How's that?"

"I'll actually feel like I belong here."

"Belong?" Snowflake asked rhetorically. "Is that ever possible?"

"Yea, that tension between the need to feel you belong and trying to remain authentic. I have struggled with it my whole life."

"Authentic---and autonomous. Same thing--right?" Snowflake asked.

"Maybe. It's probably not reconcilable. But one can always hope," Reynolds proffered skeptically.

"So you don't just look good in a dress and a football uniform. You can think also?" Snowflake flirted.

"Years of psychotherapy."

"You are full of good surprises. Maybe this lasts longer than a weekend."

"We'll see. Gotta get my legs under me again."

Reynolds got out of bed and walked naked toward the bathroom. John Roland Reynolds turned his body slightly on the way to the shower to step over a set of pom poms that lay on the floor.

Chapter 77
CLARIFY

Reverend Jessie had his secretary Dolores contact all twelve of those he had chosen and advise them to meet him at the CRC at 4:00 that afternoon, before heading to the French Quarter to stand in the storm. But there was a problem. Dolores was unable to reach all twelve. In particular she had to leave a message at the home of Spook Johnson. No-one had answered at his house only the voice mail picked up with the message: "You have reached the home of Mr. and Mrs. Thaddeus Johnson. Please leave your name and number at the tone. Have a blessed day."

When 4:00 came only 8 of the 12 chosen by Reverend Jessie had arrived at the CRC. Phillip Harvey Harrison, Timothy Mark Daigre, Spook Johnson and John Henry Calvin were not present. The men all met in a classroom usually used for teaching Sunday school classes. Those in attendance were seated in school desks and Reverend Jessie was at the front of the class, perspiring, leaning heavily on the teacher's desk.

"Men, we will wait for the other four before we get too far into this, but thanks for coming on time," Reverend Jessie said. Bartholomew Davidson stood up and then sat down and raised his hand as if in class.

"Yes, Bart," Reverend Jessie said, as the others turned tightly in their seats to look at Mr. Davidson.

"Reverend, no offense intended, but how sure are you about what the Lord told you?" he asked. Reverend Jessie smiled awkwardly and moved sluggishly away from the teacher's desk.

"Bart, you sound like that street bum with a question like that," he replied, referring pejoratively to Zarathustra II.

"Well, we trust you. You have ministered to most of us in our times of need and I feel like I need to support you on this, but you are asking a lot of us," Mr. Augustine then said. There were a few uncertain murmurs of concurrence, but these were quickly quieted.

"I appreciate that. But I'm not asking anything of you, the Lord is doing the asking. And remember I am going to be there with you," Reverend Jessie replied.

"I wish I was as free of spiritual doubt as you are. It is rather remarkable," Mr. Augustine said, with a touch of admiration.

"Intellect doubts. Faith doesn't. I'm human. I have had my moments of doubt over the years. My wife reminded me of that forcefully the other day. But God has given me my resolve," Reverend Jessie replied.

"Can you clarify how faithful you have to be in order to merit His protection? I mean I'm not a minister," Mr. Scott asked. Just then Timothy Mark Daigre came walking in.

"Sorry I'm late," he said, "but I was helping Spook load up his van."

"Well is he coming?" Reverend Jessie asked surprised.

"No. He is driving his wife and kids and my wife to Houston," Mr. Daigre said sitting down. "They are meeting up with some other members of the Comus Mardi Gras Krewe at a Houston hotel to wait the storm out there."

Reverend Jessie could not believe it. "I don't believe this!" he said involuntarily. John Henry Calvin then walked in slowly. Mr. Calvin moved at as graceful a pace as his advanced age would allow. He had shocks of white hair on both sides of his head, which had thinned to almost nothing at the forefront and a bushy white mustache. He looked a bit like a miniature Albert Einstein.

"Excuse my lateness," he said formally, and then he slowly lowered himself into a school desk chair. "Before I forget," John Henry Calvin said, just remembering there was something else he had to say. "Phillip isn't coming."

"Why not?" Reverend Jessie asked agitated.

"He did not say," Mr. Calvin responded deliberately. "Just called me this morning and said to be sure that I told you he would not be here."

Reverend Jessie's face reddened. He looked around the room as if he might find the other two men hidden there. There would only be ten.

Chapter 78
HUBIG PIES

There was a brief knock at my front door and then Ivanov opened the door and let himself in. I was startled by his appearance. He had shaved off most of his hair. He left a 2-3 inch strip of hair on the top of his head in a Mohawk. The remaining hair, the Mohawk, was spiked with some kind of gel and sticking straight up. The tips of his black hair were dyed blonde. The shaved sides of his head were very pale. It also looked like he had dark lines of mascara painted around his eye lids.

"Whoa! What did you do?" I asked instantly.

"Going for the *Green Day* early punk look," he said. "Shiloh came by my place last night to shave my head and she used some gel to make the hair at the top stand up and dyed the tips for me," Ivanov said, by way of explanation. I noticed that on one side of his head, in the shaved area, the word "Bakunin" was written. On the other side of his head in letters that leaned forward, "Zarathustra the Second" was written.

"Are those tattoos?" I asked, incredulous.

"Marks a lot. Shiloh did it for me. I asked her to write it," Ivanov replied.

Zarathustra II did not seem to immediately notice Ivanov. He nervously paced up and down in my living room. He had his hands behind his back indifferently and his trench coat was buttoned up because he was cold. Ivanov walked over and sat on the sofa watching him attentively. I remained standing near a bar stool by the kitchen counter, but with a cautious concerned eye on him as well. Suddenly, Zarathustra II stopped pacing and lowered himself to the floor harshly and kneeled. He then leaned over further and in the child's pose of Yoga, or like a Muslim facing Mecca, put his face in the carpet and his hands flat on the ground, above his head.

"Take this cup from me," he said three times in a row to the floor, but loud enough for us to hear him. He lay in that position for another minute.

"How do you feel about your pending death?" Ivanov asked, playfully, trying to draw him out. Zarathustra II sat up, looked at Ivanov, and put his hand over his mouth considering the question.

"All of life is a preparation for death, especially if you have lived philosophically."

"You have done that, I think," Ivanov replied, affirming something he felt Zarathustra II needed.

"Let's have a final glass of wine and a meal," Zarathustra II then said, standing, suddenly more relaxed. I walked over and opened the refrigerator door. There was a half filled quart of Welch's grape juice and a Hubig's pie in the refrigerator, still in its wrapper. I don't know how the Hubig pie got in the refrigerator and didn't remember buying it. I looked at the wrapper. The expiration date on the Hubig pies was two days prior. I took the grape juice and Hubig's pie and put them on the counter. Ivanov got up and found some paper plates. He opened the Hubig's pie wrapper and lifted the Hubig's pie out and broke it into 3 pieces. Each of us got a piece of Hubig's pie on a paper plate.

I was not able to find any clean glasses. However, before I realized it, Zarathustra II removed the top off the bottle of grape juice and took a big swallow out of the bottle. "Ahhh," he said, before belching "gooood" out loudly. He then handed the bottle to Ivanov who also took a swig and belched much more ineffectively. Some of the juice dripped down Ivanov's chin. He handed the bottle to me and I took a sip. Zarathustra II took a step back from us.

"As Bukowski has written: 'This thing upon me, crawling like a snake, terrifying my love of commonness...it's not death, but dying will solve its power,'" Zarathustra II recited. "I wish I had time to sit and re-read some of his poetry one last time," Zarathustra II then said. He shoved his entire piece of Hubig pie into his mouth at once. Ivanov and I ate our portions without responding. Zarathustra II gently removed his gray notepad, pencils and pencil sharpener from his trench coat pocket. He held the notebook in his hands tenderly, ceremoniously, and looked at it for a long moment.

"This is for you Luke, take it to remember me by," he said, as he placed it on the kitchen counter with the cover marked **Zarathustra the Second** facing up. Ivanov and I looked at each other knowing what this could signify.

"I'll keep my copy of *Thus Spoke Zarathustra* with me for now. By the way nice haircut. It reminds me of *The Last of the Mohicans*," Zarathustra II then said to Ivanov, without emotion. We departed in silence a minute later for the French Quarter.

Chapter 79
100 MILES DUE NORTH

The Bourbon Pub and Parade and Oz, were each packed with patrons. Both bars, in competition, had decided to charge $100 per head for an all you could drink hurricane party to ride out the hurricane. It would be a miniature Southern Decadence Festival/Hurricane Bera party, a thumbing of the nose to mother nature and to those who, out of proclaimed righteousness, thought the festival was cancelled. The coronation of Queen John Roland Reynolds would go forward inside the Bourbon Pub and Parade and the spirits would roll. The rest of the French Quarter was closed.

With its usual flair the Bourbon Pub and Parade had hastily faxed party invitations to the Governor, the Mayor, and all of the New Orleans City Council. The quickly put together invitation said: "Come drink and be Mary during the storm." The Governor's office actually replied to the RSVP indicating that he could not make it as he was out of town for a Republican fundraiser.

A few blocks away Reverend Jessie and the ten men walked hurriedly up Bourbon Street from Canal Street, in the gloaming of a light rain, towards the two bars. Bertrand Finch and his cameraman waited at the corner across from Oz. Newspaper reporters from the *Times Picayune* and *The Advocate* stood nearby. Standing on the opposite corner Zarathustra II was pacing back and forth. Ivanov and I were standing next to him. I felt out of place. My heart beat heavily. I couldn't believe we were doing this.

Under his poncho Ivanov wore a white T-shirt upon which was written in black acrylic, "Chalmette High School Anarchist Club."

"Is that original one that got you in trouble?" I asked.

"Yep."

Mrs. Rosemary Matthews and my mother were in Atlanta, at her cousin Marvin's place, eating popcorn and watching the Weather Channel. Ms. Lemoine and Ms. Dagny had checked into the hotel next to the bars with the businessman from Texas. The eye of Hurricane Bera was about 100 miles due north of Biloxi, Mississippi. The eye was currently projected to make landfall somewhere between Biloxi and Houma, Louisiana. The outer bands of the storm were dumping heavy rains on lower Plaquemine and St. Bernard parish. The tidal surge at the coast was already 30 feet high. Hurricane Bera was a category 5 storm. It was moving at 12 mph with winds exceeding 160 miles per hour.

John Roland Reynolds stepped out of the shower. His dress from the night before was on the floor. His gown for his night as Drag Queen of the Festival was hanging up in the closet. His diamond studded tiara was on the coffee table.

Chapter 80
WHAT'S WRONG JAMES?

As they approached within a block of the two bars, Bartholomew Davidson called out from the back for the group to stop. Mr. Davidson pointed back from where the group had just come, as the rest of the men, preoccupied, turned to face him. A lone figure was a half block or so behind them, walking very slowly and unsteadily, in the darkened rainy day, trying to catch up. It was the elderly John Henry Calvin, laboring heavily on his walking cane. James Simon Scott took the opportunity of this pause to approach Reverend Jessie.

"Can I ask you something, privately?" he said quietly, hoping not to be heard by the others. Reverend Jessie was distracted, looking back at Mr. Calvin struggling towards them.

"Sure," he said without forethought. Mr. Scott led Reverend Jessie by the arm off the street, where everyone was waiting, to stand under a sign that had *Tropical Isle* painted on it. Mr. Scott seemed nervous. Wind gusts now accompanied the rainfall.

"Reverend Jessie, I am not sure God can protect me," he exclaimed.

"What?" Reverend Jessie asked, looking at him incredulously, as if he was noticing him for the first time.

"Well, I am not without sin, you know," he said, fumbling with his words. Reverend Jessie seemed flustered by the remark and turned away to check on Mr. Calvin's progress. He did not respond to Mr. Scott. Suddenly

Mr. Scott kneeled down in front of Reverend Jessie as Reverend Jessie turned back to face him.

"I can't be protected. I'm an adulterer," Mr. Scott whispered. He may have been crying. Reverend Jessie could not tell because rain was on the face of both men.

"With whom?" Reverend Jessie involuntarily asked.

"Your secretary Dolores," Mr. Scott stammered. James Simon Scott stayed there kneeling and Reverend Jessie stood above him.

"What should I do? Stay or go?" James Simon Scott asked haltingly. "Reverend, I can't die, I have a wife and kids to think about," he then finished awkwardly.

"An adulterer?" Reverend Jessie muttered. He looked away from Mr. Scott and ran his entire hand over his face.

Mr. Calvin had now caught up with the rest of the disciples. "This is good exercise," he said to those around him. "Sorry to slow you good men down." They all turned as one and saw Reverend Jessie off to the side helping Mr. Scott get up from his knees. The disciples walked over toward them.

"Better put our rain coats on now men," Reverend Jessie said to all, resuming his leadership role, as if, for the moment, James Simon Scott's confession had rolled off of him like the rain which was falling. Mr. Daigre took off the canvas rucksack on his back and pulled out some red ponchos. He passed these out. Everyone put one on except Reverend Jessie. James Simon Scott stood a few steps away from the group like a child punished in time out. His head was hung down, culpable, and his shoulders drooped.

"What's wrong James?" Saul Fierke asked him innocently.

"Nothing," Reverend Jessie said affirmatively, speaking for Mr. Scott, as ministers have always spoken for vulnerable souls in the shadow lands, whom they believe are entrusted to their care. "I have decided that James needs to go home now before it is too late. It is not in God's plan for him to be with us tonight," he announced to the men, unsure himself, as a knot tightened in his stomach. The other men became confused.

"Why does he get to go home and not me?" an agitated Martin Luther Blanchfield then asked. Mr. Blanchfield, a man I once heard Mrs. Rosemary Matthews describe as having 'a big brain but no opinion,' was apparently having second thoughts about the whole endeavor.

"It is not his time," Reverend Jessie said somberly, without further explanation.

"What does that mean?" Blanchfield asked combatively, while the others remained silent, reflective, looking away from the collision. "I want to know why you say he gets to go home!" Blanchfield demanded, like an undisciplined child in conflict with a more favored sibling and seeking a parent's ruling on the matter. Reverend Jessie stood pensive. He felt the rain on his face, perhaps he thought of my mother.

"We have a right to know!" Blanchfield then said more confrontationally to Reverend Jessie. Reverend Jessie turned to walk away from the fight. At that moment James Simon Scott spoke up, like furniture overturning in a moving truck.

"Because I confessed I had sex with Dolores," he said. The wind swirled with hollow condemnation. The rain continued to fall, gently. A few of the men lowered their heads and moved, involuntarily, closer together. Mr. Blanchfield stood apart from the group, restless, and moved towards it grudgingly.

The men kept silent and did not speak to James Simon Scott. But John Henry Calvin spoke up. His hearing was not that good and the rain, wind and music from the clubs up the street made it hard for him to hear.

"What's this about singing a chorus?" he asked softly of Norton Augustine.

"No chorus today," Mr. Augustine replied reassuringly.

Chapter 81
LIKE CHAFF

As the rain fell, a sulking James Simon Scott shuffled away from the nine remaining men and Reverend Jessie. All were now huddled together, like primitive men confounded by a god of nature they did not understand, against the wind and rain of the approaching storm. The wind blew part of the back of his poncho over Mr. Scott's shoulder. He did not reach back to pull it down. He stopped, seemingly unsure, guilt ridden, about 20 feet from the group of men who were watching him. With his slump shouldered back to them he looked up, dejected, exposed, at the sky.

Martin Luther Blanchfield suddenly left the group of disciples and walked briskly toward him. "I'm going to drive him home," he said loudly, without looking back at the group of men for their approval. No-one tried to stop him from walking off. He quickly caught up with James Simon Scott. Neither spoke to the other. As the two of them walked away together, with suddenly long silent but hurried strides, the remaining eight men, and Reverend Jessie, looked at them through one uncertain eye.

God had not told Reverend Jessie anything about people not showing up, about choosing an adulterer, or possible defections in the ranks of those once chosen. Perhaps, he thought it was a test; one of those things about God he used to say we should never try to understand. The remaining men looked to him now for direction, however unsure these events momentarily made him. Their lives were in his hands and they trusted that his relationship with the Lord was as solid as he claimed. They each hoped fervently that it was God who had previously spoken to Reverend Jessie about standing together in the storm and not, just a voice in his head masquerading as God. At least all the disciples except John Henry Calvin had such thoughts. John Henry Calvin stared out vacantly, but not because he was unthinking or uncaring. Rather, he was chilled and wet and developing a mild case of hypothermia.

Reverend Jessie then steeled himself, as he had been taught by his father to do with other disappointments in his life, exhaled any doubt, and took three strong crystalline steps towards the two departing men, separating himself from the group of disciples. Facing the two men he held up his Bible in his right hand and, like shedding the husks covering grains of rice, proclaimed his verdict: "They are like chaff that the wind blows away." He turned swiftly back, forgetting James Simon Scott and Martin Luther Blanchfield, as if they were never there. "Let's go," he then said forcefully. The men, however hesitant, followed him.

Chapter 82
HEARING VOICES

As soon as Reverend Jessie and the eight remaining men approached the corner, where the Bourbon Pub and Oz were located, Bertrand Finch waved Reverend Jessie and Zarathustra II over to the stools that he had set up for the TV interviews. Several newspaper reporters present gathered round with their recorders. The sun with its six billion years left before extinguishing, if cosmology was correct, was blacked out by dark apocalyptic clouds; the universal in life, as is so often the case, blocked by the parochial. A light rain continued to fall. There were occasional heavy wind gusts. Bertrand Finch noticed Reverend Jessie was short a few of his twelve disciples. He got Reverend Jessie to sit down on the stool on his left and had Zarathustra II sit on the stool on his right, though intermittently, without apparent reason, Zarathustra II kept springing up and then sitting down. A lone cameraman shouldering a battery operated camera began to film. Reverend Jessie stared, in parental bewilderment, at Ivanov's Mohawk.

"I thought there were going to be twelve who joined you," the reporter for *The Advocate* asked Reverend Jessie.

"I lost some along the way," Reverend Jessie apologized, vaguely, not meeting the reporter's gaze.

"Listen, I'm asking the questions. This is my exclusive interview. You can take notes or tape record it, but don't ask questions," Finch rebuffed the reporter.

"Before the weather deteriorates further let's get started," Bertrand Finch then said, quickly, to all present. Ivanov and I stood by Zarathustra

II's side. The remaining eight men did the same, more leisurely, on Reverend Jessie's side. Mr. Henry looked pale, smiled weakly at me, leaning on his cane and with his other hand on Mr. Norton's forearm to steady himself. Reverend Jessie did not acknowledge my presence.

"Let's start with you Zarathustra. You have predicted that the hurricane will devastate New Orleans and that you, me and Reverend Jessie will all die. Your prediction about the hurricane hitting New Orleans has been proven true. People want to know how do you know these things? Where did this prophecy come from?" Bertrand Finch asked bluntly. Zarathustra II got up off his stool and softly touched his forehead with his right index finger.

"Voices," he said, with his own voice cracking, tangled in ambiguity, and then sat down again, without explaining.

"Are you telling us that God speaks to you?" Bertrand Finch asked, in an overly dramatic fashion, clutching his microphone tightly, while the cameraman did a close up of him. The newspaper reporters leaned in next to Zarathustra II to record his answer.

"God is no longer here," Zarathustra II answered, in a flat monotone voice, as he stood up again. "The voices I hear are my own. The one that told me the storm was going to hit New Orleans I call Samuel. The one that told me of our deaths I call Coriolanus," he said, still standing stiffly, in military formation for inspection, and looking straight ahead away from Finch.

Bertrand Finch seemed surprised by Zarathustra II's response, like he had peeled back the seal of a much anticipated dessert only to find it had spoiled.

"Voices?" Finch mumbled, baffled, hoping he heard incorrectly. The newspaper reporters glanced warily at each other.

"Yes. These are the voices that sometimes rattle around loosely, unchained, in my head. But I listen to them, because they are usually right, or as right as anyone else's voices."

Finch hesitated, unsure, and then turned to Reverend Jessie. Reverend Jessie's lips were pursed and he was shaking his head in disbelief at Zarathustra II's response.

"God has told you that you and your disciples, however many there are now, will be...will be protected by Him from the storm, correct," Bertrand Finch asked.

"The fact is that the righteous never have anything to fear," Reverend Jessie said in a very composed and commanding manner, but in a way that suddenly seemed rehearsed to me. I had heard him preach my entire life, knew the rise and fall of his voice, the placement of emphasis and the pregnant pause in his sermons. Something was missing.

"Noah was a righteous man!" Zarathustra II interrupted, in a voice that suggested that the threads in the seams of his character, which society had picked at for years, had finally unraveled. "And Nietzsche said, 'there are no facts only interpretation,'" he spilled forth while he remained standing.

Bertrand Finch paused again. He stared away from both men for a moment. Then he continued his conversation with Reverend Jessie.

"Tell us about your conversation with God," Bertrand Finch asked him. Reverend Jessie calmly leaned forward.

"It was not a conversation as you might envision. I felt His presence. I did not see Him. I saw light. He told me of the pending hurricane and its destruction. And I, like Abraham before me, asked, 'Will you sweep away the righteous with the wicked?' And He answered me, 'No, the truly faithful will be spared.'"

"So those harmed in this storm are being punished by God?" Bertrand Finch asked.

"The wicked are all destined for punishment," Reverend Jessie answered firmly and without hesitation, but again seeming to be merely reciting something from a mechanized memory. "And eventually all the wicked will be punished and the elect will be raptured to heaven," Reverend Jessie concluded.

Finch turned, reluctantly, on his stool to face Zarathustra II, who was now seated with his hands in his pockets, his eyes wide, but unfocused.

"Is the destruction of the storm because of the Southern Decadence Festival?" Finch asked tentatively, worried about the response he would receive.

Zarathustra II stood up again, like he was being reprimanded for talking in class by the school disciplinarian. "No, it's because it is a category 5 storm," he replied and then sat down with his hands still in his pockets.

"So the immorality which Reverend Jessie complains about is not a factor," he asked Zarathustra II, still unsettled.

"There is no such thing as the immorality he preaches," Zarathustra II said, standing again and gesturing. "It's just people choosing between apples, oranges and coconuts."

Bertrand Finch sat uncomfortably quiet for a moment. Reverend Jessie looked down at the ground. I saw several of the men with him shake their heads. Mr. Henry continued to lean more heavily into Mr. Augustine for support. Ivanov, staring directly at Reverend Jessie, reached over and placed a reassuring hand on Zarathustra II's shoulder, in a subtle role reversal, as if he was the father and Zarathustra II was the child. Instinctively, I also placed my hand on Zarathustra II's other shoulder. Reverend Jessie, for the first time, looked up directly at me, and then at Ivanov.

"Mr. Finch, you have played this game of setting this poor fellow against me for your own purposes long enough. You try to present us as equals, or me as the bigger fool. But let me make one thing clear to you. I don't guess when I speak of the Bible. I don't guess when I talk about God's instructions. I know these things. Do you understand?" Reverend Jessie said forcefully, regaining the judging ministerial voice I knew well. Zarathustra II slowly stood up with our hands still on his shoulders.

"As it is written in the Tao-Te-Ching, 'He who thinks he knows, doesn't know. He who knows that he doesn't know, knows,'" Zarathustra II recited.

"Oh! Cut it out! You have filled up your soul with empty words from other people's lives, and maybe you were even a smart man at some point, but you have lost your way. You are intelligent enough to know that reason cannot provide the answers to spiritual questions. And all you are doing now, with your predictions, is undermining the people who need something to believe in. You may not think you need it, but they do,"

Reverend Jessie lectured Zarathustra II, but with a tinge of compassion. I was surprised.

"And you, Reverend, have an entrenched Old Testament view of people. You can see heaven only from the depths of hell. You use the Word as punishment and prey upon people's deepest resentments, their insecurities, and you give them intolerance as their cure and prejudice to believe in! You teach them that Christianity is nothing but a listing of people to disapprove of! A fraudulent way to deal with people! You don't build them up, you keep them in their infancy!" Zarathustra II yelled back angrily.

Whatever crushing weight had been pushing down on Zarathustra II, making him emotional and erratic, left him. He accepted his crushing truths and the consequences. Zarathustra II relaxed under our collective touch. He breathed, tranquil, and paused thoughtfully, and then seemed to focus. His mood changed as he spoke, as if some implanted medication pump had finally issued forth the proper dosage. He had seemed different to me since this interview began. He had vacillated between confusion, anger, and falling apart. But now, just as quickly, he became poised, serious and composed.

"He doesn't know his Bible very well," Zarathustra II said to Bertrand Finch, while pointing a finger at Reverend Jessie. His tone became professorial, but calmly defiant. Then Zarathustra II took a confrontational step towards Reverend Jessie. Reverend Jessie sat up straight expecting to be hit. Zarathustra II then spoke directly to Reverend Jessie in a voice suddenly full, and as if no-one else was present.

"Nietzsche wrote that we should 'distrust all in whom the impulse to punish is powerful,' and that seems to be you. You are also a smart man, struggling perhaps with a role you inherited from your father. You seem to me to be in a lot of personal pain with the alienation of your son and wife, which you don't understand, but your response is a desperate need to find fault in others, instead of examining yourself. You then herald to others your finding of their supposed fault and cloak it in religious garments, like it is some treasure that you have personally unearthed. It is resentment and personal despair which fuel your moral judgment of others. But beneath it all, it is just a reflection of you turning away from the failure you find in yourself and cannot face." At that point Zarathustra II paused. He moved further away from Ivanov and I and placed his hand on Reverend Jessie's shoulder. Reverend Jessie immediately brushed his hand away, but did not look up at Zarathustra II.

He then stepped back towards his stool and sat down. Ivanov placed his hand back on Zarathustra II's shoulder.

Reverend Jessie slouched his shoulders. His eyes saddened. I wondered if it was accurate; if he had seen something in Reverend Jessie, some personal projection, that I, as a son, desiring approval, had missed all those years. Reverend Jessie stared at Zarathustra II seeking to unnerve him, or perhaps still considering what Zarathustra II had said. Bertrand Finch interrupted the silence.

"You do not agree with him about the cause of the storm---correct?" Finch interjected. Reverend Jessie's stare turned to a slight smile, or maybe it was also a sneer, and his eyes brightened again, suddenly re-charged.

"Of course not. The Bible is very clear," Reverend Jessie said routinely, a memorized line, pushing the Bible in his hand toward Bertrand Finch's chest, but not relinquishing it when Finch put his hand out expecting to receive it. "The eyes of the Lord are everywhere, keeping watch on the wicked and the good. God will not stand these abominations," Reverend Jessie said, now pointing with his Bible at the Bourbon Pub and Parade and then at Oz.

"These are people!" Zarathustra II yelled back angrily and standing up again "It's your constant condemnation that is an abomination!"

An outer band of Hurricane Bera started to come through the French Quarter. The rain stopped for a moment, but the wind gusts picked up. A strong gust blew over the desk which Finch had been sitting behind and knocked him off his stool. The wind pushed the desk on top of him and then 20 or so feet down Bourbon Street. The desk ran away, breaking against the concrete, in skips and hops, like a pebble thrown by a child across the expanse of a pond, until it completely smashed in pieces against the brick front of the *Tropical Isle*. Bertrand Finch tried quickly to grab the top of his head. His toupee had come detached on one side from the wind, and then it blew off completely, as he covered his bald head with his hand. He stood up and chased it gangly, childishly, for a few feet, but it got caught in the swirl of a wind gust and blew away.

Reverend Jessie's remaining group of men moved away from the interview and huddled together in their ponchos, in the middle of Bourbon Street, against the wind. Reverend Jessie walked over deliberately to join them. Bertrand Finch walked back towards Oz with his cameraman.

"Don't film me anymore. No more!" he told the camera man, agitated by the loss of his toupee. Zarathustra II stood in front of the stool he had been sitting on. It soon blew over as did the other stools. We watched as they were blown away from us.

Chapter 83
MY PROCLAMATION

Inside the Bourbon Pub and Parade, on the second floor, the official coronation ceremony of John Roland Reynolds, as Festival Drag Queen, had begun. It seemed an odd island of curious formality in the midst of the gathering chaos outside. To the tune of "It's Raining Men," by the Weather Girls, John Roland Reynolds walked down stairs to the first floor and then across a short red carpet, dressed in a green sequined dress wearing a Marilyn Monroe blonde wig, a fake diamond necklace, diamond earrings and opera length white gloves. On each side of him he was escorted by two muscular young men dressed in gold lame' togas with their skin painted silver, as Royal Pages. One of the young men was Nimrod "Snowflake" Rassher.

John Roland Reynolds was handed a bouquet of white roses and a faux diamond crusted scepter by the club's manager. Snowflake stepped in front of him and placed a rhinestone tiara snugly on John Roland Reynolds' wig covered head and kissed him on the cheek, placing his claim. John Roland Reynolds waved the scepter with one of his glove covered hands at the crowd who cheered and clapped in response. The music stopped for a moment and John Roland Reynolds was handed a microphone.

"Let the festival begin," he said, "that's my proclamation!" The music began again and people began to dance.

Outside the weather played a darker maniacal melody, and it was worsening. One of the patrons inside the Pub had written a message on a bed sheet that he had tied to the second floor balcony railing. It flapped restlessly in the wind and read:

Reverend Jessie
come out of your closet
and play.

Zarathustra II stepped out with purpose, from under the Bourbon Pub balcony, and walked to the center of the street like he was approaching a lectern to deliver an opening lecture to an incoming college class. He stopped a few feet in front of Reverend Jessie and his disciples. Reverend Jessie watched him closely. Zarathustra II smiled to the absent class, brought them to attention by tapping on his imagined lectern and, with the wind blowing and the rain increasing, he answered the weather, as if it were a primitive god, quoting King Lear:

Blow, winds, and crack your cheeks! Rage! Blow! You cataracts and hurricanes spout till you have drenched our steeples, drowned the cocks!

Zarathustra II paused. His courage may have momentarily deserted him as a strong gust of wind blew angrily in reply and almost knocked him over. As we all watched he regained his balance and shook his fist at the sky in defiance.

Chapter 84
COME INSIDE

As Zarathustra II lectured in the street, and the weather slowly worsened, Ivanov and I, huddled against each other for support, and walked over and leaned against the side of the Bourbon Orleans, the hotel on the opposite street corner, trying to get out of the biting wind. In an increasing rain I saw Ms. Dagny and Ms. Lemoine walking slowly towards us. At first I did not recognize them. Both were dressed sharply in the starched black tunic, woolen belt and white habits of Catholic nuns. A tall man wearing a priest's black cassock, white collar and a cowboy's hat, held a large green golf umbrella above their heads. Ms. Dagny leaned into him, patted him gently on the chest, several times and he stopped several yards from us. While she stayed under the umbrella snuggled up against him, Ms. Lemoine walked over to us.

"Why don't ya come inside the hotel and get out the rain?" Ms. Lemoine said to Ivanov. There was no seduction in her words, just a simple poetic request, that reflected her concern.

"I can't Little Love," Ivanov told her, with a private smile. She reached out and grabbed his hand and squeezed it.

"I'm worried about you," she said.

"I'll be alright," he replied.

"There are no Howard Roarks, you dip-shit! This is just a big dick contest between the two preachers! And they ain't no more preachers than we are nuns! Life is all play acting you dumbass...Pick a part, you heard me! You're an atheist. Why do you give a shit?" Ms. Dagny yelled, across the expanse of the rain and wind to Ivanov.

"Because he is a friend of mine," he replied softly, more to Ms. Lemoine than to Ms. Dagny.

Ms. Lemoine lingered for awhile longer in the rain. She then let go of his hand and walked a step back, toward Ms. Dagny and the gentleman with the umbrella.

"Hey, Big Love. I learned one of those quotes the preacher man is so fond of," Ms. Lemoine then said to Ivanov, as she turned back slightly in his direction.

"What's that?" he asked quietly, but with another intimate smile.

"'A man is a God in ruins,'" she said slowly. "It's by Emerson," she concluded, before placing a tootsie-pop back in her mouth. Ivanov did not respond, but continued to smile at her.

"We are in room 383 if you change your mind, dumbass!" Ms. Dagny yelled back to Ivanov, as the winds picked up again. Ms. Dagny and the gentleman dressed as a priest turned, as Ms. Lemoine joined them, and walked back swiftly, against the wind, to the hotel.

Chapter 85
A FEW CANDLES

Zarathustra II lay curled up on the sidewalk near Oz. He was wet and shivering. Ivanov and I were both seated, bunched tightly against the side of the Bourbon Orleans. Bertrand Finch, his cameraman and others were standing inside of Oz, watching through the glass paned doors and waiting in anticipation for something noteworthy to happen. The cameraman periodically stepped outside, when weather allowed, and filmed Zarathustra II in the street, or Reverend Jessie and his disciples.

Reverend Jessie and his disciples were standing in the middle of Bourbon Street about 25 feet from the entrances of the two clubs. The rain was now coming down in sheets. It was blinding at times. The disciples were huddled together in a circle holding on to each other. Their red ponchos flapped and rustled painfully against their bodies. A flash of lightning and the sound of thunder occurred several blocks away. The electricity in the French Quarter flickered and then it went out.

The Bourbon Pub and Parade's recently installed propane generator became operational. Within a couple of moments of the lightning strike the Bourbon Pub and Parade's electricity was back on. Oz, like the rest of the French Quarter, and perhaps the city, was dark. The bartenders at Oz lit a few candles.

The wind and rain then formed a unified voice and it howled. The voice was unhappy, dungeon like, and pained, like it was coerced into being here. The sky was an unnatural black licorice color. It was too dark to make out the shape of the clouds. Hurricane Bera was lumbering ashore and the eye of the storm was heading straight for New Orleans.

Chapter 86
I KNOW YOU

Reverend Jessie's disciples, like Ivanov and I, were soaking wet. The rain came down harder, biblically, a rain that would have concerned an unprepared Noah. The parts of my body that were exposed, like my hands and the back of my head, felt numb. My ears were ringing from the sound of the wind hurling itself down the streets and breaking itself with fury against things I could not see. Ivanov and I remained seated on the ground still leaning heavily against the Bourbon Orleans. Zarathustra II remained curled up on the side of Oz. From the huddle where the disciples stood hunched together as one, someone was knocked over, like a chair falling hard away from a table. The wind slammed him against the ground as he fell over. The group then lowered itself closer to the ground, into a kneeling position, closed the circle, and clung to each other more tightly to buffer the wind. But the person who fell to the ground was just out of their reach.

One of the disciples in the huddled group reached a hand towards the one who had been knocked down. But the fallen one was too far away. I looked and saw that it was John Henry Calvin who had been separated from the group. Mr. Calvin lay on his back as his walking cane blew away from him. He was not strong enough to buck the wind and sit upright, though he tried in vain several times to do so. The wind responded to his effort by blowing its discordant trumpet. The wind slid him, on his back, several more feet away from the group. His red poncho was blown up, covering his face. He was helpless.

One of the doors to the Bourbon Pub opened, and a lone figure emerged running, then falling, then getting up, towards John Henry Calvin. The lone figure was dressed in gold lame' and was one of the Royal Pages. A gust of wind blew him over 4-5 feet from where John Henry Calvin lay. It was Snowflake. He slowly crawled on all fours over to John Henry Calvin. He hugged John Henry Calvin into a seated position. Another larger patron of the bar ran out and the two of them helped John Henry Calvin to his feet and, holding Mr. Calvin upright, they walked, embracing him, stumbling, against the wind into the bar, while the remaining disciples stayed huddled together. The crowd inside parted and someone set out a chair in which Snowflake and the other patron set John Henry Calvin.

John Henry Calvin was soaking wet, shaking, and appeared disoriented. Snowflake removed Mr. Henry's poncho. "This is just crazy," someone said, as the music played in the background. A bartender appeared, without request, and brought a cup of hot coffee, which Snowflake placed in John Henry Calvin's hands.

"Drink some of this," a kneeling Snowflake said to John Henry Calvin. John Henry Calvin took a few sips.

"You have got to get him out of those wet clothes, honey," a very tall drag queen, in a blue sequenced dress, standing next to John Henry Calvin, said to Snowflake. Snowflake nodded in agreement. John Henry Calvin looked at Snowflake for a long moment. His hands and arms shook. His pupils got larger, which some say happens when you look at someone for whom you feel love or affection. His eyes glowed paternal.

"I know you," John Henry Calvin said, staring, in an old age whisper to Snowflake, before sipping his coffee again. Snowflake smiled.

"I'm Nimrod Rassher. I was a student in your history class at Jesuit," Snowflake said in reply. John Henry Calvin continued to look at Snowflake. His hands shook and coffee spilled into his lap though he did not seem to notice. Snowflake rubbed John Henry Calvin's arms to try to generate some heat. It was hard to tell if he understood what Snowflake had said to him. The rain had made Snowflake's mascara run down his face. Mr. Calvin sat, periodically encouraged to sip his coffee, under the influence of hypothermia, and looking intensely at Snowflake.

"I know you," he said again, still shaking.

"We all gotta know somebody honey. Now drink your coffee and hush," the tall drag queen standing next to John Henry Calvin said, patting him on the head.

Chapter 87
TOWER OF BABEL

The rain was still coming down hard. Two people tried to run from Oz to the Bourbon Pub, but either slipped or the wind shoved them onto the ground and tossed them like pieces of debris right into the huddled group of Reverend Jessie and his disciples. The two men from Oz managed to sit up against the back of the disciples, who were all facing each other in a circle. Then the two were gone, absorbed somewhere into the interior of the group of disciples, under their ponchos, all holding on to each other and seated like a large rusted gym weight on the ground.

I saw Zarathustra II still lying up against the side of Oz's building. It was hard to tell if he had run there and fell, or if the wind had carried him there and slammed him down. He lay there lifeless, his trench coat flapping and his head hanging down awkwardly.

More lightning struck, 3X, 4X, 5X. It was deafening. I thought I heard glass breaking somewhere, but could not be sure, because everything was so loud, like an actual Tower of Babel collapsing on top of us from mankind's constructed arrogance. In the background was the beat, the indecipherable beat, the never ending beat, of the music coming from the Bourbon Pub, through wind and the rain, as vibration and as echo.

Then when I looked up again Zarathustra II was no longer laying up against the side of Oz. He was now in the middle of Bourbon Street trying to walk against, or into, the wind. He looked at me for a moment.

"'Now you see my son,' as Dante wrote, 'what brief mockery fortune makes of gods we trust her with,'" he yelled out, pointing repeatedly at me.

Zarathustra II would be blown to the ground, rolled a few feet, only to get up and be slammed back down. He looked to be in great agony, but each time he was blown down he would get back up again, slipping, sneering, and try to walk forward, against the wind. I could not turn away and watched, transfixed by the spectacle.

Chapter 88
THANKS SON

Ivanov suddenly stood up, unsteadily, without a word to me. He slipped and fell down. He got up again and stumbled towards Oz. I saw Bertrand Finch and some other men open a door and help him in.

I then saw what looked like debris being blown from where the disciples kneeled. But through the rain I realized that it was a person. It was Rivet David Walker. Despite his best efforts he could not get back to the encircled group. A strong wind kept him off his feet. He struggled to his knees, but as he finally stood a gust of wind hurled him against a trash receptacle cemented to the ground. He lay there unconscious with his arms dangling unnaturally from his body. Several men in the disciple group looked at him and reached out, or pointed at him, but did not move. The wind then rolled him, a little at a time, away from the trash bin and down the street, 10, 20, 30 feet, until he was out of my sight.

Lightning cracked again 2X, 3X, 4X. Glass came raining down onto the street near me. Windows in the hotel above me were breaking. I suddenly noticed I was sitting in water. Water was filling the street slowly. From where I wondered? It was not deep, only 5-6 inches, but it seemed to be rising. I could not be sure.

I saw Zarathustra II again. He was kneeling, now standing, now blown over in the middle of Bourbon Street, facing into the winds of the storm. He was Cool Hand Luke in the prison yard fight. I was his trainer, but had no towel to throw into the ring to stop the match. And the only referee, the one Reverend Jessie prayed to and the one Zarathustra II said had disappeared, was not speaking. Zarathustra II stood up again facing into the wind.

"'Only in Christendom did everything become punishment,'" I heard him say, quoting Nietzsche, to his unseen tormentor. This time the malevolent wind lifted him up off the ground 3-4 feet and threw him sideways like a juiced curve ball. It tossed him into one of the columns holding up the balcony at the Bourbon Pub. I thought it must have broken him in half. But again he stood up, as people inside watched and he walked back into the middle of the street, bloodied but defiant.

"'Whoever is dissatisfied with himself is continually ready for revenge, and we others will be his victims!'" he yelled, again quoting Nietzsche.

Someone in the group of disciples stood up and tried to run to the Bourbon Pub. He went three steps and was knocked down by the force of the squall, so he began to crawl forward on his stomach. As he got closer to the Bourbon Pub a door opened and several people stepped out to help him inside. It looked like Bartholomew Davidson.

The lights in the Bourbon Pub flickered for a moment but remained on. The men who helped Mr. Davidson into the bar led him up the stairs to the third story apartment. There he found John Henry Calvin, who had been brought upstairs by Snowflake and given another cup of hot coffee, clothed in a pink print bathrobe. Snowflake was seated with him.

"Mister, there is a shower in there and another robe on the sofa for you after you dry off," Snowflake said to Mr. Davidson, in a very off handed matter, as he kept attentive eyes on the still shivering John Henry Calvin.

"Thanks son," Bartholomew Davidson replied.

Chapter 89
DOPPLER RADAR

The water in the street seemed to rise a bit more. Maybe there was a foot of water now. Both the Bourbon Pub and Oz were several steps above street level, so no water was inside of either bar yet, though it was close to the doorways. On one of the televisions in the Bourbon Pub the newscaster indicated that it was believed there were levee breaks somewhere along the Mississippi river above the French Quarter and two of the pumps installed by the Corps of Engineers to pump water into the lake had either mal-functioned or been abandoned by workers. Parts of the city were flooding. Property damage was going to be significant.

The Doppler radar showed the eye of the storm was approaching the city. The water in the Mississippi River and Lake Ponchartrain was ex-pected to continue rising and with it the water in the city's streets. I heard something crashing a few blocks, or maybe further, away. I could not tell what it was, but the sound lumbered towards me until I could barely hear. I tried to cover my ears but could not lift my hands to my head. It may have been a small tornado.

I looked up momentarily. I saw Zarathustra II standing in the middle of the street in the driving rain. He had Nietzsche's *Thus Spoke Zarathustra* in his right hand. It appeared that he had the book opened and was trying to read from it. Whatever he read aloud I could not hear.

Chapter 90
UNBOWED

Then it stopped suddenly. Just like the snapping of two fingers, it stopped. The hurricane's suffocating romantic embrace fell away. Everything went calm, like the still of the night, or the ending of that romantic relationship, moving from denial to acceptance. No wind. No rain. The sky remained an unnatural gray-black. I was able to stand up. I realized I had pieces of glass imbedded in my right hand and I was bleeding slightly. I felt like I had been jumped by the bullies in high school and they had kicked and punched me at will. I was soaking wet.

Those who were with Reverend Jessie also began to raise themselves up and stand. I suddenly heard things more clearly, as if the thunderous noise from the storm I had experienced had increased my primitive senses. A glass pane fell slowly onto a median blocks away. I heard it twist and dislodge from its framing. There was a splash as it fell into standing water. The water in the street was now just below my knees, but continuing to rise.

It was the eye of the hurricane passing over us. It was that surreal stillness and calm that existed at the center of such devastation, a metaphor to some, where God is found and lost like in Gödel's incompleteness theory, the god of the gap. Men from Reverend Jessie's disciple group started to move loosely, unevenly, toward the safety of the Bourbon Pub. A voice boomed out. It was Reverend Jessie. He was unbowed.

The Lord is my shepherd, I shall
not be in want,
He makes me lie down in green
pastures,
He leads me beside quiet waters,
He restores my soul.
He guides me in paths of
righteousness
for His name sake.
Even though I walk through
the valley of the shadows of
death
I will fear no evil
for you are with me
your rod and your staff
they comfort me.

When he began to speak several disciples stopped walking and stood with their heads bowed, others kept moving, broken. When he finished they left him alone, standing in the water, with his God, and the raw resonance of that fitful prayer. He did not seem to notice, as a revelation had overtaken him. He looked skyward to the bubbling cauldron above. Each of the disciples was taken, without resistance, by the arm and led to the third floor of the Bourbon Pub and Parade by the unnamed at the bar.

I did not see Zarathustra II. I also sloshed over to the Bourbon Pub and Parade. Some patrons from Oz, including Bertrand Finch and his cameraman, did the same. Others just took the time to step outside of the two bars, but they did not go far.

Chapter 91
AN UNSEEN PERSON

The Bourbon Pub and Parade was now completely packed with people. Some people on the second floor opened the doors and stepped out onto the balcony. Standing on the first floor I heard the balcony above me creak and groan, as people shuffled on to it. There was water in the bar on the first floor.

Then a slight drizzle started again. People began closing doors and running inside. The stillness, we all knew, was about to end. I stood to the side of one of the doorways of the Bourbon Pub and Parade, through which people now moved quickly to get inside, wading through water. Music was still playing in the club, but it was too crowded for people to move around much. The wind arched its back, started to pick up, and lurched forward. When I looked back outside, I saw Reverend Jessie standing in several feet of water in the middle of Bourbon Street. He held his bible aloft in his hand. Then a small figure sloshed out into the middle of the street. He was bleeding significantly from his forehead and, it appeared, from at least one eye. The blood ran from the bridge of his nose into his mustache. It was Zarathustra II. He stood thigh deep in water, four to five feet directly in front of Reverend Jessie holding up his copy of *Thus Spoke Zarathustra*. Both men were faced in the same direction, toward Golgotha.

Zarathustra II then seemed to be in physical battle with an unseen person. He fell into the water several times and was talking incessantly, while Reverend Jessie stood, hardened, stoically continuing to look skyward answering questions I could not hear. Zarathustra II would grab at the air as if trying to restrain someone, fall into the water, and then get back up immediately. Then, suddenly, Zarathustra II was hugging himself, or holding something against his body, and struggling to keep his hold on it.

There was a moment when the wind calmed and I heard Zarathustra II, still wrestling with something.

"I will not let you go," he said. But the statement by Zarathustra II seemed like one that was bullied from him after long hours of anguish. Ivanov suddenly appeared at my side. We both watched, along with countless others, helpless and yet mesmerized, as Zarathustra II was plunged repeatedly into the water, injured, only to stand up again on his own each time, with his arms wrapped around himself. His smile seemed to widen on each occasion that he regained his footing and stood again defiantly in the most unlikely of baptismal water.

Chapter 92
ZARATHUSTRA II'S ENDING

"We are waiting for you!" I suddenly heard Zarathustra II yell skyward. He bent over slightly, into the wind.

"This is painful to watch," Ivanov said. I did not know how to respond, but felt it, and said nothing.

"What has my life been?" Zarathustra II asked his absent deity, or maybe one of the voices in his head. "Beckett was right. 'Words, words, my life has never been anything but words.'"

And then an odd thing happened. Reverend Jessie suddenly lowered his gaze from the Old Testament heavens and spoke. His face shone with a light from above that seemed to break through the darkness. Above the din and clamor of the increasing wind and light rain, and the destruction around us, his voice seemed a clarion call.

"What is your name?" he bellowed. Zarathustra II must have heard him as well. Reverend Jessie, who was facing Zarathustra II's back, again yelled so loudly his voice strained:

"What...is...your...name?"

Zarathustra II stopped struggling with the elements for a moment. He dropped his copy of Nietzsche's book into the water. He looked around in front of him, standing unsteady in the water, trying to locate the voice he heard, and then cautiously he tilted his head back and raised both his arms skyward.

"Randolph!" he yelled.

"Your name will no longer be Randolph..." Reverend Jessie started to proclaim in response. At the sound of this, and as if playing his part in a scripted play, Zarathustra II started to turn toward Reverend Jessie. Perhaps, he had heard the direction of Reverend Jessie's voice. I believe their eyes met, but am not sure because the blood on Zarathustra II's face appeared to cover both of his eyes.

Just then there was a monstrous sound and simultaneous flash of light and I was temporarily blinded and deafened. People around me moaned collectively, as if we were all punched by that same primeval fist. Ivanov fell into me and I held him up. The water at our feet seemed momentarily electrified.

It took me a moment, that seemed to last forever, to realize that it was because a lightning strike had hit so close. Upon reflection I think I remember seeing Zarathustra II falling. I can't say I actually saw the lightning strike him. Zarathustra II fell face first into the water with his hands extended. At least one of his hands was clearly burnt from the strike. His trench coat ballooned away from his body on top of the water. His head seemed to float while his legs and torso sunk below the water line, and his hair splayed outward in the water. He must have been killed instantly.

The weather worsened quickly. There were three more lightning strikes nearby---1X,2X,3X, and the wind and rain now came down with a biblical vengeance. It was harsh. People laboring in congested silence, began to breathe again once the lightning strikes ceased. The crowd inched away from the doorways at the Pub into each other's embrace, as the water rose.

The music in the club ceased. The people around me seemed apprehensive, conjointly alarmed. The TV screen showed the news. The rest of the hurricane was slowly coming ashore.

I continued to look at Reverend Jessie standing, and Zarathustra II's body floating, in the water. Reverend Jessie looked permanently moored in waist deep water. I was numb but afraid to leave the bar. It appeared that he had been temporarily blinded by the lightning strike that hit Zarathustra II. He ran the sleeve of his suit across his eyes repeatedly. I saw him at that moment, through the eyes of my childhood. He was my father and he was in trouble.

Zarathustra II's body had floated to Reverend Jessie. He held the end of Zarathustra II's trench coat in his left hand keeping Zarathustra II's body near him. He raised his Bible aloft again with his right hand. He was confrontational. His demeanor was demanding and he spoke something aloud to a God it seemed he could see, but I could not hear all of his words. "I am not Job," was all that came through clearly.

Reverend Jessie was a big man, at least 260 pounds, and he leaned all that weight into the increasing gusts of wind in order to stay upright. But it still pushed him over. He went under the water but regained his footing, only to fall, or slip, once more. Each time he fell he was a few feet further away from us.

The next thing I knew John Roland Reynolds had a bullhorn in his gloved hands. He was standing near a broken glass pane on a door on the Bourbon street side of the Bourbon Pub. Rain was being blown into the bar hard by the wind.

"I need people NOW!" he yelled into the bull horn. "Everyone pick a partner. Let's make a chain to get him. NOW!" he screamed hoarsely. Several drag queens rushed through the door, holding the hems of their skirts, and facing each other began linking arms with the person next to them. At that point I saw Mr. Davidson and Saul Fierke run by me and join the chain. Mr. Davidson was in a blue bathrobe.

I turned and saw John Henry Calvin in a pink bathrobe being led by the hand by Snowflake to a chair 20 or 30 feet from the door, but still setting in water. A black man in a dress said, "Go sweetie," and at that Snowflake waded over to join the chain of people. The black man got Mr. Calvin, who seemed very pale and weak, seated and then stood in front of him shielding him from the wind. "He'll be alright," I think he told John Henry Calvin, whose eyes tried to follow Snowflake out the door.

I looked back outside and Reverend Jessie had fallen again. When he regained his footing he was still holding onto Zarathustra II's coat, which had his body wrapped up in it, and in the other hand was his Bible, which he again held aloft toward the darkened and menacing sky.

Chapter 93
DON'T YA LOSE HOPE

Mrs. Rosemary Matthews got up slowly from Marvin's couch. "Do ya want any mo of dat ice cream?" she asked Madeline, as she walked to the kitchen. Madeline did not respond. She was transfixed by the Weather Channel, watching the reports of the devastation in New Orleans. She felt safe, but helpless. Both ladies were wearing their **Zarathustra the Second's Army** T-Shirts and yellow hats.

Mrs. Rosemary Matthews realized that her friend did not respond to her. She stopped and walked back over to her.

"Oh, I'm so upset wit ma self. He was rite bout da storm hittin. Ro, do you tink he'll be rite bout da rest?" Madeline asked nervously, referring to Zarathustra II's predictions. Mrs. Rosemary Matthews sat down next to Madeline and picked up her hand.

"Look a me Madie," she said, wishing to take charge of her friend's despair, but tears came into her eyes. "Don't ya lose hope," was all she could manage to say to her.

Chapter 94
REVEREND JESSIE'S ENDING

The wind and rain were getting worse. It did not seem possible that it could rain any harder, but it did. The rain poured from the heavens like stones demanded by the God of the wandering tribe of Israelites at a biblical abomination. The human chain now stretched from inside the Bourbon Pub to within three to four feet in front of where Reverend Jessie stood in the waist deep water. John Roland Reynolds removed his wig and in his sequined dress slowly made his way down the junk DNA chain of humanity. The chain was unsteady. The wind pushed people back and forth in the foul primordial soup which filled the street. John Roland Reynolds clung to each person and moved purposely, athletically, through the water toward the end of the chain of people and towards Reverend Jessie. I overcame my fear, found my strength, and followed close behind him. Reverend Jessie was still speaking.

"The time of my departure is now at hand. I'm ready for my punishment," I heard him say.

John Roland Reynolds yelled to him. "Hang on coach." As John Roland Reynolds got to the last person on the human chain he held that person's right hand with his left hand. John Roland Reynolds reached out his right hand to Reverend Jessie, so that his hand and fingers in the white glove were extended. But Reverend Jessie stumbled slightly in the water again. When he regained his footing and stood up again he was two to three feet further away. I rushed past John Roland Reynolds and held his hand.

"Dad!"

I reached out for my father. He looked at me but I was not sure if he actually saw me, if I was part of his revelation. His face seemed sun burned and his eyes continually blinked open and then closed. He still held Zarathustra II's trench coat in his left hand, and Zarathustra II's body was still floating next to him face down and tangled in the trench coat.

He reached his right hand toward me. The right hand still held his Bible. It was completely soaked with water. He stuck the Bible in my out-stretched hand. I grabbed it and as I did he released it from his hand and he fell under the water again still clutching Zarathustra II's trench coat. I saw him roll two or three times in the water, which was above my waist, as several more lightning strikes hit nearby. I stumbled forward as well, but John Roland Reynolds grabbed me and pulled me to my feet. When my father regained his footing this time he was 8-10 feet or so from me. He stood for just a moment and then slipped under the water again with the tail of Zarathustra's trench coat wrapped around his neck; their two bod-ies entwined. I waited but did not see him stand again. I felt John Roland Reynolds pulling on my shirt yanking me toward him. "Back in!" he yelled, partially drowned out by rain slapping the standing water fist first around us in a syncopated drum beat. The mitochondrial human chain, of which we are all a part, slowly recoiled itself, a de-evolution, walking its way back as one into the Bourbon Pub and Parade.

Chapter 95
MRS. ROSEMARY MATTHEWS' ENDING

Madeline appreciated her friend's comforting hand. "What will I do if I lose him," she asked Mrs. Rosemary Matthews sorrowfully. "Dere is so much dere between us dat we neva resolv'd," Madeline then confessed. There was remorse in her tone. Mrs. Rosemary Matthews' eyes still welled with tears. She sat quietly with my mother.

"Let's see; how'd it go? My Poppa told me dis one when ma momma died," Mrs. Rosemary Matthews then said, trying hard to recall part of her own mythology. Mrs. Rosemary Matthews moved closer on the sofa next to her best friend. Comfort appeared etched on her face. She dried her eyes and cleared her throat and concentrated.

"Once upon a time," she started saying, "dere was dis king who had some health problems, like old folks sometime do." Madeline moved a bit on the sofa to face her friend directly and to better hear the story. Mrs. Rosemary Matthews straightened her shoulders involuntarily, as a childhood admonition inculcated. "Da king's doctor had told him dat fo da sake a his health he needed ta move ta da desert where da air was drier an mo betta fo his health. So kinda reluctantly da king took da doctor's advice, gave up his throne, an moved ta da desert takin his wife, servants, some cows, goats an Oh yea! Oh, yea! he took some a dem chickens too. I can't forget da chickens," Mrs. Rosemary Matthews chastised herself, as Madeline listened carefully.

"Afta da king moved he was sadden by da loss a his kingdom an his friends. You might say he had dat depression, dough dey didn't call it dat in doze days. I tink dey just called it da blues. But his servants dey built a fence ta keep in da cows, an a chicken shack fo dem chickens, an a nice fine house fo da king an his wife," Mrs. Rosemary Matthews paused. "You know a house like one a doze on St. Charles Avenue, not like doze in St Bernard," she offered.

"An den afta da king had kinda settled inta da situation a tornado came ta da desert. A tornado, can ya believe dat! Ya know dey didn't have no Nash Roberts or Weather Channel back den so it kinda caught da king by surprise," she said explaining.

"Uh-huh," Madeline replied, soothed by the sound of her friend's voice. "An dat tornado it destroyed everyting. It killed all a dem cattle, destroyed dat nice house an even destroyed dat chicken shack. It killed all da servants an it even killed da king's wife----you no da Queen," Mrs. Rosemary Matthews said remorsefully. Madeline drew her hand to her mouth in misfortune.

"But da king somehow he did survive it. Maybe it was one a dem divine intentions," Mrs. Rosemary Matthews continued. "Afta dat tornado had passed da king stood in da rubble an was tinking bout his wife, his kingdom, his animals, all dat bein gone. All dat he'd lost. He looked round at da devastation an den fell down ta his knees in shock, like I did when my momma died. He did not tink dat he could go on wit his life, ya know. An he was just about ta give up." Madeline sighed in understanding.

Mrs. Rosemary Matthews caught her breath. "Just at dat time, when he was bout ta give up on tings, dere was some movement in da collapsed chicken shack. Da dust from dat tornado was settling. Da sky was clearin as if da sun was comin up on a new day. Outta dat dust an debris da king's prize rooster came. Many a his tail feathers was missin, an his cock's comb was split, an he was bleedin. But da rooster he climbed ta da top a dat rubble dat had been da chicken shack. He flapped his wings a few times ta be sure dat dey was still woikin. An den," Mrs. Rosemary Matthews said her voice changing dramatically, "he did da most remarkable ting."

"What'd he do?" Madeline asked inquisitively, with her hand still near her mouth in anticipation. Mrs. Rosemary Matthews paused a moment for dramatic effect.

"He crowed," Mrs. Rosemary Matthews said pursing her lips, as tears then streamed down her face. "An ya know why he did dat?" Mrs. Rosemary Matthews quickly asked my mother. My mother shook her head. She did not know. "Cause honey dat's what roosters do," Mrs. Rosemary Matthews said, as she squeezed my mother's hand affectionately. My mother put her head on her friend's shoulder and wept.

Chapter 96
JOHN HENRY CALVIN'S ENDING

Once inside the Bourbon Pub I fell to my knees exhausted, into water about a foot or so deep. Many people who had been in the failed human rescue chain were piled up indiscriminately on the floor next to me. My arms were numb. In my hand was my father's Bible. I put my hands on the floor without thinking, to keep my face above the water, and the Bible in my hand went under water. On my right side I noticed Snowflake. We were both on the floor near the chair where John Henry Calvin was seated. Mr. Calvin continued to shiver, on the borderline of lucidity. Snowflake looked worn out. He rested his head on the knee of John Henry Calvin. It was an involuntary action, instinct instead of planning.

"I know you," John Henry Calvin said anciently, looking at Snowflake's wet head on his knee. Snowflake, whose makeup was now washed off, looked up at Mr. Calvin but could not speak. Exhaustion and fear had taken away his ability to speak. "I know you," Mr. Calvin repeated, as if senility had left him with only one sentence to utter. John Henry Calvin's eyes brightened. His pupils were dilated as he looked at Snowflake.

"Daniel my son, you have finally come home to me," he then said weakly to Snowflake, as tears filled his eyes. Snowflake tried to smile. He continued to rest his head on Mr. Calvin's knee. John Henry Calvin placed his wrinkled hand on Snowflake's head and ran it through his hair several times. He smiled a distant smile of contentment.

Mr. Calvin then placed both of his hands in his lap and slowly, ever so slowly, his trembling hands tried to remove the MIA bracelet with his son Daniel's name on it which he had worn around his wrist all those years. Snowflake reached up and gently grabbed Mr. Calvin's hand and held it, stopping him from trying to remove the bracelet

Chapter 97
NEW ORLEANS' ENDING

New Orleans has had many appellations: The "City that Care Forgot." "The Paris of the South." "The "Big Easy." But its true nature as a city and a culture is not so easily captured by catchy slogans, or marketing phrases.

New Orleans is a complex city where playful illusions often mask a painful subtext of unresolved issues of crime, race and poverty, that lie beneath a shifting veneer of revelry, fun and decadence. It is, somewhat uniquely, a largely Catholic city. In the ultimate metaphor of sin and redemption it revels in decadence on Mardi Gras day and goes through the motions of redemption the next day on Ash Wednesday.

At times New Orleans' 72 neighborhoods were divided by nationality or ethnicity into areas like the Irish Channel, or the lower Ninth Ward. The Vietnamese population migrated to New Orleans East joining a more affluent African American population prior to Hurricane Katrina. The neighborhood divisions would periodically blur, or disappear, with the revitalization of certain areas by younger folks returning to the city to help shore up its foundation. But it was a city often united quietly against the rest of the world, something the rest of the world did not always understand. It is a city that has a musical soul, the soul of a barrel house piano player in a Storyville brothel, and to hear it's rhythm correctly you must play all the keys on the piano, the black and the white.

It is a city full of contradictions. Those who thrive here, and become its beloved "characters," are those who, perhaps, see the same contradictions within themselves and celebrate those contradictions. Many who leave, or speak badly of it, are also blind to their own contradictions. It is a city of second and third chances that will break your heart carelessly, without reason, only to set it at ease the next day with a familiar melody.

The city was destroyed again. There was massive flooding and widespread property damage. The citizenry was again displaced. Decisions would have to be made, large and small, by everyone who was affected. People had died. People were lost. Religious beliefs were tested. Abandoned. Found. It all depended. It depended on individual truths too varied to catalogue.

Preachers of all denominations, in other parts of the country, filled the airwaves seeking to elevate their status, and perhaps confirm their narratives, by framing up the disaster with malformed scriptural explanations. Some claimed that Zarathustra II was the anti-Christ and the end times were near. Atheists claimed Reverend Jessie's death proved that there was no God. Politicians pointed fingers at each other seeking to place blame and gain political advantage. But there were no easy fits. Death and destruction knew no religious denomination, or political affiliations, and were blind to competing scriptural requirements. Those of us down here, who had endured it directly, heard only the hollow shrill cry of the insecure. If we heard them at all, as we sought to sort out our emotions. Their easy explanations were mostly meaningless in the face of the effort to move forward. The future was uncertain, but for a brief period it was coated in a primal regard for our fellow survivors, a regard which was temporarily transcendent for native New Orleanians.

Individuals had to re-plan and re-think every aspect of their lives from the mundane to the momentous: from where to live, to what to do for work, to finally what was important. So many things had disintegrated in the storm.

The social contract seemed torn asunder. The City had lost its collective voice, lost that voice as one does in the hours leading up to a long anticipated death and, just as often in life, in moments of hurt and despair.

To speak collectively one must do so in metaphor or myth. The storm had temporarily shattered that possibility.

A cacophony of individual disparate voices began to arise. Who would lead? Who had answers? Who should people believe? It was like starting over, like trying to choose between competing belief systems and being able, perhaps for the first time, to walk away from childhood cultural choices, made for us by others. Some would indeed walk away. Some would hold on more tightly and try to retrace their earlier footsteps to find a familiar worn path. Try as we might to find a larger truth in the destruction of the storm it held only indeterminate meaning for those willing to search for such answers at all. Besides, meaning, if it can be truly captured, is finite. The meaning, if any, of the storm, Zarathustra II's predictions, and its aftermath, was open ended. It would be nice, perhaps easier, if it were otherwise, but it was not.

Chapter 98
BERTRAND FINCH'S ENDING

There would be no award for television reporting for Bertrand Finch. No move to a larger television market. No discovery by a powerful TV broker. No newfound fame. His fortunes were set. His career had reached its peak.

The storm and its aftermath had forced an ill defined acknowledgment on Bertrand Finch, about his relevance and his future. His ambition was temporarily gone. There was a dull absurd feeling of nothingness in his chest that he did not understand. In that numbed state he suddenly recalled one of the many quotes that Zarathustra II had given to him and that he treated as meaningless, an annoyance, at the time.

They were standing outside the CRC together, waiting to go in before Reverend Jessie's sermon on false prophets. Zarathustra II looked disheartened and did not want to go in, wanting to avoid the confrontation. Finch ignored his reticence. Yet Finch recalled that Zarathustra II had grabbed him on the sleeve before they entered the church. He tried to pull Finch aside to talk to him. Finch resisted, pulled away from his grasp, concerned Zarathustra II would be noticed with him. As they moved slowly with the crowd into the church Zarathustra II said: "When this ends I want you to remember something Kierkegaard wrote." Finch recalled, with a lump in his throat, his impatience with Zarathustra II.

"Not now," he had told him.

"'The self must be broken in order to become a self,'" Zarathustra II had said to him, still holding onto his sleeve. Finch still didn't know what it meant.

While he had survived the storm, Zarathustra II had been wrong on that prediction, his cameraman had stumbled and submerged all his equipment in the flood waters while running from the Bourbon Pub to film the attempt to rescue Reverend Jessie. There was no film of anything that had transpired. No video footage of Zarathustra II, or Reverend Jessie, meeting their end. No images for people to take in and hold up as heroic or moronic. As is so often the case in life the heroic, the tragic, and the mundane, are not recorded anywhere, except in our own memories, where, over time, the boundaries between reality and perception, and the needs dictated by each, of which we are often unaware, fade into each other.

Bertrand Finch did not understand what he was feeling. He did not have words for it and it did not fit into his world of experience.

Bertrand Finch was alive, but part of him had momentarily died. Was he supposed to be alive, he briefly wondered. And for what purpose? He tried to process it all. But that process required reflection. And he did not know how to dive that deep. He had no answers, only questions that he wished would go away. And questioning is difficult. It is difficult because it punctures the empty veil of certainty, of ancient absolutes and their accompanying modern smugness, to which people often cling. By definition it leads to uncertainty and struggle at times. Once one allows questions to arise, without snuffing these out, it destroys the immediacy of life. Bertrand Finch just wanted things to get back to normal so he would not have to think about it.

Chapter 99
LUKE'S ENDING

I guess I should end this with some of those personal observations I told you about at the beginning, my own attempt at understanding. When someone very close to you dies you may be tempted to incorporate parts of their world view, or belief system, into your own. At least temporarily. Sometimes it is just little things; for example, a certain relaxed kindness or remembered patience towards others, that we recall. On other occasions the effect of the death is more profound. Perhaps, you are spurred on to make the deceased person's unfulfilled life's quest your own, and repress your own desires. That is often viewed as noble, but may simply be a more socially acceptable form of transcendence, to give your own life the appearance of meaning.

I have now read the Bible in its entirety. I have also read many other books and continue to do so. Mikhail Ivanov has helped me greatly in that endeavor and has remained my friend. I have tried to make my own choices, to form my own beliefs, and to follow Zarathustra II's initial Nietzschean admonition to me to develop faith in myself, to the extent that is possible. It is as difficult and rewarding as he told me it would be.

Our beliefs, it seems to me, too often only have meaning if defined in opposition to something or someone. For clarity, and to fill an emotional need it seems, there too often must be a negative other which serves as the oppositional idea in our lives, the thing which we can tell ourselves that we are not. Well, sometimes it's an idea, but mostly, the idea is superimposed on someone, or on some other group, so it can be more readily grasped and vilified. In the same way that people cannot understand a transcendent God, and need Jesus in human form so they can visualize God, they need someone, or some identifiable group, to point to in order to show what they are not.

And organized religion? That community, tradition and ritual? I think it's like when I was sick as a teenager, really sick, except that the doctors can't figure out what is wrong to make you better. You desperately want to feel better, so at some point you'll try anything to get well: herbal remedies, holistic stuff, acupuncture, anything. Organized religion is that 'anything' which we try as cure. It rises to fill that gap I mentioned, and tries to unite our divided self.

I have often wondered about the psychology of it all. The admiration of my father in the eyes of his followers, if that is what it should be called, was just a needed exaggeration. Perhaps, he needed that exaggeration to tackle the larger issues that confronted him in his life. His followers certainly needed the exaggeration of him to shield them from the same. It was an exaggeration of who he was, what he was and what they needed from him, as if he was the Catcher in the Rye and his followers were the children he sought to keep from falling into moral error. But like all exaggerations it filled an unspoken need, an emptiness in his and their lives. At its base such exaggerations are fearful. In some ways, much as they did with my father, people make their God that exaggeration also.

I guess the same could be said of Zarathustra II in Mikhail Ivanov's and my life, but I am less comfortable with that conclusion. Maybe my own needs get in the way of my objectivity. I do not see him as having been exalted, except briefly in rather extraordinary circumstances. Rather, some of the same characteristics and knowledge that brought my father approbation were used to crush Zarathustra II throughout his life, because he dared to have a different perspective, a poet's perspective, and speak of it openly. His was the heresy of an independent intellect, a life lived in five or six musical notes, and as the one who stole fire and tried to bring it to the people. My father's words brought him followers, whereas, until the last days of his life, Zarathustra II's words brought him only estrangement and exile, his right to exist chained and contested. Exaggeration, I guess, can cause either.

I have also realized that belief systems, at their core, and whatever their nature, form our unacknowledged armor with which we face the tremors of this world. Whether to protect us from the repressed fear of dying, our anxiety over an uncertain future, or to immunize us from social criticism for our failures, belief systems have developed, largely, as a protective evolutionary shield.

I read recently that the human eye is only capable of seeing about thirty percent of the spectrum of light. Other animals, who have not fallen into consciousness, who never ate from the tree of knowledge, are capable of seeing more of the light's spectrum. Indeed, single cell animals, with no self consciousness, may experience the most light. Similarly as our lives complicate, quicken and weigh us down, our belief systems often become like the human eye, trying to protect us, and blocking out much of the light, the unpleasantness, from our possible vision. That limited vision also becomes part of the armor we wear.

And remember all those different 'truths' Zarathustra II talked about? I have learned a strange dichotomy about the alleged absolute truths of belief systems. Niels Bohr, the physicist, once said that "the opposite of a profound truth is another profound truth." Indeed these days, as Zarathustra II indicated, it sometimes seems that there are more 'truths' than we can absorb and assimilate. But one would never know truth, or understand it in its various incantations, unless one takes their belief system armor off. My studies, after Zarathustra II's death, lead me to believe that Jesus and Buddha, in their own very human ways, and shorn of the corrupting influence of their denominational street barkers, were both telling us the same thing: take the armor off, drop the belief system, and face the world without it.

Sometimes I still awaken in my apartment and realize that I am in fact alone in this world. In the twilight of that awakening, when I realize that Zarathustra II and my father are gone, I am often momentarily disoriented. Since the storm I have had to learn to live without---without a father, without a teacher, and without a familiar God. Perhaps, in each case it is the same patriarchal loss, just given a different name. Freud probably would have thought so. But, among other things, I have learned that too often we allow those whom we follow, those whom we exalt with the best apparent intentions, to become our compass, to set our spiritual path, and give us their altar to kneel on. Unfortunately, that relieves us of the important burden of finding out who we are and allows us to lead unexamined and unengaged lives.

It is a cultivated illusion that provides some comfort in an often uncomfortable existence. When, or if, one comes to recognize the exaggeration, or to believe that those we follow are false prophets, or when they become lost to us, one has to question the direction of one's life. Hope may fade in that questioning, but navigating with fake reference points is simply no longer possible. As the theologian Paul Tillich wrote, life with failure is better than lifelessness without it.

ZARATHUSTRA II'S NOTEBOOK

"Dogmatism induces the fanatic religionist to split himself into a cruel judge and a hopeless sinner." Erik Erikson

"Yet no pain has been able or shall be able to tempt me into giving false testimony about life as I recognize it." Nietzsche.

"Every man takes the limits of his own field of vision for the limits of the world." Schopenhauer.

"There are no whole truths; all truths are half truths. It is trying to treat them as whole truths that plays the devil." Alfred North Whitehead.

"To dare is to lose one's footing momentarily. To not dare is to lose oneself." Kierkegaard.

"The battle over truth is often reduced to a distracting battle over the language we use, divorced from substance. Whomever's language prevails and is accepted, whoever wins the game of defining the 'facts,' can claim 'truth' as the prize; at least within their own tribe." Zarathustra II.

"An ideology which has to persuade and mobilize people cannot choose its victim arbitrarily." Hannah Arendt.

"We must realize once and for all that the meanings which make up our world are simply an historically determined and continuously developing structure in which man develops and are in no sense absolute." Karl Mannheim.

"It is unwise for Christians to claim any knowledge of either the furniture of heaven or the temperature of hell." Reinhold Niebuhr.

"It's better to be driven around in a red Porsche than to own one. The luck of the fool is inviolate." Bukowski.

"During difficult or uncertain times, be those times economic or spiritual, the absolutes of Plato and Augustine descend as a dark shadow on the minds of a frightened mankind. During more prosperous times, when fears seem less immediate, the light of reason from Aristotle and Aquinas shines down ascendant." Zarathustra II.

"Genesis, or most of the Bible for that matter, was not written to chronicle a set of historical facts. To read it solely as a historical narrative is to strip it of its larger meaning. Rather, it was written with purported history as metaphor, to try to answer spiritual questions; existential questions, and to try to explain our relationship to each other and to, and through, the divine." Zarathustra II.

"The very word Christianity is a misunderstanding------the truth is, there was only one Christian and he died on the cross." Nietzsche.

"The problem with the biblical focus on an afterlife, or a heavenly reward, is that we too often neglect solving the problems of this existence; we minimize the importance of the present and shirk our responsibility to our fellow man. The thought of an imagined glorious afterlife may calm our fears of a future death, but it too often denigrates our current humanity." Zarathustra II.

"The mass of men cannot handle the world as it is really is. We need a characterological lie as a defense, or for someone else to shoulder the burden of life's meaning for us. It is the poet and the artist, on the other hand, who takes the world into themselves, transforms it and sets it out anew, removing the supposedly unbreakable veneer, for others to see. But unfortunately for the poet and the artist, sometimes the world, as it really is, gets lodged in their throat and it slowly suffocates them." Zarathustra II.

"Philosophy as I have understood it and lived it to this day, is a life voluntarily spent in ice and high mountains-----a searching out of all that is alien and questionable in existence." Nietzsche.

"God is to be found in goodness itself and nowhere else." Boethius.

"He who risks and fails can be forgiven. He who never risks and never fails is a failure in his whole being." Paul Tillich.

"The smaller the world one inhabits, the smaller one's view of the world and the narrower one thinks. Intolerance is a seed that oft finds the most fertile soil on a small planet." Zarathustra II.

"Ideas cannot be fought except by means of better ideas." Ayn Rand.

"Is it possible to find a rule of conduct outside the realm of religion and its absolute values? That is the question raised by rebellion." Albert Camus.

"There is a bluebird in my heart that wants to get out, but I'm too tough for him. I say, stay in there, I'm not going to let anybody see you." Charles Bukowski.

"My enemies are those who want to destroy without creating their own self." Nietzsche.

"Stereotypes simplify. Labels are used as a substitute for thought or analysis, and as a means of narrowly defining something, or someone, we do not wish to think about further. We want simplicity, not complexity, and as a result meaning is loss in the exchange of 25 cent catch phrases and TV sound bites." Zarathustra II.

"If I conduct myself like others I shall be a betrayer; if I separate myself from them I betray myself." Kierkegaard.

"It is those who defy us, those who quarrel with us and who are not afraid to articulate their disagreements with us, those who we categorize as the 'negative other' in our lives and to whom we point to show what we are not, who give us our language and, ultimately, our temporal meaning." Zarathustra II.

"Be kind because everyone you meet is fighting a great battle." Philo.

"Man has always been his most vexing problem." Reinhold Niebuhr.

"...the insistent resolution, like the rosebud or the anarchist, is eventually wasted, like moths in towers or bathing beauties in New Jersey." Charles Bukowski.

"Few are made for independence----it is the privilege of the strong. And he who attempts it, having the completest right to it but without being compelled to, thereby proves that he is probably not only strong but also daring to the point of recklessness." Nietzsche.

"Too often we spend large parts of our life unknowingly kneeling on someone else's altar and sacrificing to someone else's idol, an altar constructed by a father, or mother, or someone else. Perhaps, this is how we are guided initially in our attempt to define ourselves, but ultimately we must choose our own path, our own altar upon which to kneel and to devote our life, or whether to kneel at all." Zarathustra II.

"...the more reason we have to feel guilty, the more fervent our propaganda." Eric Hoffer.

"We are a false Free Market culture where distorted Darwinian ideas have become more important economically than those of Adam Smith, where the Free Market ethos, of letting the 'market' set our values has trampled underfoot or co-opted its ethical competitors. And what does this have to do with religion? The Free Marketers have used the Christian Fundamentalists as foot soldiers and somehow convinced them that Jesus would have been a proponent of a free market culture. This ethos has replaced thought with propaganda and along the way we have lost the tools that allow us to separate spiritual truth from orchestrated economic fiction." Zarathustra II.

"I have refused the discipline of art and government and God and all that which destroy my seeming...." Charles Bukowski.

"Truth is born only of freedom." Bonhoeffer.

"When we cannot handle reality, when we are fearful of it, we create symbols and then invest those symbols with the fabricated reality that our fears demand." Zarathustra II.

"He who has seen deeply into the world knows what wisdom there is in the fact that men are superficial. It is their instinct for preservation which teaches them to be fickle, light and false." Nietzsche.

"Cheap Grace means grace as a doctrine, a principle, a system. It means forgiveness of sins proclaimed as a general truth." Bonhoeffer.

"What is the fabric of our culture made of? One thread is clearly economic; a second thread is organized religion, or the religious instinct, wherever manifested. Or perhaps the second thread is just illusion and religion often serves to fill that role. The third thread, which too often binds the first two threads, is conflict with others and the accompanying intolerance." Zarathustra II.

"I worry that Christians who have only one foot on earth can also only have one foot in heaven." Bonhoeffer.

"And we are now men and must accept in the highest mind the same transcendent destiny; and not minors and invalids in a protected corner, not cowards fleeing before a revolution, but guides, redeemers, and benefactors, obeying the almighty effort, and advancing on chaos and the dark." Ralph Waldo Emerson.

"We age in darkness like wood and watch our phantoms change their clothes of shingles and boards for a purpose that can only be described as wood." Richard Brautigan.

"Ultimately, with Constantine's embrace of Christianity, a defining but often overlooked pillar of what would become Western culture was put in place. That aspect, heavily influenced by Greek philosophy, was monotheism. It had existed long before Constantine of course, most notably with Judaism. But it was Constantine's embrace of it, his role in defining the Trinity, co-opting Bishops with tax collection duties and empowering the emerging Church, that chartered the course. And with the gradual demise of polytheism, monotheism sowed the cultural seeds for religious intolerance, which over time provided the moral sanction for all forms of hatred." Zarathustra II.

"We cannot forgive the mass of men for their refusal to think, for their blind transference to a leader, because it was the mass of men who followed Hitler and Mussolini and who brought mankind near to annihilation before quietly murmuring a mea culpa that they were misled. One needs moral independence in order to stand up to evil and to the degradation of others. Those who blindly follow religious leaders generally lack such moral independence." Zarathustra II.

"Fanaticism consists in redoubling your efforts when you have forgotten your aim." Santayana.

"Fundamentalists, those who claim biblical inerrancy, are by nature undemocratic and opposed to equality for all, because the Bible stories are undemocratic, written at a time when the concept was unknown. So the Fundamentalist takes the biblical stories and places them in opposition to modernity, thereby clothing his stand against equality in finer raiment, as if these were pre-ordained by a God given hierarchy." Zarathustra II.

"Righteousness too often correlates with one's sense of being victimized, of being attacked by those outside the person's tribe or community. This is in direct conflict with how Jesus handled his victimization, even to his death. Lately, elements of Christianity have portrayed themselves as being under attack by nonbelievers, by government, by other denominations and by the media. Christianity's street barkers have responded by portraying themselves, and their belief system, as more righteous than their opponents. The lie of victimization fuels this self-righteousness, which then becomes the basis for more intolerance. In the process Jesus' admonition to forgive, and turn the other cheek, is lost." Zarathustra II.

"Perhaps a true sense of community, of kinship with others, is only possible in times of crisis, in an emergency. Most other times it is feigned. Religion, by demonizing certain groups and/or exaggerating their potential harm, seduces its followers with an elevated sense of community, of belonging to that kinship which opposes the ever present and imagined threat." Zarathustra II.

"Western Civilization is not Christian. It has embraced Christianity and used it to sanctify its acts. Our nationalism is only tribalism raised to the Nth degree." Reinhold Niebuhr.

"We must be careful not to place too high a price on obtaining meaning and truth. It must be open to all and affordable without the taxation of condemnation, or the penalty of isolation." Zarathustra II.

"We ask people to know God when they don't even know themselves. We want them to be literate about the world when they are illiterate as to their own thoughts and feelings. How can this change?" Zarathustra II.

"When men hate they also need to believe that the object of their hatred is worthy of the hatred bestowed on it. Hatred over matters that appear petty impugn the hater and make him appear small. So the hater must inflate the object of his hatred, enlarge its potential danger, so it appears to merit the level of hatred and thereby turn the hatred into a heroic or sacred cause." Zarathustra II.

"Doubt is not the opposite of faith; it is one element of faith." Paul Tillich.

"Given the nature of spiders, webs are inevitable. And given the nature of human beings, so are religions. Spiders can't help making flytraps and men can't help making symbols. That's what the human brain is there for----to turn the chaos of given experience into a set of manageable symbols." Aldous Huxley.

"Is it our individual memory or our individual notion of truth which creates our identity and governs our behavior?" Zarathustra II.

"A god is a personification of a motivating power or a value system that functions in a human life and in the universe." Joseph Campbell.

"Always go too far, because that's where you'll find the truth." Albert Camus

"I have seen all the works that are done under the sun; and indeed, all is vanity and grasping for the wind." Ecclesiastes 1:14.

"When we do science, we are pantheists; When we do poetry, we are polytheists; When we moralize we are monotheists." Goethe.

"Whether we like it or not, the one justification for the existence of all religions is death." Jose Saramago.

"It was a piece of subtle refinement that God learned Greek when he wanted to become a writer----and that he did not learn it better." Nietzsche.

"Every culture and every belief system needs transgression and excess to function. Ironically, both are creations of the culture as assuredly as the values and cultural mores which oppose those same transgressions." Zarathustra II.

"I do not believe in a fate that falls on man however they act; but I do believe in a fate that falls on them unless they act." Buddha.

"Meaning used to be based upon immediate perception, but it has not been so since at least Rousseau. Now meaning is disjointed and separated from perception by analysis and it has become largely a creation of one's culture or belief system." Zarathustra II.

"In the primitive's world things do not have the same sharp boundaries they do in our 'rational societies.'" Jung.

"Man's use of reason, in his pursuit of enlightenment over blind faith, is an aberration in history. The time of enlightenment is bracketed on either side by religious intolerance, religious wars and blind faith." Zarathustra II.

"All gods who receive homage are cruel. All gods dispense suffering without reason. Otherwise they would not be worshipped. Through indiscriminate suffering men know fear and fear is the most divine emotion. It is the stones for altars and the beginning of wisdom." Zora Neale Hurston.

"Man has tried to explain the existence of evil in many ways. Augustine's formulation of original sin is but one of those ways. But evil, intolerance, harming others, is transmitted, at least in part, culturally. Perhaps, hate is ingrained, but man is taught who to hate by the culture that sustains him. The object of our hate is refined and focused, if not created, by our culture." Zarathustra II.

"Objection, evasion, joyous distrust, and love of irony are signs of health; everything absolute belongs to pathology." Nietzsche.

"The great epochs of our life are the occasions when we gain the courage to rebaptize our evil qualities as our best qualities." Nietzsche.

"Propaganda by itself succeeds mainly with the frustrated." Eric Hoffer.

"In our youthful years we respect and despise without that art of nuance which constitutes the best thing we gain from life, and, as is only fair, we have to pay dearly for having assailed men and things with yes or no in such a fashion." Nietzsche.

"Religion has embraced absolutism and literalism in a dim witted attempt to claim supremacy in its battle with science over the veracity of scientific truths." Zarathustra II.

"When there is no vision, the people perish." Proverbs 29.

"To recognize untruth as a condition of life: that, to be sure, means to resist customary value-sentiments in a dangerous fashion; and a philosophy which ventures to do so places itself, by that act alone, beyond good and evil." Nietzsche.

"Hypocrisy [is] an inevitable byproduct of all virtuous endeavors." Reinhold Niebuhr.

"That nostalgia for unity, that appetite for the absolute illustrates the essential impulse of human drama." Albert Camus.

"The more abstract the truth you want to teach, the more you must seduce the senses to it." Nietzsche.

"Perhaps the soul and the self are the same thing. Just different words for the same idea at different points in our cultural development." Zarathustra II.

"Absolutes are probably imperative when raising a child, restrictive to the development of an adolescent and the convenient foundation of intolerance as an adult." Zarathustra II.

"It feels good to be driven around in a red Porsche by a woman better read than I am." Charles Bukowski.

"Our vanity would have just that we do best count as that which is hardest for us. The origin of many a morality." Nietzsche.

"Christianity gave Eros poison to drink---he did not die of it, to be sure, but degenerated into vice." Nietzsche.

"Take away our holy duties and you leave our lives puny and meaningless." Eric Hoffer.

"There is but one truly serious philosophical problem and that is suicide." Albert Camus.

"There can be no real freedom without the freedom to fail." Eric Hoffer.

"I shall continue to be an impossible person so long as those who are now possible remain possible." Bakunin.

"The devil has the widest perspective for God, and that is why he keeps so far away from him----the devil being the oldest friend of knowledge." Nietzsche.

" I saw the best minds of my generation destroyed by madness, starving hysterical naked...." Allen Ginsberg.

"We live in a culture of screams, polarizing screams, where no one seems to listen and the 'winner' is too often seen as the one who yells the loudest. It is a culture where opposing opinions are demonized, rather than considered; where the unconscious masses, through their self anointed leaders, attack reflective thought as anathema, and where beneath the luster of a polished patina, there is the ever constant and droning fear of there being no meaning, of dying without allegiance to a larger idea." Zarathustra II.

"In our contemporary social and intellectual plight, it is nothing less than shocking to discover that those persons who claim to have discovered an absolute are usually the same people who pretend to be superior to the rest." Karl Mannheim.

"Between the certainty of my existence and the content I try to give to that assurance, the gap will never be filled." Albert Camus.

"People who live in exile, whether internally or externally imposed, evolve their beliefs and their ideas, due to the influence of their exiled status, much quicker than those who are accepted within a community." Zarathustra II.

"Sometimes the curses of the godless sound better than the hallelujahs of the pious." Luther.

"Man defines himself by his make believe as well as by his sincere impulses." Albert Camus.

"The end of man is knowledge, but there is one thing he can't know. He can't know whether knowledge will save him or kill him. He will be killed alright, but he can't know whether he is killed because of the knowledge which he has got or because of the knowledge which he hasn't got and which, if he had it, would save him." Robert Penn Warren.

Made in the USA
Columbia, SC
12 May 2017